Angel

Colleen McCullough

Angel

McArthur & Company
Toronto

First published in Canada in 2005 by
McArthur & Company
322 King St. West, Suite 402
Toronto, Ontario
M5V 1J2
www.mcarthur-co.com

This paperback edition published in 2006 by
McArthur & Company

Library and Archives Canada Cataloguing in Publication

McCullough, Colleen, 1937-
   Angel / Colleen McCullough.

   ISBN 1-55278-588-2

   I. Title.

PR9619.3.M24A65 2006   823'.914   C2006-903330-7

Printed in Canada by Webcom

10 9 8 7 6 5 4 3 2 1

For Max Lambert
Much loved friend

Colleen McCullough was born in western New South
Wales in 1937. A neuroscientist by training she worked
in various Sydney and English hospitals before settling
to ten years of research and teaching in the Department
of Neurology at the Yale Medical School in the US.

In 1974 her first novel, *Tim*, was published and
followed by the bestselling *The Thorn Birds*
in 1977, and a string of successful novels.

She lives on Norfolk Island with her husband
Ric Robinson and a cat named Poindexter.

For automatic updates on McCullough,
visit www.mcarthur-co.com

Friday,

January 1st, 1960 (New Year's Day)

How on earth can I get rid of David? Don't think that I haven't contemplated murder, but I wouldn't get away with murder any more than I got away with the bikini I bought myself with the five quid Granny gave me for Christmas.

"Take it back, my girl, and bring home something one-piece with a modesty panel across the business area," Mum said.

Truth to tell, I was a bit horrified when the mirror showed me how much of me that bikini put on display, including sideburns of black pubic hair I'd never noticed when they lurked behind a modesty panel. The very thought of plucking out a million pubic hairs sent me back to exchange the bikini for an Esther Williams model in the latest colour, American Beauty. Sort of a rich, reddish pink. The shop assistant said I looked ravishing in it, but who is going to ravish me, with David Bloody Murchison hovering over my carcass like a dog guarding a bone? Certainly not David Bloody Murchison!

It was up over the hundred today, so I went down

to the beach to christen the new costume. The surf was running high, pretty unusual for Bronte, but the waves looked like green satin sausages—dumpers, no good for body surfing. I spread my towel on the sand, slathered zinc cream all over my nose, pulled on my matching American Beauty swim cap, and ran towards the water.

"It's too rough to go in, you'll get dumped," said a voice.

David. David Bloody Murchison. If he suggests the safety of the kids' bogey hole, I thought, girding my modesty-panelled loins, there is going to be a fight.

"Let's go round to the bogey hole, it's safe," he said.

"And get flattened by kids bombing us? No!" I snarled, and launched into the fight. Though "fight" is not the correct word. I yell and carry on, David just looks superior and refuses to bite. But today's fight produced a new rocket—I finally got up the gumption to inform him that I was tired of being a virgin.

"Let's have an affair," I said.

"Don't be silly," he said, unruffled.

"I am *not* being silly! Everybody I know has had an affair—except me! Dammit, David, I'm twenty-one, and here I am engaged to a bloke who won't even kiss me with his mouth open!"

He patted me gently on one shoulder and sat down on his towel. "Harriet," he announced in that toffee-nosed, super-genteel Catholic boys' college voice of his, "it's time we set a wedding date. I have my doctorate, the C.S.I.R.O. has offered me my own lab and a research grant, we've been going out together for four years, and engaged for one. Affairs are a sin. Marriage isn't."

Grr!

"Mum, I want to break off my engagement to David!" I said to her when I got home from the beach, my new costume unbaptised.

"Then tell him so, dear," she said.

"Have you ever tried telling David Murchison that you don't want to marry him any more?" I demanded.

Mum giggled. "Well, no. I'm already married."

Oh, I *hate* it when Mum is funny at my expense!

But I battled on. "The trouble is that I was only sixteen when I met him, seventeen when he started taking me out, and in those days it was terrific to have a boyfriend I didn't need to fight off. But Mum, he's so— so *hidebound*! Here I am of an age to consent, but he doesn't treat me any differently than he did when I was a mere seventeen! I feel like a fly stuck in amber."

Mum's a good stick, so she didn't start moralising, though she did look a bit concerned.

"If you don't want to marry him, Harriet, then don't. But he is a very good catch, dear. Handsome, well-built— and such a bright future ahead of him! Look at what's happened to all your friends, especially Merle. They take up with chaps who just aren't mature and sensible like David, so they keep getting hurt. Nothing comes of it. David's stuck to you like glue, he always will."

"I know," I said through my teeth. "Merle still nags me on the subject of David—he's divine, I don't know how lucky I am. But honestly, he's a pain in the bum! I've been with him for so long that every other bloke I know thinks I'm already taken—I never have an opportunity to find out what the rest of the male world is like, dammit!"

But she didn't really listen. Mum and Dad approve of David, always have. Maybe if I'd had a sister, or been closer in age to my brothers—it's *hard* being an accident of the wrong sex! I mean, there are Gavin and Peter in their middle thirties, still living at home, shagging hordes of women in the back of their van on top of a waterproof mattress, partnering Dad in our sporting goods shop and playing cricket in their spare time—the life of Riley! But I have to share a room with Granny, who pees in a potty which she empties on the grass at the bottom of the backyard. Pongs a treat.

"Think yourself lucky, Roger, that I don't chuck it on next-door's washing" is all she says when Dad tries to remonstrate.

What a good idea this diary is! I've encountered enough weird and wonderful psychiatrists to realise that I now have a "medium through which to vent frustrations and repressions". It was Merle suggested I keep a diary—I suspect she'd like to peek in it whenever she visits, but no chance of that. I intend to store it propped against the skirting board underneath Granny's bed right in line with Potty.

Tonight's wishes: No David Murchison in my life. No Potty in my life. No curried sausages in my life. A room all to myself. An engagement ring so that I could chuck it in David's face. He said he wasn't giving me one because it's a waste of money. What a miser!

Saturday,
January 2nd, 1960
I landed the job! After I sat my finals at the Sydney Tech last year, I applied to the Royal Queens Hospital X-ray Department for a position as a trained technician, and today the postie brought a letter of acceptance! I am to start this Monday as a senior X-ray technician at the biggest hospital in the Southern Hemisphere—*more than a thousand beds*! Makes Ryde Hospital, my old alma mater, look like a dinghy alongside the *Queen Elizabeth*. From where I am now, I should never have done my training at Ryde Hospital, but at the time I thought it was a brilliant idea when David suggested it. His elder brother, Ned, was a registrar there—a friend at court. Hah! He acted as my watchdog. Every time someone male gave me a come-hither look, Ned *Bloody* Murchison warned him off—I was his brother's girl, so no poaching on taken preserves! In the

5

early days I didn't mind, but it became a colossal bog as I grew out of my teenage uncertainty and humility, started thinking occasionally that X or Y looked like he'd be fun to go out with.

Training at Ryde did have one advantage, though. It takes two hours on public transport to get there from Bronte, and studying on public transport beats trying to study in the Purcell residence, between Granny and Mum watching television and the men usurping the whole evening to wash the dishes while they yarn cricket, cricket, cricket. Clint Walker and Efrem Zimbalist Junior in the lounge room, Keith Miller and Don Bradman in the kitchen, and no doors between all this and the only spot to study, the dining room table. Give me a bus or a train any day. Guess what? *I topped everything!* Highest marks possible. That's why I got the job at Royal Queens. When the results came out, Mum and Dad nagged a bit because when I'd finished at Randwick High, I refused to go to Uni and do a degree in science or medicine. Topping X-ray rubbed my lack of ambition in, I suppose. But who wants to go to Uni and suffer the slings and arrows of all those males who don't want women in men's professions? Not me!

**Monday,
January 4th, 1960**
I started work this morning. Nine o'clock. Royal Queens is so much closer to Bronte than Ryde! If I

walk the last mile-and-a-bit, I only have a twenty-minute bus ride.

Because I applied at Tech, I'd never been to the place before, only gone past it on a few occasions when we went south to visit someone or have a picnic. What a place! It's got its own shops, banks, post office, power plant, a laundry big enough to contract out to hotels, workshops, warehouses—you name it, Royal Queens has got it. Talk about a maze! It took me fifteen minutes at a fast clip to walk from the main gates to X-ray through just about every sort of architecture Sydney has produced for the last hundred or so years. Quadrangles, ramps, verandahs lined with pillars, sandstone buildings, red brick buildings, lots of those ghastly new buildings with glass on their outsides—stinking hot to work in!

Judging by the number of people I passed, there must be ten thousand employees. The nurses are wrapped up in so many layers of starch that they look like green-and-white parcels. The poor things have to wear thick brown cotton stockings and flat-heeled brown lace-up shoes! Even Marilyn Monroe would have trouble looking seductive in opaque stockings and lace-up flatties. Their caps look like two white doves entwined, and they have *celluloid* cuffs and collars, hems mid-calf. The registered nursing sisters look the same, except that they don't have aprons, flaunt Egyptian headdress veils instead of caps, and wear nylons—*their* lace-up shoes have two-inch block heels.

Well, I've always known that I don't have the temperament to take all that regimented, mindless discipline, any more than I have to put up with being maltreated by male Uni students protecting masculine turf. Us technicians just have to wear a white buttondown-the-front uniform (hems below the knee), with nylons and moccasin flatties.

There must be a hundred physios—I *hate* physios! I mean, what are physios except glorified masseuses? But boy, are they up themselves! They even starch their uniforms *voluntarily*! And they all have that gung-ho, jolly-hockey-stick-brigade air of superiority as they nip around smartly like army officers, baring their horsey teeth as they say things like "Jolly D!" and "Oh, supah!"

It's lucky I left home early enough to make that fifteen-minute walk yet still arrive at Sister Toppingham's office on time. What a tartar! Pappy says that everyone calls her Sister Agatha, so I will too—behind her back. She's about a thousand years old and was once a nursing sister—still wears the starched Egyptian headdress veil of a trained nurse. She's the same shape as a pear, right down to the pear-shaped accent. Fraightfullehfraightfulleh. Her eyes are pale blue, cold as a frosty morning, and they looked through me as if I was a smear on the window.

"You will commence, Miss Purcell, in Chests. Nice, easy lungs at first, don't you know? I prefer that all new staff serve an orientation period doing something simple. Later on we shall see what you can really do, yes? Jolly good, jolly good!"

Wacko, what a challenge! *Chests.* Shove 'em against the upright bucky and get 'em to hold their breath. When Sister Agatha said Chests, she meant OPD chests—the walking wounded, not the serious stuff.

There are three of us doing routine chests, me and two junior trainees. But the darkrooms are in furious demand—we have to hustle our cassettes through at maximum speed, which means anyone who takes longer than nine minutes gets yelled at.

This is a department of women, which amazes me. Very rare! X-ray technicians are paid the male award, so men flock to X-ray as a profession—at Ryde, almost all of us were men. I imagine the difference at Queens is Sister Agatha, therefore she can't be all bad.

I met the nurses' aide in the dreary area where our lockers and the toilets live. I liked her at first glance, a lot more than any of the technicians I met today. My two trainees are nice kids, but both first-years, so a bit boring. Whereas Nurse-aide Papele Sutama is *interesting.* The name is outlandish—but then, so is its owner. Her eyes do have upper lids, but there's definitely a lot of Chinese there, I thought when I saw her. Not Japanese, her legs are too shapely and straight. She confirmed the Chinese later on. Oh, just the prettiest girl I've ever seen! A mouth like a rosebud, cheekbones to die for, feathery eyebrows.

She's known as Pappy, and it suits her. A tiny little thing, about five feet tall, and very thin without looking as if she's out of Belsen like those anorexia nervosa cases Psych sends me for routine chests— why on earth do teenage girls starve themselves? Back to Pappy, whose skin is like ivory silk.

Pappy liked me too, so when she found out that I'd brought a cut lunch from home, she invited me to eat it with her on the grass outside the mortuary, which isn't very far from X-ray, but Sister Agatha can't see you from X-ray as she patrols. Sister Agatha doesn't eat lunch, she's too busy policing her empire. Of course we don't get the full hour, especially on Mondays, when all the routine stuff from the weekend has to be squeezed in as well as the normal intake. However, Pappy and I managed to find out a great deal about each other in just thirty minutes.

The first thing she told me was that she lives at *Kings Cross*. Phew! It's the one part of Sydney that Dad put out of bounds—a den of iniquity, Granny calls it. Riddled with vice. I'm not sure exactly what vice is, apart from alcoholism and prostitution. There are a lot of both at Kings Cross, judging by what the Reverend Alan Walker has to say. Still, he's a Metho—very righteous. Kings Cross is where Rosaleen Norton the witch lives—she's always in the news for painting obscene pictures. What *is* an obscene picture—people copulating? I asked Pappy, but all she said was that obscenity is in the eye of the beholder. Pappy's very deep, reads Schopenhauer,

Jung, Bertrand Russell and people like that, but she told me that she doesn't have a high opinion of Freud. I asked her why she wasn't up at Sydney Uni, and she said she'd never had much formal schooling. Her mother was an Australian, her father Chinese from Singapore, and they got caught up in World War Two. Her father died, her mother went mad after four years in Changi prison camp—what tragic lives some people have! And here am I with nothing to complain about except David and Potty. Bronte born and bred.

Pappy says that David is a mass of repressions, which she blames on his Catholic upbringing—she even has a name for the Davids of this world—"constipated Catholic schoolboys". But I didn't want to talk about him, I wanted to know what living at Kings Cross is like. Like any other place, she says. But I don't believe that, it's too notorious. I'm *dying* of curiosity!

Wednesday,
January 6th, 1960
It's David again. Why can't he get it through his head that someone who works in a hospital does not want to see some turgid monstrosity of a Continental film? It's all very well for him, up there in his sterile, autoclaved little world where the most exciting thing that ever happens is a bloody mouse growing a bloody lump, but I work in one of those

places where people suffer pain and sometimes even die! I am surrounded by gruesome reality—I cry enough, I'm depressed enough! So when I go to the pictures I want to laugh, or at least have a good old sniffle when Deborah Kerr gives up the love of her life because she's in a wheelchair. Whereas the sort of films David likes are so *depressing*. Not sad, just depressing.

I tried to tell him the above when he said he was taking me to see the new film at the Savoy Theatre. The word I used wasn't depressing, it was sordid.

"Great literature and great films are not sordid," he said.

I offered to let him harrow his soul in peace at the Savoy while I went to the Prince Edward to see a Western, but he gets this look on his face which long experience has taught me precedes a lecture that's sort of a cross between a sermon and a harangue, so I gave in and went with him to the Savoy to see *Gervaise*—Zola, David explained as we came out. I felt like a wrung-out dishrag, which isn't a bad comparison, actually. It all took place in a Victorian version of a giant laundry. The heroine was so young and pretty, but there wasn't a man worth looking at within cooee—they were fat and *bald*. I think David might end up bald, his hair isn't as thick as it was when I met him.

David insisted on taking a taxi home, though I would far rather have walked briskly down to the Quay and grabbed the bus. He always lets the taxi go outside our place, then escorts me in up the side passage, where, in the dark, he puts a hand on either side of my waist and squishes my lip with three kisses so chaste that the Pope wouldn't think it sinful to bestow them. After which he watches to see I'm safely in the back door, then walks the four blocks to his own house. He lives with his widowed mother, though he's bought a roomy bungalow at Coogee Beach which he rents out to a family of New Australians from Holland—very clean, the Dutch, he told me. Oh, is there *any* blood in David's veins? Never once has he put a finger, let alone a hand, on my breasts. What do I have them for?

My big Bros were inside, making a cup of tea and killing themselves laughing at what had gone on in the side passage.

Tonight's wish: That I manage to save fifteen quid a week at this new job and save enough by the beginning of 1961 to take that two-year working holiday to England. Then I'll lose David, who can't possibly leave his bloody mice in case one grows a bloody lump.

**Thursday,
January 7th, 1960**
My curiosity about Kings Cross is going to be gratified on Saturday, when I am to have dinner at Pappy's place. However, I shan't tell Mum and Dad exactly whereabouts Pappy lives. I'll just say it's on

the fringe of Paddington.

Tonight's wish: That Kings Cross isn't a let-down.

Friday,
January 8th, 1960

Last night we had a bit of a crisis with Willie. It's typical of Mum that she insisted on rescuing this baby cockatoo off the Mudgee road and rearing it. Willie was so scrawny and miserable that Mum started him off on a dropper of warm milk laced with the three-star hospital brandy we keep for Granny's funny little turns. Then, because his beak wasn't hard enough yet to crack seed, she switched to porridge laced with three-star hospital brandy. So Willie grew up into this gorgeous, fat white bird with a yellow comb and a daggy breast caked with dried porridge. Mum has always given him his porridge-and-brandy in the last of the Bunnyware saucers I had when I was a toddler. But yesterday she broke the Bunnyware saucer, so she put his dinner in a bilious green saucer instead. Willie took one look, flipped his uneaten dinner upside down and went bonkers— screeched high C without letting up until every dog in Bronte was howling and Dad had a visit from the Boys in Blue, who arrived in a paddy wagon.

I daresay it's all those years of reading whodunits sharpened my deductive powers, because, after a hideous night of a screeching parrot and a thousand howling dogs, I realised two facts. One, that parrots are intelligent enough to discern a saucer with cute little bunnies running around its rim from a saucer of bilious green. Two, that Willie is an alcoholic. When he saw the wrong saucer, he concluded that his porridge-and-brandy had been withdrawn, and went into withdrawal himself—hence the racket.

Peace was finally restored to Bronte when I got home from work this afternoon. I'd grabbed a taxi at lunchtime and dashed into the city to buy a new Bunnyware saucer. Had to buy the cup as well—*two pounds ten*! But Gavin and Peter are good scouts, even if they are my big brothers. They each donated a third of the two-and-a-half quid, so I'm not much out of pocket. Silly, isn't it? But Mum so loves that dippy bird.

**Saturday,
January 9th, 1960**
Kings Cross is certainly not a let-down. I got off the bus at the stop before Taylor Square and walked the rest of the way with Pappy's directions memorised. Apparently they don't eat very early at Kings Cross, because I didn't have to be there until eight, so by the time I got off the bus it was quite dark. Then as I passed Vinnie's Hospital it began to rain—just a drizzle, nothing that my frilly pink brolly couldn't handle. When I reached that huge intersection I believe is the actual Kings Cross, seeing it on foot

with the streets wet and the dazzle of all those neons and car lights rippling across the water was completely different from whizzing through it in a taxi. It's beautiful. I don't know how the shopkeepers avoid the Sydney Blue Laws, because they were still open *on a Saturday evening*! Though it was a bit disappointing when I realised that my route didn't lie along the Darlinghurst Road shops—I had to walk down Victoria Street, in which The House is situated. That's what Pappy calls it, "The House", and I know she says it with capital letters. As if it is an institution. So I admit that I hiked past the terraced houses of Victoria Street eagerly.

I love the rows upon rows of old Victorian terraced houses inner Sydney has—not kept up these days, alas. All the lovely cast-iron lace has been ripped off and replaced by sheets of fibro to turn the balconies into extra rooms, and the plastered walls are dingy. Even so, they're very mysterious. The windows are blanked out by Manchester lace curtains and brown-paper blinds, like closed eyes. They've seen so much. Our house at Bronte is only twenty-two years old; Dad built it after the worst of the Depression, when his shop started making money. So nothing's happened in it except us, and we are boring. Our biggest crisis is Willie's saucer— at least, that's the only time the police have called on us.

The House was a long way down Victoria Street, and as I walked I noticed that at this far end some of the terraced houses still had their cast-iron lace, were painted and well kept-up. Right at the end beyond Challis Avenue the street widened into a semicircular dead end. Apparently the Council had run out of tar, because the road was cobbled with little wooden blocks, and I noticed that within the semicircle no cars were parked. This gave the crescent of five terraced houses which filled it an air of not belonging to the present. They were all numbered 17—17a, b, c, d and e. The one in the middle, 17c, was The House. It had a fabulous front door of ruby glass etched in a pattern of lilies down to the clear glass underneath, the bevels glittering amber and purple from the light inside. It wasn't locked, so I pushed it open.

But the fairytale door led into a desert waste. A dingy hall painted dirty cream, a red cedar staircase leading upward, a couple of fly-dirt-speckled naked lightbulbs on long, twisted brown cords, awful old brown linoleum pitted from stiletto heels. From the skirting boards to a height of about four feet, every single bit of wall I could see was smothered in scribbles, aimless loops and whorls of many colours with the waxy look of crayon.

"Hello!" I yelled.

Pappy appeared from beyond the staircase, smiling a welcome. I think I stared quite rudely, she looked so different. Instead of that unflattering bright mauve uniform and hair-hiding cap, she wore a skin-tight tube of peacock blue satin embroidered in dragons, and it was split so far up her left leg that

I could see the top of her stocking and a frilly lace suspender. Her hair cascaded down her back in a thick, straight, shining mass—why can't I have hair like that? Mine is just as black, but it's so curly that if I grew it long it'd stick out like a broom in an epileptic fit. So I hack mine really short with a pair of scissors.

She led me through a door at the end of the passage beside the stairs and we emerged into another, much shorter hall which went sideways and seemed to end in the open air. It held only the one door, which Pappy opened.

Inside was Dreamland. The room was so chocka with books that the walls were invisible, just books, books, books, floor up to ceiling, and there were stacks of books lying around that I suspect she'd cleared off her chairs and table in order to entertain me. During the course of the evening I tried to count them, but there were too many. Her collection of lamps knocked me sideways, they were so gorgeous. Two dragonfly stained-glass ones, an illuminated globe of the world on a stand, kerosene lamps from Indonesia converted to electricity, one that looked like a white chimney six feet tall, overlaid with slashed purple swellings. The ceiling bulb was inside a Chinese paper lantern dripping silk tassels.

Then she proceeded to cook food that bore no relationship to the chow-meow from Hoo Flung's up Bronte Road. My tongue smarting gently from ginger and garlic, I shovelled in three helpings. There is nothing wrong with my appetite, though I never manage to keep enough weight on to graduate from a B to a C cup bra. Darn. Jane Russell is a full D cup, but I've always thought that Jayne Mansfield is only a B cup on top of a huge rib cage.

When we'd finished and drunk a pot of fragrant green tea, Pappy announced that it was time to go upstairs and meet Mrs. Delvecchio Schwartz. The landlady.

When I remarked that it was a peculiar name, Pappy grinned.

She led me back to the front hall and the red cedar staircase. As I followed her up, consumed with curiosity, I noticed that the crayon scribbles didn't stop. Rather, they increased. The stairs continued upward to a higher floor, but we went forward to a huge room at the front of the house, and Pappy pushed me inside. If you want to find a room that is the exact opposite of Pappy's, this one is it. *Bare*. Except for the scribbles, which were so thick that there wasn't a scrap of space for more. Maybe because of that, one section had been roughly painted over, apparently to provide the artist with a fresh canvas, as a few scribbles already adorned it. The place could have held six lounge suites and a dining table to seat twelve, but it was mostly empty. There was a rusty chrome kitchen table with a red laminex top, four rusty chairs with the padding of their red plastic seats oozing out like pus from a carbuncle, a velvet couch suffering from a bad attack of alopecia,

and an up-to-the-minute refrigerator/freezer. A pair
of glass-panelled doors led out onto the balcony.

"Out here, Pappy!" someone called.

We emerged onto the balcony to find two women
standing there. The one I saw first was clearly from
the Harbourside Eastern Suburbs or the upper
North Shore—blue-rinsed hair, a dress that came
from Paris, matching shoes, bag and gloves in burgundy kid, and a weeny hat much smarter than the
ones Queen Elizabeth wears. Then Mrs. Delvecchio
Schwartz stepped forward, and I forgot all about the
middle-aged fashion plate.

Phew! What a mountain of a woman! Not that
she was fat, more that she was gigantic. A good six
foot four in those dirty old slippers with their backs
trodden down, and massively muscled. No stockings. A faded, unironed old button-down-the-front
house dress with a pocket on either hip. Her face
was round, lined, snub-nosed and absolutely dom-
inated by her eyes, which looked straight into my
soul, pale blue with dark rings around the irises, little pupils as sharp as twin needles. She had thin
grey hair cut as short as a man's, and eyebrows that
hardly showed against her skin. Age? On the
wrong side of fifty by several years, I reckon.

As soon as she let my eyes go, my medical training clicked in. Acromegaly? Cushing's Syndrome?
But she didn't have the huge lower jaw or the jutting
forehead of the acromegalic, nor did she have the
physique or hairiness of a Cushing's. Something

pituitary or midbrain or hypothalamic, for sure, but what, I didn't know.

The fashion plate nodded politely to Pappy and me, brushed past us and departed with Mrs. Delvecchio Schwartz in her wake. Because I was standing in the doorway, I saw the visitor reach into her bag, withdraw a thick wad of brick-coloured notes—*tenners!*—and hand them over a few at a time. Pappy's landlady just stood there with her hand out until she was satisfied with the number of notes. Then she folded them and slipped them into one pocket while the fashion plate from Sydney's most expensive suburbs left the room.

Back came Mrs. Delvecchio Schwartz to throw herself onto a mate of the four chairs inside, bidding us sit on two more with a sweep of a hand the size of a leg of lamb.

"Siddown, princess, siddown!" she roared. "How the hell are youse, Miss Harriet Purcell? Good name, that— two sets of seven letters—strong magic! Spiritual awareness and good fortune, happiness through perfected labour—and I don't mean them lefty politicians, hur-hur-hur."

The "hur-hur-hur" is a kind of wicked chuckle that speaks volumes; as if there is nothing in the world could surprise her, though everything in the world amuses her greatly. It reminded me of Sid James's chuckle in the *Carry On* films.

I was so nervous that I picked up her comments about my name and regaled her with the history of the Harriet Purcells, told her the name went back many generations, but that, until my advent, its owners had all been quite cuckoo. One Harriet Purcell, I said, had been jailed for castrating a would-be lover, and another for assaulting the Premier of New South Wales during a suffragette rally. She listened with interest, sighed in disappointment when I finished my tale by saying that my father's generation had been so afraid of the name that it didn't contain a Harriet Purcell.

"Yet your dad christened you Harriet," she said. "Good man! Sounds like he might be fun to know, hur-hur-hur."

Ooooo-aa! Hands off my dad, Mrs. Delvecchio Schwartz! "He said he liked the name Harriet, and he wasn't impressed by family claptrap," I said. "I was a bit of an afterthought, you see, and everybody thought I'd be another boy."

"But you wasn't," she said, grinning. "Oh, I like it!"

During all of this, she drank undiluted, uniced three-star hospital brandy out of a Kraft cheese spread glass. Pappy and I were each given a glass of it, but one sip of Willie's downfall made me abandon mine— dreadful stuff, raw and biting. I noticed that Pappy seemed to enjoy the taste, though she didn't glug it nearly as fast as Mrs. Delvecchio Schwartz did.

I've been sitting here debating whether I might save a lot of writer's cramp by shortening that name to Mrs. D-S, but somehow I don't have the courage. I don't *lack* courage, but Mrs. D-S? No.

Then I became aware that *someone else* was on the balcony with us, had been there all along but stayed absolutely invisible. My skin began to prickle, I felt a delicious chill, like the first puff of a Southerly Buster after days and days of a century-mark heatwave. A face appeared above the table, peering from around Mrs. Delvecchio Schwartz's hip. The most bewitching little face, chin pointed, cheekbones high beneath the orbits, flawless beige skin, drifts of palest brown hair, black brows, black lashes so long they looked tangled— oh, I wish I was a poet, to describe that divine child! My chest caved in, I just looked at her and loved her. Her eyes were enormous, wide apart and amber-brown, the saddest eyes I have ever seen. Her little pink rosebud mouth parted, and she smiled at me. I smiled back.

"Oh, decided to join the party, have youse?" The next moment the little thing was on Mrs. Delvecchio Schwartz's knee, still with her face turned to smile at me, but plucking at Mrs. Delvecchio Schwartz's dress with one tiny hand.

"This is me daughter, Flo," said the landlady. "Thought I had the Change four years ago, then got a pain in the belly and went to the dunny thinkin' I had a dose of the shits. And—bang! There was Flo, squirmin' on the floor all covered with slime. Never even knew I was up the duff until she popped out— lucky I didn't drown youse in the dunny, ain't that right, angel?" This last was said to Flo, who was fiddling with a button.

"How old is she?" I asked.

"Just turned four. A Capricorn who ain't a Capricorn," said Mrs. Delvecchio Schwartz, casually unbuttoning her dress. Out flopped a breast which looked like an old stocking with its toe stuffed with beans, and she stuck its huge, horny nipple in Flo's mouth. Flo shut her eyes ecstatically, leaned back into her mother's arm and began to suck away with long, horribly audible slurps. I sat there with my mouth catching flies, unable to think of a thing to say. The X-ray vision lifted to focus on me.

"Loves her mother's milk, does Flo," she said chattily. "I know she's four, yeah, but what's age got to do with it, princess? Best tucker of all, mother's milk. Only thing is, her teeth are all in, so she hurts like hell."

I went on sitting there with my mouth catching flies until Pappy said, quite suddenly, "Well, Mrs. Delvecchio Schwartz, what do you think?"

"I think The House needs Miss Harriet Purcell," said Mrs. Delvecchio Schwartz with a nod and a wink. Then she looked at me and asked, "Ever think of movin' outta home, princess? Like into a nice little flat of your own?"

My mouth shut with a snap, I shook my head. "I can't afford it," I answered. "I'm saving to go to England on a two-year working holiday, you see."

"Do youse pay board at home?" she asked.

I said I paid five pounds a week.

"Well, I got a real nice little flat out in the backyard, two big rooms, four quid a week, electricity included. There's a bath and dunny inside the laundry that only you and Pappy'd use. Janice Harvey, me tenant, is movin' out. It's got a *double* bed," she added with a leer. "Hate them piddly-arse little single beds."

Four pounds! Two rooms for *four pounds*? A Sydney miracle!

"You stand a better chance of getting rid of David living here than at home," said Pappy persuasively. She shrugged. "After all, you're on a male award, you could still save for your trip."

I remember swallowing, hunting desperately for a polite way to say no, but suddenly I was saying *yes*! I don't know where that yes came from—I certainly wasn't thinking yes.

"Ripper-ace, princess!" boomed Mrs. Delvecchio Schwartz, flipped the nipple out of Flo's mouth and lumbered to her feet.

As my eyes met Flo's, I knew why I'd said yes. Flo put the word into my mind. Flo wanted me here, and I was putty. She came over to me and hugged my legs, smiling up at me with milky lips.

"Will youse look at that?" Mrs. Delvecchio Schwartz exclaimed, grinning at Pappy. "Be honoured, Harriet. Flo don't usually take to people, do you, angel?"

So here I am, trying to write it all down before the edges blur, wondering how on earth I'm going to break it to my family that, very shortly, I am moving into two big rooms at Kings Cross, home to alcoholics, prostitutes, homosexuals, satanic artists, glue-sniffers, hashish-smokers and God knows what else. Except that what I saw of it in the rainy dark I liked, and that Flo wants me in The House.

I'd said to Pappy that perhaps I could say that The House was in Potts Point, not Kings Cross, but Pappy only laughed.

"Potts Point is a euphemism, Harriet," she said. "The Royal Australian Navy owns Potts Point whole and entire."

Tonight's wish: That the parents don't have a stroke.

Sunday,
January 10th, 1960

I haven't told them yet. Still getting up the courage. When I went to bed last night—Granny was snoring a treat—I was sure that when I woke up this morning, I would change my mind. But I haven't. The first thing I saw was Granny squatting over Potty, and the iron entered my soul. That's such a good phrase! I never realised until I started writing this that I seem to have picked up all sorts of good phrases from reading. They don't surface in conversation, but they certainly do on paper. And though this is only a few days old, I'm already well into a fat exercise book, and I'm quite addicted. Maybe that's because I can never sit still and *think*, I always have to be *doing* something, so now I'm killing two birds with the same stone. I get to think about what's happening to me, yet I'm doing something at the same time. There's a discipline about writing the stuff down, I see it better. Just like my work. I give it all my attention because I enjoy it.

I haven't quite made up my mind about Mrs. Delvecchio Schwartz, though I do like her very much. She reminds me of some of my more memorable patients, those who manage to stay with me for as long as I've been doing X-rays, maybe are going to stay with me for the rest of my life. Like the dear old bloke from Lidcombe State Hospital who kept neatly pleating his blanket. When I asked him what he was doing, he said he was folding sail, and then, when I settled to talk to him, he told me he'd been bosun on a windjammer, one of the wheat clippers used to scud home to England loaded to the gunwales with grain. His words, not mine. I learned a lot, then realised that very shortly he was going to die, and all those experiences would die with him because he'd never written them down.

Well, Kings Cross is not a windjammer, and I'm no sailor, but if I write it all down, someone sometime in remote posterity might read it, and they'd know what sort of life I lived. Because I have a funny feeling that it isn't going to be the boring old suburban life I was facing last New Year's Day. I feel like a snake shedding its skin.

Tonight's wish: The parents don't have a stroke.

Friday,
January 15th, 1960

I still haven't told them, but it's going to happen tomorrow night. When I asked Mum if David could eat steak-and-chips with us, she said of course; best, I think, to wallop the whole lot of them at the same time. That way, maybe David will get used to the idea before he has enough time alone with me to nag and hector me out of it. How I dread his lectures! But Pappy is right, it *is* going to be easier to get rid of David if I don't live at home. That thought alone has kept my course steering for the Cross, as the natives call it. Up at the Cross, to be exact.

I saw a man today at work, on the ramp leading from X-ray to Chichester House, which is the posh red brick building housing the Private Patients in the lap of luxury. A room and a bathroom each, no less, instead of a bed in a row of about twenty down either side of a whacking great ward. Must be awfully nice not to have to lie listening to half the patients vomiting, spitting, hacking or raving. Though there's no doubt that listening to half the patients vomiting, spitting, hacking or raving is a terrific incentive to get better and get out, or else get the dying over and done with.

The man. Sister Agatha grabbed me as I finished hanging some films in the drying cabinet—so far I haven't had one ponk film, which awes my two juniors into abject submission.

"Miss Purcell, kindly run these to Chichester

Three for Mr. Naseby-Morton," she said, waving an X-ray envelope at me.

Sensing her displeasure, I took it and hared off. Pappy would have been first on her invitation list, which meant Sister Agatha hadn't been able to find her. Or else she was holding a vomit bowl or dealing with a bedpan, of course. Mine not to reason why— I hared off like the juniorest junior to the Private Hospital. Very swanky, Chichester House! The rubber floors have such a shine on them that I could see Sister Chichester Three's pink bloomers reflected there, and you could open a florist shop on the amount of flowers dotted around the corridors on expensive pedestals. It was so quiet that when I bounded off the top step at Chichester Three level, six different people glared at me and put fingers to lips. Ssssssh! Oooooo-aa! So I looked contrite, handed the films over and tiptoed away like Margot Fonteyn.

Halfway down the ramp I saw a group of doctors approaching—an Honorary Medical Officer and his court of underlings. You don't spend a day working in any hospital without becoming aware that the H.M.O. is God, but God at Royal Queens is a much superior God to God at Ryde Hospital. Here, they wear navy pinstriped or grey flannel suits, Old School ties, French-cuffed shirts with discreet but solid gold links, brown suede or black kid thin-soled shoes.

This specimen wore grey flannel and brown

suede shoes. With him were two registrars (long white coats), his senior and junior residents (white suits and white shoes), and six medical students (short white coats) with stethoscopes ostentatiously displayed and nail-bitten hands full of slide cases or test tube racks. Yes, a very senior version of God, to have so many dancing attendance on him. That was what caught my attention. Doing routine chests doesn't bring one into contact with God, senior or junior, so I was curious. He was talking with great animation to one registrar, fine head thrown back, and I think I had to slow down and shut my mouth, which does have a tendency to catch flies these days. Oh, what a lovely man! *Very* tall, a good pair of shoulders, a flat tummy. A lot of dark red hair with a kink in it and two snow-white wings, very slightly freckled skin, chiselled features—yes, he was a *lovely* man. They were talking about osteomalacia, so I catalogued him as an orthopod. Then as I slid by them— they did rather take up all the ramp—I found myself being searchingly regarded by a pair of greenish eyes. Phew! My chest caved in for the second time in a week, though this wasn't a surge of love like Flo's. This was a sort of breathless attraction. My knees sagged.

At lunch I quizzed Pappy about him, armed with my theory that he was an orthopod.

"Duncan Forsythe," she said without hesitation. "He's the senior Honorary Medical Officer on

Orthopaedics. Why do you ask?"

"He gave me an old-fashioned look," I said.

Pappy stared. "*Did* he? That's odd coming from him, he's not one of the Queens Lotharios. He's very much married and known as the nicest H.M.O. in the whole place—a thorough gentleman, never chucks instruments at Sister Theatre or tells filthy jokes or picks on his junior resident, no matter how ham-fisted or tactless."

I dropped the subject, though I'm sure I didn't imagine it. He hadn't stripped the clothes off me with his eyes or anything silly like that, but the look he gave me was definitely man-woman. And as far as I'm concerned, he's the most attractive man I've ever seen. The *senior* H.M.O.! Young for that post, he couldn't be more than forty.

Tonight's wish: That I see more of Mr. Duncan Forsythe.

**Saturday,
January 16th, 1960**
Well, I did it at the dinner table tonight, with David present. Steak-and-chips is everybody's favourite meal, though it's hard on Mum, who has to keep frying T-bones in a huge pan and keep an eye on the deep fryer at the same time. Gavin and Peter get through three each, and even David eats two. The pudding was Spotted Dick and custard, very popular, so the whole table was in a contented mood

when Mum and Granny put the teapot down. Time for me to *strike*.

"Guess what?" I asked.

No one bothered to answer.

"I've rented a flat at Kings Cross and I'm moving out."

No one answered that either, but all the sounds stopped. The tinkling of spoons in cups, Granny's slurps, Dad's cigarette cough. Then Dad pulled out his packet of Ardaths, offered it to Gavin and Peter, then lit all three of their smokes *off the same match*—oooooo-aa, that was trouble!

"Kings Cross," said Dad finally, staring at me very steely. "My girl, you're a fool. At least I hope you're a fool. Only fools, Bohemians and tarts live at Kings Cross."

"I am not a fool, Dad," I said valiantly, "and I am not a tart or a Bohemian either. Though these days they call Bohemians Beatniks. I've found myself a most respectable flat in a most respectable house which just happens to be at the Cross—the *better* end of the Cross, near Challis Avenue. Potts Point, really."

"The Royal Australian Navy owns Potts Point," Dad said.

Mum looked as if she was going to cry. "Why, Harriet?"

"Because I'm twenty-one and I need space of my own, Mum. Now I'm through training, I'm earning good money, and flats at Kings Cross are cheap enough for me to live yet still save to go to England next year. If I moved out to some other place, I'd have to share with two or three other girls, and I can't see that that's any better than living at home."

David didn't say a thing, just sat on Dad's right looking at me as if I'd grown another head.

"Well, come on, bright boy," Gavin growled at him, "what have you got to say?"

"I disapprove," David answered with ice in his voice, "but I would rather talk to Harriet on her own."

"Well, I reckon it's bonza," said Peter, and leaned over to give me a cuff on the arm. "You need more space, Harry."

That seemed to decide Dad, who sighed. "Well, there isn't a lot I can do to stop you, is there? At least it's closer than old Mother England. If you get into trouble, I can always yank you out of Kings Cross."

Gavin burst into a bellow of laughter, leaned across the table with his tie in the butter and kissed my cheek. "Bully for you, Harry!" he said. "End of the first innings, and you're still at the crease. Keep your bat ready to deal with the googlies!"

"When did you decide all this?" Mum asked, blinking hard.

"When Mrs. Delvecchio Schwartz offered me the flat."

The name sounded very peculiar said in our house. Dad frowned.

"Missus who?" asked Granny, who had sat looking rather smug throughout.

"Delvecchio Schwartz. She's the landlady." I remembered a fact I hadn't mentioned. "Pappy lives there, that's how I got to meet Mrs. Delvecchio Schwartz."

"I knew that Chinky girl was going to be a bad influence," Mum said. "Since you've met her, you haven't bothered with Merle."

I put my chin up. "Merle hasn't bothered with me, Mum. She's got a new boyfriend, and she can't see any farther. I'll only come back into favour with her when he dumps her."

"Is it a proper flat?" Dad asked.

"Two rooms. I share a bathroom with Pappy."

"It isn't hygienic to share a bathroom," said David.

I lifted my lip at him. "I share a bathroom here, don't I?"

That shut him up.

Mum decided to bite the bullet. "Well," she said, "I daresay you'll need china and cutlery and cooking utensils. Linen. You can have your own bed sheets from here."

I never thought, the answer just popped out. "No, I can't, Mum. I've got a whole double bed to myself! Isn't that terrific?"

They sat gaping at me as if they envisioned the double bed with a bus conductor's bag on the end of it to collect the fees.

"*A double bed?*" asked David, paling.

"That's right, a double bed."

"Single girls sleep in single beds, Harriet."

"Well, that is as may be, David," I snapped, "but this single girl is going to sleep in a double bed!"

Mum leaped to her feet. "Boys, the dishes don't wash themselves!" she chirped. "Granny, it's time for 77 *Sunset Strip*."

"Kooky, Kooky, lend me your comb!" carolled Granny, skipping up lightly. "Well, well, did you ever? Harriet's moving out and I've got a room to myself! I think I'll have a double bed, hee-hee!"

Dad and the Bros cleared the table in double-quick time, and left me alone with David.

"What brought this on?" he asked, tight-lipped.

"Lack of privacy."

"You have something better than mere privacy, Harriet. You have a home and a family."

I pounded my fist on the table. "Why are you such a myopic git, David? I share a room with Granny and Potty, and I have nowhere to spread my things without picking them up the minute I've finished with them! Whatever space I have here is also occupied by others. So now I'm going to luxuriate in my own space."

"At Kings Cross."

"Yes, at Kings bloody Cross! Where the rents are affordable."

"In a lodging house run by a foreigner. A New Australian."

That killed me, I laughed in his face. "Mrs. Delvecchio Schwartz, a foreigner? She's an Aussie, with an Aussie accent you could cut with a knife!"

"That is an even greater indictment," he said. "An Australian with a name that's half Italian and half Jewish? At the very least, she married beneath her."

"You bloody snob!" I gasped. "You bigoted git! What's so posh about Australians? We all came out as bloody convicts! At least our New Australians have come out as free settlers!"

"With SS numbers tattooed in their armpits or tuberculosis or stinking of garlic!" he snarled. "And 'free settlers' is right—they all came out here for a mere ten-pound subsidised passage!"

That did it. I jumped up and started whacking him on both sides of his head right over his ears. Wham, wham, wham! "Piss off, David, just bloody piss off!" I yelled.

He pissed off, with a look in his eyes that said I was having one of Those Days, and he'd be back to try again.

So there you have it. I do like my family—they're good scouts. But David is exactly what Pappy called him—a constipated Catholic schoolboy. Thank heavens I'm Church of England.

Wednesday,
January 20th, 1960
I've been so busy I haven't had time to sit and write this, but things are looking all right. I managed to talk Dad and the Bros out of inspecting my new

premises (I went last Sunday to have a look, and they're not fit yet for inspection), and I'm working like stink to get my things together for next Saturday's move. Mum has been colossal. I've got heaps of china, cutlery, linen and cooking utensils, and Dad shoved a hundred pounds at me with a gruff explanation that he didn't want me touching my savings for England to buy what by rights belonged in my Hope Chest anyway. Gavin presented me with a tool kit and a multimeter and Peter donated his "old" hi-fi, explaining that he needed a better one. Granny gave me a bottle of 4711 eau de Cologne and a set of doilies she'd crocheted for my Hope Chest.

There's a sort of an archway between my bedroom and my living room in my new flat—no door—so I'm going to use some of Dad's hundred quid to buy glass beads and make my own bead curtain. The ones you can buy are plastic, look awful and sound worse. I want something that *chimes*. Pink. I'm going to have a pink flat because it's the one colour no one at Bronte will permit anywhere. And I like pink. It's warm and feminine, and it cheers me up. Besides, I look good against it, which is more than I can say for yellow, blue, green and crimson. I'm too dark.

My flat is in the open air passage that goes down alongside Pappy's room and leads to the laundry and the backyard. The rooms are big and have very high ceilings, but the fixings are pretty basic. There's a kitchen area with a sink, an ancient gas stove and a fridge, and it's impossible to make it look nice, so I rang Ginge the head porter at Ryde and asked him if he could find me an old hospital screen—no trouble, he said, then started moaning about how dull the place is since I left. What rubbish! One X-ray technician? The Ryde District Soldiers' Memorial Hospital isn't *that* small. Ginge was always one to exaggerate.

Matron came to visit X-ray yesterday. What a tartar she is! If the H.M.O. is God, Matron has equal rank with the Virgin Mary, and I think virginity is a prerequisite for the job, so it isn't an invalid comparison. No man would ever get up the courage, it would take a dove flying in the window to quicken any matron. They're always battleships in full sail, but I must say that the Queens Matron is a very trim craft. Only about thirty-five, tall, good figure, red-gold hair, aquamarine eyes, beautiful face. You can't see much of the hair for the Egyptian headdress veil, of course, but the colour's definitely not out of a dye bottle. Her eyes would freeze a tropical lagoon, though. Glacial. Arctic. Oooooo-aa!

I felt rather sorry for her, actually. She's the Queen of Queens, so she can't possibly be a woman too. If you want to slap a coat of paint on a wall or you stick up a poster to amuse the patients, Matron decides what colour the paint will be or if the poster can stay there. She wears a pair of white cotton gloves, and while she can't do it in X-ray (strictly speaking, she's the guest of Sister Agatha in X-ray), on all ground where nurses work or play she runs the tip of one finger along skirting boards, window ledges, you name it, and God help a ward sister whose premises produce the faintest tinge of grey on that white glove! She heads the domestic as well as the nursing staff, she ranks equally with the General Medical Superintendent, and she's a member of the Hospital Board, which I have found out is chaired by Sir William Edgerton-Smythe, who just happens to be my dishy Mr. Duncan Forsythe's uncle. The reason why he's senior H.M.O. of Orthopaedics at his age becomes clearer. Unk must have been a great help. What a pity. I rather thought, looking at Mr. Forsythe, that he was the sort of man who doesn't stoop to string-pulling Upstairs. Why do idols always turn out to have feet of clay?

Anyway, I was introduced to Matron, who shook my hand for the precise number of milliseconds courtesy and rank demand. Whereas when I met Sister Agatha, she stared straight through me, Matron held my eyes à la Mrs. Delvecchio Schwartz. It seems Matron came to discuss the purchase of one of those new rotating set-ups for X-ray theatres, but a tour of the whole place was obligatory.

Tonight's wish: That I stop thinking of Forsythe the Crawler.

Saturday,
January 23rd, 1960

I'm here! I'm in! I hired a taxi truck this morning and hied myself and my cardboard cartons full of loot to 17c Victoria Street. The driver was a great bloke, never passed any sort of remark, just helped me inside with my loot, took the tip graciously, and pissed off to his next job. One of the cartons was chocka with tins of pink paint—ta much for the hundred quid, Dad—and another held about ten million assorted pink glass beads. I started in without any further ado. Got out the drum of ether soap (handy to work in a hospital and know the value of ether soap), my rags and scrubbing brush and steel wool, and set about cleaning. Mrs. Delvecchio Schwartz had said she'd clean it up when she showed me the place, and she hasn't done a bad job, really, but there are cockroach droppings everywhere. I'll have to ring Ginge at Ryde again and ask him for some of his cockroach poison. I *hate* the things, they're loaded with germs—well, they live in sewers, drains and muck.

I scrubbed and scoured until Nature called, then went out to look for the toilet, which I remembered was in the laundry shed. Pretty awful, the laundry shed. No wonder Mrs. Delvecchio Schwartz didn't include it in the tour. It has a gas-fired copper on a meter that eats pennies and two walloping big concrete tubs with an ancient mangle bolted to the floor. The bathroom is behind it to one side. There's an old tub with half its enamel missing, and when I put my hand on it, it tipped down with a thump—one of its ball-and-claw feet has been knocked off. A wooden block will help that, but nothing short of several coats of bicycle enamel will help the bath itself. A gas geyser on the wall provides hot water—another meter, more pennies. The wooden latticed mat I put straight into a laundry tub for a soak in ether soap. The toilet was in its own wee (good pun!) room, and it's a work of art—English china from the last century, its bowl adorned inside and out with cobalt blue birds and creepers. The cistern, very high on the wall and connected to the bowl by a squashed lead pipe, is also blue birds. I sat down pretty gingerly on the old wooden seat, though it is actually very clean—the thing is so high off the floor that even I can't pee without sitting down. The chain is equipped with a matching china knob, and when I pulled on it, Niagara Falls cascaded into the bowl.

I've worked all day and never seen a soul. Not that I had expected to see anybody, but I'd thought that I'd hear Flo in the distance—little kids are always laughing and squealing when they're not bawling. But the whole place was as silent as the grave. Where Pappy was, I had no idea. Mum had provided a hamper of edibles, so I had plenty of fuel for all the hard labour. But I wasn't used to being so absolutely *alone*. Very strange. The living room and the bedroom each had only one power point, but as I'm very knacky at stringing my own power, I got out Gavin's tool kit and multimeter and popped in a few extra outlets. Then I had to go to the front verandah to examine the fuse box. Yep, there was me! One of those ceramic plug-ins with a piece of three-amp wire between its poles. I took it out, shoved a fifteen-amp wire in it, and was just closing the box when this crew-cut young bloke in a rumpled suit with tie askew came through the gate. "Hullo," I said, thinking he was a tenant. "New here, eh?" was his answer. I said I was, then waited to see what happened next. "Whereabouts are you?" he asked. "Out the back near the laundry." "Not in the front ground floor flat?" I produced a scowl, which, when you're as dark as I am, can be very fierce. "What business is it of yours?" I demanded.

"Oh, it's my business all right." He reached inside his coat and produced a scuffed leather wallet, flipped it open. "Vice Squad," he said. "What's your name, Miss?"

"Harriet. What's yours?"

"Norm. What do you do for a living?"

I finished closing the fuse box door and put my hand under his elbow with a sultry look modelled on Jane Russell. At least I think it was sultry. "A cup of tea?" I asked.

"Ta," he said with alacrity, and let me escort him inside.

"If you're on the game, you're awful clean about it," he said, looking around my living room while I put the kettle on. *Pennies!* I'll have to buy bags of the ruddy things, there are so many gas meters to feed.

"I'm not on the game, Norm, I'm a senior X-ray technician at Royal Queens Hospital," I said, pottering about.

"Oh! Pappy brought you here."

"You know Pappy?"

"Who doesn't? But she doesn't charge, so she's apples."

I gave him a cuppa, poured one for myself, and found some sweet bikkies Mum had put in the hamper. We dunked them in our tea in silence for a minute, then I started to pump him about Vice. What a beaut learning experience! Norm was not only a mine of information, he was what Pappy would call a "complete pragmatist". You couldn't keep prostitution out of the social equation, no matter what all the wowsers like archbishops and cardinals and Metho ministers said, he explained, so the thing was to keep it quiet and orderly. Every girl on the street had her territory, and the trouble started when a new girl tried to poach on an established beat. All hell would break loose.

"Teeth and nails, teeth and nails," he said, taking another crunchy bikky. "Then the pimps get out their knives and razors."

"Um, so you don't arrest known prostitutes?" I asked.

"Only when the wowsers start making it impossible not to—stir up the Mothers' Leagues and the

Legions of Decency from the pulpit—flamin' pains in the arse, wowsers. Jeez, I hate them! But," he went on, suppressing his emotions, "your front ground floor flat is always a problem because 17c isn't in the trade. Mrs. Delvecchio Schwartz tries, but they come in all sorts, and then the feathers get ruffled in 17b and 17d."

Front ground floor flats at the Cross, I discovered, are just ideal for a girl on the game. You can bring the customers in via the French doors onto the verandah and shove them out the same way fifteen minutes later. And no matter who Mrs. Delvecchio Schwartz puts in our front ground floor flat, that woman or women always turn out to be on the game. I did a bit more probing, and learned that the two houses on either side of The House were brothels. What *would* Dad say about that? Not that I am going to tell him.

"Do you raid the brothels next door?" I asked.

Norm—a nice-looking bloke, by the by—looked utterly horrified. "I should bloody think not! They're the two poshest brothels in Sydney, cater to the very best clients. Sydney City Councilmen, politicians, judges, industrialists. If we raided them, we'd get strung up by the balls."

"Ooooooo-aa!" I said.

So we finished our tea and I chucked him out, but not before he'd invited me up to the Piccadilly pub ladies' lounge for a beer next Saturday afternoon. I accepted. Norm didn't even know there was a David

Murchison on my horizon—oh, thank you, Mrs. Delvecchio Schwartz! Here less than twelve hours, and I already have a date. I don't think that Norm is going to be my first affair, but he's definitely presentable enough to have a beer with. And a kiss?

Tonight's wish: That my life overflows with interesting men.

Sunday,
January 24th, 1960
I met several of The House's tenants today. The first two happened after I'd had a bath (there's no shower) and decided to visit the backyard. One of the things about Victoria Street that had intrigued me was that it had no streets or lanes leading off its left side, that our little cul-de-sac was a dead end, that there aren't any houses lower than number 17. The brick paving of my side passage continued in the backyard proper, which was crisscrossed with washing lines, a good few of them festooned in sheets, towels, and clothes which seemed to belong to a man and a woman. Cute little lace-trimmed Gorgeous Gussie panties, boxer shorts, men's shirts, girls' bras and blouses. I pushed through them—they were dry—and discovered why there were no side streets off the left side, and why we were a dead end. Victoria Street was perched on top of a sixty-foot sandstone cliff! Below me the slate roofs of Woolloomooloo's rows of terraced houses marched

off toward the Domain—for this time of year, its grass is lovely and green. I like the way it divides Woolloomooloo from the City, though I never realised it did until I stood at the back fence to look. All those new buildings in the City! So many storeys. But I can still see the AWA tower. To the right of Woolloomooloo is the Harbour, flaked with white because it's Sunday and the whole world has gone sailing. What a view! Though I'm very happy with my flat, I felt a twinge of envy for the inhabitants of 17c who are upstairs and whose flats look this way. Heaven, for a very few quid a week.

When I parted the sheets to go back to my painting, a young man carrying an empty basket was striding down the passage.

"Hullo, you must be the famous Harriet Purcell," he said as he reached me and stuck out a long, thin, elegant hand.

I was too busy staring to take it as quickly as I ought have.

"I'm Jim Cartwright," "he" said.

Oooooo-aa! A Lesbian! Close up it was obvious that Jim was not a man, even one with a limp wrist, but she was dressed in men's trousers—fly up the front instead of side placket—and a cream men's shirt with the cuffs folded up one turn. Fashionable men's haircut, not a trace of make-up, big nose, *very* fine grey eyes.

I shook her hand and said I was delighted, whereupon she left off laughing silently at me, took a tobacco pouch and papers out of her shirt pocket and rolled a cigarette with one hand only, as deftly as Gary Cooper did.

"Bob and I live on the second floor, up above Mrs. Delvecchio Schwartz—beaut-oh! We look this way and to the front."

From Jim I obtained more information about The House—who lives where. Mrs. Delvecchio Schwartz has the whole first floor except for the end room, right above my living room; it's rented by an elderly teacher named Harold Warner, though when Jim spoke of him, she screwed up her face in what looked like detestation. Directly above Harold is a New Australian from Bavaria named Klaus Muller, who engraves jewellery for a crust, and cooks and plays the violin for amusement. He goes away every weekend to friends near Bowral who hold apocalyptic barbecues with whole lambs, porkers and vealers on spits. Jim and Bob have the bulk of that floor, while the attic belongs to Toby Evans.

Jim started to grin when she said his name. "He's an artist—boy, will he like you!"

The cigarette disposed of in a garbage tin, Jim began taking the washing down, so I helped her fold the sheets and get the lot neatly tucked into the basket. Then Bob appeared, scurrying and frowning, tiny feet in blue kid flatties skittling like mouse paws. A little blonde Kewpie doll of a girl, much younger than Jim, and dressed in the height of female fashion four years ago—pastel blue dress with a great big full skirt held out by six starched petticoats, nipped-in waist, breasts squeezed into sharp points that my Bros always say mean "Hands off!".

She was late for her train, Bob explained in a fluster, and there were no taxis. Jim leaned to kiss her—now *that* was a kiss! Open mouths, tongues, purred mmmmms of pleasure. It did the trick; Bob calmed down. Washing basket on one inadequate hip, Jim guided Bob down the passage, turned the corner and vanished.

Eyes on the ground, I wandered toward my flat, busy thinking. I knew that Lesbians existed, but I had never met one before—officially, anyway. There have to be plenty of them among the heaps of spinster sisters in any hospital, but they give nothing of it away, it's just too dangerous. Get a reputation for that, and your career is on the garbage dump. Yet here were Jim and Bob making no secret of it! That means that while Mrs. Delvecchio Schwartz might object to girls on the game in her front ground floor flat, she isn't averse to housing a pair of very public Lesbians. Good for her!

"G'day, love!" someone screamed.

I jumped and looked toward the voice, which was feminine and issued from one of 17d's mauve lace windows. 17d's windows intrigued me greatly, between their mauve lace curtains and the boxes of puce-pink geraniums under each of them—the effect was actually quite pretty, and made 17d look like a seedy private hotel. A young, naked woman with masses of hennaed hair was leaning out of one window, lustily brushing the hair. Her breasts, very full and oh so slightly pendulous, swung merrily in time with the brush, and the top of her black bush peeked among the geraniums.

"G'day!" I called.

"Movin' in, eh?"

"Yes."

"Nice to see ya, hooroo!" And she shut the window.

My first Lesbians and my first professional whore!

Painting was a bit of a let-down after that, but paint I did until my arms ached and every wall and ceiling had a first coat. Some of me was missing my Sunday game of tennis with Merle, Jan and Denise, but swinging a paintbrush has much the same effect as swinging a tennis racquet, so at least I was getting my exercise. I wonder if there are any tennis courts near the Cross? Probably, but I don't think too many Crossites play tennis. The games here are a lot more serious.

Around sunset, someone knocked on my door. Pappy! I thought, then realised that it wasn't her knock. This one was authoritatively brisk. When I opened the door and saw David, my heart sank into my boots. I just hadn't expected him, the bastard. He came in before I issued an invitation and stared around with this look of fastidious distaste, how a cat might look if it found itself standing in a puddle of beery pee. My four dining chairs were good, stout wooden ones I hadn't started to sand down yet, so I poked one forward with my foot for David and perched myself on the edge of the table so I could look down on him. But he didn't fall for that—he stood so he could look me in the eye.

"Someone," he said, "is smoking hashish. I could smell it in the hall."

"That's Pappy's joss sticks—incense, David, incense! A good Catholic boy like you should recognise the whiff, surely," I said.

"I certainly recognise licentiousness and dissipation."

I could feel my mouth go straight. "A den of iniquity, you mean."

"If you like that phrase, yes," he said stiffly.

I made my tone conversational, tossed the words off like mere nothings. "As a matter of fact, I am living in a den of iniquity. Yesterday a Vice Squad constable checked up on me to make sure I'm not on the game, and this morning I said hello to one of the top-flight professionals next door when she leaned stark naked out of a window. This morning I also met Jim and Bob, the Lesbians who live two floors up, and watched them kiss each other with a great deal more passion than you've ever shown me! Put *that* in your pipe and smoke it!"

He changed tack, decided to back down and beseech me to come to my senses. At the end of his dissertation about how nice girls belong at home until marriage, he said, "Harriet, I *love* you!"

I blew a raspberry of thunderclap fart proportions, and I swear that as I did, a lightbulb flashed on above my head. *Suddenly I saw everything!* "You, David," I said, "are the sort of man who deliberately picks a very young girl so that you can mould her to suit your own needs. But it hasn't worked, mate. Instead of moulding me, you've broken your precious bloody mould!"

Oh, I felt as if I'd been let out of a cage! David had always cowed me with his lectures and sermons, but now I didn't give a hoot about his pontifications. He'd lost his power over me. And how cunning, never giving me an opportunity to judge him as a man by kissing or fondling or—perish the thought!—producing his dingus for my inspection, let alone use. Because he's so handsome and well-built and such an enviable catch, I'd stuck to him, convinced that the end result would be worth waiting for. Now, I realised that he'd always been his own end result. I wasn't ever to know his faults as a man, and the only way he could ensure that was to keep me from sampling other merchandise. I had had it all wrong—it wasn't David I had to get rid of, it was my old self. And I did get rid of my old self, right in that moment when I blew my raspberry.

So I let him prose on for a while about how I was going through a phase, and he'd be patient and wait until I came to my senses, yattata, yattata, yattata.

I'd found a packet of Du Mauriers in the laundry

and slipped it into my pocket. When he got to the bit about feeling my oats, I fished the cigs out of my pocket, stuck one in my mouth and lit it with a match from the gas stove.

His eyes popped out on stalks. "Put that thing out! It's a disgusting habit!"

I blew a cloud of smoke in his face.

"The next thing it will be hashish, and after that you'll start sniffing glue—"

"You're a narrow-minded bigot," I said.

"I am a scientist in medical research, and I have an excellent brain. You've fallen into bad company, Harriet, it doesn't take a Nobel Prize winner to work that out," he said.

I stubbed the cigarette in a saucer—it tasted vile, but I wasn't going to let him know that—and escorted him outside. Then I marched him to the front door. "Goodbye forever, David," I said.

Tears came into his eyes and he put his hand on my arm. "This is utterly wrong!" he said in a wobbly voice. "So many years! Let's kiss and make up, please."

That did it. I doubled my right hand into a fist and whacked him a beauty on the left eye. As he staggered—I do pack a punch, the Bros made sure of that—I saw a newcomer over his shoulder, and gave David a shove off the step down onto the path. I looked, I hoped for the benefit of the newcomer, like a particularly dangerous Amazon. Caught in a ridiculous situation by a stranger, David scuttled out the front gate and bolted down Victoria Street as if the Hound of the Baskervilles was after him.

Which left the newcomer and I to look each other over. Even given the fact that I was on the step and he on the path below it, I picked him as barely five foot six. Nuggety, though, standing lightly balanced on his toes like a boxer, his reddish-brown eyes gleaming at me wickedly. Nice straight nose, good cheekbones, a mop of auburn curls trimmed into discipline, straight black brows and thick black lashes. *Very* attractive!

"Are you coming in, or are you just going to stand there and decorate the path?" I asked coldly.

"I'm coming in," he said, but made no move to do so. He was too busy looking at me. A peculiar look, now that the wickedness was dying out of his eyes— detached, fascinated in an unemotional way. For all the world like a physician assessing a patient, though if he was a physician, I'd eat David's Akubra town hat. "Are you double-jointed?" he asked.

I said no.

"That's a pity. I could have put you in some grouse poses. There's not much meat on you and what there is looks sporty, but you've got very seductive breasts. They belong to your body rather than a bra manufacturer." He hopped up the step as he said this, then waited for me to precede him inside.

"You have to be the artist in the garret," I said.

"Dead on the knocker. Toby Evans. And you must

be the new girl in the back ground floor flat."

"Dead on the knocker. Harriet Purcell."

"Come upstairs and have a coffee, you must need one after the wallop you gave that poor silly coot outside. He's going to have a shiner for a month," he said.

I followed him up two flights of stairs to a landing which had a huge female symbol on one of its doors (Jim and Bob, undoubtedly) and an alpine view on the other (Klaus Muller, undoubtedly). Access to the garret was up a sturdy ladder. Toby went first, and as soon as I'd climbed onto firm ground he pulled a rope which plucked the ladder off the floor below, folded it against the ceiling.

"Oh, that's terrific," I said, staring about in amazement. "You can pull up the drawbridge and withstand a siege."

I was in an enormous dormered room with two alcoved windows at its back and two more at its front, where the ceiling sloped. The whole place was painted stark white and looked as sterile as an operating theatre. Not a pin out of place, not a smear or a stain, not a speck of dust or even the outline of a dried-up raindrop on the window panes. Because it was an attic, the windows had seats with white corduroy cushions on them. The paintings were turned with their faces to the wall in a white-painted rack and there was a big professional easel (painted white), a dais with a white chair on it and a little white chest of drawers beside the easel. That was the business area. For leisure he had two easy chairs covered in white corduroy, white bookshelves with every book rigidly straight, a white hospital screen around his kitchen nook, a square white table and two white wooden chairs. Even the floor had been painted white! Not a mark on it either. His lights were white fluorescent. The only touch of colour was a grey army blanket on his double bed.

Since he'd got personal first with that bit about my breasts—the cheek!—I said exactly what I was thinking. "My God, you must be obsessional! I'll bet when you squeeze the paint out of a tube, you do it from the bottom, then carefully bend the empty bit over and make sure it's perfectly squared."

He grinned and cocked his head to one side like an alert little dog. "Sit down," he said, disappearing behind his screen to make the coffee.

I sat and talked to him through the crisply ironed cotton folds of the screen, and when he came out with the coffee in two white mugs, we just kept on talking. He was a bush boy, he said, grew up around the enormous cattle stations of western Queensland and the Northern Territory. His father had been a barracks cook, but first and foremost a boozer, so it was Toby who did most of the cooking, kept his father in a job. He didn't seem to hold that against the old boy, who eventually died of the booze. Back then, Toby's paints were children's watercolours and his drawing blocks cheap butcher's paper, his pencils HB pilfered from the station office. After his dad's death, he headed for the Big Smoke to learn how to paint properly, and in oils.

"But it's grim, Sydney, when you don't know a soul and the hay sticks out from behind your ears," he said, pouring three-star hospital brandy into his second coffee. "I tried working in the cook trade—hotels, boarding houses, soup kitchens, Concord Repat Hospital. Awful, between the voices that didn't speak English and the cockroaches everywhere except Concord. I'll give hospitals this, they're clean. But the food is worse than station food. Then I moved to Kings Cross. I was living in a six-by-eight shed in the backyard of a house on Kellett Street when I met Pappy. She brought me home to meet Mrs. Delvecchio Schwartz, who told me I could have her attic for three quid a week and I could pay her when I had the money. You know, you see those statues of the Virgin Mary and Saint Teresa and the rest, and they're all beautiful women. But I thought Mrs. Delvecchio Schwartz, the ugly old bugger, was the most beautiful woman I've ever seen. One day, when I'm more confident, I'm going to paint her with Flo on her knee."

"Do you still cook?" I asked.

He looked scornful. "No! Mrs. Delvecchio Schwartz told me to get a job tightening nuts in a factory— 'Youse'll earn big bikkies and suffer not a bit, ace,' was how she put it. I took her advice, I tighten nuts in a factory in Alexandria when I'm not up here painting."

"How long have you been in The House?" I asked.

"Four years. I turn thirty in March," he said.

When I offered to wash the coffee mugs, he looked horrified—I daresay he thought I wouldn't do it properly. So I took myself off down to my own flat in a very thoughtful mood. What a day! What a weekend, for that matter. Toby Evans. It has a nice ring to it. But when he'd mentioned Pappy, I caught the shadow of a new emotion in his eyes. Sadness, pain. Light dawned—he's in love with Pappy! Whom I haven't seen since I moved in.

Oh, I'm tired. Time to put the light out and enjoy my second-ever sleep in a double bed. One thing I know—I am never going to sleep in a single bed again. What luxury!

**Wednesday,
February 3rd, 1960**
All I've been doing when I'm not doing routine chests is slapping pink paint on everything in my flat that stays still long enough. Though I've been around the Cross in daylight enough now to have my bearings. It's fabulous. The shops are like nothing I've ever seen, and I've eaten more strange things in a week than in the whole of the rest of my life put together. There's a French bakery produces long thin sticks of bread that are a dream, and a cake shop called a patisserie with these fantastic cakes of many

layers thin as wafers instead of jam rolls and cream sponges and lamingtons like an ordinary cake shop. Nectar and ambrosia whichever way I look. I bought something called potato salad—oh, the taste! And a cabbage salad called coleslaw—I gobbled a whole little plastic bin of it and farted all night, but I don't care. There's a brick of mince with a hard-boiled egg in the middle of it called Hungarian meatloaf. Salami instead of Devon, Tilsiter cheese instead of the sweating soapy stuff Mum buys from the grocer—I feel as if I've died and gone to heaven when it comes to food. It isn't very expensive either, which amazed me so much I remarked on it to the New Australian chap in my favourite delicatessen. His answer solved my vexed question about Blue Laws and opening hours—he said that all the businesses were run by family members, though he put his finger against the side of his nose when he said it. No employees in the union sense! And it keeps the prices down.

There are a couple of underwear shops have me goggling. The windows are full of transparent black or scarlet bras and bikini bottoms, negligees that would make David keel over in a seizure. Underwear for tarts.

Pappy tried to talk me into buying some as we walked home one evening, but I declined firmly.

"I'm just too dark," I explained. "Black or scarlet make me look as if I've got terminal cirrhosis of the liver."

I tried fishing for information about the situation between her and Toby, but she eluded every bait I put on my hook. That alone is highly suspect. Oh, if only I can work out a way to get them together! Neither with a family, each immersed in important activities—Pappy her studies, Toby his canvases. They were made for each other, and they'd have *beautiful* children.

Sister Agatha called me to her office today and informed me that from next Monday I'm coming off Chests and going to work in Casualty X-ray. *Cas!* I'm tickled pink. The best work of all, no end of variety, every case serious because the unserious stuff is shunted to main X-ray. And at Queens, Cas X-ray is Monday to Friday! That's because Queens doesn't have many emergencies at weekends. It's surrounded by factories to north, south and west, and east of it for miles are parks and sporting grounds. Its residential districts it shares with St. George Hospital, though it does have its share of ancient dilapidated terraces. Of course the State Government keeps trying to close Queens down, put the money Queens eats like candy floss into St. George and the small hospitals out in the west, where Sydney's population is mushrooming. However, I'll back Matron against the Minister for Health any day. Queens is not about to close, my new job in Cas is safe.

"You are an excellent technician, Miss Purcell," said Sister Agatha in her round-vowels accent, "and excellent with the patients too. These facts do not escape us."

"Yes, Sister, thank you, Sister," I said, backing out bowing.

Yippee, Cas!

Tonight's wish: That Pappy and Toby get married.

Saturday,
February 6th, 1960

Bash your head against a brick wall, Harriet Purcell, until the brain inside it *thinks*. What a fool you are! What a drongo!

Pappy and I went shopping this morning, armed with our string bags and our purses. On a Saturday morning, you can hardly move for people along Darlinghurst Road, but nobody's ordinary up at the Cross. This stunningly beautiful woman came stalking past with a poodle dyed apricot-pink on a rhinestone lead, dressed from head to foot in apricot silk and apricot kid. Her hair was the exact-same colour as the poodle's.

"Phew!" I breathed, staring after her.

"A knockout, isn't he?" asked Pappy, grinning.

"*He?*"

"Commonly known as Lady Richard. A transvestite."

"Camp as a row of tents, you mean," I said, flabbergasted.

"No, he's so into clothes that he's asexual, but a

lot of transvestites are heterosexual. They just like women's clothes."

And that was how the conversation started. Though I haven't seen Pappy at The House, we see a lot of each other during the week, so by this time I thought I knew her. But I don't know her at all.

She told me that it was high time I had an affair, and I fully agreed. But Norm the Vice Squad constable turned out to be a lousy kisser—drowned me in spit. We parted after our beer on the best of terms, but each of us knew there wasn't going to be anything in it. And, though I couldn't very well mention that to Pappy, Toby Evans is taken. A pity. I'm very attracted to him, and he looks as if he knows his way around a bed. Which was what Pappy was going on about as we walked, that My First Time couldn't possibly be with anyone insensitive, ignorant, dopey or up himself.

"He has to be experienced, considerate and tender," she said.

I started to laugh. "Listen to the expert!" I chortled.

Turns out she *is* an expert.

"Harriet," she said, sounding a bit exasperated, "haven't you wondered why you don't see much of me at the weekend?"

I said I had wondered, but presumed she was deep in a book.

"Oh, Harriet, you're dense!" she exclaimed. "I spend the weekends having sex with men."

"Men?" I asked, winded.

"Yes, men."

"In the plural?"

"In the plural."

Where does one go from there? I was still looking for what to say next when we turned into Victoria Street. "Why?" "Because I'm looking for something." "The perfect lover?" She rocked her head from side to side as if she'd like to shake me rather than it. "No, no, no! It's not about sex, it's about the spirit. I'm looking for a soul mate, I suppose."

I nearly suggested that he was sloshing paint on a canvas in the attic, but I bit my tongue and didn't. There was a young chap sitting on the stairs when we came in. Pappy flicked me a small smile of apology as he rose to his feet, and I scuttled ahead of them to my pink flat, where I sat down rather suddenly to get my wind back. So that was what Norm the Vice Squad constable had meant when he said Pappy didn't charge! No doubt she'd had sex with him too.

Time to sort out your priorities, Harriet Purcell. Everything you've been brought up to believe in is hanging in the balance. Pappy can't qualify as a "nice girl", yet she's the nicest girl I've ever met. But nice girls do not distribute sexual favours freely to any amount of men. It's only trollops do that. *Pappy* a trollop? No, that I won't admit! I am the sole member of my Bronte–Bondi–Waverley group hasn't had at least one affair, but Merle, for instance, doesn't think of herself as a trollop any more than she really is. Oh, the emotional gyrations I've witnessed as Merle plunged into love! The rhapsodies, the furies, the doubts, the eventual disillusionment. And those awful days once, while she waited for her overdue period to appear. It did, and the relief was something I'd felt as keenly as she, putting myself in her place. If anything keeps us on the straight and narrow, it's the fear of pregnancy. The only people who do abortions use knitting needles, but the alternative is a ruined reputation. Usually what happens is a sudden four-month disappearance, or a very hasty wedding and a "premature" baby. But whether a girl chooses to go into a home for four months and then adopt her baby out, or whether she marries the bloke, the talk follows her for the rest of her days. "She *had* to get married!" or "Well, we all know, don't we? She walks round with a face as long as a wet week, the fellow isn't to be seen, she looks fat in the waist, and then suddenly she visits her granny in Western Australia for a few months— who does she think she's fooling, eh?"

I don't believe I've ever subscribed to that sort of malice, but it is a fact of every girl's life. Yet here is Pappy, whom I love, playing with fire in all directions from pregnancy to V.D. to the possibility of being bashed up. Using sex to look for a soul mate! But how can sex find the soul in a man? The trouble is, I don't know any answers. What I do know is that I can't think any the worse of Pappy. Oh, poor Toby!

How must he feel? Has she had sex with him? Or is he the one she doesn't fancy? Yes, I don't know why I think that, but I do.

I couldn't settle, so I decided to go for a walk, lose myself in those crowds of fascinating people up at the Cross. But as I went through the front hall, there was Mrs. Delvecchio Schwartz sweeping it. To little effect. She used the broom so hard and fast that the dust just rose in clouds and then crusted on the floor behind her. It was on the tip of my tongue to ask if she'd ever thought of sprinkling wet tea leaves before she swept, but I wasn't game.

"Ripper-ace!" she said, beaming. "Come upstairs and have a wee snort of brandy."

"I haven't seen hide nor hair of you since I moved in," I said as I followed her up the stairs.

"Never intrude on people when they're busy, princess," she said, flopping down on her chair on the balcony and glugging brandy into two Kraft cheese spread glasses. Flo had been clinging to her skirts throughout, but now she scrambled onto my lap and lay looking up at me with those tragic amber eyes, yet smiling.

I sipped at the revolting stuff, but I couldn't like it. "I never hear Flo," I said. "Does she talk?"

"All the time, princess," said Mrs. Delvecchio Schwartz.

She was handling a pack of over-sized cards, then she fixed her X-ray eyes on me and put the cards down. "What's bothering you?" she asked.

"Pappy says she sleeps with a lot of men."

"Yep, that she does."

"What do you think about it? I always thought that landladies evicted girls who have men in their flats, and I know you do when it's the front ground floor flat."

"It ain't right to make real good women think they're wicked just because they like a bit of nooky," she said, drinking deeply. "Nooky's as normal and natural as pissin' and shittin'. As for Pappy, what's there to think about? Sex is her way of voyaging." Another X-ray glare at me. "It ain't your way, but, is it?"

I felt inadequate and squirmed. "Not so far, anyway," I said, and sipped again. Willie's tipple was beginning to taste better.

"You and Pappy are the opposite ends of women's life," said Mrs. Delvecchio Schwartz. "To Pappy, no touch means no love. She's a Libran Queen of Swords, and that ain't strong. Her Mars, mostly. Very poorly aspected. So's her Jupiter. Moon in Gemini squared to Saturn."

I think I've remembered that correctly.

"What am I?" I asked.

"Dunno 'til you tell me when you was born, princess."

"November the eleventh, nineteen thirty-eight," I said.

"Ah! Knew it! Scorpio woman! Very strong! Where?"

"Vinnie's Hospital."

"Right next door to the Cross! What time?" I racked my brains. "A minute past eleven in the morning."

"Eleven, eleven, eleven. Oh, bonza! Ripper-ace!" She huffed and creaked her chair, leaned back in it and closed her eyes. "Um, lessee . . . You rise in Aquarius— well, well!" The next minute she was on her hands and knees at a little cupboard to bring out a book so well worn it was falling to pieces, a few sheets of paper, and a cheap little plastic protractor. One of the sheets of paper, blank, was thrown to me together with a pencil.

"Write it all down as I tell youse," she said, and looked at Flo. "Angel, gimme some of your crayons." Flo slid off my lap and trotted into the living room, returned bearing a handful in blue, green, red, purple and brown.

"I do it all in me head—oughta be able to, after all these years," said Mrs. Delvecchio Schwartz, consulting her ratty book and making mysterious marks on a sheet already drawn up like a pie separated into twelve equal slices. "Yep, yep, real interesting. Write, Harriet, write! Three oppositions, all potent—Sun to Uranus, Mars to Saturn, Uranus to Midheaven. Most of the tension is removed by squares—lucky, eh?"

As she spoke at normal pace, I had to do a Flo and scribble to get all this down.

"Jupiter in the first house in Aquarius, your rising

sign—*very* powerful! You're gunna have a fortunate life, Harriet Purcell. Sun's in the tenth house, means you're gunna make your career your whole life."

That made me sit up straight! I scowled at her. "No, I am not!" I snapped. "I'm darned if I'll keep on taking X-rays until I'm old enough to retire! Carry a lead apron on my shoulders for forty years and have blood tests once a month? Bugger that!"

"There are careers and careers," she smirked. "Venus is in the tenth house too, and your Moon's in Cancer. Saturn's on the cusp of the second and third houses, means you'll always look after them what can't look after themselves." She sighed. "Oh, there's lotsa stuff, but none of it's worth a tuppenny bumper compared to your perfect quincunx between the Moon and Mercury!"

"*Quincunx?*" It sounded absolutely obscene.

"That's the aspect will do for me," she said, brushing her hands together in huge satisfaction. "You gotta look at everything in a chart before the quincunx makes sense, but the way your stars have progressed since you was born says the quincunx is *it*." The X-ray vision eyed me again, then she got to her feet, went inside and opened the fridge. Back she came with a plate holding chunks of what looked like horizontal sections through a snake. "Here, have some, princess. Smoked eel. Very high brain food. Klaus's mate Lerner Chusovich catches 'em and smokes 'em himself."

The smoked eel was delicious, so I tucked in.

"You know a lot about astrology," I said, chewing away.

"I should bloody hope so! I'm a soothsayer," she said.

Suddenly I remembered the blue-rinsed lady from the upper North Shore, the several others I had encountered in the front hall, and a lot of things fell into place. "Those prosperous-looking women are clients?" I asked.

"Bullseye, ace!" She speared me on those icy searchlights yet again. "D'you believe in the here-after?"

I thought about that before I answered. "Only maybe. It's a bit hard to believe in the reason and justice behind God's immutable purpose when you work in a hospital."

"This ain't about God, it's about the hereafter."

I said I wasn't sure about that either.

"Well, I deal in the hereafter," said Mrs. Delvecchio Schwartz. "I cast horoscopes, deal out the cards, scry into me Glass"—she said it with a capital letter— "communicate with the dead."

"How?"

"Haven't got a clue, princess!" she said cheerfully. "Didn't even know I could until I was past thirty."

Flo climbed onto her lap for some mother's milk, and was put down gently but firmly. "Not now, angel, Harriet and I are talking." She went to the lit-tle cupboard and brought out a very heavy object covered with dirty pink silk, put it on the table. Then she handed me the deck of cards. I turned them over expecting to see the usual hearts, diamonds, clubs, spades, but these were pictures. The one on the bottom showed a naked woman surrounded by a wreath, all of it brightly coloured.

"That's the World," said Mrs. Delvecchio Schwartz.

Underneath was a card showing a hand holding a chalice which poured out thin streams of liquid. A dove with a small circular object in its beak hovered upside down over the chalice, on which was written what looked like a W.

"The Ace of Cups," she said.

I put the deck down very gingerly. "What are they?"

"A tarot pack, princess. I can do all sorts of things with it. I can read your fortune if you like. Ask me a question about your future, and I'll answer it. I can sit down all by meself and deal out a gypsy spread to get the feel of what's happening in The House, to the people in my care. The cards have mouths. They speak."

"Rather you to hear them than me," I said, shivering.

She went on as if I hadn't interrupted. "This is the Glass," she said, whipping the dirty pink silk off the object she'd taken from the cupboard. Then she reached across the table to take my hand, and put it on the cool surface of that beautiful thing. Flo, standing watching, suddenly gasped and fled to hide behind her mother, then peered at me from around that bulk with wide eyes.

"Is it glass?" I asked, fascinated at how it held everything inside it—the balcony, its owner, a plane tree—but upside down.

"Nope, it's the real thing—crystal. A thousand years old. Seen everything, has the Glass. I don't use it much, it's like a fit of the dry horrors."

"Dry horrors?" How many questions were there to ask?

"The gin jitters, the whisky wackos—delirium tremens. With the Glass, youse never knows what's gunna come screamin' up to push its face against the inside of the outside. Nope, I use the cards most. And for me ladies, Flo."

The moment she uttered Flo's name, I knew why I was being made privy to all this. Mrs. Delvecchio Schwartz, for what reason I had no idea, had decided that I must be told about this secret life. So I asked the ultimate question. "Flo?"

"Yep, Flo. She's me medium. She just knows the answers to the questions me ladies ask. I wasn't born with the gift meself—it just sorta snuck up on me when I was—oh, Harriet, *desperate* for money! I started the fortune telling as a racket, and that's honest. Then I discovered I did have the gift. But Flo's a natural. Scares the bejeezus outta me sometimes, does Flo."

Yes, and she scares the bejeezus out of me too, though not with revulsion. I could believe it all. Flo doesn't look as if she belongs to this world, so it isn't much of a surprise to find that she has access to another world. Maybe it is her natural one. Or maybe she's an hysteric. They come in all ages, hysterics. But knowing, I simply loved Flo more. It answered the riddle of the sorrow in her eyes. What she must see and feel! *A natural*.

After drinking a full glass of brandy, I got down the stairs rather clumsily, but I didn't flop on my bed to sleep it off, I wanted to get all this down before I forgot it. And I'm sitting here with my Biro in my hand wondering why I'm not outraged, why I'm not of a mind to give Mrs. Delvecchio Schwartz the sharp edge of my tongue for exploiting her weeny daughter. I do have a sharp edge to my tongue. But this is so far from anything I know or understand, and even in the short time I've lived here, I've grown a lot. At least that's how I feel. Sort of new and changed. I like that monstrosity named Mrs. Delvecchio Schwartz, but I *love* her child. What stills the sharp edge of my tongue, Horatio, is the realisation that there are indeed more things in heaven and earth than Bronte's philosophy ever dreamed of. And I can't go back to Bronte any more. I can never go back to Bronte.

Flo the medium. Her mother had implied that she herself communicated with the dead through the Glass, but she hadn't really described Flo's mediumistic activities as concerned with the dead. Flo knows the answers to the questions "me ladies" ask.

I conjured up visions of "me ladies" and had to admit that they didn't look like women chasing beloved phantoms. All different, but none with that air of unassuaged grief. Whatever drove them to seek help from Mrs. Delvecchio Schwartz was, I somehow knew, connected to this world, not the next. Though Flo was not of this world.

Perhaps in the beginning, when it was a racket to earn the money she was desperate for, Mrs. Delvecchio Schwartz valued money. I imagine it bought her The House. But these days? In that bare, bleak, awful surrounding? Mrs. Delvecchio Schwartz doesn't give tuppence for comfort, and nor does Flo. Wherever they dwell, it isn't among pretty dresses and comfy couches. I can even understand why Flo is still feeding off the breast. It's a link with her mother she needs. Oh, Flo! Angel. Your mother is the whole of your world, its beginning and its end. She's your anchor and your refuge. And I am honoured that you've welcomed me into your affections, angel. I feel blessed.

Monday,
February 8th, 1960
I started in Casualty X-ray this morning, I must confess not quite such an eager beaver as I used to be. My life is getting a weeny bit complicated, between nymphomania and soothsaying. Though I'm not sure that confining one's sexual activity to the week-

end qualifies as nymphomania. However, within ten minutes of starting, I forgot that there was any other world than Cas X-ray.

There are three of us—a senior, a middleman (me), and a junior. I'm not sure that I *like* Christine Leigh Hamilton, as my boss introduced herself. She's in her middle thirties, and, from overhearing the occasional conversation between her and Sister Cas, she's just starting to suffer what I call the "Old Maid Syndrome". If I'm still single when I hit my middle thirties, I will cut my own throat rather than go through the Old Maid Syndrome. It arises out of spinsterhood and contemplation of an old age spent living with another female in relative penury unless there's money in the family, which there usually isn't. And the chief symptom is an overwhelming determination to catch a man. Get married. Have some babies. *Be vindicated as a woman.* I sympathise, even if I'm determined not to contract the malady myself. I'm never sure which drive is uppermost in the O.M.S.—the drive to find someone to love and be loved back, or the drive to achieve financial security. Of course Chris is an X-ray technician, so she's paid a man's wage, but if she went to a bank and asked for a mortgage so she could buy a house, she'd be turned down. Banks don't give mortgages to women, no matter what they're paid. And most women are paid poorly, so they never manage to save much for their old age. I was talking to Jim about it—she's a master printer, but she doesn't get equal pay for equal work. No wonder some women go funny and abrogate men altogether. Bob is a secretary to some tycoon, isn't exactly overpaid either. And if you work for the Government, you have to leave when you get married. That's why all the sisters and female department heads are old maids. Though a very few are widows.

"If it wasn't for Mrs. Delvecchio Schwartz, we'd lead a dog's life," Jim told me. "Running scared of being found out and evicted, not able to afford to buy a place. The House is our lifeline."

Anyway, back to Chris Hamilton. The trouble is that she's not a man-trap. Blocky sort of figure, hair she can't do a thing with, glasses, the wrong make-up, grand piano legs. Which could be overcome if she had any sense, but she doesn't. Man sense, I mean. So whenever a man, especially one in white, enters our little domain, she simpers and rushes around and turns cartwheels trying to impress him. Oh, not the New Australian porters (they're beneath her notice), but even the ambulancemen get cups of tea and coy chats over the bikkies. If we're not busy, that is, give her her due. Her best friend is Marie O'Callaghan, who happens to be Sister Cas. They share a flat together in Coogee, are both middle-thirties. And they *both* have the Old Maid Syndrome! Why is it that women aren't deemed real women unless they've got a husband and kids? Of course if Chris could read this, she'd sneer and say it's all very well for me, I'm a mantrap. But why are we categorised like that?

The junior is very shy and, as usually happens in a busy unit, spends most of her day in the darkroom. Looking back on my own training, there were times when I thought I was better qualified to work for Kodak than in X-ray. But somehow it all evens out in the end, we do get enough experience with the patients to pass our exams and turn into people who send the junior to the darkroom. The trouble is that it's a question of priorities, especially in Cas, where you can't make mistakes or have ponk films.

Five minutes hadn't gone by before I realised that I wasn't going to have it all my own way in Cas X-ray. The Cas surgical registrar came in accompanied by his senior resident, took one look at me and started laying on the charm with a trowel. I don't know why I have that effect on some doctors (some, not all!), because I honestly am not after anything in a white coat. I'd rather be an old maid than married to someone who's always rushing off on a call. And all they can talk about is medicine, medicine, medicine. Pappy says I'm sexy, though I haven't got a clue what that term means if Brigitte Bardot is sexy. I do *not* wiggle my bottom, I do *not* pout, I do *not* give men languishing glances, I do *not* look as if I haven't got a brain in my head. Except for Mr. Duncan Crawler Forsythe on the ramp, I look straight through the bastards. So I didn't do a thing to encourage that pair of doctors, but they still dawdled and got in my way. In the end I told them to piss off, which horrified Chris (and the junior).

Luckily a suspected fracture of the cervical spine came in through our double doors at that moment. I got down to business, determined that Chris Hamilton wasn't going to be able to lodge any complaints about my work with Sister Agatha.

I soon discovered that I wouldn't have time to eat lunch with Pappy—we eat on the run. By the time I'd been in the place four hours, we'd had three suspected spinal fractures, a Potts fracture of tibia, fibula and ankle bones, several comminuted fractures of the long bones, a fractured rib cage, a dozen other oddments and a critical head injury who came in comatose and fitting and went straight on up to neurosurgery theatre. Once she got over her miff at the way that couple of eligible doctors had behaved, Chris was smart enough to see that I wasn't going to be a handicap when it came to the patients, and we soon had a system going.

The unit was officially open between six in the morning and six in the evening. Chris worked the early shift and knocked off at two, I was to start at ten and knock off at six.

"It's a pleasant fiction that we ever knock off on time," Chris said as she buttoned her coat over her uniform about half-past three, "but that's what we aim for. I don't approve of keeping the junior any longer than necessary, so make sure you send her off at four unless there's a huge flap on."

Yes, ma'am.

I finally got off a bit after seven, and I was tired enough to think of hailing a taxi. But in the end I plodded home on foot, though people are always saying that Sydney isn't a safe city for women to walk in after dark. I took my chances anyway, and nothing happened. In fact, until I reached Vinnie's Hospital, I hardly saw a soul. And so to bed. I'm buggered.

Tuesday,
February 16th, 1960

I finally saw Pappy tonight. When I pushed the front door open I nearly knocked her over, but it can't have been an important appointment, because she turned and walked to my flat with me, came in and waited while I made coffee.

Settled in my own easy chair, I looked at her properly and realised that she didn't look well. Her skin had a yellow tinge and her eyes looked more Oriental than usual, with black rings of fatigue under them. Her mouth was all swollen, and below each ear was an ugly bruise. Though it was a humid evening, she kept her cardigan on—bruises on the arms too?

Though I'm a terrible cook, I offered to fry some sausages to go with the coleslaw and potato salad I can't get enough of. She shook her head, smiled.

"Get Klaus to teach you to cook," she said. "He's a genius at it, and you've got the right temperament to cook well."

"What sort of temperament cooks well?" I asked.

"You're efficient and organised," she said, letting her head flop back against the chair.

Of course I knew what was wrong. One of the weekend visitors had been rough with her. Not that she would admit it, even to me. My tongue itched to tell her that she was running a terrible risk going to bed with men she hardly knew, but something stopped me, I let it lie. Though Pappy and I were better friends in many ways than Merle and I had been—oooooo-aa, that's an interesting tense!—I had a funny feeling that there were fences I'd be wise not to try to peek over. Merle and I were sort of equals, even if she had had a couple of affairs and I hadn't had any. Whereas Pappy is ten years older than me and immensely more experienced. I can't summon up the courage even to pretend that I'm her equal.

She mourned that we weren't seeing much of each other these days—no lunches, no walks to and from Queens. But she knows Chris Hamilton, and agrees that she's a bitch.

"Watch your step" was how she put it.

"If you mean, don't look at the men, I've already taken that point," I answered. "Luckily we're awfully busy, so while she bustles around making a cuppa for some twit in white pants, I get on with the work." I cleared my throat. "Are you all right?"

"So-so," she said with a sigh, then changed the subject. "Um, have you met Harold yet?" she asked very casually.

The question surprised me. "The schoolteacher above me? No."

But she didn't lead the conversation down that alley either, so I gave up.

After she left I fried myself a couple of snags, wolfed down potato salad and coleslaw, then went upstairs looking for company. Starting at ten means not getting up early, and I had enough sense to know that if I went to bed too early I'd wake with the birds. Jim and Bob were having a meeting, I could hear the buzz of voices through their door, a loudly neighing laugh which didn't belong to either of them. But Toby's ladder was down, so I jingled the bell he's rigged up for visitors, and got an invitation to come on up.

There he was at the easel, three brushes clenched between his teeth, four in his right hand, the one in his left hand engaged in scrubbing the tiniest smidgin of paint on a dry surface. It looked like a wisp of vapour.

"You're a southpaw," I said, sitting on white corduroy.

"You finally noticed," he grunted.

I supposed that the thing he was working on was an excellent piece of work, but I'm not equipped to judge. To me, it looked like a slag heap giving off steam in a thunderstorm, but it caught the eye—very dramatic, wonderful colours. "What is it?" I asked.

"A slag heap in a thunderstorm," he said.

I was tickled! Harriet Purcell the art connoisseur strikes again! "Do slag heaps smoke?" I asked.

"This one does." He finished his wisp, carried his brushes to the old white enamel sink and washed them thoroughly in eucalyptus soap, then dried them and polished the sink with Bon Ami. "At a loose end?" he asked, putting the kettle on.

"Yes, as a matter of fact."

"Can't you read a book?"

"I often do," I said a little tartly—oh, he could rub one up the wrong way!—"but I'm working in Casualty now, so when I get off duty I'm in no fit condition to read a book. What a rude bastard you are!"

He turned to grin at me, eyebrows wriggling—so attractive! "You talk as if you read books," he said, folding a laboratory filter paper, inserting it into a glass laboratory funnel, and spooning powdery coffee into it. I was fascinated, not having seen him making coffee before. The screen was shoved out of the way for a change—it must have got a mark on it.

The coffee was brilliant, but I thought I'd stick to my new electric percolator. Easier, and I'm not all that fussy. Naturally he'd be fussy, it's in his soul.

"What do you read?" he asked, sitting down and throwing one leg over the arm of his chair.

I told him everything from *Gone With The Wind* to *Lord Jim* to *Crime and Punishment*, after which he said that he confined his own reading to tabloid newspapers and books on how to paint in oils. He suffered, I discovered, a huge inferiority complex about his lack of formal education, but he was too prickly about it for me to attempt any repair measures.

Artists traditionally dressed like hobos, I had thought, but he dresses very well. The slag heap in a thunderstorm had received his attentions in clothes the Kingston Trio wouldn't have been ashamed to perform in—crew-neck mohair sweater, the beautifully ironed collar of his shirt folded down over it, a pair of trousers creased sharp as a knife, and highly polished black leather shoes. Not a skerrick of paint on himself, and when he'd leaned over me to put my mug down I couldn't smell a trace of anything except some expensive piney-herby soap. Obviously tightening nuts in a factory paid extremely well. Knowing him a little bit by now, I thought that his nuts would be perfect, neither too loose nor too tight. When I said that to him, he laughed until the tears ran down his face, but he wouldn't share the joke with me.

"Have you met Harold yet?" he asked later.

"You're the second person tonight to put that question to me," I said. "No, and I haven't met Klaus either, but no one asks if I've met him. What's so important about Harold?"

He shrugged, didn't bother to answer. "Pappy, eh?"

"She looks terrible."

"I know. Some bastard got a bit too enthusiastic."

"Does that happen often?"

He said no, apparently oblivious to the hard stare I was giving him. His face and eyes looked concerned but not anguished. What a good actor he was! And how much it must hurt him to have to endure that kind of rejection. I wanted to offer him comfort, but that tongue of mine has developed a habit lately of getting too tied up to speak, so I said nothing.

Then we talked about his life in the bush following his dad around, of this station and that station out where the Mitchell grass stretches to infinity "like a silver-gold ocean", he said. I could see it, though I never have. Why don't we Aussies know our own country? Why do we all have this urge to go to England instead? Here I am in this house stuffed with extraordinary people, and I feel like a gnat, a worm. I don't know *anything*! How can I ever grow tall enough to look any of them in the eye as equals?

Wednesday,
February 17th, 1960

My goodness, I was in a self-abnegatory frame of mind last night when I wrote the above! It's Toby, he has that effect on me. I would really like to go to bed with him! What's the matter with Pappy, that she can't see what's right under her nose?

Saturday,
February 20th, 1960

Well, I did it at last. I've had the family to dinner in my new flat. I invited Merle too, but she didn't come. She rang me in January while I was still in Chests, and I had to have a junior tell her that I couldn't come to the phone, that staff are not allowed to receive private calls. Apparently Merle took it as a personal rebuff, because whenever I've phoned her at home since then, her mother says she's out. The trouble is that she's a hairdresser, and they seem to spend half their lives on the phone making personal calls. At Ryde the policy wasn't so strict, but Queens isn't the same kind of institution. Anyway.

I'd wanted to have Mrs. Delvecchio Schwartz and Flo to dinner as well, but that lady just grinned and said she'd come down later to say hello.

It wasn't a huge success, though on the surface it was smooth enough. We had to wedge up at the table, but I'd grabbed extra chairs from the front ground floor flat, which is vacant again. Two women and a man who said they were siblings had rented it, but I tell you, men are not fussy when it comes to getting rid of their dirty water. The prettier of the two "sisters" made Chris Hamilton look like Ava Gardner, and both of them stank of stale, horribly cheap scent over the top of their B.O. The "brother" just had B.O. They were doing a roaring trade until Mrs. Delvecchio Schwartz rang the Vice Squad and the paddy wagon arrived. There's an American air-craft carrier in port, and when I pushed the front door open on Thursday night, I saw sailors from arsehole to breakfast—sitting on the stairs, leaning against Flo's scribbles in the hall, spilling into Pappy's hall and trooping by the dozen to the upstairs toilet, which was flushed so often that it took to groaning and gurgling. Mrs. Delvecchio Schwartz was not amused. The "brother" and his "sisters" were hauled off to the pokey in the paddy wagon, and the sailors scattered far and wide at the sight of the Boys in Blue behind Norm and his sergeant, a hugely beefy bloke named Merv. Good old Norm and Merv, stars of the Kings Cross Vice Squad!

It really hurt that I didn't dare tell this story to the family.

As I haven't met Klaus yet, let alone started to learn to cook, I cheated and imported all these deli-cious foods from my favourite delicatessen. But they didn't like any of it, from the macaroni salad to the dolmades and the shaved ham. I'd bought this divine orange liquer gateau for pudding, skinny layers of cake separated by thick layers of aromatic butter cream. They just picked at it. Oh, well. I daresay steak-and-chips followed by Spotted Dick and cus-tard or ice-cream with choccy syrup are what they dream of when their tummies rumble in the middle of the night.

They walked around like cats in a strange place they've made up their mind not to like. The Bros pushed through the bead curtain to inspect my bed-room a bit bashfully, but Mum and Dad ignored it, and Granny was too obsessed with the fact that she needed to pee every thirty minutes. Poor Mum had to keep taking her outside and down to the laundry because my blue-birded toilet is too high for Granny to get up on by herself. I apologised for the state of the toilet and bathroom, explained that when I had the time I was going to do everything out in bicycle enamel so it would look absolutely spiffy. Cobalt blue, white and a scarlet bathtub, I rattled feverish-ly. Most of the conversation fell to me.

When I asked if anyone had seen Merle, Mum told me that she was convinced I didn't want to have anything to do with her now I had moved. She wouldn't believe that Queens refused to let its staff take personal phone calls. Mum spoke in the gentle tones mothers use when they think their children are going to be bitterly disappointed, but I just shrugged. Goodbye, Merle.

They had more news about David than about Merle, though he hadn't visited them—didn't dare, was my guess, until that wacko shiner I'd given him faded.

"He's got a new girl," Mum remarked casually.

"I hope she's a Catholic," I remarked casually.

"Yes, she is. And she's all of seventeen."

"That fits," I said, breathing a sigh of relief. No more David Murchison! He's found a new bit of female clay to mould.

After I'd cleared the uneaten gateau away and made a pot of tea, Mrs. Delvecchio Schwartz and Flo materialised. Oh, dear. The family didn't know *what* to make of them! One didn't talk, the other's grammar wasn't the best, and the most that could be said for their unironed dresses was that they were clean. Flo, barefoot as always, was clad in the usual snuff-brown pinny, while her mother sported orange daisies on a bright mauve background.

After giving my tall, athletic-looking Dad the unmistakable glad-eye, my landlady sat down and monopolised him, much to Mum's annoyance. As her excuse, Mrs. Delvecchio Schwartz chose the Harriet Purcells, and quizzed him as to why, when there wasn't one in his generation, he'd bestowed the dread name on his only daughter. Normally oblivious to feminine advances, Dad absolutely glowed at all this attention— even *flirted*! He might be pushing eighty, but he doesn't look more than sixty-five. In fact, I thought, watching the pair of them, they went well together. By the time she got up to go, Mum was so livid that poor Granny, legs and eyes crossed, was desperate to go too. Only when Mrs. Delvecchio Schwartz was well and truly gone did Mum oblige Granny. I'd never seen Mum jealous before.

"That kid gave me the jitters," Gavin said. "Looks as if God intended to make her retarded, then forgot and gave her a brain."

My hackles rose as high as Mum's; I glared at him, the myopic git! "Flo is special!" I snapped.

"She looks half-starved to me," was Granny's verdict when she and Mum returned from the toilet. "What a great lump of a woman her mother is! Very common." That is the most damning thing Granny can say about anyone. *Common.* Mum agreed fervently.

Oh, dear. I ushered them out at ten, stood and waved goodbye as Dad drove off in the new Ford Customline, and hoped they would never return. What they said about me, my flat, The House, Flo and Mrs. Delvecchio Schwartz as they went home I can only guess, except that I had a fair idea Dad's opinion of my landlady was a bit different from Mum's. My bet is that the old horror was just making enough mild mischief to make sure the Purcell Family did not make The House a regular stop whenever they went out.

What makes me want to cry is that I was so bursting with opinions and impressions and conclusions about everything that's happened to me in the last four weeks, yet the moment I looked at their faces as they eyed Flo's scribbles in the front hall, I knew that I couldn't air a one of them. Why is that, when I still love them to death? I do. I do! But it's like going down to the Quay to farewell a friend heading off for England on the old *Himalaya.* You stand there looking up at the hundreds of faces clustered at the rail, holding your brightly coloured paper streamer in your hand, and the tugs get the ship under way, it unglues itself from the wharf, and all the streamers, including yours, snap and float on the dirty water with no purpose left except to contribute to the flotsam.

In future I am going to Bronte to see them. I know I said in here somewhere that I could never go back to Bronte, but I meant inside my soul. My body is going to have to do its duty, however.

**Sunday,
February 28th, 1960**
Tomorrow I can propose marriage to some bloke I fancy because this is a Leap Year, February has twenty-nine days. Fat chance.

Today I met Klaus, who didn't go to Bowral for the weekend. He's a chubby little bloke in his middle fifties with big round pale blue eyes, and he told me that he'd been a soldier in the German army during the War, a paper pusher in a depot near Bremen. So it was the British who interned him in a camp in Denmark. They offered him his choice of Australia, Canada or Scotland. He picked Australia because it was so far away, worked as a clerk for the Government for two years, then went back to the work he was trained for, goldsmithing. When I asked him if he'd teach me to cook, he beamed all over his face and said he'd be delighted. His English is so good that his accent is almost American, and he doesn't have any SS tattoos in his armpits because I saw him hanging out his washing in his singlet. So poop to you, David Murchison, with your petty biases against New Australians. Klaus and I made a date for nine o'clock on next Wednesday night, which he assured me wasn't too late an hour for a Continental. I was fairly sure I'd be home by then even if Cas was a nightmare.

On Friday night I had stopped in at the Piccadilly pub's bottle department to buy a quart of three-star from Joe Dwyer, whom I'm getting to know quite well now that brandy doesn't taste so foul. This afternoon I trotted it up the stairs to the lady herself, who greeted it and me with great enthusiasm. She fascinates me, I want to find out heaps more about her.

While Flo took her dozens and dozens of crayons and drew her aimless squiggles on a freshly painted section of wall just inside, we sat on the balcony in the steamy salty air with our Kraft cheese spread glasses, a plate of smoked eel, a loaf of bread, a pound of butter and all the time in the world, or so it seemed. She never once gave me the impression that perhaps someone else was due to visit, let alone tried to hustle me out quickly. I noticed, though, that she always kept an eye on Flo, sat herself where she could see Flo scribbling, and nodded and grunted whenever the little sprite turned her head with an enquiring look.

I yattered on about my continued virginity, about David, about Norm's disappointingly sloppy kiss; she listened as if it was important and assured me that the breaking of my hymen was definitely in the offing because it had appeared in the cards.

"Another King of Pentacles, another medical man," she said, making a sandwich out of smoked eel, bread and butter. "He's right next to your Queen of Swords."

"Queen of Swords?"

"Yep, Queen of Swords. Except for Bob, we're all Queens of Swords in The House, princess. Strong!" She went on about this King of Pentacles next to me. "A ship what passes in the night. Which is real good, princess. You ain't gunna fall in love with him. It's murder to do it for the first time with someone you think you're in love with." Her face took on an expression of mingled malice, amusement and smugness. "Most men," she said conversationally, "ain't very good at it, y'know. Oh, they brag a lot among themselves, but braggin' is all it is, take me word for it. See, men are different from us in more ways than havin' dinguses, hur-hur-hur. They *gotta* come—they gotta fire the old mutton gun, or they go barmy. That's what flogs the poor bastards on like lemmings to the cliff." She sighed. "Yeah, lemmings to the cliff! But we don't need to come, so for us it's kinda— I dunno, less important." She huffed with exasperation. "No, that ain't the right word, important."

"Compulsive?" I suggested.

"Spot on, princess! Compulsive. So if your first time is with someone you think shits caramel custard, you're likely to be disappointed. Pick a real experienced bloke who loves pleasurin' women as much as he loves shootin' his load. And he's there in the cards for youse, I promise."

Finally I got around to telling her about my family's dismay, even though she was a big part of it—she can take stuff like that on the chin—and about the ship with the broken streamers.

As we talked she fondled the cards like friends, occasionally turning one up and sliding it back into the pack, I fancied a bit absently. Then she asked me whether I was on the ship or the shore, and I said on the shore, definitely on the shore.

"Good, good," she said, pleased. "It ain't you who's lost hold of the ground, princess. You never will either. Feet as firmly planted as a big old gum tree. Not even an axe can chop you down. You ain't one to drift with the tide, which is what our Pappy does. Like a bit of weed at the mercy of the current. You're the bringer of light to The House, Harriet Purcell, the bringer of light. I've been waitin' for youse for a long time." She glugged down the last of her brandy and poured another. Then she shuffled the cards properly and began to lay them out.

"Am I still there?" I asked selfishly.

"Large as life and twice as beautiful, princess."

"Am I ever going to fall in love?"

"Yeah, yeah, but not yet, so hold your horses. There's tonsa men, but. Ah, here's the other medical bloke! See? That's him there, the King of Pentacles I keep seein' for youse every time. Hur-hur-hur."

Wait, and all will be answered. I'd wondered what she was on about with her Kings of Pentacles, now I found out.

"This one's a real posh chap, talks plummier than Harold. A mile of letters after his name. Not in the first flush of youth, as they say."

My heart did a funny flip inside my chest as I thought of Mr. Duncan Forsythe the orthopod. No, surely not. A senior H.M.O. and a lowly X-ray technician? Not on. But I listened as closely as Chris Hamilton would to the minister supervising her wedding vows.

"There's a wife and two sons in their teens. Heaps of money in the family—he don't need to work, but he works like a navvy 'cos work's all that keeps him goin'. The wife is as cold as a stepmother's breast, so he don't get nothin' at home except a hot meal. Ain't in the habit of playin' around, but he's hooked on you, the poor fish."

That, no matter what the cards said, was a fallacy. I'd only seen Mr. Forsythe once. Mrs. Delvecchio Schwartz gave me a wicked grin, but kept on dealing her cards.

"That's the lot about you. Now let's look at the rest of 'em. Ah! I see a man for Pappy too! This one ain't in the first flush of youth either, and he's got as many letters after his name as your bloke does. Jeez! What's this? Oh, shit!"

She stopped, frowning, and studied the cards,

pulled another, grunted, shook her head a little sadly, I thought. But she didn't volunteer any information. "Toby's caught in a net he didn't make," she said when she resumed her spread, "but he's gunna break out of it after a while. Good young fella, Toby." She gave a rumble as she saw the next card. "There I am, the Queen of Swords! Real well placed. Yeah, yeah, I keep shovin' 'em back in."

I was growing a little bored, perhaps, because she didn't always inform me what each card meant, or how it fitted into the general picture. But about four or five cards after the Queen of Swords, she put down a card showing a figure lying prone with ten separate swords stuck in its back—what sex it was you couldn't tell. The moment she saw it she jumped, shivered, took a swig of brandy. "Shit!" she hissed. "There's the fuckin' Ten of Swords again, with Harold right next to it."

I was so busy swooning with delight that I hardly heard all she said—she'd used the Great In-And-Out Word without turning a hair! Maybe one day I'd get up the courage to do the same. But as I couldn't very well comment on that, I asked about the Ten of Swords, what it meant.

"If you're the Queen of Swords, princess, it's the death card. If you're the queen of a different suit—Wands or Pentacles or Cups—then it's more likely to mean ruin than death. And Harold right next to it. Always Harold right next to it."

The skin around my mouth went numb, I looked

at her in terror. "Are you seeing your own death?" I asked.

She laughed and laughed, genuinely hearty laughter. "No, no! It ain't that, princess! Youse can never see things like death for yourself! As far as the seer's concerned, the cards are dumb as mummies in a tomb about the future. I'm discombobulated because I dunno what Harold and the Ten of Swords means. I just keep on turning the pair of them up, have done since New Year's Eve."

Harold was upside down. "The King of Wands reversed" was how Mrs. Delvecchio Schwartz put it. I gathered that when a card was pulled upside down, it meant that it held the opposite meanings to the ones it had the right way up. *But why was this Harold so important?* I wasn't game to ask.

Flo dropped her crayons and came outside to us. As she slid by me she brushed one satiny cheek against my arm, but instead of climbing up for some mother's milk, she grabbed her mother's brandy glass and drank from it. I was paralysed with shock.

"Oh, let her have it," said Mrs. Delvecchio Schwartz, reading me like a book. "It's Sunday and she knows what's comin'."

"But she might turn into an alcoholic!" I squeaked.

That provoked a tremendous raspberry. "Who, Flo? Nah!" she said with wonderful lack of concern. "Ain't in her cards or her horoscope, princess. Brandy ain't just booze, it's good for the soul." She leered.

"Keeps a man's pecker up too. If he drinks other spirits—or beer!—limp as a wet sock on the line."

The next bit happened so quickly that I hardly saw it. Flo jerked and jumped, flung the half-empty glass away in a shower of brandy, then fled as if all hell was after her, into the living room and straight under the couch.

"Ah, shit, here comes Harold." Mrs. Delvecchio Schwartz sighed, getting up to retrieve the unbroken glass. Still shaken by Flo's frenzy, I followed her from the balcony to the living room.

In he came, daintily, something like a seized-up old ballet dancer. Every step measured, pricked out on some paper pattern of movements. He was a faded, shrunken little chap in his late fifties, and he peered at us over the top of a pair of half-glasses perched on his thin, sharp nose. With utter malevolence. But I inherited the full focus of that terrible gaze, not Mrs. Delvecchio Schwartz. I don't quite know how to describe something I've never encountered before, even from a demented patient with homicidal tendencies. He glared at me with such hate, such venom! And I suddenly remembered that Mrs. Delvecchio Schwartz had said I too was a Queen of Swords. It crossed my mind that maybe it was *my* death she was looking at in the cards. Or Pappy's. Or Jim's.

She didn't seem to notice that anything was wrong, booming out, "This is Harold Warner, Harriet. He's me live-in lover."

I bleated something polite which he answered with a frosty nod of his head, then he turned it away as if he couldn't bear to look at me a moment longer. If I weren't a healthy five foot ten, I swear I would have joined Flo under the couch. Poor little thing! Harold obviously affected her the way he affected me.

"He's me live-in lover." So that was why everybody wanted to know whether I'd met Harold!

The pair of them left the room, he preceding her, she in his wake like a sheepdog rounding up a stray lamb. Presumably they went off to her bedroom. Or perhaps to Harold's quarters, right above my living room. When I realised that they weren't coming back I lay flat out on the floor, lifted the tatty edge of the couch skirt and stared at a huge pair of eyes glowing in the gloom like the glass bobbles buried in a road. It took some time to coax Flo out, but in the end she skittled across the lino like a crab and kept on going until she hung by her arms around my neck. I got her weight distributed on my hip and looked at her.

"Well, angel," I said, stroking her flyaway hair, "how about we go down to my flat and sort out your crayons?"

So she and I picked all of them up off the floor— there must have been over a hundred, and they weren't cheap children's crayons, they were German artist's quality in every hue. Flo could have worn a pretty new dress every day for a week on what they must have cost her mother.

I've learned a great deal about Flo this afternoon. That she doesn't speak, at least in my presence, but that her mind is clear, alert, intelligent. We pleated cardboard into grooved trays, then I asked her to pick out all the green crayons, which she did. Then I told her to arrange them in gradations of colour in a tray, and watched her deciding whether a greeny-yellow one belonged with the greens. We sorted out the reds, the pinks, the yellows, the blues, the browns, the greys, the purples and oranges, and she was never wrong. It wasn't difficult to tell that she was enjoying herself very much, because after a while she began to hum a shut-mouthed tune, a pretty melody unshaped by lips or tongue. Not once did she try to scribble on my walls, though I had wondered. We sat down on two chairs and ate potato salad and coleslaw and shaved ham, we drank lemonade, then we lay down together on my bed and had a nap. Whenever I moved about, she hung onto my leg and moved with me. I have never been as happy as I was this afternoon, being with Flo, getting the feel of her world. While her mother, that astonishing mass of contradictions, cavorted upstairs on a bed with a very sick man. What did Flo do on other Sunday afternoons? For this tryst with Harold was a weekly event; Mrs. Delvecchio Schwartz had indicated that. The Ten of Swords, the Queen of the same suit, the death.

I returned Flo when I heard her mother bellowing for her angel. The wee child trotted along with her hand in mine, greeted her mother with no visible sign of resentment at being abandoned for two hours. I left them, my mind whirling, my heart aching. As I shut their door I glanced along the lightless hall which ran toward the back, feeling a prickle of terrible fear. And there was Harold standing in the dark, giving nothing of his presence away. I had a fancy that he had managed to fuse himself into the wall, scribbles on his bottom half, dingy cream on his top half. Our eyes met and my mouth went bonedry. The hate! It was palpable. I couldn't get down the stairs fast enough, though only his eyes had acknowledged me.

And now, even though it's high time I was in bed, I'm sitting here at my table studded with goose pimples. What have I done to that awful little man to earn such hatred? And *who* is the relevant Queen of Swords? Mrs. Delvecchio Schwartz, Pappy, Jim or me?

Wednesday,
March 2nd, 1960

The best thing about using an ordinary exercise book as a diary is that you don't have blank pages reproaching you because you haven't entered it faithfully. All I do is write in the date and start my entry right after the one before, even if it was a fortnight ago. I'm onto my second fat book already. Though my door has a mortice lock, I can pick it myself when I forget my key, so anybody with a smidgin of resource can do the same. Therefore I am hiding my finished exercise book(s) in the back of the cupboard where I keep my hunk of Tilsiter cheese. My theory is that no one, even Harold, could summon up the strength to stick his or her head inside that cupboard to hunt for anything. The pong is *unbelievable*! I manage to confine the stench to the interior of the cupboard by wadding up the door with plasticine, and the door bears a warning underneath a radioactive symbol and a skull-and-cross-bones: BEWARE OF THE CHEESE! This achieves two purposes. One, unpicking the plasticine is laborious, so I don't eat Tilsiter more than once a week—once I start eating it, I can't stop. Two, my finished exercise book(s) will be safe. I make sure by embedding a hair in the plasticine, a ruse I saw in a who-dunit film. The exercise book in current use goes everywhere with me, be it to Queens or the shops. One cannot be too careful with anything that contains secrets.

An odd thing happened at work today. There was a big flap on in Cas—a twenty-seater plane crashed on the Mascot runway, so half went to St. George and the other half came here, the living and the dead. I hate burns. Everybody does. Six of the passengers and the two pilots went straight through Cas to the morgue, but two of the passengers were still alive when I left. Oh, the stench! Like charred roast meat, and impossible to get rid of, which meant that the other Cas patients became restive and afraid, the nurses were scared as nurses rarely are, and the sisters couldn't be in enough places at one and the same time.

Chris was off at a meeting Sister Agatha had called, and the junior was tidying up the darkroom while I mended sandbags—we weren't busy for a change. And in walked Mr. Duncan Forsythe! I was sitting at our lone desk in the patient waiting area plying my needle, didn't look up for a moment. When I did, my mouth fell open. Such a smile he was giving me! He really is a very good-looking man. I managed a polite grimace and got to my feet with my hands behind my back like an obedient inferior in the presence of God. Chin and tummy tucked in, feet at attention. After a couple of years of hospital work, it comes naturally.

All he wanted was the phone—the ones in Cas were running hot because of the crash, he explained. I indicated ours and stood, still at attention, while he told Switch to page his team of underlings to meet him in Chichester Four. After he replaced the receiver I expected him to depart, but he didn't. Instead, he sat on one corner of the desk swinging one leg and staring at me. Then he asked me my name, and when I told him, he repeated it.

"Harriet Purcell. It has a nice, old-fashioned sound."

"Yes, sir," I answered, stiff as a post.

Green eyes are mysterious. In romantic novels they're always the colour of emeralds, but in my experience they're more of a swampy green, change-ful. My eyes are black, you can't easily tell the pupil from the iris, which I daresay is why I like his eyes so much—different from mine, but not opposite. He continued to sit looking at me, quietly smiling, for long enough to make me feel the skin of my face heat up, then he slid off the desk and wandered to the door in that wonderfully absent way surgeons do, as if external forces propel them from place to place.

"Goodbye, Harriet," he said as he went out.

Phew! He must be six-three, because I have to look up. Oh, what a lovely man! But Mrs. Delvecchio Schwartz is *not* going to trap me with those wretched cards!

And then tonight I had my first cooking lesson. Klaus had all the ingredients ready when I knocked on his door a bit after eight; I'd heard the sound of his violin and knew that meant he wouldn't mind if I was early. He plays like a virtuoso, classical stuff full of yearning. I'm not up on classical stuff, but if what Klaus plays is anything to go by, I'm going to buy whatever LPs he cares to suggest. It leaves Billy Vaughan for dead.

We made Beef Stroganoff with spaetzle (I asked Klaus to spell it—just as well, because it isn't in my *Oxford*), and I think I've died and gone to heaven. He showed me how to slice the half-frozen beef fil-let very thinly, how to slice the mushrooms and the onions, gave me a lecture about keeping my knives sharp with a steel. The spaetzle have the same composition as Granny's dumplings, only he forces the dough through a colander into boiling salted water and cuts it off regularly to make what look like short, thick macaronis.

"Fry the meat lightly and quickly, put it in your pot, fry the onions golden, add them to your pot, fry the mushrooms until they're soft, add them to your pot. Heat the frying pan until the drippings are brown, then add a dash of cognac."

When he put the cognac in (he sneers at the old three-star), it hissed and bubbled, evaporated. "Put some fresh cream in the pan before you start with the sour cream, Harriet. If you do not, your sauce will curdle as it nears its boiling point. I for one prefer my food piping hot, so I use fresh cream first to stop the sour cream curdling. Squash the sour cream into bits, then use a French whisk to stir as you heat—it takes all the lumps out. Then pour your sauce into the pot, mix it all up, and *voila*! Beef Stroganoff."

The whole meal took less than half an hour to prepare, and I have never tasted anything that good. "Do not put tomato paste or pickles in it," he scolded, as if I was going to dash off and commit these crimes immediately. "The way I make Stroganoff is the right way, the only way." He thought for a minute, then said, "Except for the cognac, but cognac is excusable. Keep your flavours simple and make sure that what you use in a sauce does not camouflage the main ingredients. With fillet of beef, mushrooms and onions, who needs disguising flavours?"

End of lesson. Next week we're going to make Chicken Paprika—on *sweet* Hungarian paprika! We had a bit of a squabble about who was going to pay for the raw materials—he insisted, I wouldn't let him. In the end we agreed to split the cost down the middle.

Next Saturday I'm going looking for knives, a steel and a French whisk. And I can't wait to tell Mum how to make lump-free gravy! Stir it with a French whisk.

**Friday,
March 11th, 1960**
I refuse to believe those cards!

Today we had a head injury day. I don't know why things fall out like that, they just do. On any one day we tend to get more of a certain kind of patient than others. And today it was heads, heads, heads.

Chris was still there when Demetrios the New Australian Cas porter wheeled the umpteenth head injury through the door on a trolley. Demetrios is Greek, and has organised an interpreter service to cope with all the nationalities we get in these days of New Australians galore. I like the N.A.s very much and I think they're good for the country—less steak-and-chips, more Beef Stroganoff. But my family loathes them, and so does Miss Christine Hamilton. A pity, because Demetrios thinks Chris is a bit of all right. He's single, quite tall and not bad-looking in a slightly alien way, and he told me that portering is only temporary. He's going to Tech at night to learn car mechanics because he wants to own his own garage one day. Like all N.A.s, he works very hard and he saves every penny. I think that's why most Old Australians loathe the N.A.s. N.A.s think of a job as a privilege, not a right. They're so happy to be somewhere that their tummies are full and their bank books have a bit in them.

Anyway, after casting Chris a languishing look and getting a glare in return, Demetrios pushed off and left us with the patient. Said patient was turpsed to the eyeballs, stank of beer, wouldn't keep still, refused to co-operate. Then when I bent over him to shove a sandbag on either side of his neck, he puked beery vomit all over me. Oh, what a mess! I had to leave Chris cursing and the junior wiping up the floor, get myself to the Cas women's staff room and take off my uniform, shoes, stockings, suspender belt, bra, panties, the lot. I had another uniform in my locker, but no underwear and no spare pair of shoes, so I had to wash them in the sink, wring them as dry as possible and put them back on, even my stockings. It is strictly forbidden to have bare legs. My beloved old shoes will never be the same again, a tragedy. For three years they've pampered my feet, now I'll have to buy a new pair and break them in—

hell when you're permanently on your feet. As you can't wring out shoes, I put them on soaking wet and squelched back to Cas X-ray leaving a set of wet footsteps behind me. Matron was visiting, eyed me up and down.

"Miss Purcell, you are wetting the floor, and that is very dangerous for other people," she said icily.

"Yes, Matron. I am aware, Matron. I apologise, Matron," I said, and bolted through our door. You don't try to justify yourself to Matron or Sister Agatha, you just escape as fast as possible. But isn't she amazing? She's only met me once, but she knows who I am and what my name is.

It went on like that—one of "those days". But I sent the junior off at four and battled on alone, so it was well after eight when I took the dirty laundry to the Cas chute and hunted someone up to put in a request for special treatment to our floor from the cleaning staff. Having entered the register and prepared tomorrow's cassettes, I was free to go.

When I got outside, I found that one of those March storms had built up and was about to burst. Of course I had my brolly, but a look up and down South Dowling Street revealed that all the taxis had decided to get off the road before the deluge broke. It was either walk home, or sleep on a plastic sofa in Cas, and I didn't think Matron would approve of the latter.

Someone came out of the Cas pedestrian door just as a huge gust of wind howled down to send leaves, bits of paper and tin cans flying. I didn't bother to look until whoever it was stood so close to me that I realised it must be someone I know. Mr. Forsythe, no less! He gave me that dazzling smile and pointed with the tip of his big black ebony-handled umbrella toward the H.M.O.s' parking area. All the Rollses and Bentleys had gone, leaving a Mercedes from the 1930s and a sleek black Jaguar saloon. His, I took a private bet with myself, was the Jag.

"It's going to pour in a minute, Harriet," he said. "Let me drive you home."

I dared to give him a proper smile in reply, but I shook my head emphatically. "Thank you, sir, but I'll manage."

"It's no trouble, truly," he persisted, then gave a hoot of triumph when the heavens opened and the rain bucketed down. "You can't possibly wait for a bus in this, Harriet, and there isn't a taxi for miles. Let me drive you home."

But I wasn't going to budge. Hospitals are seething hotbeds of gossip and we were standing in a very public place, people coming and going constantly. "Thank you, sir," I said firmly, "but I stink of vomit. I'd prefer to walk."

My chin was up, my mouth was down. He gazed into my face for a moment, then shrugged and put up his umbrella, which had a silver band around its handle engraved with some message from Geoffrey and Mark. Off he ran to the black Jaguar. Good guess, Harriet! A 1930s Mercedes was the sort of car a psychiatrist or a pathologist drove. Orthopods were orthodox. As the black Jaguar swished by me I could see the blur of his face behind the fogged window, and a hand giving me a wave. I didn't return it. Instead I waited a bit longer, then put up my brolly and started the three-mile plod home. Better this way. Much better.

**Monday,
March 28th, 1960**
Between Cas and cooking, I haven't had the energy to write in my exercise book for a long time. But tonight something happened which I can't get out of my mind, so maybe if I write it down, I can banish the ghosts and get some much-needed sleep.

Jim summoned me to an emergency meeting upstairs in their flat, which is a curious mixture of frilly Bob and unvarnished Jim. I've known for ages that the Harley Davidson motorbike chained to our plane tree on Victoria Street belongs to Jim, so it wasn't a surprise to find Harley Davidson posters plastered on the walls. They are always at me to come to their meetings, a regular event, but I've resisted them until tonight—sheer cowardice, I admit. I just didn't think I wanted to get mixed up too closely with a group of women who mostly seem to have men's names—Frankie, Billie, Joe, Robbo, Ron, Bert and so on. I love Jim and Bob because they are a part of The House and Mrs. Delvecchio

COLLEEN McCULLOUGH

Schwartz has told me sternly that Lezzos have a hard row to hoe (her metaphors are always wonderful, but I never know when she's pulling my leg, the old horror). When Jim begged me to come tonight, I understood that I was on trial, so I went.

Much to my surprise, Toby was there. So was Klaus. No Mrs. Delvecchio Schwartz, however. There were six women I didn't know. One, who was introduced to me as Joe, is a barrister—a Q.C., in fact. That's awesome, to get to the top of the legal tree in a skirt. Or rather, a tailored suit. Stop it, Harriet! This is not the time to digress. I think my idle remarks are because I'm dodging having to put the subject of the meeting on paper.

The players in the drama weren't present—Frankie and Olivia. I gathered that Frankie is a bit of a Lesbian idol, very dynamic and attractive, also very masculine. She had just taken up with Olivia, who is nineteen, very pretty, and from a stinking-rich family. When Olivia's father found out about his daughter's sexual inclinations, he didn't just hit the roof, he set out to teach her a lesson. So he pulled a few strings that saw Frankie and Olivia snatched off the footpath where they were walking their dog and hauled to the holding-cells in a cop shop somewhere on the outer rim of Sydney. There they were raped non-stop by a dozen of the Boys in Blue all last night, then this morning at dawn they were chucked onto the road outside Milson's Point station, their dead dog too.

Both of them are in the Mater Hospital, brutally damaged.

I sat there feeling so sick that I thought I'd have to excuse myself and lose my dinner, but pride kept my gorge down, I hung on. After one look at my face, Toby transferred himself from the far side of the room and sat down on the floor next to me, sneaked his hand out to grab mine. I clenched it like grim death. Joe the Q.C. was talking about legal action, but Robbo said that Frankie refused to give evidence, and poor little Olivia was going to be transferred to the acute psych unit at Rozelle as soon as she was physically well enough to be discharged from the Mater.

After the anger and the bluster died down, they started to talk about what it was like to be a Lez, probably because I was there. Robbo said that she'd once been married and had a couple of kids, but her husband divorced her citing a female co-respondent, and she isn't allowed to see her children unless she can prove that she isn't a "corrupting influence". Two of them had been sexually assaulted by their fathers as young children, one's mother had "sold" her to a rich old man whose preference was for anal sex with little girls. They all bore some sort of scars, physical or psychic. Jim and Bob were tame compared to the rest. All Jim had suffered was to be thrown out by her parents because she liked to wear men's clothes. Bob's parents, who live in the bush, have no idea that Jim is a female.

Afterwards Toby took me up to his garret and fed me coffee laced with brandy while I shivered like an old soldier with a bout of malaria.

"I didn't know it was a crime to be a Lesbian," I said after the hot liquid settled my stomach and steadied my thumping heart. "I know it is a crime for a man to be a homosexual, but someone told me that when the legislation arrived for her consent, Queen Victoria struck out the clauses affecting women, refused to believe women could be homosexual. But if Frankie and Olivia were arrested, it must be a crime."

"No, you're right," he said, refilling my mug. "It's not a crime to be a Lez."

"Then how could it have happened?" I asked.

"Under the lap, Harriet. Secretly. You won't find Frankie and Olivia on the cop shop books. Some copper big-wig obliged Olivia's daddy. I imagine the idea was to show Olivia what a good man could do, but it got out of hand. Probably after Frankie started in on the rapists. She's not the sort to knuckle under, even in a situation like that."

He's so detached, Toby. I suppose all good artists are, they watch the world looking for subjects.

I'm not an ignoramus about the more repellent side of life. No one who's worked in a hospital for over three years can be. But you never really hear the full story, especially in disciplines like X-ray, where the patients come in for their tests and then go somewhere else, and we're rarely unbusy enough to have

the time to listen to a patient's story. When we meet
for lunch or at a party or have a moment to talk
among ourselves, it's always the hot item on the gossip grapevine that's discussed. The horror's in seeing
what comes in, what's been done by another human
being. No, I'm not an ignoramus. But I've been *shel-
tered*. Until I moved up to the Cross, into The
House.

Tonight has been a blinding enlightenment. I can
never think the same about people again. Publicly
one thing, behind closed doors something very different. Dorian Gray everywhere. I don't know who
on earth Olivia's father is, but I've grown up enough
tonight to think that he is at peace with himself, that
he blames it all on Frankie and his daughter. And I
can't *bear* to think of the people who prey on little
children! It is a terrible world.

Friday,
April 1st, 1960 (April Fool's Day)
I got home fairly early tonight, and for once Pappy
was at a loose end. I don't know where she was last
Monday night when Jim and Bob held their meet-
ing—I hardly ever see her now that I'm in Cas X-ray.
Toby offered to take us to Lorenzini's, a wine bar at
the end of Elizabeth Street in the City.

"They gave me two bits of news at work this
arvo," Toby said as we walked down the McElhone
Stairs to Woolloomooloo, which is the shortest route

to Lorenzini's. "One good and one bad."

I asked when Pappy didn't. "What's the good news?"

"I've been given a hefty pay rise."

"So what's the bad news?"

"The company accountants sat down and did some calculations," he said, pulling a face. "The result is that from early next year I'm out of a job, along with almost everybody else. Between pay rises, strikes, shop stewards calling go-slows, and investors who want to see a big return for their money, the company's decided to replace men with robots. The robots can tighten nuts and shove parts together twenty-four hours a day without needing meal breaks or to go to the dunny."

"But robots cost a fortune," I objected.

"True, but the accountants worked out that they'll pay for themselves pretty quickly, and after that, with no human staff, it'll be beer and skittles for the investors."

"That's terrible!" Pappy gasped. She was always militant about crimes against the workers. "It's disgraceful!"

"It's just the way of the world, Pappy, you ought to know that," Toby lectured. "There's a bit of right on both sides. The bosses try to exploit us, and we try to exploit the bosses. If you want to blame any-one, blame the boffins who invent robots."

"I do!" she snapped. "Science is what's wrong!"

I contributed my mite by saying that I thought

what was really wrong were human beings, who can bungle a booze-up in a brewery.

There are always more young men at Lorenzini's than available women, so we soon lost Pappy, who has probably slept with the entire male complement anyway. Toby found a small table with two chairs down the back, and we sat in pleasant silence watching the eddies and swirls as people table-hopped madly. Poor Toby! It must be frightful to be in love with someone like Pappy.

We hadn't been there long when there was a stir at the door and about a dozen people entered, almost all young girls. Pappy came flying over to us, eyes wide.

"Harriet! Toby! See who's just come in? That's Professor Ezra Mar-mumble-mumble, the world-famous philosopher!"

I tried to make her repeat what was undoubtedly a peculiar name, but she was already gone to join the crowd around Professor Ezra Mar-supial? Yes, Marsupial sounds good. A bit long in the tooth for Lorenzini's, I thought, when the crowd parted and the Prof emerged like the sun from behind a cloud.

He isn't going to win any Mr. America contests, for sure. His face was ugly, he was a skinny, weedy little man, he grew his hair very long and combed it sideways to conceal his baldness, and he wore the sort of clothes you see on authors of important non-fiction books if they have their photos inside the back cover—tweed jacket with leather patches on the elbows, Aran sweater, corduroy trousers, a pipe in one hand. As the night was humid and hot, he must have been stewing like a casserole.

I can never work out how Pappy does it. The Prof was three-deep in female students, all at least ten years younger than Pappy, some of them as pretty as film starlets. Yet within two minutes, Pappy had managed to oust the girls and was sitting at his right hand, her adoring face turned up to his, some of her thick, glossy black hair straying over his hand. Maybe it's the hair. She's the only woman I know with long hair, and they do say men love it.

I sniffed. "That," I said to Toby, waving my hand to indicate the Prof, "is the Knight of Cups reversed."

Toby stared at me in surprise. "Are you taking lessons from the old girl?"

I said no, but she'd seen him in Pappy's cards. "She's an old villain, too, pretended to me that the Knight of Cups reversed is just what Pappy needs. I know the court card only reveals the person, that it's the other cards fill the person out and show how the person relates to someone else, but Mrs. Delvecchio Schwartz lied to me. She could see as clear as crystal what sort of bloke Pappy's new man is, and she saw something else that really upset her. But she wouldn't say a word to me about it. I don't remember what the cards were that followed the Knight of Cups, but I went out and bought a book on the tarot and looked *him* up, even if I couldn't put the whole picture together."

"I thought the knights were young men. He's fifty-odd."

"Not necessarily," I said, showing off my new-found knowledge. "They can be called knaves as well as knights."

He leaned back and looked at me through half-shut eyes. "You know, *princess*, there are times when you remind me awfully of our landlady."

I took that as a compliment.

When Pappy and the Prof got up together and departed, leaving his students looking as if they were contemplating suicide, Toby and I decided to go home too. We weren't far behind them, but when we emerged onto Elizabeth Street there wasn't a sign of them. I didn't want Toby to follow me down to my flat in case Pappy and the Prof were in her room, but he insisted on accompanying me.

Oh, good! No light under Pappy's door, no cackles of carnal content. Perhaps the Prof had a lair of his own, considering his liking for droves of nubile students.

Toby and I had coffee and talked about the brothels on either side of 17c. He had names for all the whores—Chastity, Patience, Prudence, Temperance, Honour, Constance, Verity, Columba—and he had christened the proprietress of 17d Madame Fugue, the proprietress of 17b Madame Toccata. In fact, given that the love of his life was probably in bed with a bald old coot with tickets on himself, Toby was in excellent form, had me laughing until the tears came. He disapproved of so much pink and dismissed my bead curtain as a subconscious wish to be shut up in a harem, but I enjoyed myself.

"I'm surprised you haven't walloped me the way you did David," he said, and looked at me sharply. "I don't get on with women."

"Unless they're Lezes."

"Lezes don't weigh a bloke up on the marriage scales. No, I reckon I don't get on with women because I say what I think." He sighed and stretched, let his eyes roam over me. "You'll be a lovely, lanky old lady one day, and I still think you've got a terrific pair of breasts."

Time to change the subject. "What do you think of Harold?"

Toby lifted his lip. "I don't. Why?"

"He hates me."

"That's a bit strong, Harriet."

"It's true!" I insisted. "I've encountered him quite a few times now, and he scares me witless. The hate in his eyes for me! Even worse, I can't work out what I've done to him."

"Wormed your way into Mrs. Delvecchio Schwartz's affections, is my guess," he said, getting up. "But don't worry about him—he's on the skids. The old girl's fed up with his shenanigans."

I walked to the door with him, where he balked on the step.

"Would you mind hopping down onto the path?" he asked.

I obliged. It put him slightly above me.

"That's better. I need all the altitude I can get."

His hands gripped my shoulders firmly but gently.

"Goodnight, princess," he said, and kissed me.

I thought, after the traumatic evening he'd had, that he was fishing for a warm and beautiful salute of consolation. But it wasn't like that at all. He slid his hands under my arms and across my back, pulled me against him, and kissed me *properly*. My eyes flew open in shock as a quiver of some highly emotional sensation crept along my jaws until it got to my lips. Then I closed my eyes and got into the mood. Oh, it was wonderful! After David and Norm, I couldn't believe what I was feeling. I know his hands on my back never moved, but I fancied that they burned their way into my very bones. It was all for me; he just cruised along at my pace, and when I needed to come up for air he pushed his face into the side of my neck and kissed it hard. Ooooooo-aa! That provoked all sorts of reactions! Come on, Toby, I was thinking, cop a feel of those terrific breasts!

The bastard let me go! I opened my eyes indignantly to see his glowing at me impishly.

"Goodnight," I said, struggling for the upper hand.

His eyes danced with unholy laughter, he flicked me carelessly on the cheek and went off up the path without a backward glance.

"April fool!" he called.

117

I leaped inside and slammed the door, ground my teeth for a minute, then simmered down. April fool or not, I'd just had my first decent kiss, and I loved it. Finally I have an inkling of the pleasure being with a man might be. My blood is dancing.

Monday,
April 4th, 1960

Pappy came home for long enough to have coffee with me before she left for work, even though this meant she dragged me out of bed two hours earlier than necessary. I was so anxious to find out what was going on that I didn't care about the two lost hours of sleep. She was radiant—so beautiful!

"Where did you go?" I asked.

She explained that he keeps a weeny flat in Glebe, near Sydney University. "We went there, bolted the door, took the telephone off the hook, and never moved outside until six this morning. Oh, Harriet, he's wonderful, perfect—a king, a god! Nothing like it has ever happened to me before! Would you believe that we lay naked together and played with each other for *six hours* before he took me the first time?" Her eyes glazed at the memory. "We tormented each other—licked and sucked until we nearly came, then stopped, then started all over again—our climax was simultaneous, isn't that incredible? At one and the same moment! And then we plunged into a sadness so deep and full that we both wept."

These confidences were so embarrassing that I begged her to keep the gory details to herself, but Pappy lacks inhibitions, she really does.

"You're embarrassing yourself, Harriet," she said in tones of disapproval. "It's high time you came to terms with your body."

I stuck my chin up. "There's no one I fancy," I lied. Toby, Toby, Toby.

"You're afraid."

"Of getting pregnant, for sure."

"Mrs. Delvecchio Schwartz says that if a woman doesn't want a baby all the way through to her soul, she won't conceive."

I snorted. "Thank you, I have no intention of testing the Delvecchio Schwartz Theory, Pappy, and that's that. So you had a jolly time with the Prof. Was it all sex, or did you talk too?"

"We talked endlessly! We smoked a little hashish, lay in each other's arms, inhaled a little cocaine—I never realised how some substances can heighten one's pleasure almost unbearably!"

I knew if I started to remonstrate with her about that, we'd quarrel, so instead I asked if the Prof was married.

"Yes," she said quite happily, "to a sad, dreary woman he detests. They have seven children."

"He can't detest her that much, then. Where do they live?"

"Somewhere out near the Blue Mountains. He

drives out there occasionally for the sake of the children, but he and his wife sleep in separate bedrooms."

"That's one method of birth control," I said, a bit waspishly.

"Ezra told me that he fell in love with me the moment he set eyes on me. He says I've brought him joy no other woman ever has."

"Does Ezra mean that your weekend parade of men is a thing of the past?" I asked.

Pappy looked genuinely shocked. "Of course it does, Harriet! My search is over, I've found Ezra. Other men are meaningless."

Well, I honestly don't know how much of all that I ought to believe. Pappy believes, so for her sake I hope my own doubts are without foundation. Hashish and cocaine. The Prof certainly knows how to indulge in ultimate pleasures. Married, too. Lots of men do have unhappy marriages, no reason to think that Ezra Marsupial—what *is* his name?—isn't one of them. Oh, but what truly does set my teeth on edge is the way darling Ezra chooses to live his life. He keeps his wife and seven kids far enough away from his place of work to negate them, and he keeps this weeny flat in the Glebe. Very handy, a weeny flat right next door to a bottomless supply of nubile young maidens. For the life of me I can't see why the wretched man is so attractive to those idiotic girls, but obviously he's got something, though I doubt that his dingus is as long as Dad's garden hose. It's the hashish and cocaine, I reckon.

He's just using Pappy, I know it in my bones. But why did he pick her, with all those others gazing at him with their tongues hanging out? Why, for that matter, is Pappy so desirable to so many men? When sex is uppermost on a man's mind, the beauty of a woman's nature isn't what draws them. There's a mystery here that I have to solve. I love Pappy, and I think she's the prettiest creature in the world. But there's more to it than that.

Harriet Purcell, you're a novice in the love department, what gives you the right to speculate? Hurry up, King of Pentacles number one! I need a basis of reference.

Thursday,
April 7th, 1960
Ooooo-ah! That dolt Chris Hamilton made a right mess of our busy but placid little world today. I wish the hell she'd give Demetrios a proper look-over instead of snapping at the poor chap every time he pushes a patient in.

We nearly had a death on our hands this morning, and that is the most awful thing that can happen. A suspected fracture of the skull decided to develop acute swelling of the brain while we were X-raying him. I found myself pushed aside by an unknown registrar, who acted very promptly and had the patient off to neurosurgery theatre in a trice. But ten minutes later he was back to look at Chris and me more coldly than Matron can.

"You bloody bitches, why didn't you see what was happening?" he snarled. "That man coned because you left it too late to call for help! You *stupid* bloody bitches!"

Chris put the cassettes she was holding into my hands and stalked to the door. "Kindly accompany me to Sister Toppingham's office, Doctor," she said in freezing tones. "I would be grateful if you repeated your remarks to her."

Sister Cas rushed in a minute later, eyes out on stalks. "I heard!" she cried. "Oh, he's a bastard, Doctor Michael Dobkins!"

The junior had flown off to neurosurgery theatre with the X-rays and I had no patient on my hands, so I stared at her with a few ideas germinating in my head. "They know each other, don't they?" I asked. "Chris and Dr. Dobkins, I mean." Since she and Chris shared digs, I figured she'd be privy to the dirt.

"They certainly do," she said grimly. "Eight years ago, when Dobkins was a junior resident, he and Chris were so wrapped in each other that Chris rather took it for granted they were engaged. Then he dumped her, no explanation. Six months later he married a physio with a company director father and a mother on the Black and White Committee. As she was still virgo intacta, Chris couldn't even threaten to sue him for breach of promise."

Well, that would do it, all right.

Chris came back with Sister Agatha and Dr. Michael Dobkins and I had to give my version of the incident, which tallied with Chris's. As a result of my testimony, the Super, the Clinical Super and Matron appeared in that order, and I had to retell the story to three very disapproving faces. Chris had charged Dobkins with unprofessional conduct, namely hurling unpardonable epithets at female staff. Surgeons do it in the operating theatre all the time, but surgeons have to be allowed their little foibles. Dr. Dobkins, a mere senior registrar, is supposed to sit on his feelings.

The worst of it is that it ought never to have happened. If Chris had kept her head and kept the tempest local—maybe hauled Dobkins into a private corner and chewed his arse off for bad manners—then Upstairs would never have got into the act. As it is, she switched on a million-watt searchlight that has hampered our work and called our integrity into question.

By the end of the afternoon, it was Dobkins on the carpet, not us. The patient *had* coned—his brain had suddenly swollen until its vital centres in the brain stem were squashed against the surrounding bony ridges—but a gigantic subdural haematoma had been successfully aspirated in neurosurgery theatre and the patient had survived intact thanks to the proximity of Cas and resuscitation equipment. The judgement delivered from Upstairs and relayed to us by Sister Agatha was that we had *not* been derelict in our duty.

Chris knocked off looking like Joan of Arc at the stake, left me to finish what was a rather awful day.

It was nearly nine o'clock when I searched South Dowling Street for a taxi. Not a one. So I walked. At the Cleveland Street lights, a sleek black Jaguar slid into the kerb beside me, the passenger's door opened and Mr. Forsythe said, "You look very tired, Harriet. Would you like a lift home?"

I threw caution to the winds and hopped in. "Sir, you're a godsend!" I said, snuggling into the leather seat.

He flashed me a smile, but said nothing. However, at the next big junction he automatically turned into Flinders Street, and I realised that he had no idea where I lived. So I had to apologise and tell him that I lived at the Potts Point end of Victoria Street. Shame on you, Harriet Purcell! What's happened to Kings Cross? He apologised for not asking me where I lived, drove down to William Street and back-tracked.

As we purred into that visual cacophony of neons I said, "Um, I really live at Kings Cross. The Royal Australian Navy owns Potts Point whole and entire."

His brows rose, he grinned. "I wouldn't have picked you as living at Kings Cross," he said.

"And just what sort of person does live at the Cross?" I growled.

That startled him! He took his eyes off the road for long enough to see that I looked militant, and tried to mend his fences. "I really don't know," he said pacifically. "I suppose I suffer all the misconceptions of those whose only acquaintance with the Cross is via the yellow press."

"Well, the postie did tell me that the whores next door have their mail addressed to Potts Point, but as far as I'm concerned, *sir*, Victoria Street is Kings Cross from end to end!"

Why was *I* so angry? It was me who mentioned Potts Point first! But he must be very well house-trained, because he didn't try to justify himself, he just fell silent and drove to my directions.

He pulled into the section the parking police keep reserved for august clients of 17b and 17d; the caduceus on the Jag's back bumper is protection from parking tickets absolutely anywhere.

Then he was out and around to open my door before I could find the right handle. "Thank you for the ride," I muttered, dying to get away as quickly as I could.

But he stood looking as if he had no intention of moving. "Do you live here?" he asked, waving at our cul-de-sac.

"The middle house. I have a flat."

"It's charming," he said, waving that hand about again.

I stood beside him desperately trying to think of something to say that would tell him I appreciated his kindness but was not going to ask him in. But what came out was "Would you like a cup of coffee, sir?"

"Thank you, I would."

Oh, *shit*! Praying that no one was about, I pushed the front door open and headed down the hall, hideously conscious of him behind me taking in the scribbled walls, the tatty lino, the fly-poop on the naked lightbulbs. Things were in full swing at 17d next door as we hit the open air; the faint sounds of whores working hard were quite as audible as Madame Fugue having a screaming fight with Prudence in the kitchen, her subject a graphic description of what a girl had to do to please a gentleman with rather peculiar tastes.

"Don't fuckin' piss before you go in when they want to be pissed on, and drink a gallon of fuckin' water!" was the crux of the matter.

"An interesting altercation," he said, as I wrestled with the old mortice lock.

"It's a very high-class brothel, and so's the one on the other side of us," I said, flinging the door open. "Patronised by Sydney's highest and finest."

He confined his next remarks to my flat, which he called pretty, charming, homey.

"Sit down," I said, a little ungraciously. "How do you take your coffee?"

"Black, no sugar, thank you."

At which moment came the sound of a violin playing what I now could identify as Bruch.

"Who's that?" he asked.

"Klaus upstairs. Good, isn't he?"

"Superb."

When I emerged from behind my screen with two mugs of coffee, I found him sitting in an easy chair, very relaxed as he listened to Klaus. Then he looked up and took the mug with a smile of such genuine pleasure that my knees turned to water. I felt less afraid of him, could sit down with reasonable composure. Hospitals condition more lowly staff to regard H.M.O.s as beings from another planet—beings who didn't visit the Cross unless they were patronising the Mesdames Fugue and Toccata.

"It must be great fun living here," he said. "Lowbrow and highbrow."

Well, he certainly wasn't judgemental. "Yes, it is great fun," I said.

"Tell me about it."

Oh, really! How could I do that? Sex is behind everything that happens here, hadn't he got that message from Madame Fugue? So I elected to tell him about the front ground floor flat.

"At the moment," I finished, "we think we've actually found an elderly couple who aren't in the business."

"Too old, you mean?"

"Oh, you'd be surprised, sir," I said chattily. "The women on the streets are pretty decrepit. The young and beautiful ones work in established brothels—the pay's better, they live better, and there are no pimps to beat them up."

His swampy green eyes held a mixture of amusement and sadness; I thought the amusement was on my account, but I wasn't so sure about the sadness. Maybe, I decided, it was permanent.

He glanced at his very expensive gold watch and rose. "I must go, Harriet. Thanks for the coffee and the company—and the lesson about how the other half lives. I've enjoyed myself."

"Thanks for the lift home, sir," I said, and took him to the front door. After I shut it behind me I leaned against it and tried to work out what had just happened. I seem to have made a new friend. Thank God he'd made no advances to me! But I keep remembering the sadness in his eyes, and I wonder if all it is is a need to talk to someone? How strange. You don't stop to think that maybe God the H.M.O. needs someone to talk to.

Monday,
April 11th, 1960
I saw Pappy again this morning, but this time she didn't have to wake me up. I was lying in wait for her when she came in from her weekend rendezvous at Glebe, and dragged her into my place for a decent breakfast. She may be in love, but she's even thinner.

Thinner, but idyllically happy.

"A good weekend?" I asked, handing her Eggs Benedict.

"Wonderful, wonderful, wonderful! Harriet, I can't believe it!" she cried, threw her head back and laughed delightedly. "My Ezra wants to marry me!

Next weekend he's going to tell his wife."

Now why doesn't that ring true? But I kept my face smiling and interested. "That's marvellous news, Pappy."

She yawned, frowned at the plate and pushed it away.

"Eat it!" I snapped. "You can't live on hashish and cocaine!"

Cowed, she pulled it back and shoved the first forkful in her mouth listlessly. Then she started to eat with enthusiasm—my lessons with Klaus are bearing fruit. I sat down opposite her and leaned forward, feeling very uncomfortable but determined to say my piece. "Um, I'm very aware that what I'm going to ask you is rude and prying, but—" I floundered, not sure where to go next. In for a penny, in for a pound, Harriet—*do it!* "Pappy, you hardly know Ezra, and he hardly knows you. In fact, I gather that neither of you is capable of much logical thought from Friday night to Monday morning. Two weekends together, and he wants to marry you? On what sort of basis? That you don't bat an eyelid about his little pharmaceutical recreations? I can see why he'd think you're safer to be with than his nubile young students—you're very much a woman of the world. You're not going to dob him in to the Boys in Blue, even by accident. But *marriage*? Isn't that taking two weekends a bit far?"

My scepticism didn't offend her. I doubt it

penetrated the fog. "It's sex," she said. "Men need sex to be truly in love."

"That's begging the question," I objected. "You're not talking about love, you're talking about marriage. He's a world-famous philosopher, you say. That means he has status in his bit of the intellectual empire, so he can't possibly have avoided all the obligations things like tenure and university seniority demand. I'm not an academic, but I do know a bit about academia, and it's pretty stuffy. If he dumps his wife and kids for you—" I broke down in a mire of my own making, just looked at her helplessly.

Her head shook back and forth slowly. "Dear Harriet, you don't know anything," she said. "There's sex and there's sex."

"Oh, why all this harping about sex?" I growled. "Peculiar tastes don't go with marriage, if that's what you mean by sex."

"You're so *young*!"

I did my nana, started to yell. "Oh, for Chrissake, Pappy, I'm fed up with being dismissed as an ignoramus! I'm not sitting here quizzing you because I'm eaten up with sick curiosity! I simply want to know exactly why Ezra wants to *marry* you rather than go on having a wonderful weekend relationship! I know you, you're not the type to hang out for a wedding ring, so why is he? It doesn't fit, it just doesn't fit!"

"Fellatio," she said.

"Fell-what?" I asked blankly.

"Fellatio. I suck his penis until he ejaculates in my mouth. That's every ordinarily sexed man's dream," she said, "yet few women are keen on doing it. Especially wives, who—just like you, really—don't know about it until the husband asks for it. Then they're outraged, think he's some sort of pervert. Whereas I *love* fellating Ezra. His penis is perfect for me, small and always a little flaccid. And that's why he wants to marry me. If I'm his wife, he can have fellatio every single day." She sighed. "Oh Harriet, it would be lovely to be married to Ezra!"

My lower jaw was on the table, but I managed to grin. "Well, I daresay it's an efficient method of birth control," I said.

"Oh, we do it the accepted ways too," said Pappy.

So there you have it. The recipe for married bliss.

**Tuesday,
April 12th, 1960**

Chris is pursuing a vendetta against Dr. Michael Dobkins, aided and abetted by Sister Cas. Turns out he's the new senior registrar in Cas, but did Upstairs remove him after the kerfuffle with us? No! The fur flies regularly, and I predict that Dr. Dobkins is shortly going to decide that he'd be much happier at Hornsby Hospital, a lot closer to his home in Pymble than Queens is. I'd say Royal North Shore, posh and suitably huge, but it sticks to its own. Fellatio aside, men who irritate women in positions

131

of power are stupid. Dobkins wasn't wrong about our being bloody bitches, but stupid? *He's* the stupid one.

Chris ticked me off in front of the junior because I was nice to Demetrios. I saw red and rounded on her, claws out.

"Listen, you bigoted bloody bitch, that's a darned decent man with a brain in his head and a bright future! He fancies you, only God knows why, but you wouldn't even spit on him simply because he porters patients and he's a Wog! If I want to treat Demetrios like a human being, I will, and nothing you or Sister Agatha can say will stop me! What you need, Christine Leigh Hamilton, is a good *fuck*!"

I said it, I said it! The junior almost fainted, then fled to the darkroom voluntarily, and Chris stood gaping at me as if she'd been savaged by a guinea pig.

I waited for her to march me off to Sister Agatha, but this time she decided discretion was the better part of valour, said not a word, even to me. However, the next time Demetrios brought us a patient, Chris stared at him as if the scales had fallen from her eyes. She even gave him a smile. I'll bet that tomorrow he gets offered a cuppa and a bikky.

Just call me Cupid.

Monday,
April 25th, 1960 (Anzac Day)
Almost two weeks, and my exercise book hasn't

been pulled out of my dilly-bag. We had to work today despite the public holiday, but there wasn't much to do, and I knocked off on time.

When I came in my door I could still smell the spices—mace, turmeric, cardamom, fenugreek, cumin. Such exotic words. So I sat down at the table, had a bit of a weep at the silence and those smells, then dug out my book.

The Friday after Pappy gave me her theory on happy marriage and I told Chris Hamilton that she needed a good fuck was Good Friday, but up at the Cross Good Friday isn't very different from any other Friday. Business as usual. Toby, Pappy and I went to the Apollyon, a basement coffee lounge. It's too intellectual for my taste—everybody seems to sit there playing chess—but Pappy loves it and Toby thought his friend Martin might turn up there. Rosaleen Norton came down the stairs with her poet friend, Gavin Greenlees—the first time I'd seen the Witch of the Cross. Nothing much to frighten a person there, is my conclusion. She does herself up to look satanic— peaked black brows, scarlet lipstick, black hair and eyes and stark white make-up—but I don't feel any satanic emanations, as Mrs. Delvecchio Schwartz might put it.

Then Martin arrived arm-in-arm with this stunner of a bloke. Even the most ardent chess players stopped to stare at him, so did Rosaleen Norton and Gavin Greenlees. I was riveted, and tickled to death when the newcomers moved toward our humble table.

"Mind if we sit with you?" Martin lisped.

Mind? I couldn't shuffle my chair to make room quickly enough. Though Martin is an unabashed and vociferous member of the Cross's homosexual contingent, he doesn't lisp because he's poofterish. He lisps because he has no teeth. One of those peculiar people who refuse to darken a dentist's door.

"This," he said, waving a graceful hand in the direction of the smiling Adonis, "is Nal. He's being singularly difficult to seduce—I'm absolutely worn out from trying."

"How do you do?" asked the reluctant seducee in an Oxford accent before seating himself opposite me. "My full name is Nal Prarahandra, I am a doctor of medicine, and I am in Sydney for a week to attend a World Health Organisation congress."

He was so *beautiful*! I'd never thought of men as beautiful, but there isn't another word that adequately describes him. His lashes were as long and thick and tangled as Flo's, the brows above his perfectly arched orbits were drawn in as if with a charcoal pencil, and the eyes themselves were black, liquid, languishing. His skin shared Flo's colouration too. The nose was high-bridged and faintly aquiline, the mouth full but not too full. And he was tall, broad-shouldered, narrow-hipped. Adonis. I sat looking at him the way a country bumpkin looks at the Queen.

Then he reached across the table, picked up my

hand and turned it over to look at the palm. "You're a virgin," he said, but not out loud. I had to read his lips.

"Yes," I said.

Toby had Martin rattling away in one ear, but his eyes were on me, and he looked angry. Then Pappy put her hand on his arm and he looked at her; the anger faded, he smiled at her. Poor, poor Toby!

"Do you live in a suitable place?" he—Nal—whispered.

"Yes," I said.

My hand was still in his when he stood up. "Then let us go."

And we went, just like that. I wasn't even remotely tempted to wallop him, but I suspect Toby was. I suppose Toby was worried because I was leaving with a stranger.

"What is your name?" he asked as we emerged into the lights and blare of the Cross.

I told him, my hand still wrapped in his. "How on earth did you fall in with Martin?" I asked him as we crossed William Street.

"This is my first day in Sydney, and everyone said I must go to Kings Cross. When Martin accosted me, I was contemplating an interesting window, and as I found him amusing, I consented to accompany him. I knew that he would lead me to someone I liked, and I was right," he said, giving me a smile that isn't *quite* as wonderful as Mr. Forsythe's, I think because such amazing beauty isn't suited to smiling.

"Why on earth me?" I asked.

"Why on earth not you, Harriet? You are not yet fully awake, but you have great potential. And you are very pretty. It will make me very happy to teach you a little about love, and you will endow my week in Sydney with memorable pleasure. We will not know each other long enough to feel true love, so when we part, we will do so as good friends."

I don't think there's much of Pappy in me, because I find that I don't want to write down all the gory details.

Except that he made love to me for the first time in the bathtub off the laundry—thank God I'd had time to paint it out with scarlet bicycle enamel! And that he was wonderful, tender, considerate, all the things everybody kept telling me I had to have in my first lover. He loved my breasts, and I loved his attentions to my breasts, but I suppose the best part was his sensuousness. He really made me feel that he was enjoying himself, yet his lovemaking was geared to me and my feelings. As I wasn't ignorant about any aspect of the act, especially after nearly four months in The House, I daresay I could appreciate it and him a great deal more than virgins did in the old days. It must have been a shock to them!

He moved in with me that night, and stayed in my flat for the whole week with Mrs. Delvecchio Schwartz's blessing. The only landlady in Sydney so broad-minded, I reckon. When Flo came down on

Sunday afternoon, her muteness fascinated him. I assured him that her mother says she talks to her, but he doubts that very much.

"They may communicate on a different plane," he said, having met Mrs. Delvecchio Schwartz when she came to collect Flo after her two hours entertaining Harold. "The mother is an extraordinary woman. Very powerful, and a very old soul. Thoughts are like birds that can fly straight through solid objects. I think Flo and her mother speak without words."

Speaking without words. Well Nal, who is a psychiatrist, and I did a lot of that ourselves. Despite his alien way of looking at things, I liked him enormously, and I think he liked me for more than just sex. We did a lot of talking with words too.

He taught me to cook two Indian dishes, a korma and a vegetable curry, taking care to explain that a real curry isn't made with our "curry powder" because every dish requires a different selection of spices and herbs. On Sunday morning we went down to Paddy's Markets and bought the mace, the turmeric, the cardamom, the cumin, the fenugreek, the garlic. I don't think Indian food compares to Klaus's Beef Stroganoff or Veal Piccata, but I suppose it takes a bit of time to tune the tastebuds to such foreign flavours.

The one item we disagreed about is Pappy. Isn't that peculiar? All he would say is that she is a typical half-caste. Indians can be as prejudiced as Old

Australians, it seems. Of course he's very high caste, his father is some sort of maharajah. He told me that his bride has already been chosen for him, but for the time being she's too young for marriage. I already knew the answer to the question I didn't bother asking—that, after he married, he would still seek out women like me whenever he went abroad. Well, his ways are his ways. They're not ours. No doubt his wife will think no worse of him, so how can I?

Every evening he was waiting in Cas to walk me home, sitting on one of the hideous plastic sofas reading the *Mirror* until I came out and locked my door. Then he would take my bag and we'd leave, strewing a trail of delicious gossip behind us. Sister Cas works an early shift like Chris, but I'm sure that Sister Herbert, who's in charge on the evening shift, reports all the news about us. Chris gave me some funny looks, but that little outburst of mine has improved our relationship no end. Chris is, besides, starting to go out with Demetrios. They'll probably have very nice children, her stolid Pommy blood spiced with his Wogness. *Provided* that she doesn't get cold feet. Sister Cas is looking down her nose at the pair of them and feeding Chris subtly poisonous remarks. If Chris marries, she'll have to find another flatmate, won't she?

Nal flew out to New Delhi at the crack of dawn last Saturday. Somehow I couldn't face the thought of spending the weekend alone at The House, so I retreated to Bronte and the lounge room couch until this morning. Mum eyed me sharply, but didn't say a word. Nor did I.

Coriander. I forgot coriander. A whiff of it just came stealing out from behind my screen. But Nal was right. We didn't know each other long enough to develop a grand passion, but we did indeed part good friends, my first King of Pentacles and I.

Tuesday,
April 26th, 1960

I had an odd encounter with Toby this evening, the first time I've seen him since Nal and I left the Apollyon together.

He's been slogging away at a portrait of Flo for two months, and it's been driving him mad with frustration. So when I saw him in the front hall, I asked him how it was going.

"Oh, a thousand thanks for your highness's interest!" he snarled. "Am I expected to kowtow to show you how terrifically grateful I am for the enquiry?"

My head rocked as if he'd slapped me—what on earth was he angry about? "No," I answered politely, "of course not. Last time we were talking, you weren't happy about it, which is why you were looking for your mentor, Martin."

That good-mannered reply made him look ashamed of himself. He stuck out a hand. "Sorry, Harriet. Shake?"

I shook.

"Come up and see for yourself," he said then.

To my admittedly unschooled eyes, the portrait was stunning—also unbearably sad. My wee angel! Toby had succeeded in making Flo's flesh tissue-thin without suggesting ill treatment, her face was just a frame for those huge amber eyes, and the whole background was peopled with shadows like ghosts forming out of a grey fog. Toby and I had never talked much about Flo, so to see that background came as a shock. Was her otherworldliness that obvious to everybody? Or was it just Toby, with the discerning eye of the artist?

"It's brilliant," I said sincerely. "Last time I saw it, Flo looked as if she lived in a concentration camp. Now, you've managed to retain the essence without making her look abused."

"Ta," he said gruffly, but he didn't invite me to sit down or partake of coffee. "Is love fled?" he asked suddenly.

"Yes, last Saturday."

"Broken-hearted? Want to cry on Uncle Toby's shoulder?"

I laughed. "No, idiot! It wasn't like that at all."

"What was it like?"

Toby, to ask something so personal? "Very nice," I said.

His eyes went quite red, his face twisted up ferociously. "You're not hurt?"

So that was it! God bless Toby, always protecting

the women of The House. I shook my head. "Not a bit, cross my heart. It was a flutter, mate. A flutter I needed rather badly after years and years of David."

The anger rose even higher, he bared his teeth. "How can you call *that* a flutter?" he demanded.

"Oh, honestly! You sound like someone in a Victorian novel!" I said, baring my own teeth. "I gave you more credit, Toby Evans, than to think that you subscribe to the double standard! Men can dip their wicks from their early teens, but women have to sit on it until they're married! Well, get stuffed!" I yelled.

"Keep your shirt on, keep your shirt on!" he said, getting over his anger, but not sure what his next mood was going to be. Or that was what I fancied. I might be wrong, I don't know, it was all so strange, so unlike him.

"I intend to keep *all* my clothes on, Mr. Evans!" I snapped. "A flutter with an Indian peacock does not mean that I intend to go flying with any Australian crows!"

"Peace, peace!" he cried, holding both hands up, palms out.

I was still smouldering, but the last thing in the world I ever want is to be at outs with Toby, his friendship is far too precious to me. So I changed the subject. "I know Ezra was going to ask his wife for a divorce two weekends ago," I said, "but I haven't seen Pappy to find out what the wife said."

His mood had gone from red to brown; now it

went a sort of flat black. "Ezra didn't turn up last weekend, so she doesn't know how it's going. Except that he phoned on Friday to say the wife was being very difficult, so he'd have to visit her again."

"Maybe she's desperate enough to offer a bit of fellatio," I said without thinking.

Toby stared at me as if paralysed, then turned abruptly away from me, grabbed the bottle of three-star from the table, and poured himself a whole glassful. It was only as I went down the stairs that I realised he must have thought it was Nal informed me of that term, probably in practice. I'd understood for some time that for all his liberality, Toby was old-fashioned about women and their activities. In his catalogue I was a woman. Jim, Bob and Mrs. Delvecchio Schwartz weren't. Aren't men peculiar?

Friday,
April 29th, 1960
I do like Joe Dwyer, who works the bottle depart-ment at the Piccadilly pub. Tonight I stopped in to buy a quart of three-star for my Sunday afternoon session with Mrs. Delvecchio Schwartz. He wrapped it in a brown paper bag and handed it over with a big grin. "For the seeing-eye tigress upstairs," he said.

I remarked that that sounded as if he knew the seeing-eye tigress upstairs extremely well, which made him laugh. "Oh, she's one of the great Cross characters," he said. "You might say I've known her for at least a couple of lifetimes."

Something in his voice suggested knowledge in the biblical sense, and I found myself wondering how many of the elderly—and not so elderly—men Mrs. Delvecchio Schwartz knows are past lovers. Whenever I see the shy, shadowy Lerner Chusovich, who smokes our eels and sometimes eats with Klaus, he speaks of our landlady with tender yearning. Why ever she might choose a man, it wouldn't be for anyone else's reasons. She is a law unto herself.

As the upstairs toilet is in a separate room from the upstairs bathroom, I often use the upstairs bathroom because it has a shower head over the bath, and I prefer a shower to a bath any day. My odd working hours mean that when I need a shower, the rest of The House are either gone or immersed in the evening's activities, so I don't inconvenience a soul. Truth to tell, one bathroom isn't enough for a four-storey house. No one goes down to the laundry.

Get to the point, Harriet! *Harold.* The upstairs bathroom and toilet lie between Harold's domain just above my living room and Mrs. Delvecchio Schwartz's bedroom and kitchen, which I've never seen because their doors are always closed. He seems to know when I'm coming, though I swear I'm silent-footed, nor do I arrive at the same hour thanks to Cas X-ray's irregularities. But he's always there in that hall, which is always plunged into darkness— the bulb seems to blow every day, though when I remarked on it to Mrs. Delvecchio Schwartz, she looked surprised and said it worked for her. Does that mean that Harold slips it from its bayonet when his antennae tell him I'm coming? It's possible to see because the toilet light is always on and its door is always ajar, but the hall itself is pitch-black corners, in one of which he's always standing when I come round the stairs. He never says a word, he just stands fused into the wall and glares his hatred at me, and I confess that I walk warily, ready to elude him if he goes for me with a knife or a bit of washing-line wire.

Why don't I content myself with a bath downstairs? Because there's a stubborn streak in me, or maybe it's more accurate to say that I'm more afraid of cowardice than I am even of Harold. If I give in and don't have my shower, I'm telling Harold that I'm too frightened of him to invade his territory, and that gives him the advantage over me. It hands my power over to him. That can't happen, I can't let it happen. So I go upstairs for my shower, and I pretend that Harold isn't there in the darkness, that I'm not the only target of the evil in him.

Sunday,
May 1st, 1960
The crystal ball was sitting uncovered on the table in the living room when I came in. Summer's well gone, and the air has a nip in it, which I suppose is why

Mrs. Delvecchio Schwartz has removed herself from the balcony. Today it's raining as well.

Flo ran to hug me, face lit up, and when I sat down she chose my knee. Why do I feel as if she's flesh of my flesh? I love her more and more as time goes on. Angel.

"The Glass must be very valuable if it's a thousand years old," I said to Mrs. Delvecchio Schwartz, who had the table set with our usual luncheon fare.

"It'd probably buy me the Hotel Australia if I sold it, but no one sells a glass, princess. Especially not one that works."

"How did you come by it?"

"Its last owner gave it to me. In her will. They get passed from one seer to another. When I go, I'll be passing it on."

Suddenly Flo gave a convulsive leap, flew off my lap and dived under the couch.

Not half a minute later, Harold sidled through the open door. How did Flo know he was coming? There's nothing wrong with my ears, but I didn't hear the softest scuff of a shoe.

Mrs. Delvecchio Schwartz looked at him with a face like thunder. "What the hell are you doing here?" she growled. "It ain't four o'clock, it's one o'clock. You ain't welcome, Harold, so piss off."

His eyes were fixed on me, full of hate, but he swung them now to her and stood his ground. "Delvecchio, it is a disgrace!"

Delvecchio? Was that her Christian name?

She put the bottle of brandy down with a thump and turned her eyes to him, though I was sitting at the wrong angle to see what exactly they contained. "A disgrace?" she asked.

"Those two disgusting sexual deviates on the floor above us have stolen the money out of the gas meter in the bathroom!"

"Any proof?" she asked, her bottom lip jutting out.

"Proof? I don't need proof! Who else in this house would do a thing like that? It was you asked me to go the rounds of the gas meters every Sunday!" His face twisted. "You're too tall to get down that far, you said, but *I've* got duck's disease!"

Mirth rumbled, she looked at me. "He has too, princess. You know what duck's disease is?"

"No," I said, wishing she wouldn't joke at Harold's expense.

"Arse too close to the ground." She heaved herself to her feet. "Come on, Harold, let's have a look."

I knew it was pointless to try to persuade Flo to come out of her hiding place. Harold seemed likely to come back, and Flo would know that. Extra-sensory perception. I'd read somewhere that it was being investigated. Bugger Harold! This was a ploy to spoil my time with Mrs. Delvecchio Schwartz. Jim and Bob, stealing pennies from a gas meter? Ridiculous.

A lot of things were telling me that this repressed and hate-filled elderly man was a maelstrom of negative emotions. Suddenly I remembered a lecture given by a psychiatrist. He'd talked of "mummy's boys"—the single male who remained in the grasp of his mother until she died, when, doomed by his own inadequacies, he then fell into the clutches of another dominant woman. Was Harold a mummy's boy? He fitted the picture. Only that didn't explain the hatred for me. They were usually quite harmless people, and if one did become violent, the violence was sometimes directed at the dominant woman, more often at himself. According to the bloke who gave that lecture. Today indicated that Harold's hatred was not purely for me. Today his targets were Jim and Bob. And Jim was another Queen of Swords.

I could hear Mrs. Delvecchio Schwartz returning because she was bellowing with laughter. "Ripperace!" she roared as she erupted into the room, Harold behind her with a face like flint. "Oh, it's flamin' terrific!"

"What?" I asked dutifully.

"The buggers pinched the pennies out of the bathroom meter all right, but not by bustin' the padlock, oh no! They used a hacksaw and cut through the hinges on the back of the penny door. Looked perfect! What really kills me is that the buggers went to so much trouble for the sake of about two bob in pennies."

"Delvecchio, I *insist* that you evict those women!" Harold cried.

"Listen, ace," said Mrs. Delvecchio Schwartz

through her teeth, "it ain't Jim and Bob, it's Chikker and Marge in the front ground floor flat. Gotta be."

"They are respectable people," Harold said stiffly.

"Grow up, dickhead! Don't you hear him beatin' the shit outta her every Fridee night after he comes home turpsed? Respectable, my arse!" Her shoulders shook. "Fancy takin' so much trouble for a few pennies! Can't pin it on 'em, either. What's more, I don't wanta pin it on 'em. At least they ain't on the game, and apart from Fridee nights, they're good tenants."

"I must take your word for that," said Harold, who obviously didn't care a hoot about Chikker and Marge. "However, I insist that you get rid of that pair of Lesbians! Riding a motorcycle, indeed! They're disgusting, and you are a fool!"

"And you," said Mrs. Delvecchio Schwartz conversationally, "couldn't organise a free fuck in 17d! Piss off! Go on, piss off! And don't bother comin' back at four. I ain't in the mood."

His dismissal seemed to fall on deaf ears; he was too busy glaring at me. And I, uncomfortably aware that I really ought not to be listening to any of this, was staring intently into the huge crystal ball and its upside-down view of the room.

"Training another charlatan?" Harold sneered.

Mrs. Delvecchio Schwartz didn't answer. She simply picked him up by the scruff of the neck and the seat of the pants and threw him out of the door as if he weighed nothing. I heard the crash of his landing, almost jumped up to see if she'd hurt him, then subsided. If she had, he might calm down a bit.

"Piss off, you fuckin' little turd!" she yelled into the hall, then sat down beaming in content. Then, to the couch, "Youse can come out now, Flo, Harold's gone."

"Why is she so frightened of him?" I asked, sipping brandy while Flo, on her mother's lap, drank from the breast.

"I dunno, princess."

"Can't you persuade her to tell you?"

"She don't want to. And I ain't sure I wanta know."

"He—he wouldn't interfere with her, would he?" I asked.

"No, Harriet, he wouldn't do that. I ain't stupid, honest. It's spiritual."

"I didn't realise anybody in The House minded Jim and Bob."

"Harold minds everyone."

"Is he a mummy's boy?"

The X-ray vision flared into action. "Now ain't you the cluey one? Yeah, as a matter of fact. She was what I call a professional invalid—lay in bed while Harold waited on her hand and foot. But when she died, he was like a chook with its head cut off, didn't know what to do. Worse, she left everything she had to a cousin in the Old Country she hadn't seen since they were children. The cousin sold up the house, and Harold had nowhere to go. He'd spent every penny he earned on the selfish old cow. So when he come to me askin' for a room, I felt sorry for him. One of the other chaps what teaches at his posh private school useta be a tenant here ages ago—that's how Harold knew about The House. I turned up the cards, and they said he had an important job to do for The House, so I took him in. Then," she said, leering, "I found out he was an old maid in more than his manners—yep, a virgin! Take me word for it, princess, you gotta have a virgin before you die."

I wanted desperately to tell her that I thought Harold was a very sick man, but these days my tongue tends to get me into hot water, so I bit it and said nothing, even about the way he stalked me and looked at me. Instead I said, "You're very tired of him."

"Fed up to the back teeth, princess."

"Then why don't you get rid of him?"

"Can't. The cards still say he's got an important job to do for The House, and they ain't to be disobeyed." She topped her glass up, took a bite of bread-and-eel, and said, mumbling, "So the King of Pentacles went home to Curry Land?"

"Eight days ago. I spent last weekend at Bronte."

"Lovely lookin' bloke! Reminded me of Mr. Delvecchio, only Mr. Delvecchio was an Eyetie, didn't have a touch of the tarbrush like your bloke. But proud and handsome! King of the world, that was Mr. Delvecchio." She sighed and sniffled. "I useta lie in bed and watch him strut around like a rooster."

One of her pale eyes mocked me, the other closed speculatively. "Was your first King of Pentacles a nice hairy man?"

"No. He was more like an ivory sculpture."

"Pity. Mr. Delvecchio was smothered in hair. I useta comb his chest, and as for the you-know-where"—she laughed hugely—"tangles 'n' snarls, princess, tangles 'n' snarls! A regular jungle. I useta *love* prowlin' through it! Combed it with me tongue."

Somehow I kept my face straight. "How long ago was that?"

"Oh, seems like a hundred years! About thirty, really. But, aaaah, I remember him like it was yesterday! Youse always does remember your men like that, you'll find as they start addin' up. Yeah, like yesterday. That's what keeps youse young."

"There were no children?" I asked.

"Nah. Ain't that peculiar? A nice hairy man like that, and no children. I'd say it was me. Flo come on that hormone stuff."

"What happened to Mr. Delvecchio?"

She shrugged. "Dunno. He just up and left one day. Never even packed a port. I waited a few days, but he never come back. So I turned up the cards and they said he'd gone for good. The Tower. The Lovers reversed. The Hanged Man. The Nine of Swords. The Four of Wands reversed. Ruin of the house, y'know. But the Queen of Swords—me—was well placed, so I got over it. I saw him in the Glass once, a long time after. He looked real well and happy, and he was surrounded by kids. When we was first together, he gave me a blue bunny rug for the son we never had. Oh, well!"

The story moved me unbearably, though she didn't tell it with a shred of regret or self-pity. "I'm so sorry!" I said.

"No need, princess. There's a time for things to be over, is all. You know that after your week with the ivory statue."

"Yes, I suppose I do."

"Is your heart broken?"

"Not even dented."

"So there youse are. The sea is chocka with fish, me young Harriet Purcell. Youse ain't the sort to get a broken heart, you're the sort will break 'em. Youse ain't like me, but that bit is. Life's just too good and the sea's too chocka with fish for the likes of us, young Harriet Purcell. We're unbreakable."

Willie's tipple had long ceased to taste revolting, but the truth is that the more of it I drink, the better I like it. So I was well enough away by this to go on asking questions. "Did you and Mr. Delvecchio divorce?"

"Wasn't necessary."

"You weren't officially married, you mean?"

"That's as good a way of puttin' it as any." Mrs. Delvecchio Schwartz refilled our glasses.

"But you and Mr. Schwartz were married."

"Yeah. Funny, ain't it? And in plenty of time for

Flo. I was at that age. Y'know, you're gettin' on in years and suddenly feel a bit chilly without a husband to warm the feet."

"Was Mr. Schwartz like Mr. Delvecchio?"

"Total opposite, princess, total opposite. That's the way it oughta be. Never repeat your mistakes! Never pick the same sorta bloke twice. Variety is the spice of life."

"Was Mr. Schwartz handsome?"

"Yeah, in a poetic sorta way. Dark eyes but real fair hair. A nice face, fresh and young. Flo looks sorta like her daddy."

A deliciously muzzy feeling was crawling inside me, and perhaps because of it, as I squinted at Mrs. Delvecchio Schwartz I suddenly saw how she must have looked thirty or forty years ago. Not beautiful, not pretty, but very attractive. Men must have felt like Sir Edmund Hillary on top of Mount Everest when they scaled her heights.

"You were extremely fond of Mr. Schwartz," I said.

"Yep. You always are of the ones what won't make old bones," she said tenderly. "Mr. Schwartz didn't make old bones. He was twenty-five years younger'n me. A lovely Jewish gentleman."

I gaped. "And he *died*?"

"Yep. Just never woke up one morning. A real grouse way to go, princess. A dicky heart, they said at the inquest. Maybe it was. But the cards said if it hadn't been that, it woulda been something else. A bus or a bee sting. Youse can't escape the old gent with the scythe when it's your time to go."

I pushed my glass away. "If I don't go now, Mrs. Delvecchio Schwartz, I'll start wuddling my merds." Then I thought of one more question. "Harold called you Delvecchio. But that's not your Christian name. What is, if I may ask?"

"Seems a funny way to describe a first name when most of the world ain't Christian," she said, grinning. "I dropped me first name donkey's years ago. Me magic's in Delvecchio Schwartz."

"Is my magic in Harriet Purcell?" I asked.

She pinched my cheek. "Dunno yet, princess." A stretch. "Oh, what a relief! No fuckin' Harold this arvo!"

I went downstairs, fell on my bed and slept for two hours. When I woke a while ago, I felt wonderful. Today I learned heaps about my landlady. Flo? *Hormone stuff*? Darn! I didn't ask.

Wednesday,
May 11th, 1960

A poor old boy came in late this afternoon with crush injuries to both legs from just below the pelvis. One of those insanely freaky accidents that aren't even supposed to happen at all. He'd been walking along minding his own business when a block of concrete fell off an elderly factory's cornice. If it had hit him, there wouldn't have been enough of him left to scrape up, but what hit him was the sheet of iron attached to it just far enough from the ground when it met it to squash his legs flat, and then, rebounding, to release him, let the ambulancemen rush him to Queens. There was no hope for him, of course, not at his age. Eighty.

I was returning from the female staff room to my own domain when Sister Herbert, on evening shift, grabbed me and asked me if I was busy. I said no.

"Look, the place is a shambles and I've got more nurses coming any minute, but I need someone *trained* to see what's bothering my poor old boy in Seven. He's terribly distressed, he won't settle, and I don't want him pegging out unhappy. We've done what we can—he's going to meet his Maker tonight for sure, but he keeps crying for someone called Marceline. I can't bear the thought that we're not making his last moments what they should be, but I can't spare anybody to talk to him. He insists he's got no family or kin—oh, he's fully conscious, it's that sort of shock. Could you talk to him for me?" Off she dashed—the place really was a shambles.

He was so sweet, the poor old boy, and scrupulously clean. They'd taken his false teeth, so he smiled at me gummily, clasped my hand. The drips, the cradle, the monitors didn't seem to impinge on him. All he could think about was Marceline. His cat.

"I won't be home to feed her," he said. "Marceline! Who will look after my angel?"

The words hit me like a ton of bricks. His angel.

My heart always aches for the old and forgotten—there are so many of them around the inner city, living in those dreary, neglected terraced houses between Royal Queens and the Cross. BOARD AND LODGING, MEN ONLY the hand-lettered cardboard signs say, and men like my poor old boy eke out an existence in a tiny room a thousand times over. Subsisting on dignity and the smell of an oil rag, or else sodden with drink. Eating in the soup kitchens, resigned to their solitude. And here was this one, dying before my eyes, with no one to care for his angel.

A fourth-year nurse arrived not five minutes after me, and between us we managed to convince him that I would feed his cat, care for her until he came home. Once he believed us, he closed his eyes and drifted contentedly away.

I borrowed Chris's canvas shopping bag and a supply of safety pins, walked up to Flinders Street, found the house, knocked. When no one answered I pushed the front door open and started knocking on every door inside. Absentee landlord because no one in authority challenged me. An old boy with a bad case of the shakes and enough alcohol on his breath to make my head spin pointed toward the backyard, such as it was. A mean little rectangle full of junk. And there, sitting on the skeleton of a gas stove, was my poor old boy's angel. A skinny tortoiseshell cat which stood up and mewed at me plaintively.

I held out my hand. "Marceline? Are you Marceline?"

She jumped down, came to rub around my legs purring loudly. When I put Chris's bag flat on the ground and lifted one edge of it to make a cave, the cat calmly walked inside it, and when I set it on its flat bottom and began to shove safety pins in it to close it, the cat just kept on purring. So I carried my burden home with no trouble except the fear that Mrs. Delvecchio Schwartz would refuse to let me keep Marceline angel. No one else has a pet except Klaus, who keeps two budgies in a cage and lets them fly around his room.

She knew what was in the shopping bag, though it neither moved nor emitted a meow. How *does* she know? Because she sees it in the cards or the Glass.

"You keep it, princess," she said, waving a dismissal.

I didn't tell her that Marceline was an angel. That I had brought the animal home as an omen.

When I undid the shopping bag, there was Marceline in its bottom, paws tucked under, snoozing. Maybe my poor old boy had some reason on his side, to be so attached to this only other living thing in his life. Marceline was special. I fed her on smoked eel, which she devoured ravenously, and when I pointed to the partially open window, she stared at me solemnly, then waddled to it with distended belly, jumped to the sill, and vanished.

I wonder will I still have a cat in the morning?

Thursday,
May 12th, 1960

Yes, I still have a cat. When I woke, Marceline was curled on the foot of my bed. I picked her up and examined her closely for fleas, sores, mange, but she was as scrupulously clean as her old boy. Just skinny, probably because he couldn't afford to feed her lavishly. We breakfasted together on scrambled eggs and toast—she certainly isn't a fussy eater. She does like top-of-the-milk, however. That should put weight on her. There's no problem in The House about keeping a window open; to get into our backyard, you have to scale a sixty-foot cliff. Though why would you bother, when the front door's always open?

My poor old boy had met his Maker at about the same time as I appropriated his angel from the house on Flinders Street.

As I would have to take Marceline to the vet's for worming and maybe spaying, I kept Chris's canvas shopping bag, gave her a new and nicer one I bought on my way to work.

Saturday,
May 14th, 1960

Would you believe it? David Murchison turned up not long after I got in from the vet's. My poor old boy had certainly spent what he could on his angel, because the vet told me that she was already spayed.

All I had to pay for were worming and yeast tablets, plus a couple of injections for feline fevers. Five bloody quid! So when David turned up on my doorstep, my mind was on my expensive cat and what a good lurk vets have.

When he saw Marceline curled up in my lap, David shuddered and made no attempt to come closer to me than the other side of the fireplace, where (on another meter, more pennies!) I had the gas fire going. Winter's around the corner.

"Where did you get that?" he asked with a moue of distaste.

"From heaven, I suspect," I answered. "I'm just back from the vet's, and I can tell you that her name is Marceline, she's spayed, and she's about three years old."

His only response was a noise of revulsion, but he sat down opposite me in the other easy chair, stared at me out of the blue eyes I used to think so divine, and steepled his fingers.

"I hear you have a new girlfriend," I said chattily.

His skin flushed, he looked annoyed. "No, I do not!" he said with a snap in his voice.

"Broke your mould, did she?"

"I am here," he said stiffly, "to ask you to change your mind and come back to me. Rosemary was a rebound, that's all."

"David," I said patiently, "you're out of my life. I don't want to see you, let alone go out with you."

"You're cruel," he muttered. "You've changed."

"No, I haven't changed, at least not where you're concerned. But I am a different person. I've gained the courage to be direct and the hardness not to relent when people play on my sympathy. You may as well get your bum off my chair and piss off, because I don't want you."

"It isn't fair!" he cried, hands unsteepled. "I love you! And I'm not going to take no for an answer."

Right, Harriet Purcell, bring out the Big Bertha cannon. "I am not a virgin," I said.

"*What?*"

"You heard me. I am not a virgin."

"You're joking! You're fabricating!"

I laughed. "David, why can't you believe the truth?"

"Because you wouldn't! You *couldn't!*"

"I bloody could, and I bloody did. What's more, I thoroughly enjoyed myself." Fire the ten-ton shell, Harriet! "Added to that, he wasn't precisely a white man, though he was a beautiful colour."

David got up and left without another word.

"So," I said to Toby later, "I've finally got rid of David for good, though I suspect it was more because my lover was an Indian than because I've had a lover."

"No, a bit of both," Toby said, grinning. "The silly clot! He ought to have seen the writing on the wall years ago. It's women who choose their mates. If a man's interested, he simply has to wait around with his cap in hand until she makes up her mind.

And if she decides to give him the royal heave-ho, that's too bad. I've seen it happen from dogs to dicky-birds. As for spiders"—he shuddered—"the ladies eat their mates."

"I am not a bitch on heat, thank you!" I snarled.

He laughed. "Maybe not, Harriet, but you certainly do have an effect on us poor old dogs." His eyelids lowered, he considered me like a sniper his target. "You're sexy. There's no slapping a label on that, it's underneath the skin."

"I do not pout, wiggle or stick my tongue out!"

"That's confusing advertisement with essence. If a man says a woman's sexy, he simply means that he thinks she'd be fun in bed. Some of the homeliest women I know are sexy. Look at Mrs. Delvecchio Schwartz. She's the back end of a bus, but I'll bet the men have been turning somersaults over her since she was twelve. I rather fancy her myself, as a matter of fact. I always did like women who are taller than me. I must have Sherpa blood."

He strolled over to my chair and put a hand on its back, then lowered himself onto its arm, his knee pinning me hard. "It's my experience of genuinely sexy women that they *are* fun in bed."

I looked suspicious. "Is that a hint or an invitation?"

"Neither. I don't intend to let you grab me by the short and curlies at this stage, thank you very much. Which doesn't mean I'm not going to kiss you, mind."

He did so, forcefully enough to be painful until my head lifted off the chair back and turned to accommodate him, then he fitted his mouth luxuriously into mine and played with my tongue.

"That's as far as I intend to go," he said, releasing me.

"That's as far as I intend to let you go," I said.

Interesting man, Toby Evans. In love with Pappy, but yet attracted to me. Well, I'm attracted to him too, though I'm not in love with him. Why does everything in life seem to boil down to sex?

Pappy's at home again this weekend. Ezra's wife, she told me when I invited her to have something to eat and meet Marceline, is being hideously difficult.

"With seven kids, I'm not surprised," I said, putting the beef braise on the table so we could take as much as we wanted. Pappy, I noticed, wrinkled her nose and started to hunt out the carrots and potatoes, leave the meat. "What's this?" I demanded.

"Ezra deplores eating flesh. The beasts of the field are innocents we subject to horrible torture in slaughterhouses," she explained. "Man wasn't intended to eat flesh."

"That's complete bullshit! Man started as a hunter, and our gums are populated by as many teeth for tearing flesh as for grinding plants!" I snapped. "Slaughterhouses are policed by government officials, and all the animals that go to them wouldn't exist at all if we didn't eat them. Who says that carrot you're busy masticating with your

omnivorous teeth wasn't subjected to horrible torture when it was yanked from the soil, decapitated,
scrubbed hard enough to exfoliate it, cruelly
chopped into chunks and then got the living day-
lights simmered out of it? And all that is nothing
compared to the fate of the potato you're relishing—
I not only flayed it, I took a sharp knife, screwed it
round in its flesh and dug out its eyes! The brisket's
good for you, you're so thin you must be burning tissue protein. *Eat the lot!*"

Oh, dear. I'm turning into a shrew. Still, it worked.
Pappy helped herself to beef and enjoyed the taste of
it enough to forget darling stupid drongo flipping
Ezra.

Luckily she liked Marceline, and Marceline liked
her enough to climb on her lap and purr away. Then
I set out to do a bit of fishing for information on
Ezra, and learned some very interesting stuff, such as
how he can afford to maintain a wife and seven kids
as well as a flat in the Glebe and very pricey substances the Law says he can't have. He holds a chair,
but academics don't get paid what managing direc-
tors do because intellect and education don't rank
with money-making. His salary, Pappy said, goes to
his family. But he has written a couple of books that
sell to a popular market, and he keeps that income
for himself. Oh, the more I hear about Ezra, the less
I like him! Utterly, totally, completely selfish.

On the other hand, Pappy's so happy, and every
day that she's happy is one more day that she isn't

unhappy. Not an ounce of practicality in her, but we can't all be like me, I suppose.

Saturday,
May 28th, 1960

An animal is good company. Today was one of the really quiet Saturdays, Jim and Bob off tooling around the Blue Mountains on the Harley Davidson, Klaus off down to Bowral, Chikker and Marge in the front ground floor flat sleeping off a binge, Toby off with his sketching block and a tin of water-colours to some site in Iron Cove that's caught his fancy, Mrs. Delvecchio Schwartz dealing with a cav-alcade of blue-rinsed clients (they love to come on Saturdays), and Pappy somewhere in dreamland at Glebe. Harold was here, of course. I don't know what he does when he isn't teaching school, but he certainly doesn't go out. Mrs. Delvecchio Schwartz does his washing when she does her own, so the one part of The House I can be sure not to find him is the laundry and backyard. There's never a sound from his room, though it's right above me—no music, no creaking of my ceiling, and when I'm outside and lift my head to look at his window, its blind is drawn, both panes shut all the way. Yet I'm conscious of him somewhere in the back of my mind all the time. It used to be just when I went upstairs to have a shower, but during the last couple of weeks I've noticed that if I go upstairs anywhere to see anybody, as I come down again I think I can hear feet whispering shoeless behind me. I turn around, but there's no one there. And if it's Mrs. Delvecchio Schwartz I go to visit, he's always on the landing outside her door when I leave, not moving, just staring at me.

It must have been about six o'clock when someone knocked on my door. The days have drawn right in, so it's dark by six now, and I've taken to sliding the bolt on the inside of my door when the back regions of The House are deserted except for me and Harold. Even worse indication of my creeping paranoia, I've driven six-inch nails from my window frames deep into the architraves around them, which allows me to keep them open at top and bottom, but not wide enough for anyone to slither inside. Sydney's not cold enough to close windows all the way in winter, neither wind nor rain beats in along the side passage, and in summer I don't get the sun. If I am inside and the big bolt is engaged, I am *safe*. When I think about that, I get the shivers. That awful little man upstairs is waging psychological warfare against me, and for all my horror of cowardice, in some ways he's winning. Yet I can't say anything to anybody about it—when I did to Toby, he pooh-poohed it. Paranoid.

So when the knock fell on my door, I jumped. I was reading a whodunit by a snobby Pommy woman and Holst's *Planet Suite* was playing on Peter's hi-fi, the gas fire was going, and Marceline was curled up in the other easy chair, fast asleep. A part of me wanted to call out and ask who was there, but that's cowardice, Harriet Purcell. So I walked to the door, slid the bolt and opened it with a rush, every muscle poised not for flight, but for fight.

Mr. Forsythe was standing there. My muscles sagged.

"Hello, sir," I said brightly, and held the door wider. "Ah, um, er, come in." *Feeble*.

"I do trust that I'm not inopportune?" he asked, entering.

What an incredible turn of phrase! God speaketh in a superior tongue, none of this "I'm not in the way, am I?" stuff.

"You're perfectly opportune, sir," I said. "Sit down."

Marceline, however, was not about to budge. She likes the fire too much. His solution was to pick her up, ensconce himself in the chair, put her on his lap and stroke her back to sleep.

"I can offer you coffee or three-star hospital brandy," I said.

"Coffee, thank you."

I disappeared behind my screen and stood looking at the sink as if it held the answer to the meaning of life. The sound of his voice jolted me into action, I filled the percolator, spooned coffee into it, turned it on.

"I've been to see an aged patient of mine at Elizabeth Bay," he was saying, "and I have to return later tonight. Unfortunately it's over an hour's drive to my house, so I wondered if perhaps you might be free to join me for dinner in this area."

Oh, lord! It's got to be almost two months since I last saw him, that night when he gave me a lift home and drank a mug of my coffee. Since then, not hide nor hair of him.

"I'll be out in a minute," I called, wondering why percolators took so long to get their only job over and done with.

Why was he here? *Why?*

"Black, no sugar," I said, finally reappearing. Then I sat down opposite him and looked at him as Chris Hamilton had looked at Demetrios on that famous day when I'd gone up her like a rat up a drainpipe. The scales fell from my eyes. Those wretched cards are right, Mr. Forsythe wants me. *He wants me!* So I sat staring at him stupidly, too astounded to find a thing to say.

I don't think he noticed the mug of coffee or the cat on his lap, he was too intent on me, chin up, eyes calm and steady. A bit like a film star playing a spy going to his execution. Prepared to suffer, prepared to die for what he believed in. Suddenly I realised that I knew nothing like enough about men to understand what forces would impel a Duncan Forsythe to do this. All I did know was that if I accepted his invitation, I was going to trigger a chain of events that had the power to ruin both of us.

How fast is thought? How long did it take me to

sit there, wordless, and make up my mind? Harold aside, I'm happy with my lot—with myself, my sexuality, my code of behaviour, my life. But he, poor man, doesn't even know who or what he is. I don't have the remotest idea why he wants me, only that he's brought himself to the necessary pitch to come asking. On the strength of three little encounters.

"Thank you, Mr. Forsythe," I said. "I would be delighted to have dinner with you."

For a moment he looked absolutely taken aback, then that smile that turns me into a melted puddle lit up his face and his eyes. "I've booked a table at the Chelsea for seven o'clock," he said, finally saw the coffee and picked it up to sip at it.

The Chelsea. Gord Aggie! The hospital grapevine is definitely right, he's not a philanderer. He was planning to take me to eat at the poshest restaurant between the City and Prunier's, where half the customers would recognise him in an instant.

"Not the Chelsea, sir," I said gently. "I don't have that sort of wardrobe. Would you mind the Bohemian up the street? Russian Egg and Rostbraten Esterhazy for ten bob."

"Wherever you like," he said, looking as if some huge burden had been lifted from his shoulders. Then he put the mug down and rose to his feet, deposited Marceline back in her chair. "I'm sure you'd like to have some time to yourself," he said then with the courtesy he was famous for, "so I'll sit in my car outside and wait for you to come out." At the door he stopped. "Ought I to go ahead of you, make a reservation?"

"It's not necessary, sir. I'll join you outside shortly," I said, and shut the door behind him.

Nal had been a flutter, but what I was about to get myself into couldn't possibly end up a friendly, short-term indulgence. That wasn't in Duncan Forsythe's nature, I could see that without needing to consult Mrs. Delvecchio Schwartz. Oh, bugger! What drives us on to make potential messes of our lives? I should have politely sent him packing, I knew it. But I just didn't have the strength of character. No Matron, I. So I put on my new winter suit of pink knobbly tweed, slid my feet into the highest heels I own—no risk of towering over *him*—and hunted for my only pair of gloves. White cotton numbers, not matching kid. Hats I cannot abide, they're so utterly useless, especially on epileptic hair.

We ate Russian Egg and Rostbraten Esterhazy at the Bohemian, hardly said a word to each other. But he did insist upon a bottle of sparkling burgundy, which almost doubled the cost of the meal. Mr. Czerny waited on us himself, and when Duncan Forsythe bunged a crisp blue five-pound note on the table and told him to keep the change, Mr. Czerny nearly swooned.

We'd walked up, and we walked back. When the bulk of St. Vincent's girls' school loomed, I plunged diagonally across the road without stopping to think about traffic, and he reached to grab my arm, deter me. The touch made me panic, I blundered into a plane tree and found myself backed against it with him in front of me. I heard him gasp, then felt his mouth slide across my cheek, and I closed my eyes, found his lips and clung to them with a fierce joy heightened by my fears for the future.

After that I persuaded him by look and touch to come inside. The lights were on against our return, and there was Marceline looking up from her chair, yawning pinkly.

His head was thrown back, the pupils of his eyes still widely dilated from the night, and he breathed as if he'd been running. Oh, he looked so *alive*! And I knew that he was going to pay for this so dearly that I had to do everything in my power to make it worth the price.

So I loved him with skin and mouth and fingertips, delicately and smoothly, strongly and passionately. It was beautiful to be with a man again, especially this man. Nal had been a learning experience, heartfree and carefree, a means and an end combined. But Duncan Forsythe *mattered*. There could be no divorcing him from my life. The emotion! I kissed his hands and feet, rode him until his back arched between my slippery thighs, wrapped him within my arms and legs and fought him, muscles against muscles, until his greater strength bore me down and away.

He stayed until a little after eleven, I thought, completely lost to awareness of passing time, then suddenly he was out of my bed and looking down at me.

"I have to go," he said, nothing more, but when he'd dressed and used his comb at my mirror, he came back to me, leaned over and touched his cheek against mine. "May I come tomorrow about four?"

"Oh, yes," I said.

Oh, yes. I think I must be in love. Otherwise, why would I have let this happen?

Sunday,
May 29th, 1960
By the time I went upstairs at one for my session with Mrs. Delvecchio Schwartz, I'd already encountered Toby. I have no idea how news gets around so fast, because Toby knew, yet how could he?

"You're a fool," he snapped, eyes more red than brown. "If it's possible, a bigger fool than Pappy."

I didn't bother to reply, just pushed past him and went into Mrs. Delvecchio Schwartz's living room.

"The King of Pentacles is here," she said as I sat down and reached for my Kraft cheese spread glass of brandy.

"I don't believe this place," I said, sipping abstemiously—best go easy, with Mr. Forsythe returning in a couple of hours. "How *does* the news get around?"

"Flo," she said simply, jigging our angel up and down on her knee. Flo smiled at me, but sadly, then got off her mother's lap and went to scribble on the wall.

"It don't worry you none that he's married?" my landlady asked, doling out smoked eel and bread-and-butter.

I thought about that, then shrugged. "Actually, I think I'm glad that he's married. I'm not sure I know what I want, but I do know what I don't want."

"And what don't youse want?"

"To settle down in a posh house and play Missus Doctor."

"Just as well," she said with a grin. "The cards don't hold out much hope of a life in the suburbs for you, Harriet Purcell."

"Do I have a life at Kings Cross?" I asked.

But she went vague on me, wouldn't commit herself. "All depends on what happens to *that*." And she pointed to the crystal ball.

I studied it curiously and with closer attention than I'd ever done before. It wasn't flawless, though it contained no cracks or bubbles. Just wisps of cloud as thin as the nebulae of stars in our southern skies. It sat on a black ebony base that must have been concave to hold the huge ball—it was at least eight inches in diameter—so firmly, and I noticed that a little fold of black fabric overlapped the rim of the base. Yes, she'd have to cushion it against the ebony wood in case it scratched. I'd looked up quartz crystal in the Queens library *Merck*, to find that it had a "soft" hardness. Unsuitable for gemstones but able to be carved and highly polished. *Why did she say that?* Significant, but how?

"It all depends what happens to the Glass," I said.

"S'right." So she intended to remain cryptic.

I probed by asking casually, "I wonder who first thought of rounding rock crystal into a ball and using it to see the future?"

"Oh, mightn't be the future. Might be the past. I dunno, but they was old when Merlin was a boy," she said, refusing to be drawn.

I left a little early so I'd be downstairs when Mr. Forsythe arrived, but some things weren't going to change just because he existed. Flo would come for her two hours with me, and he could either like it or lump it. Mrs. Delvecchio Schwartz demurred, but I won. When Harold arrived, angel would come down to me.

He was there outside, in the darkness, Harold. Waiting. Eyes filled with hate. I ignored him, started down the stairs.

"Whore!" he whispered. "Whore!"

Mr. Forsythe turned up on time. I was down on the floor with Flo and the crayons because she refuses to play with anything else. I'd brought some of my old toys from Bronte, a doll with a wardrobe of clothes, a weeny trike, building blocks with a letter of the alphabet on each side. But she wouldn't even look at them. It was always the crayons.

"Door's open!" I called.

So the first thing the poor man saw was his girl-friend down on the braided rug playing crayons with a four-year-old child. His face was a study, I could-n't help laughing.

"No, she's not mine," I said, getting up and going to him to put my hands on either side of his neck, pull his head down until I could put my lips and nose against the snow-white hair of his temple. He smelled delicious, of expensive soap, and he didn't muck up that wonderful hair with oil. Then I took him by the hand and brought him over to Flo, who stared up at him without a trace of fear and smiled immediately.

"This is Flo, my landlady's daughter. I mind her every Sunday from four to six, so if you're in a hurry, I'm afraid all you can do with me is talk."

He squatted down and stroked Flo's hair, smiling at her. "How do you do, Flo?" Orthopods were always good with children because a good propor-tion of their patients were children, but try though he would, he couldn't get Flo to talk.

"She appears to be mute," I said, "though her mother says she talks. You may be sceptical about it, but a friend of mine and I believe that she commu-nicates with her mother without words, by a sort of telepathy."

He was sceptical—well, he's a surgeon. They don't have any flights of fancy, at least about things like telepathy and extra-sensory perception. You need a psychiatrist for that, and maybe one from Asia somewhere into the bargain.

Harold, however, got short shrift today. Flo hadn't been in my flat more than half an hour when Mrs. Delvecchio Schwartz thundered through the door, still open.

"Oh, *there* you are, angel!" she squeaked in an artificial voice, as if she'd been searching The House high and low. She then propped like a hammy comedian and pretended she hadn't seen a man until that very millisecond. "Oho! The King of Pentacles!" she bellowed, and grabbed the bewildered Flo. "Come on, angel, don't be a nuisance. Give 'em some privacy, hur-hur-hur."

I cast her a glance which informed her that it was the worst performance I'd ever seen, and said, "Mrs. Delvecchio Schwartz, this is Dr. Duncan Forsythe. He's one of my bosses at Queens. Sir, this is Flo's mother and my landlady."

The old horror actually dropped him a curtsey. "Tickled to meet youse, sir." Flo tucked under one arm, she marched out with another hur-hur-hur.

"Ye Gods!" said Mr. Forsythe, staring at me. "Is she Flo's biological mother?"

"She says she is, and I believe her."

"She must have been menopausal when she had the little thing."

"Didn't even know she was up the duff, she told me."

Which were the last words spoken for at least an hour. Oh, he is a lovely man! We fit together so well.

"You'll have to stop thinking of me as Mr. Forsythe and calling me sir," were the first words spoken after that hour. "My name is Duncan, which you must already know. I'd like to hear it from your lips, Harriet."

"Duncan," I said. "Duncan, Duncan, Duncan."

That led to another interlude, after which I heated up the lamb neck chop casserole I'd made this morning, and boiled some potatoes to go with it. He ate as if he was starving.

"Don't you mind my being married?" he asked as he sopped up the gravy dregs with a piece of bread.

"No, Duncan. I realised yesterday that you'd thought it out before you arrived. It doesn't matter a bit to me that you're married, as long as it doesn't matter to you."

But of course it does matter to him that he's married, as he proceeded to explain to me at greater length than I honestly cared to hear. What a burden guilt can be. The truth lies in the fact that he sought me out—his wife is a cold fish, and to her, he's a meal-ticket. That's what a lot of doctors are to the women who marry them. I knew from listening to Chris and Sister Cas that he'd married a classmate of Sister Cas's—the prettiest and most vivacious nurse of her year, just as the Duncan of those days was the most eligible and attractive bachelor registrar at Queens. Added to which, his family is quite sinfully wealthy. *Old money*, Sister Cas contributed, sounding awed. Old money *is* awesome in a country that only started yesterday, though I don't think that the Australian definition of old money is the same as the English one.

He and Cathy had been happy enough for the first few years, while he was establishing his specialist practice and she was having their two boys. Mark is thirteen, Geoffrey eleven. He loves them dearly, but he sees hardly anything of them, between the miles and miles his Jaguar clocks up and the long hours in operating theatres, consulting rooms, wards and Out Patients. It was on the tip of my tongue to ask him why on earth they all seemed to live way up on the North Shore when so often their hospitals are at the opposite end of Sydney, and their rooms *have* to be in Macquarie Street, convenient neither to hospitals nor residences. The H.M.O.s at Vinnie's Hospital, which is convenient, are mostly Catholics or Jews who sensibly live in the Eastern Suburbs.

But I didn't say any of it because my why is not the reason Duncan would give me. My why is that their *wives* love the upper North Shore. They cluster between Lindfield and Wahroonga, where they can drive their smart little British cars safe from the worst traffic, can congregate for bridge, solo, committee meetings and tennis. Their children go to posh private schools in the area and there are heaps of trees, snatches of real forest. The upper North Shore is idyllic for a wealthy wife.

Anyway, Cathy Forsythe sounds like a right bitch to me, though Duncan defended her staunchly and blamed his infidelity on himself. And perhaps—entirely subconsciously!—a weeny bit on me.

"You're a witch, my dark darling," he said, holding my hand across the table. "You've cast a spell on me."

How to answer that? I didn't try.

He carried my hand to his lips and kissed it. "You don't know what it's like to be too successful," he said, "so I'll tell you. The very last thing the people who love you understand is that you enjoy the work for the work's sake. You're caught up in an image which belongs to everyone but you. Even with the work, half of it consists in keeping other people happy, of not creating an adverse ripple on the big hospital pond. My uncle is Chairman of the Hospital Board, which has been a damned nuisance over the years. I was content as a junior H.M.O.— I had more time for research and more time for my patients. But as the senior on Orthopaedics, I seem to spend a disproportionate amount of my time in meetings— hospital politics are like any other form of politics."

"That must be a terrible bog," I said warmly, tickled that he hadn't crawled to Unk after all. Duncan Forsythe is exactly what he appears—a thoroughly nice, decent, educated, brilliant man. "Never mind, Duncan. You're welcome at 17c Victoria Street whenever you can spare the time."

That wasn't the answer he wanted to hear, of course. He wanted me to tell him that I loved him madly, would shift mountains for him, wash his socks, give him fellatio. Well, I'd wash his socks and

I'm into semi-fellatio, if that's the correct term for not quite all the way. But I am not sure that I want to hand him the key to my soul. I pity him deeply and I like him enormously and I adore our lovemaking and we have an extra bond, professional companionship. But love? If it's the key to my soul, not love.

After he left about nine o'clock tonight, I sat for an hour just thinking about us, and at the end of it I still wasn't sure that I love him madly. Because I'm darned if I'll give up my freedom for him. It's as I told Mrs. Delvecchio Schwartz, I don't want to live in a posh house and play Missus Doctor.

A re-read of Saturday night's entry tells me how quickly my attitude has changed. Then, I saw it as having to be love. Now, I see it as everything except love. What's swung me around over a mere twenty-four hours? I think it has to be listening to him talk about his life and his wife. *She* wangled him the senior post!

Monday,
May 30th, 1960
He picked me up at the Cleveland Street lights tonight as I walked home in the dark, but though he gave me that melting smile and his eyes shone, I could tell at once that his mind wasn't on lovemaking. Which made me feel a little better about us; clearly I was more to him than a female body he happened to fancy.

"I don't have very much time," he said as he drove, "but I realised today that I've made no effort to care for you, Harriet."

What an odd thing to say! "Care for me?"

"Yes, care for you. Or perhaps it would be better to ask how you care for yourself."

The penny dropped, the lightbulb went on. "Oh!" I said. "Oh, that! I'm afraid I haven't given it a thought. My career as a mistress is barely off and running, you know. But I ought to be safe enough for the moment. I'm due for my period tomorrow, and I'm as regular as clockwork."

I could hear his sigh of relief, but having been reassured, he said nothing further until I ushered him into my flat. There he picked Marceline up and cuddled her, then put his little black bag on my table. Until he did, I hadn't noticed him carrying it, that's how he affects me.

He unearthed his stethoscope and sphygmomanometer, listened to my lungs and heart, took my blood pressure, inspected my legs for varicosities, pulled my lower eyelid down, looked carefully at the tips of my fingers and the colour of my ear lobes. Then he took his prescription pad out of the bag and wrote on it rapidly, tore the top sheet off and handed it to me.

"This is the best of the new oral contraceptives, my darling Harriet," he said, tucking everything back inside the bag. "Start taking it the moment you finish your next period."

"*The Pill?*" I squawked.

"That's what they call it. You shouldn't have any problems, you're in the absolute pink of health, but if you get any pain in the legs, shortness of breath, dizziness, nausea, swelling of the ankles or headaches, go off the medication at once and let me know the same day," he ordered.

I stared down at the illegible writing, then at him. "How does an orthopod know about The Pill?" I asked, grinning.

He laughed. "Every sort of medical man from psychiatrist to gerontologist knows about The Pill, Harriet. As every specialty sees some side of unwanted pregnancies, we're all breathing sighs of relief at this little beauty." He took my chin in his hand and gazed at me very seriously. "I don't want to cause you any more trouble than I need to, my dearest love. If I can't do more for you than prescribe the most effective contraception yet devised, I have at least done something."

Then he kissed me, told me he'd see me next Saturday at noon, and left.

How lucky I am! There are single women travelling all over Sydney in search of a doctor reputed to prescribe The Pill. It's very much with us, but only if we're married. But my man wants to care for me properly. In some ways I *do* love him.

Monday,
June 6th, 1960

It had to happen sooner or later. Though Pappy knew I had a boyfriend, his identity remained a mystery until early this morning. She came in the front door around six, just as Duncan was leaving. Of course he didn't recognise her, just smiled and stood aside courteously, but she knew exactly who he was, and came straight to my flat.

"I don't believe it!" she cried.

"Neither do I."

"How long has this been going on?"

"Two weekends in a row."

"I didn't realise you knew him."

"I hardly do know him."

A funny conversation for two good friends to have, I thought as I made us some breakfast.

"Mrs. Delvecchio Schwartz told me that the King of Pentacles had arrived, and Toby told me that you had acquired a lover, but I never dreamed of Mr. Forsythe," she said.

"I didn't dream of him either. Still, it's nice to know that The House's grapevine isn't as efficient as I thought it was. Toby told me I was a fool, since when I haven't seen so much as his back going up the stairs, and Mrs. Delvecchio Schwartz approves after barging in to meet him," I said, giving Marceline her top-of-the-milk.

"Are you quite well?" Pappy asked, eyeing me doubtfully. "You sound awfully detached."

I sat down, hunched my shoulders and looked at my boiled egg without a shred of appetite. "I'm well, but am I good? That's the real question. I don't know why I did it, Pappy! I know why he did it—he's lonely and afraid, and he's married to a cold fish."

"He sounds like Ezra," she said, gobbling up her egg.

I didn't like that comparison, but I understood why she made it, so I let it pass. Half-past six on a dark winter's morning is no time to quarrel, especially after each of us had spent two days of illicit love with a very much married man.

"He hasn't done this sort of thing before, so why he picked me is a mystery. He's in love with me—or he thinks he is—and when he turned up here out of the blue, I didn't have the heart to turn him down," I said.

"You mean you're not in love with him?" she asked, as if that was a worse sin than Sodom and Gomorrah had ever dreamed of.

"How can you love someone you hardly know?" I countered, but that was the wrong thing to say to Pappy, who definitely didn't know Ezra at all.

"All it takes is a glance," she said rather stiffly.

"Does it? Or is that what my brothers call elephant love? I've really only got my mother and father to gauge, and they're very much in love. But Mum says they built it, that it took years, and it keeps getting better." I looked at her, feeling helpless. "I can look after myself, Pappy, it's him I'm worried about. Did I start something he's going to have to do all the paying for?"

Her exquisite face went suddenly hard. "Don't feel too sorry for him, Harriet. Men have all the advantages."

"You mean that Ezra is still dickering with his wife."

"Eternally." She shrugged, looked at my egg. "Do you want that? Eggs are the perfect protein."

I shoved it across the table. "It's all yours, you need it more than I do. You sound a bit disillusioned."

"No, I'm not disillusioned," she sighed, dipping a finger of toast in the runny yolk as if it interested her far more than the subject of our conversation did. "I suppose I just assumed that Ezra would be able to start committing himself to me utterly. I love him so much! I'll be thirty-four in October—oh, it would be so nice to be married!"

I hadn't realised she was quite that old, but middle thirties accounted for it, all right. Pappy is suffering from the Old Maid Syndrome. Going from many men to the only man hasn't rewarded her with the safety and security she craves. Oh, please, please, God, don't let the Old Maid Syndrome happen to me!

**Thursday,
June 23rd, 1960**
This evening when I walked upstairs to the bath-

room to have my shower, I decided that it isn't a sort of hopeful attack of imagination, it's real. Ever since Duncan entered my life, Harold has given up stalking me. The light in the hall is always on, and he's nowhere to be seen. I don't hear the sound of socked feet whispering on the stairs behind me, nor is he outside the door when I leave Mrs. Delvecchio Schwartz's living room. In fact, the last time I encountered him was that day he called me a whore. Is that what it takes to discourage these psychopathic types? The advent of a powerful man?

Tuesday,
July 5th, 1960
I am neglecting my exercise book. This is number three, but it isn't filling very fast since Duncan entered my life. I never understood how much of one's time a man can occupy, even if he's only part-time. He's worked out how to see the most of me. On Saturdays I'm a golf game that extends late enough to incorporate a "drink with the boys" in the club house after eighteen holes. On Sundays he comes in the morning and stays until Flo comes down—yes, she does cramp his style a bit, but I refuse to put his needs ahead of Flo's. I'm a session catching up with his records for a part of that, and then I'm either an emergency operation or some sort of meeting.

I can't believe that his wife doesn't smell a rat, but

he assures me that she's completely unaware anything unusual is going on. Her own schedule, it
seems, is fairly hectic. She's a bridge fanatic, and
Duncan loathes the game, won't play it. I daresay
when your other half is seemingly considerate of
your own interests, it's easy to lull your suspicions.
But she can't be very bright, his Cathy. Or maybe
she's just terribly selfish? There have been some illu-
minating confidences, like the separate bedrooms (so
he doesn't wake her up when he's called out in the
middle of the night) and the fact that she's relegated
him to what she calls the "boys' bathroom". He
hates "her" bathroom, which is attached to "her"
bedroom— wall to wall mirrors. Apparently she's
one of Sydney's best-dressed women, and now she's
pushing forty, she keeps an eye on everything from
crow's feet around the eyes to any thickening in her
waist. She's almost as addicted to tennis as she is to
bridge because it keeps her figure trim. And if her
photo is in the weekend society pages of one of the
newspapers, she's in seventh heaven. That's why he
can't be with me on Saturday evenings—she needs
him to squire her out to some black-tie function or
other, preferably one where the photographers and
journalists who feed the society pages are hovering.

What an empty life. But that's only me talking. To
her, it is exactly the life she dreamed of living since
her schooldays, I imagine. Heaps of money, two
handsome sons who sound as if she's kept them very
young for their ages, a divine house way out in the

Wahroonga backblocks, where the ground covers two acres, there's a swimming pool, and she can't see the neighbours. She has a gardener, a slushie to scrub the floors, vacuum, wash and iron, a woman who comes in to cook on the evenings she expects Duncan home, a Hillman Minx car, and unlimited accounts at the best department stores and Sydney's two fashion salons. How do I know all this? Not from Duncan, but from Chris and Sister Cas, who admire Cathy Forsythe with heart and soul. She's got what women yearn for.

As for me, I suppose you might say that I'm happy to take Cathy Forsythe's leavings. The part of Duncan she most definitely doesn't want is the part of him that I appreciate. We do a lot of talking, he and I, about everything from his fascination with sarcoma to the private secretary in his Macquarie Street rooms, Miss Augustine. She's into her fifties, another old maid, and she treats Duncan like her only begotten son. A model of efficiency, tact, enthusiasm, you name it. She's even invented a special sort of filing system, which made me smile to myself when he told me about it. What a way to ensure your own indispensability! The poor man can't find a thing without her.

It's just over five weeks since he knocked on my door with that invitation to dine at the Chelsea, and he's changed. For the better, I flatter myself. The laugh comes easier and those dark, muddy green eyes aren't as sad as they were. In fact, his looks have improved so much that Sister Cas is going around remarking that she always knew Mr. Forsythe was a handsome man, but she'd never noticed just how handsome. He's blooming, simply because someone esteems him as a man. Unlike the habitual philanderers, he's not conscious of his attractiveness to women, so he thinks that capturing me is miraculous.

Anyway, as long as Cathy Forsythe doesn't get wind of me, I keep hoping everything stays as it is. Only my exercise book is suffering, and that's a small price to pay for the love and the company of a very desirable, terrifically nice man.

Friday,
July 22nd, 1960
I've finally seen Toby. It's worried me that he's kept himself completely invisible. When I've gone up the stairs to Jim and Bob and Klaus's level, his ladder has always been pulled up to the ceiling and his bell's been disconnected. Jim and Bob haven't changed toward me, though there's a certain sorrow present for my obtuseness in choosing a man, and Klaus continues to tutor me in the kitchen every Wednesday night. I can now fry and grill as well as braise and stew, but he won't teach me how to make puddings.

"The stomach has a separate compartment for desserts," he said earnestly, "but if you train that compartment to close down now, dear Harriet, you will benefit when you get to my age."

I suspect, however, that he hasn't managed to close his own dessert compartment down, judging by his figure.

I didn't go up to see Jim and Bob or Klaus tonight, I went up to see if Toby's ladder was down. And it was! What's more, the bell was back on its string.

"Come up!" he called.

He was wrestling with a vast landscape he couldn't fit on his easel, and so was attacking it on a makeshift frame—painted white, of course—rigged on top of the easel. I'd never seen him paint anything like it before. If he did a landscape, it was always some blast furnace or dilapidated powerhouse or smoking slag heap. But this was a stunner. A great valley filling up with soft shadows, sandstone cliffs reddened by the last light of the sun, a hint of mountains that went on forever, endless still forests.

"Where did you see that?" I asked, fascinated.

"Up the other side of Lithgow. It's a valley called the Wolgan, cut off all around except for one four-wheel-drive track that winds back and forth down a cliff and ends at a pub that's a real relic. Newnes. They used to mine oil shale there during the War, when Australia was desperate for fuel. I've been spending every single weekend up there, doing sketches and watercolours."

"It's a beauty, Toby, but why the change in style?"

"There's a contract being let for paintings in the

foyer of a new hotel in the City, and this is the sort of stuff the management is looking for, so Martin says." He grunted. "Usually the hotel's interior designers have a graft going with some gallery owner, but Martin wangled me a chance at it. He can't landscape, he's purely a portrait man when he isn't into cubism."

"Well, I think this one should hang in the Louvre," I said sincerely.

He flushed and looked quite absurdly pleased, put his brushes down. "Want some coffee?"

"Yes, please. But I really came to ask if we could make a date for you to taste my newfound culinary skills," I said.

"And disturb you when the boyfriend might turn up? No, thanks, Harriet," he said curtly.

I saw red. "Listen, Toby Evans, the boyfriend doesn't intrude unless I want him to intrude! I don't remember that you had much to say about Nal apart from an intolerant attitude toward my levity, but the way you've cut me since Duncan arrived in my life, you'd think I was having an affair with the Duke of Edinburgh!"

"Come on, Harriet," he said through the screen, "you know why! The House grapevine says that he's not the sort of bloke who visits girls who live in Kings Cross. Unless, that is, they're working girls like Chastity and Patience."

"Toby, you're a bigot! I wouldn't touch a man who patronised the Mesdames Fugue and Toccata!"

"Dirty water's dirty water."

"Don't be crude! And you're begging the question. What about dear Professor Ezra Marsupial?"

"Ezra doesn't slum it here. Pappy goes to his place. And just who is your lordly bloke, anyway?"

"Do you mean The House hasn't informed you of that snippet?" I asked sarcastically. "He's an orthopod at Queens."

"A what?" he asked, arriving with the coffee.

"An orthopod is an orthopaedic surgeon."

"But Mrs. Delvecchio Schwartz called him Mister, not Doctor."

"Surgeons inside their own hospitals are always called Mister," I explained. "Though you didn't hear that from our landlady. I introduced Duncan to her as Doctor."

He wasn't rattled, simply lifted his brows. "Then I must have heard it from Harold," he said, sitting down.

"*Harold?*"

"What's peculiar about that?" he asked, surprised. "I often stop to have a word with Harold, we usually come in about the same time. And he's the biggest gossip in The House, he knows the lot."

"I'll bet he does," I muttered.

Because Toby's good opinion matters to me, I tried to explain why I was involved with Duncan, tried to make him see that it isn't immoral, even if it is illicit. But he retained his scepticism, I couldn't dent it. Bloody men, with their double standard! Tainted by the venom of a snake like Harold Warner, no doubt. He was one who wouldn't ignore the chance to make trouble for me with those I love. Oh, but it hurts when Toby condemns me unjustly! He's so decent and straightforward himself, so incapable of being underhanded. Why couldn't he see that my own openness about my affair with Duncan was evidence that I too am not underhanded? If it were up to me, the whole world could know. It's Duncan wants to keep our secret so his precious Cathy isn't embarrassed.

I changed the subject back to the painting on his easel, very glad that his absences weren't on my account. Truth to tell, it is Pappy's plight drove him up the other side of Lithgow. Then he floored me by telling me that he'd bought a piece of land on the wrong side of the tracks at Wentworth Falls, and was building a shack on it.

"You mean that you're going to leave The House?" I asked.

"Next year I'll have to," he said. "Once the robots take my job, I'll be back to living from hand to mouth if I stay in the City, whereas if I'm living in the Blue Mountains I can grow all my own vegetables, keep fruit trees, buy cheaply because prices are much lower. And if I get the hotel contract, I'll be able to build a decent house, own my own place free and clear."

I just wanted to cry, but I managed to smile and tell him how happy I was for him. Damn and blast Pappy! This is all her fault.

**Wednesday,
August 24th, 1960**

Oh, dear. A whole month since the last entry. But what is there to write when life has settled into a routine and nothing comes along to disturb it? I suppose I've become a Crossite, and what used to knock me sideways doesn't have that capability any more. Duncan and I are as settled as an old married couple, though we haven't lost our enthusiasm for bed. For a while he tried to persuade me to increase his visits by adding Tuesday and Thursday evenings, but I stood firm. Even idiots as myopic as Cathy F. do have eyes. Absences during the week above and beyond what she's used to might start her wondering about Duncan's sudden passion for golf at the Lakes, a lot closer to Queens than to Wahroonga, his excuse for choosing to play on a links where he's not known.

Maybe I'm just a little tired of the furtiveness, but my instinct for self-preservation says that as long as Cathy F. lives in blissful ignorance, I don't have to make any choices about posh houses and a future playing Missus Doctor. It irks him, though he won't hurt her by confessing. She's the mother of his sons, after all, and Unk on the Hospital Board thinks the sun rises and sets in her. What had Duncan said? Don't create adverse ripples on the big hospital pond. Well, I don't want any adverse ripples on my own Kings Cross pond, thank you very much.

Today has seen a tidal wave on the Cas X-ray

pond. Chris and Demetrios are getting married, and she's absolutely ecstatic about it. All of Cas has seen the engagement ring, a very nicely unusual cluster of diamonds, rubies and emeralds that belonged to the prospective groom's mother. Such is hospital snobbery that our humble Greek porter, having caught himself a senior X-ray technician, is now spoken of as "up-and-coming". Helped by Chris's raves about the motor mechanics course and the garage, which Demetrios has put a down-payment on. Shrewdly chosen, because it's on the Princes Highway in Sutherland and there's no competition within cooee. He's bound to do well. Poor old Sister Cas has bitten the bullet nobly, which is smart of her. She's talking about moving into the Nurses' Home until she finds just the right one to share a flat with. And there's the agreeable prospect of being Chris's bridesmaid. Chris asked me to be a bridesmaid too, but I declined tactfully, said that I'd come to the wedding. Then I teased Sister Cas by saying I used to be a champion basketball player, so I intended to outmanoeuvre the competition and catch the bride's bouquet. Dr. Michael Dobkins is staying at Queens. Once Demetrios came on the scene, Chris forgot all about her feud, and Sister Cas has decided that he's worth keeping because he's so alert and competent.

Well, well. Even if she dies tomorrow, Chris isn't going to die wondering. Demetrios struts around the place like a turkey cock, and Chris has a new facial expression— the "I know what it's like to have a good fuck" look. I was right, it has done her the world of good.

The wedding's set for next month, and will be a Greek Orthodox ceremony. Chris is busy taking lessons from the priest, and will, I suspect, end up more orthodox than the orthodox. Converts are usually a pain in the arse.

**Sunday,
September 11th, 1960**

I was seeing Duncan out this afternoon, Flo clinging to my leg, when Toby came clattering down the stairs. The moment he saw us he propped, the debate clearly written on his face—so far he's managed to avoid meeting Duncan. But then he shrugged, kept on coming down. It's always hard for a short man to have to look all that way up as he sticks out his hand for the introductory shake, but Toby did his duty, tried to look a very tall man's equal.

As he made his escape out the door, he flung a question at me. "What's the matter with our Pappy? She looks terrible." Then he was gone.

I don't see much of her, is the trouble. But tomorrow morning I'm going to get up early and tackle her.

Monday,
September 12th, 1960

Toby was right, she looks terrible. I don't think she's any thinner—that would be hard without going to complete bones—but she seems to have lost *substance*. Her beautiful mouth is dragged down at its corners, and her eyes flicker nervously here and there, won't settle on anything. Including me.

"What's wrong, Pappy?" I asked.

She panicked. "Harriet, I'll be late for work, and I've been in so much trouble with Sister Agatha for months— I look tired, I'm not applying myself to my job properly, I tend to be late or absent on Mondays—if I don't go now, I'll be in the soup!"

"Pappy, I will undertake to visit Sister Agatha this morning and tell her any tale that comes into my mind— you've been run over by a bus, or abducted into the slave trade, or you've had this man stalking you for months and it's affecting your work—I'll fix Sister Agatha, you've got my word on it. But you're not moving from this room until you've told me what's the matter, and that is that!" I said fiercely.

Suddenly Pappy bowed her head, covered her face with her hands and wept so desolately that I found myself crying too.

It took a long time to quieten her. I gave her brandy, helped her to an easy chair and half-lay her in it with her feet up on a low stool. Until this moment I had always gone a little in awe of Pappy, so much older, more intellectual, more experienced, more loving and giving. *Too* loving and giving, I realised now. All of a sudden I felt myself her equal because I understood that I owned heaps of something she utterly lacked—commonsense.

"What is it?" I asked gently, sitting beside her, holding her hand strongly.

She gazed at me out of blurred, drowned eyes. "Oh, Harriet, what am I going to do? I'm pregnant!"

Funny, that. When a girl is filled with joy, she always says she's going to have a baby. But when she's filled with horror, she says she's pregnant. As if the phrase she chooses is an emotional and cerebral distinction between a lovely fact of life and a much dreaded disease. I looked into her ravaged face with overwhelming sadness: there, but for the grace of a considerate man, go I.

"Does Ezra know?" I asked.

She didn't answer.

"Does Ezra know?" I repeated.

She swallowed, shook her head, tried to wipe away the fresh tears with her hand.

"Here," I said, giving her another handkerchief.

"I tried everything," she whispered dully. "I threw myself down the stairs. I beat my stomach against the corner of my table. I gave myself a douche with ammonia, then I tried to push a soap-and-water douche right up. I bought some ergotamine tartrate from a wardsman, but it just made me vomit. I even resorted to melting hashish with cheese on a piece of toast and eating that, but it made me sick too. I've tried everything, Harriet, everything! But I'm still pregnant." Her face became a mask of terror. "What am I going to do?"

"Sweetie, the first thing you have to do is tell Ezra. It's his child too. Don't you think he has a right to know?"

"Harriet, I was so happy! What am I going to do?"

"Tell Ezra," I insisted.

"I was so happy! This is going to spoil it. He wants an emancipated sexual partner, not more babies."

"How far gone are you?" I asked.

"I'm not sure. Almost twenty weeks, I think."

"Oh, God Jesus! You're halfway there!"

"Nothing shifted it, nothing!"

"You don't want it, obviously."

Pappy began to shiver, then the shivering turned to shaking. "Yes, yes, I want it! But how can I have it, tell me that? Ezra can't help me, he's already got seven children! His wife refuses to give him a divorce, even though she knows all about me. How can I possibly tell him?"

"It takes two to make a baby, Pappy. You have to tell him! No matter how many children he already has, he's got to answer for this one too, it's his responsibility." I gave her more coffee laced with brandy. "Why have you kept this to yourself for so long? Surely you knew that we'd all stick by you."

"I—just—couldn't get the words out, even to Mrs.

Delvecchio Schwartz," she whispered, mopping the tears. "I must have skipped two periods before I even began to suspect. Then I counted, but I must have been too far gone already for things like the ergotamine to work. Oh, Harriet, what am I going to do?" came that cry.

"First off, you're going to phone Ezra at the University and tell him that you have to see him here today. After he knows, we'll take it as it comes," I said, more optimistically than I felt.

When she refused, I marched to the phone in my bedroom which Duncan insisted I have installed, called Sister Agatha and told her that Pappy was so ill neither of us would be in to work, then I located Ezra and ordered him to report in one hour. Had it been Pappy, he might have argued, but listening to my strange voice and the iron in it, he said he'd come.

Pappy fell asleep while I tried to read a book, my mind too busy to make sense of a single word. The Pill represents true emancipation of the female, I thought. Which is why, now that it's with us in all its awesome fact, it's so decried, so impossible to get. It's in the hands of mostly men. Some religious bodies call it evil, and those hypocritical bastards of politicians have fled screaming. But men won't be able to control its distribution much longer. The Pill is going to belt the balls to the women's end of the court. The Pill is *Power*.

I did understand, however, that Ezra isn't one of

The Pill's opponents. As Pappy works in a hospital, he probably assumed that she had access to it. He's not a health worker, how would he know how hospitals operate? But he should have asked her. Maybe he had. She'd told me once that she always used a diaphragm. But the pair of them spent each weekend they were together expanding their emotions with hashish and cocaine. Probably they hadn't been as careful as they thought during a session of ordinary intercourse. Oh, Pappy, you should have stuck to fellatio!

I let her sleep for half an hour, then roused her and told her to have a shower, get ready for Ezra.

"I'm all swollen from crying," she objected.

"The sleep dealt with that, now you have to deal with Ezra," I said, adamant.

"I'm sorry I didn't confide in you, Harriet, but the words kept getting stuck in my throat. I couldn't get them out. And I kept telling myself, if I don't say a word to anyone, it will go away—if I wait a little longer, it won't exist. Isn't that strange? You'd think that anything so unwanted would vanish from sheer despair. But not *it*. Not *it*."

"Then you definitely don't want to go on with the pregnancy," I said, helping her down the passage.

"I wish I could! Oh, how much I wish I could!" she cried. "I want it because I love him so much, and this is his child. I want it because I'd like to have a child to live for. But it's utterly impossible. How would I support myself? They don't give unmarried mothers anything, Harriet, you know that."

"I believe there is a tiny subsistence payment, but it's far too small to make ends meet without working. What about having it and giving it up for adoption?"

"No, no, no! I'd rather kill it in embryo than give it away! To have it grow up thinking its natural mother didn't want it? I would go through the whole thing like a starving baker shaping a loaf of bread for someone else to eat. No, an abortion is the only way out." Her eyes filled again. "Oh, Harriet, it's so hopeless! I'll never be the same again. But what else can I do?"

"Ezra will help," I said with a confidence I didn't feel.

"He hasn't the money to help," she said.

"Rubbish! He has a house big enough for a wife and seven kids, a flat in Glebe, and the income to buy illegal drugs," I said. "Now get ready, Pappy, Ezra will be here in twenty-five minutes."

He didn't stay long. I heard the front door slam, and sat waiting for Pappy. When she hadn't come ten minutes later, I went to her.

"He's gone!" she said in tones of wonder.

"Gone for *good*?"

"Oh, yes, definitely for good. He can't help me, Harriet, he just doesn't have the money."

"He had the money to get you into this mess," I said tartly. The bastard! If he'd been anywhere within catching distance, I would have taken a nice sharp scalpel to his scrotum. The world-famous philosopher would have to change his career to singing in the Vienna Boys Choir.

Then the battle really began, and I lost it. Why do people's feelings rule them to the exclusion of the smallest particle of commonsense? Pappy wants this baby, but she won't hear of taking her precious Ezra to court, or even going to his wife and asking her to help. No, no, no, Ezra mustn't suffer! Ezra's career and position must be preserved at all and any cost! She kept talking about abortion being the only answer, kept saying the child was cursed because its father didn't want it, kept insisting that she wouldn't bring a child into the world whose father didn't want it. And on, and on, and on. Finally she asked if she might borrow the cost of an abortion from me. Apparently she'd been helping dear Ezra buy those expensive illegal drugs, so she was skint.

Eventually I left her and went upstairs to see Mrs. Delvecchio Schwartz, who had to be told. This time I was the one broke down, cried and cried while Mrs. Delvecchio Schwartz fussed and clucked with the brandy.

"But don't you *dare* say it was in the cards!" I yelled when I could speak again. "If it was, you should have done something!"

"Bullshit, princess," she said. "You can't run other people's lives for them, and if they don't ask what's in the cards, you can't go runnin' off to tell them. The cards don't work that way. Or the Glass, or Progressions."

"For one thing, she's almost twenty weeks," I said, calming down. "For another, I know she wants this baby desperately, no matter how much she talks about abortion. Couldn't we all chip in a bit each and help her keep the baby?"

"No, we can't," said the woman I had always thought so kind, so generous, so forgiving. "Think, Harriet Purcell, *think*! Yeah, we could do that for a while, but Toby's movin' out soon, Jim an' Bob ain't gunna want to divert what spare cash they got from women's causes to Pappy and a baby, and what about you, eh? What happens if you decide on a life in the suburbs after all, and trot off too? You reckon I'll be here to take the responsibility?"

She got up and walked around the table to stand over me and pin me on those terrible eyes. "D'youse really think I don't know there's somethin' wrong with me?" she demanded. "I got a tumour in me brain, and it's let me live an awful lot longer than anyone thought it would. I might live an awful lot longer still, but there's no guarantee. I saw the great Gilbert Phillips himself, an' he *said* I got a tumour in me brain. He never made mistakes—if he said you got a brain tumour, you got a brain tumour. It ain't malignant, but it's there, an' I suppose it grows a bit from time to time. Some fuckin' Vinnie's doctor put me on a newfangled hormone nearly five years ago, and bang! I had Flo. So I stopped takin' the stuff. All I do is get on with livin'. That's what we all gotta do. So you leave

Pappy alone to make up her own mind, hear me, princess?"

I sat paralysed and stared at Mrs. Delvecchio Schwartz as if I'd never seen her before.

When I got my breath back I embarked on a last-ditch stand, said I could afford to support Pappy. But what, she asked, would my husband have to say about that when I got married? And so on.

"All right," I said, beaten. "I'll leave the decisions to Pappy. Except that I *know* she'd keep the baby if she could only wait long enough to regain her senses. At almost twenty weeks, she can't, of course. But who would do such a late abortion?"

"Ask your Dr. Forsythe," she said.

I can't write any more, I'm stonkered. How many shocks can a person sustain in one day without going mad? I feel as if the whole world has shifted under my feet so mightily that I'm standing in an alien land, lost and alone. But if that's how I feel, how must poor Pappy feel? And that giant upstairs with the little kernel growing inside her brain?

Tuesday,
September 13th, 1960
Duncan and I have arranged a system whereby I can let him know if I need to see him urgently, and he can let me know on his side. So he picked me up at the Cleveland Street lights shortly after eight, and drove me home passing the time in idle chat. I like

that about him. He's so unruffled, so considerate, so aware what are the right circumstances and time for serious talk.

Poor chap, I hit him squarely in the solar plexus with it by asking as soon as we got inside, "Duncan, do you know anyone who would be willing to perform an abortion at about twenty weeks?"

"Why?" he asked, calmly but warily.

"For Pappy," I said.

"I take it that the po-faced Prof has done a bunk?" he asked, going to the cupboard where the brandy lives.

The rest of my story came out in a rush, including the bit about Mrs. Delvecchio Schwartz and her brain tumour.

"I am very sorry for Pappy," he said, giving me a full glass. "Hasn't she thought about having the baby and then giving it up for adoption? That's the usual solution."

"She flew at me like a harpy when I suggested that."

He took a mouthful of his own brandy and shuddered. "I think I must be getting used to this cat-pee. Speaking of cats, where is the magnificent Marceline?"

For several minutes he occupied himself making love to her—she's putty in his hands, the trollop. Then he said, "If the late Gilbert Phillips diagnosed a brain tumour, Mrs. Delvecchio Schwartz must have one. He must have found an unambiguous calcification on a plain X-ray of the skull."

My teeth chattered against the rim of the glass. "Oh, Duncan, what would happen to Flo if she—if she did die? The ruin of The House. I can't bear the thought."

He put Marceline down and sat on the arm of my chair. "That is for the future, Harriet, and the presence of a tumour doesn't say she won't live out her threescore years and ten, maybe more. Our present problem is Pappy, not Mrs. Delvecchio Schwartz. Would Pappy consider having the baby and keeping it?"

"I think she'd love to, but she can't afford to. If she can't work, she can't eat or pay rent. Dammit, Duncan, why does this Fallen Woman myth persist into the last half of the twentieth century? Are we never going to be rational? God made pregnancy, not marriage! Marriage was invented to help men ensure that their offspring are theirs—it makes women second-class citizens!"

"Stop sounding like the po-faced Prof, Harriet. Let's talk brutal reality," he said, looking into my face sternly.

"She wants an abortion, and I can't talk her out of it."

"And you want me to refer her to an appropriate person," he said, very seriously. "Do you understand that you're asking me to break the law?"

I snorted. "Don't be silly, Duncan! I'm not asking you to do it yourself, I just want to know someone who will. Give me a name, just give me a name! I'll do the rest."

"I doubt the Ethics Committee or the Disciplinary Board are so inclined to split hairs, Harriet. The moment I give you a name, I'm culpable too."

Yes, of course he is! "But what else can I do?" I demanded. "The alternative is someone in a back alley with a knitting needle—if they'd touch someone so far gone. I suppose I could ask one of the Mesdames next door, but I imagine any little mistakes that happen there are dealt with at six weeks by ergotamine."

"It's all right, my darling," he said, kissing me. "I've got you where I want you at last. Every gift I've offered you since we've been together has been rejected. Now I can finally give you something you'll accept. There's a very nice and secluded sanatorium in the country which specialises in cases like Pappy's. The surgery is first class, so are the medicine and the nursing. I'll give the man a ring on your phone and arrange for her to be admitted first thing in the morning." He got to his feet. "But first, I want to talk to Pappy myself, on our own."

"How much will it cost?" I asked, enormously grateful. "I have a thousand pounds in my bank book."

"Professional favours don't cost anything, Harriet."

He was with Pappy for over half an hour, returned looking very sad. "May I use your phone to ring the man?" he asked.

I followed him into the bedroom, took off my clothes and crawled into bed, which startled him. I don't think he had expected me to offer him physical consolation on this terrible evening, but I like to pay my debts. Odd, I thought, watching him undress—we're usually throwing our clothes away together, so I never have a chance to look at him properly. For forty-two, he's an asset to his tailor, not a liability.

"You have an absolutely beautiful body," I said to him.

That floored him. He caught his breath and stood immobile. Do women never pay a man compliments? Obviously his wife didn't, and I knew enough now to know that when he married her, his sexual experience consisted of a few drunken encounters half-remembered.

Wednesday,
September 14th, 1960

I was woken at six o'clock by someone pounding on my door in a way that suggested it wasn't going to stop until I answered.

Toby pushed inside and stood looking at me grimly. "Mrs. Delvecchio Schwartz sent me down," he said. "I wanted to know about Pappy, but she wouldn't tell me, and Pappy's not home."

I went to make coffee, scowling at him.

"Here, let me do it," he said, shoving me out of

the way. "I want to know what's the matter with Pappy, you concentrate on that."

So I told him. He listened painfully, grinding his teeth and beating his fist on the counter.

"I'm going to find that bastard and wallop him to death!"

"Before you do, you'd better listen to Mrs. Delvecchio Schwartz on the subject," I said, hiding my face in my mug. "Pappy doesn't want a single hair on Ezra's head harmed, she's determined to protect him at all costs, including her baby. She refuses to sue him for child support, or inform his wife— *anything* that might upset the Marsupial apple cart! And Mrs. Delvecchio Schwartz will rub salt into that wound by telling you that you're not Pappy's husband, father, brother, uncle or cousin, so you have absolutely no right to say or do a thing."

"Isn't love a good enough excuse?" he asked. "Pappy has no one of her own blood left. If we don't look after her, who will?"

"We are looking after her, Toby, in the way she wants us to," I said quietly. "The damage is done, and thank God for Duncan Forsythe. If she's not next door, then she's already gone to the sanatorium—and no, I don't know its name or where it is, because Duncan wouldn't tell me. Nor can you breathe a word about this to anyone, so mind your temper! And if you yap to Harold Warner as you meet on the way in—even thinking to throw dust in his eyes—I swear, Toby Evans, that I'll castrate you!

That evil little man is nobody's fool, and he's dangerous."

But I doubt he heard a word I said, he was so upset. *And* he bitterly resented the fact that Duncan could help more than he could. I felt for him terribly. What he must have gone through over Pappy and Ezra is something I find hard to think about.

The second mug of coffee calmed him down a bit, he recovered enough to look me up and down with— *contempt*?

"You look very satisfied," he said harshly.

"Satisfied? What do you mean?"

"Pappy's plight notwithstanding, you look as if, once the big surgeon had tidied Pappy's future up, you and he had a fine old time of it," he sneered.

I whacked him with my open hand so hard that he staggered. "Don't you dare come the judge of me!" I whispered. "Don't you damned well dare! Or come the judge of Duncan Forsythe either, for that matter! Your whole trouble is that you resent other people being able to do more for Pappy than you can yourself! Well, that's too bloody bad! Live with it, don't take it out on me!"

He was so white that the mark of my hand stood out on his skin like a naevus. "I'm sorry," he said stiffly. "You're right. Don't worry, I'll live with it."

I put my arm across his shoulders and gave him a quick hug. He returned it, slid out from under my arm, grinned at me and was gone.

Not a good start to the day. I had to go to Sister

Agatha's office and explain that Pappy would be away for two weeks.

"This is *most* irregular, Miss Purcell!" she said. "Why did Nurse Sutama not report to sick bay?"

"She went to her local practitioner," I lied. "I expect he refers his patients to places like Vinnie's and private hospitals in the Eastern Suburbs." Oh, why does everybody have to make it so complicated?

"That is immaterial, Miss Purcell. Nurse Sutama is Staff and therefore entitled to a Queens bed no matter who her physician is. She would simply have been transferred to the care of one of our own Honoraries— who, as I am sure I do not need to remind you—are the very best."

I persevered. "Sister Toppingham, truly I cannot give you any more information. All I know is that Nurse Sutama preferred to remain under the care of her own practitioner."

"Most, most irregular!" Sister Agatha clucked, giving me a horribly shrewd glance from those pale blue eyes. She smells a rat, I'm sure of it. A starchy old biddy she might be, but you can't be in command of a small army of young women for thirty years without realising that sometimes one and one add up to a total of three.

"I apologise, Sister," I said, giving the standard answer.

"Quite all right, Miss Purcell, quite all right." She bent to look at the papers on her desk. "You may go."

I walked into another catastrophe, though of a routine kind. Disorientated patient, Harriet Purcell's soothing skills required.

Luckily things died down about an hour later, and we sat to have a cup of tea. Sister Cas joined us—the wedding draws ever closer. But Chris had a bone to pick with me first.

"Why were you late?" she demanded.

"I had to report to Sister Agatha. Pappy's still sick."

"What's the matter?"

"Nothing much, but her local doctor's put her into hospital."

"Poor little beggar! Which hospital is she in, Vinnie's or Sydney? Marie and I will call in on our way home."

"You can't. She's in a sanatorium in the country."

Chris and Marie exchanged a glance of complete comprehension and changed the subject to the wedding.

Thank God that Pappy isn't involved with someone on the staff! Chris and Sister Cas were all right, but the news of Pappy's sudden illness will go on the grapevine for sure. Everybody knows her, she's been a fixture in X-ray for thirteen years. Chris and Sister Cas gave me a fit of the willies, I can tell you. It's one thing to think vaguely about the prospect of discovery, even to decide you don't care about discovery, but when suddenly discovery stares you in the face because a beloved friend's business is going to become public property—oh, that puts the world in perspective!

What if Mum and Dad found out? God in heaven, I'd *die* if Mum and Dad thought their daughter was a home-wrecker! Because if Cathy F. finds out, that's what I'll be branded. A home-wrecker.

**Saturday,
September 17th, 1960**

When Duncan arrived at noon today, I broke it off.

"I just can't bear the suspense," I tried to explain without going into details like the hospital grapevine and walloping Toby for making nasty remarks. "I know I've picked a great moment, right on the tail of your wonderful care of Pappy—how ungrateful I must seem! But it's Mum and Dad, don't you see? Duncan, what I do with myself and my life is my business, but not if it involves a married man. Then it's everyone's business. How could I face Mum and Dad? If we continue, it's bound to come out. So it stops."

His face! His eyes! The poor man looked as if I had killed him. "You're right, of course," he said, voice shaking. "But I have a different solution. Harriet, I can't live without you, I honestly can't. What you say is inarguable, my love. The last thing I ever want is to make you feel that you can't even look at your mother and father. So it's best that I ask Cathy for a divorce immediately. Once the divorce is through, we can marry."

Oh, dear God! That was the one response I hadn't counted on, and the last I wanted to hear. "No, no, no!" I shouted, and beat my hands in a frenzy. "No, not that—never that!"

"The scandal, you mean," he said, still ashen. "But I will keep you out of it, Harriet. I'll hire a woman to pose as the co-respondent, and we won't see each other again until I'm free. Let Cathy trumpet her injuries to the yellow press, let the yellow press do its worst! As long as you're not involved, it doesn't matter how sordid things get." He took my hands in his, chafed them. "My love, Cathy can have whatever she wants, but that doesn't mean you will want. There's money enough, believe me."

Oh, God! He didn't see what I meant because it hadn't occurred to him that I don't want to play Missus Doctor. That I *couldn't* play Missus Doctor, even for him. Maybe if I loved him that little bit more, I could make the sacrifice. But the trouble is that I only love him in some ways, not in all ways.

"Duncan, listen to me," I said like steel. "I'm not ready to marry anyone, I'm not ready to settle down. Truthfully, I doubt that I'll ever be ready to settle down, at least to the sort of life I would have had with David, that I would with you."

Jealousy, even at this moment! "Who is David?" he asked.

"My ex-fiancé—he's nothing," I said. "Go back to your wife, Duncan, or find a woman who wants to live in your world if you can't face it with Cathy. But forget me. I don't want affairs with married men, and I don't want you to dream of me as the second Mrs. Forsythe. It's over, and that's as plain as I can say it."

"You don't love me," he said dully.

"Yes, I do love you. But I don't want to build any nests in the suburbs, and I don't want to feel grubby."

"But children! You must want children!" he floundered.

"I don't deny that I'd like at least one child, but it has to be on my terms, and I'd rather do without a child if that means asking a man to assume responsibility for my fate. You're no Ezra, Duncan, but you come from the same world, you expect the same commitments, you compartmentalise women identically. Some for fun, some for procreation. I take it as a great compliment that you'd rather I was your wife than your mistress, but I don't want to be either."

"I don't understand you," he said, utterly bewildered.

"No, sir, and you never will." I went to the door and held it open. "Goodbye, sir. I mean it."

"Goodbye, then, my love," he said, and left me.

Oh, that was awful! I must love him, because I hurt terribly. But I'm so glad it's over before it could get worse.

**Saturday,
September 24th, 1960**
Christine Leigh Hamilton became Mrs. Demetrios

Papadopoulos today. It was a wonderful do, though a bit peculiar. I suspect that a great deal of diplomatic wrangling had gone on, conceding this custom to the bride, that custom to the groom, until both bride and groom reached conciliation. The groom's relatives and friends were on one side of the church, and the bride's on the other. His side was chocka, hers was about a third full of almost all spinsters, except for a few doctors and their wives. Dr. Michael Dobkins was there with his physio wife, which solved a mystery. She was the spitting image of Chris right down to the grand piano legs, except that, having money, she could afford to wear contact lenses. How do I know? She has that blind-as-a-bat-without-my-glasses look. No matter how well their optical aids allow them to see, they still have that muzzy myopic gaze.

The last person I expected to see was Duncan, but there he was complete with the Missus. Of course, I realised, Chris must know him very well from her days in main X-ray—orthopods look at a lot of pictures of bones. I lurked in the back of the church with a pink lace hanky on my head because I refuse to wear a hat, even for Chris's wedding. Until I set eyes on Mrs. Duncan Forsythe, I had been pleased with my slinky pink jersey dress. But the Missus—phew! Jacques Fath, if the draping of her clinging beige number was anything to go by. Beige kid gloves with seven buttons, beige kid shoes by Charles Jourdan, a beige hat *nobody* in the Royal

Family would be seen dead in, it was so elegant. In amongst us over-dressed New and Old Australian peasants, she stuck out like dog's balls, despite the fact that her hair, skin and eyes are as beige as her outfit was. She should have faded into the background, but she surely didn't. Her jewellery consisted of pearls, too dingy and dull to be fake.

Duncan looked awful, though the Missus had made sure he was perfectly clad for an occasion I'm positive she despised. Only one little week, and he's faded. Not to her beige, but to various shades of grey. Grey skin and grey hair—can so much grey appear in a week? I daresay it can, if hair can go silver overnight. To me, he seemed as if he was cooking a heart attack, but he's too fit for that. *No, Harriet Purcell, he's plain suffering, and it's all your fault, you flaming selfish bitch!* Though I was glad to get a look at the Missus, probably never will again.

Turns out that Chris has no close relatives, so Sister Agatha gave the bride away! The bride wore a Scarlett O'Hara crinoline of white tulle covered with millions of lace frills, its back cut to form an imposingly long train held up by two weeny Greek girls who staggered adorably, and everybody oohed and aahed when she came down the aisle on Sister Agatha's arm. Sister Agatha wore pastel blue guipure lace and a hat the Queen Mother would have died for—a punch-bowl of matching pastel blue straw embellished with stiff quiffs of mauve net and a couple of violent purple orchids the same as her corsage. Sister Cas—Marie O'Callaghan today, I suppose—was the only bridesmaid, in cream lace over daffodil yellow satin. The bride carried the sort of bouquet you only see in wedding photos from the 1920s and 1930s—trailing masses of white lilies and orchids. The bridesmaid carried another stunner made of creamy roses. As it's the groom's job to buy the flowers, I dipped me lid to Demetrios.

The reception was held in a Greek restaurant at Kensington, and it was, in my view, brilliant. Demetrios's parents were so proud of him! He'd managed to catch an Old Australian, the ten-quid trip out from Greece on some ghastly old cockroach of a ship was vindicated. The Papadopouloses have entered the Australian mainstream. The Forsythes, I saw, contented themselves with the church, shook hands with the groom and pecked the bride outside among the tons of confetti, then purred away in a huge black Rolls, no doubt to attend some more palatable occasion. I don't think either of them noticed me because I hid behind a pillar in the church and skulked inside the vestibule until the Rolls had gone.

So I could relax at the reception, danced with a dozen Greek blokes who all undressed me with their flashing eyes, threw plates with the best of them, and tried that *Never on Sunday* stuff, but decided it was more fun to sit back and watch the men do it the right way. They were graceful and passionate, the music was magic. I don't think there was much enthusiasm for the food among the bride's contingent, but I shovelled it in with gusto. Moussaka, dolmades, weeny meatballs, tabouli, spitted roast lamb, eggplants, olives, artichokes, octopus, squid. The rice pudding was out of this world, sweet creamy mush laced with brown ribbons of nutmeg and cinnamon. I made an absolute pig of myself.

Despite the divine food and the admiring throng of men all asking me to dance or sleep with them, I found the time to observe the table on the dais. Chris and Demetrios sat in a daze and ate nothing, but Sister Cas and the best man, Constantin, gazed into each other's eyes and fed each other coyly when they weren't in fits of giggles from the Retsina. There is going to be another Cas wedding, mark my words! When it came time for Demetrios and Chris to leave and Chris summoned up her sandbag-enhanced strength to chuck that colossal bouquet at a screaming horde of desperate women, I *did* use my old basketball skills, just not in the way I'd threatened. I manoeuvred Sister Cas into the right spot, flipped my knuckles at the correct flower as the thing whizzed straight at me, and deflected it into Sister Cas's delighted hands.

Cupid strikes again.

Sunday,
September 25th, 1960

Neither Harold nor I saw Mrs. Delvecchio Schwartz last Sunday because she had her most important client, Mrs. Desmond Thingummy—I always forget their names. It may be that she'd arranged that with malice aforethought, thanks to Pappy's crisis. Incidentally, Pappy isn't home yet. A real worry, but I'm *sure* if anything has gone wrong, the sanatorium knows how to contact us. Duncan wouldn't do it any other way. Perhaps her general health is so run down that they had preferred to wait a few days before acting, and keep her a few extra days after acting.

At least that's what I told Mrs. Delvecchio Schwartz today, and she's sensible enough to agree with my theory.

Of course she already knew that I had dismissed Duncan, though I did it very quietly, there was absolutely no one around, and last Sunday I didn't see her. I told no one about Duncan, but she knew. *It was in the cards.* It's always in the cards. Is it her tumour makes her prescient? They say that there are parts of our brains we don't utilise, that there are powers we don't know we have. Or can some people genuinely summon up the elements? Force events to go their way? See into the mists of time? I wish I knew, but I do not. All I know is that either Mrs. Delvecchio Schwartz has the best espionage system in the world, or she actually can see what's happening by spreading her cards.

I had to report on the wedding in every tiny detail, from the six crystal wine glasses I'd given the happy couple to how Sister Agatha danced the hours away on twinkling little feet. Who would have guessed it? Retsina is potent.

Flo looked exhausted, yet her mother says she's had no clients this weekend. When I came in Flo stared at me as if she knew just what I was going through, though I've tried to keep that from the whole world, haven't even given my emotions any space in this book. Nobody's business, including whoever broke the hair on my Tilsiter cupboard when they picked away the plasticine and stuck their head inside. My old books have been read, they aren't how they should be, standing neatly upright. I found them lying down, and they hadn't fallen either. Someone knows my business almost up to the present day, because I'm just starting a new book. It's left a sour taste in my mouth, though I know who's guilty. *Harold.* So I went one better when I drew all my curtains closed, stood on my bed and put the books in through the manhole in my ceiling. He'd need a ladder even if he thought of looking in the crawl space. I wish there was someone I could talk to about Harold. With Duncan gone, is he about to start his horrible little war against me all over again?

But Flo knows or senses or feels some of what I've gone through, I swear she does. It's in her eyes, my angel. She came to me the minute I sat down and climbed onto my lap, kissed my face all over, snuggled down and played with her fingers. Then her hand stole toward my brandy glass.

"Not from mine, Flo darling," I said. "If you want some, ask your mother."

"Oh, let her have a bit," Mrs. Delvecchio Schwartz rumbled. "I've finally got her off the breast, so she deserves something."

"What made you do that?" I asked, astonished.

"Saw it in the cards, princess." She reached over to take my right hand, turned it over to study the palm, then closed it into a fist and chuckled. "Youse'll be all right, Harriet Purcell. This ain't gunna keep *you* down. Sent him back to the missus, eh?"

"Yes. He was getting more and more possessive, then told me he was going to ask his wife for a divorce so he could marry me and we could live respectably. But I couldn't stomach so much as the thought of it." I sighed. "I did *try* to let him down easily."

"Men got so much pride there's no such thing as lettin' 'em down easy when it's the woman doin' the heave-ho. He's a real fine bloke—a gentleman and a scholar, as they useta say. Youse'd be good together part-time, but permanent? It just ain't in the cards. All that water and all that fire—sooner or later the pair of youse woulda gone up like a volcano meetin' the sea."

"You did his horoscope?" I asked, surprised.

"Yep. Solid Leo, Aries, Sagittarius. Looks and acts

like a Virgo with a touch of Libra and Sagittarius, but underneath he's on a permanent slow burn—there's an afflicted square between Venus and Saturn, though he ain't got the selfish streak of that—it hobbles him terrible, but. Pity I dunno what he rises in."

"How did you find out his birth date? Even I don't know!"

"Looked him up in *Who's Who in Australia*," she said smugly.

"You went out to a library?"

"Nah, princess! I got me own library."

If she does, it isn't kept in this room. Her attitude helped me a lot—this will pass, the sea is chocka with fish, my Queen of Swords is well placed, I am unbreakable. Though Flo helped me more. She never budged from my lap until Harold arrived, when she bolted under the couch.

He looks frightful. Ill, unkempt. He's crumbling, his self-esteem is eroding badly. He used to be so immaculately groomed—a prissy, fussy little man in ancient three-piece suits with a gold watch and fob across the waistcoat. Now he reminds me of a derelict. His shirt collar is frayed, his trousers are rumpled, his thin grey hair is flaked with dandruff. Oh, Mrs. Delvecchio Schwartz, try to be kind to him!

But that isn't in her. She resents him, she wants to be rid of him, yet the cards say he has a job to do for The House, and she will never go against the cards.

So she picks away at him like a crow at a carcass, the softest and most vulnerable bits first.

"You're early," she snarled.

Even his voice has lost its edge, its pernickety genteel vowels more nasal, flatter, Australian. "It is precisely four o'clock by my watch," he said, his eyes on me. Hate, hate, hate.

"Bugger the time!" she roared. "You're early, so piss off."

Harold actually rounded on her! "Shut up!" he screamed shrilly. "Shut up, shut up!"

Oh, Flo, you shouldn't be listening to this, but you are from under the couch! I shrank in my chair and prayed a silent babble that the cards released Flo's mother from this hideous, self-inflicted bondage.

Mrs. Delvecchio Schwartz simply laughed at him. "Garn, Harold, you ain't even a danger to all them little boys at school!" she said contemptuously. "You don't impress me one little bit with your shut ups. Or with your trouser snake, ace." She winked broadly at me, but made sure that he could see her do it. "Truth of the matter is, princess, that if it was half an inch shorter, it'd be a hole."

"Shut up, shut up!" he screamed again. Suddenly he turned on me, the hate flaring up in his eyes like a fire doused in petrol. "It's your fault, Harriet Purcell! It's all your fault! Things have changed around here since you arrived!"

If I could have answered, she would have cut me short. "Lay off Harriet!" she thundered. "What's

Harriet ever done to you?"

"She's changed things! She's changed things!"

"Bullshit!" she scoffed. "The House needs Harriet."

That set him off around the room, wringing his hands, screwing his head down into his shoulders, shaking and shuddering. Dear God, I thought, he's genuinely demented! "The house, the house, the wretched house!" he cried. "Do you know what I think, Delvecchio? I think you have an unhealthy attachment to this—this female! Harriet wants, Harriet gets. There's no difference between you and that filthy pair upstairs! Oh, why are you so *cruel*?"

"Bugger off, Harold," she said with dangerous quietness. "Go bugger off. The cards may say I gotta keep youse here, but you just done your dash in the nooky department, ace. From now on you can masturbate. *Fuck off!*"

One more scorching look at me, and he went.

"Sorry about that, princess," she said to me, then, to the couch, "Youse can come out, angel, Harold ain't ever comin' back into this room."

"Mrs. Delvecchio Schwartz, there's something seriously wrong with Harold's mental processes," I said with all the authority I could summon. "If you insist on keeping him in The House, please, I *beg* of you, treat him more kindly! He's deteriorating, surely you can see that! And he stalks me—or at least he did until Duncan came. Now that Duncan's gone, he might go back to stalking."

Oh, how can she be so intelligent and wise, yet so *thick*? Her response was to blow me a derisive raspberry. "Don't youse worry none about Harold, princess," she said. "The cards say you ain't in any danger from a little wart like Harold."

The cards, the cards, the *bloody* cards!

Still, I got Flo to myself for two hours, which delighted me. That scene between the two unlikely lovers had been awful to endure, but even in the midst of it, my heart had turned to lead at the thought that the breach between them would mean no more Flo on late Sunday afternoons. I think Flo was feeling the same as she huddled under the couch, because when her mother handed her to me, she lit up so vividly that I melted the way I used to when Duncan smiled at me. *Used to*. Past tense, Harriet, past tense. Oh, I miss him! Thank God I don't have to miss my angel too.

She loves the other angel, Marceline. If only Flo would put on weight the way Marceline has! My five-pound cat is now ten pounds, and still expanding. The pleasure in watching the pair of them roll around the floor! But I have made up my mind that Flo must start playing with the alphabet building blocks. I've tried sending my thoughts at her, but they don't get through. So if I teach her to read and write, then we'll be able to communicate.

She listened intently while I showed her A and B and C and T and a few others, seemed to comprehend completely when I built CAT and DOG. Yet when I give the bricks to her, what comes out is CTB or DAC. She can't even hand me A or B. Meaningless to her. The reading centre in her brain must be damaged or nonexistent. Oh, Flo!

**Monday,
September 26th, 1960**

Pappy must have returned very late last night, while Marceline and I were asleep. Yet there must be some sort of supernatural force in The House, because I woke two hours early and I knew that she was home. When I came around the corner to her room with the coffee percolator in my hand, her door was wide open.

She was sitting at the table, looked up at me and smiled. Oh, so much better than she had looked when she went away! I hugged her and kissed her, poured both of us coffee, sat down. There were sheets of paper spread on the table, some blank, some with a few words written on them in purple ink.

"Ezra Pound—another Ezra!—had huge hand-writing," she said. "I wrote to him while he was in jail, and he answered me. Isn't that amazing? I must show you his letter—written in pencil on a page torn out of an exercise book. His wonderful poetry! I've been trying to write a poem, but I can't find the right words."

"You will, later. How was it?"

She didn't dodge the question. "Not too bad. I had a post-operative haemorrhage that kept me longer than usual. They treated me as if I had a fibroid tumour—that was the diagnosis on my chart. It's a very well-run place. I had a private room, and they don't let you see any of the other patients—very prudent. The food was good, and they were sympathetic to my going off meat. A dietician came and explained to me that I'd have to balance my food very carefully to get all the necessary amino acids— eggs, cheeses, nuts. So in future you won't be able to rouse on me, Harriet, I'll be eating sensibly."

All this was spoken in a gentle voice that utterly lacked any kind of vitality.

"Harriet," she said suddenly, "do you ever feel as if you're nailed to the same spot by one foot only, going round and round?"

"Of late, often," I said wryly.

"I'm so tired of going round and round."

I swallowed, tried to think of something to say that wouldn't open up her wounds, yet might comfort her. In the end I just sat and looked at her, my eyes full of tears.

"Can you teach?" she asked.

"Teach? Me? Teach what?"

"I want to sit for the nurses' entrance examination, but I lack even elementary schooling. Funny, I can read and write like a real author, yet I can't analyse or parse a sentence, I can't add or subtract or multiply or divide beyond kindergarten level. But

I'm fed up with being an aide. I want to do nursing," she said.

What a relief! Her words didn't indicate a return to those hectic, men-by-the-dozen weekends. Ezra may have almost killed her in one way, but in another he seemed to be freeing her.

I told her I'd try, suggested that she go and see Sister Tutor at Queens for an idea of what the examination was going to demand.

"Do you think Duncan would give me a reference?" she asked. "I'm quite sure he'd leap at the chance, Pappy." She drew a breath, sighed. "Did you know that he offered to support me and my child? To give me enough money not to need to work, to educate it properly?" Oh, Duncan! How good and kind you are, and how cruel I am! "No," I said, "he didn't tell me."

"It upset him dreadfully when I refused. He didn't understand."

"I don't either," I said.

"It's the father's place to care for his child and its mother. If he isn't willing to honour his moral and ethical obligations, no other man can take his place. If another man did, then in a court of law, lawyers could prove that that man was the father."

"The Law is a ass," I said, disgusted.

"I need to thank Duncan for everything he's done. Ask him to visit me next time he's here, please, Harriet?"

"You'll have to leave a note in his box at Queens.

I broke it off with Duncan," I said.

That seemed to upset her more than dealing with her fibroid had. Nor could she grasp why I'd sent him packing. To her, I'd betrayed him, the finest man in the world. I didn't try to explain my side of it. Why upset her even more?

Wednesday,
October 19th, 1960

I'm losing my enthusiasm for everything, including entering this book, though the finished ones seem to be safe in the ceiling.

Harold's back at his old tricks, and maybe because I'm missing Duncan so much, the crazy old bastard has won at least the battle, if not the war. I don't go upstairs for a shower any more, I use the laundry bathroom. Oh, I just got to the point where my hair was standing on end and my flesh was crawling before I got to the top of the stairs. When I peered around the corner, the bulb would be out and the toilet door shut. Pitch darkness, and terrifying.

"Whore!" he'd whisper. "Whore!"

So I'm going to buy a shower head, some pipe and a couple of elbow joints and see if I can't rig up a shower myself. I did ask Mrs. Delvecchio Schwartz if she'd have one installed, but she has been in a peculiar mood lately too. I don't think she even heard what I said. Malefic influences are at work, was all she would say, and that at a mutter. From which it's obvious that lunches on Sunday are not happening. I still get Flo, which is the main thing. But Flo can't seem to learn her alphabet.

Toby is never here at weekends, too busy building his shack up at Wentworth Falls, and during the week he has his work cut out tutoring Pappy, who is determined to sit the entrance examination this year, at the end of November. I did try to tutor her, but I'm so good at maths that I can't understand anyone who has trouble doing simple arithmetic. *Not* a born teacher, unfortunately. Toby, on the other hand, is proving wonderfully patient and considerate. I am delighted. The pair of them are spending hours together from Monday to Friday. She still looks all right, just quenched.

Thanks to Klaus, I am now a very good cook of European food, and can make a few Indian and Chinese dishes, thanks to Nal and Pappy. Isn't it funny, though, that I can't be bothered cooking for myself? I save my talents for dinner guests, of whom there are very few. Jim and Bob, really. They come down on Tuesday evenings, sometimes with Joe the Q.C. and her friend Bert. I've found out their real names. Jim is Jemima, which I don't blame her for hating. Fancy parents being inconsiderate enough to do that to a baby! Bob and Bert are both Robertas, and Joe is Joanna. After that awful business with the Boys in Blue, Frankie (Frances) moved away from the Cross, lives somewhere in Drummoyne these days. That's because poor little Olivia was discharged from Rozelle into Callan Park—she's gone quite mad, poor soul, just drifts around in another world. But Frankie won't abandon her, though her family has. Pathetic, isn't it?

When I had Norm to dinner—roast chook, roast potatoes, good old Aussie-type vegies for Norm—I found out that word of the Frankie-Olivia outrage has filtered through the system, and our own Kings Cross coppers are as livid as they are mortified. Well, coppers are like any other large group—some good, some bad, some indifferent. Our own blokes leave the Lezes alone, don't think any the worse of a girl for being a Lez any more than they think the worse of a girl for being on the game. They just keep the wowsers at bay. Seems to me that the wowsers generate the worst of vice simply by stirring people up against what is inevitable, while the politicians serve their own interests by sucking up to the wowsers. Beware of people who are addicted to power. In politicians, it's ambition allied to no talent. They're either failed lawyers or failed schoolteachers, with an occasional shop steward thrown in.

Off your soap box, Harriet Purcell!

I did mention Harold to Jim and Bob, who believe me.

"You don't think he'd take to haunting the laundry, do you?" I asked with a shiver.

Jim considered it, shook her head. "No, I don't, Harry. He seems glued to Mrs. Delvecchio Schwartz's floor, that's where the centre of his universe is located. He wants to separate you from the old girl, that's all. If he was really going to do you in, I think he would have tried already."

"He hates you too," I said gloomily.

"Yes, but that's the wowser in him. Oh, he's jealous of us, but he knows we don't matter to the old girl the way you do."

What a splendid person Jim is! She sat there looking like whipcord and sprung steel, slim and muscular, that bony face very definitely more a man's than a woman's. No wonder the world sees her as a young man when she thunders through on her Harley Davidson with Bob perched on the pillion—a hell-for-leather chap out for a ride with his sweetheart. I can even understand why Bob's parents, elderly and real bushies, have never woken up to the fact that Jim is a woman. So wise of them!

Jim offered to help me install my shower.

Monday,
November 7th, 1960
Well, I am now officially in charge of Cas X-ray. Chris left last Friday after a little party organised by Sister Cas, who in the old days would have been weepy and crotchety, but kept up a cheerful face because she confidently hopes to follow Chris's example next year. Constantin (a chef at Romano's restaurant) is still very keen on her. When Chris announced that a Happy Event was on the way, the

little gaggle of technicians and sisters gooed and gushed, squeaked and giggled. Luckily a couple of multiple emergencies broke the party up, and we all went back to our work.

I have a new technician to take my place—older and more experienced than me, but engaged to be married to a senior resident, so perfectly happy to be the middleman. Her name is Ann Smith and she's facing a long engagement because Dr. Alan Smith (no name change necessary!) has to sort out his career preferences before they can tie the knot. But why *me* for the charge position?

"Your work is excellent, Miss Purcell," said Sister Agatha to me as I stood at attention in front of her desk. "I have decided to replace Miss Hamilton with you because you are efficient, very well organised, and you can think on your feet—an essential for good casualty work."

"Yes, Sister, thank you Sister," I said automatically.

"Unless—" and she paused ominously.

"Unless what, Sister?" I asked.

"Unless you are planning to be married, Miss Purcell."

I couldn't help it, I grinned. "No, Sister, I can assure you that I am *not* planning to be married."

"Excellent, excellent!" And she actually smiled. "You may go, Miss Purcell."

It makes a difference to be in charge. Chris was a very good technician, but ran the place in a way I thought could be improved. Now I can do what

I like—provided that neither Matron nor Sister Agatha objects.

What it does mean is that I now commence work at six in the morning, have the junior between eight and four, and Ann from ten onward in my old slot. I don't think Ann was too pleased about that, but hard cack. If her hours mean that she will see less of her Alan, she'll just have to lump it. See what a position of power does? I've turned into an unsympathetic bitch.

Friday,
November 11th, 1960 (My Birthday)
I overheard a wonderful little conversation between Matron and the General Medical Superintendent shortly after six this morning. God knows what the Super was doing in at such an hour, but Matron, of course, hasn't got the words "off duty" in her vocabulary.

"I would never have believed it of Dr. Bloodworthy," she said stiffly just outside my door.

Now what *has* Dr. Bloodworthy been up to? He is a pathologist whose specialty is blood—isn't it odd how people with suggestive names espouse them completely? Like Lord Brain the neurologist.

"It's flaming hysterical!" replied the Super, clearly in fits of laughter. "Maybe it will teach all those old chooks in the Sisters' dining room to mind their own business for a change."

"Sir," said Matron in tones producing instantaneous icicles on all my equipment, "as I remember it, there were just as many old chooks in the Doctors' dining room. I believe, in fact, that Mr. Naseby-Morton actually managed to lay an egg, which you put on your spoon and ran with all the way downstairs."

There was a moment of silence, then the Super spoke. "One of these days, Matron, I am going to have the last word! And when I do, I will not be an old chook! I will be *cock* of the walk! Good day to you, ma'am."

Oooooo-aa! And poop to birthdays. I went to Bronte tonight.

Wednesday,
November 23rd, 1960

I saw Duncan today. Professor Sjögren is over from Sweden, and gave a lecture on hypothermic techniques for contending with vascular anomalies in the brain. All of Queens above the domestic level wanted to go, but our lecture theatre only holds five hundred, so the competition for a seat was fierce. The old Swede is a great neurosurgeon with a worldwide reputation in pioneering this idea of freezing the patient to slow down heart and circulation before going in to clip the aneurysm or close the shunt or whatever. As technician in charge of Cas X-ray, I rated a seat, found myself wedged between Sister

Cas and none other than Mr. Duncan Forsythe. Oh, it was agony! We couldn't help but be in bodily contact, and my whole right side burned for hours after. He acknowledged me with a curt nod but no smile, then stared at the podium throughout when he wasn't chatting to Mr. Naseby-Morton on his other side.

Sister Tesoriero, who runs Kids' Bones, was on Sister Cas's far side, and they were having their usual scrap.

"*I* really work," Marie O'Callaghan was saying, "whereas you ward charges are pure decoration. You run around peeing in the H.M.O.s' pockets and giving them tomato sandwiches for their cuppa instead of the peanut butter the rest of the poor mortals get."

"Ssssh!" I hissed. "I'm sitting next to you-know-who!"

Sister Cas merely smirked, but Sister Tesoriero took a horrified look and shut up. Her darling Mr. Forsythe, chief of Kids' Bones, might not approve of eating tomato sandwiches if he realised that the rest of the poor mortals got peanut butter. He was so *nice*.

For a while I debated whether I could clap my hand to my mouth and bolt pretending I was sick on the stomach, but as we were in the very centre of the long wooden bench, I'd earn more attention than I would if I just endured it.

I don't think I heard a word of the lecture, and the second it was over I was up and ready to join the mass exodus. He'd leave with Mr. Naseby-Morton by the far aisle, thank God. But he didn't. He followed me, with the chief of cardiac surgery following him to continue their chat. Then he put his hands on either side of my waist, the idiot! Isn't he aware that half the feminine eyes in any crowd are riveted on him? The touch was a caress, not a squeeze, and it all came back in a rush, those big, well-cared-for hands that could crunch through bone in one swoop yet were so reverent as they roamed my skin, so shiversome. My head spun, I staggered. Which was the best thing I could have done, looking back on it now. He could keep his hands there, steady me, even turn me so that he could see my face.

"Thank you, thank you, sir!" I gasped, broke free and bolted to the Sisters Cas and Tesoriero, well ahead of me.

"What was that all about?" Sister Cas asked as I reach them.

"I tripped," I said, "and Mr. Forsythe caught me."

"Half your luck!" sighed Sister Tesoriero.

Half my luck, nothing. The bastard did it deliberately to see how I reacted, and I bloody obliged him.

Sister Cas, who knows me much better, simply looked thoughtful. *What was wrong with my face?*

Thursday,
December 1st, 1960
Incredible to think that 1960 is almost over. Last

year at this time I was still at Ryde Hospital, had just completed my exams, hadn't yet seen the Royal Queens booth at Sydney Tech, let alone contemplated working there. Didn't know Pappy, didn't know about Mrs. Delvecchio Schwartz or The House. Didn't know that my angel existed. Ignorance is bliss, they say, but I do not believe that. Ignorance is a trap which leads people to make the wrong decisions. Harold and Duncan notwithstanding, I am so glad that when I emerged from my chrysalis, I became a big, handsome Bogong moth, not a frail butterfly.

If it's been a fairly decent sort of a day, I'm home by four or half-past. Today being only middling, I knocked off a bit after five, and so walked home with Pappy, who has just finished her exams. She thinks she scraped a pass, and I'm sure she has. There are never enough nurses, thanks to the grinding discipline, the hard labour and the obligation to live in a nurses' home. It's the last worries me the most; after all, as a nurses' aide she's been subjected to even more stringent discipline because aides are the lowest of the low. But how will Pappy manage to live in a weeny room if she's at a hospital with a big home, or share a weeny room if she's at a hospital less well endowed?

"You'll keep your room at The House," I said as we strode out.

"No, I can't afford to," she said, "and quite honestly, dear Harriet, I'm not sure that I want to."

Oh, what is *happening*? Toby saying he's going, now Pappy! I'm going to be left with Jim, Bob, Klaus and Harold. And two new tenants, one of whom will live next door to me. Without those floor-to-ceiling books, I'll hear everything when I'm in bed—there is a sealed-off door between us with Victorian panels in it as thin as plywood. That sounds so selfish, and I suppose it is selfish, but no Pappy doesn't bear thinking of. God rot Professor Ezra Marsupial! When she killed his child, she killed something in herself that has nothing to do with foetuses.

"I think you should try to make the effort to keep a bolt-hole in The House," I said as we crossed Oxford Street. "For one thing, you'll never be able to take a twentieth of your books with you, and for another, you're too old for all that jolly, giggly sort of communal life. Pappy, they're *babies*!"

Oh, what an unfortunate slip of the tongue! She ignored it.

"I shall probably be able to rent something halfway between a shed and a cottage at Stockton," she said. "I'll keep my books in it, and spend my days off there."

I only heard "Stockton". "*Stockton?*" I gasped.

"Yes, I'm applying to go psychiatric nursing at Stockton," she said.

"Jesus, Pappy, you can't!" I cried, halting outside Vinnie's Hospital. "Psych nursing is bad enough—everybody knows that the nurses and doctors are loonier than the patients, but Stockton is the dumping ground to end all dumping grounds! Out there in the sand dunes on the far side of the Hunter estuary, with all the aments, dements and biological nightmares—it'll kill you!"

"I'm hoping it will heal me," she said.

Yes, of course. It's exactly what a Pappy would do. It's so easy for Catholics, they can renounce the world, take the veil and enter a convent. But what can non-Catholics do? Answer: take the cap and go psych nursing at Stockton, a hundred miles to Newcastle and then catch the ferry to nowhere. She's expiating her sins in the only way she knows.

"I understand completely," I said, started walking again.

Mrs. Delvecchio Schwartz was lurking in the front hall when we came in, greeted us in the most peculiar way. "Oh, do I need the pair of youse!" she exclaimed, looked agitated and worried, then had to muffle a laugh.

The laugh calmed me immediately—Flo was all right, then. If something had happened to Flo, there would have been no laugh.

"Well?" I asked.

"It's Harold," said Mrs. Delvecchio Schwartz. "Can youse take a squizzy at him, Harriet?"

The last thing I wanted to do was to take a look at Harold, but this was definitely a medical request. In medical matters, I outrank Pappy in our landlady's eyes.

"Of course. What's the trouble?" I asked as we ascended.

Whereupon she clapped her hand over her mouth to stifle a guffaw, then waved the hand about and burst into a huge bellow of mirth. "I know it ain't funny, princess, but Jeez, it is funny!" she said when she could. "The funniest thing I seen in years! Oh, Jeez, I can't help meself! It's fuh-fuh-funny!" And off she went again.

"Stop it, you old horror!" I snapped. "What's wrong with Harold?"

"He can't pee!" she yelled, in fits once more.

"I beg your pardon?"

"He can't pee! He—can't—*pee*! Oh, Jeez, it's funny!"

Her mirth was so infectious that it was an effort to keep my face straight, but I managed. "Poor Harold. When did this happen?"

"I dunno, princess," she said, wiping her eyes on her dress and revealing an amazing pair of pink bloomers almost down to her knees. "All I know is that he's been hoggin' the dunny lately. I thought it was the constipation—keeps it all bottled up, does Harold. Anyway, Jim and Bob complained, Klaus complained, and Toby just gallops down to the laundry dunny. I told Harold to take some Epsom salts or cascara or something, and he turned all huffy. It's been goin' on for days! This arvo he forgot to bolt the dunny door when he come in, so I barged in to give 'im a piece of me mind." The laughter threatened, she suppressed it heroically. "And there he was standin' in front of the dunny, floggin' his poor old dingus and cryin' like his heart was broken. Took him ages to come clean—you know what an old maid he is. He—can't—pee!" Off she went into another convulsion.

I'd had enough of her. "Well, you can stand there howling your head off if you want, but I'm going to see Harold," I said, and marched up to his room.

I'd never seen it before, of course. Like its owner it was drab, neat and utterly lacking in imagination. A silver-framed photo of an old and haughty woman with spite in her eyes stood on his fireplace mantel; on each side of it was a posy of flowers in matched little vases. So many books! *Beau Geste. The Scarlet Pimpernel. The Prisoner of Zenda. The Dam Busters. The Wooden Horse. The Count of Monte Cristo. Tap Roots. These Old Shades. The Foxes of Harrow.* All the Hornblower novels. An extraordinary collection of derring-do, knights in shining armour and the kind of romantic fantasy I'd finished with by the time I was twelve.

I smiled at him and said a soft hello. The poor man was sitting hunched on the side of his single bed; when I spoke, he looked at me with pain-racked eyes. Then when he realised who it was, the pain vanished, was replaced by outrage.

"You told her!" he shrieked at Mrs. Delvecchio Schwartz, who was standing in the doorway.

"How could you tell *her*?"

"Harold, I work in a hospital, that's why Mrs. Delvecchio Schwartz told me. I'm here to help you, so come on, no nonsense, please! You can't manage to urinate, is that right?"

His face was twisted, his arms were clasped protectively across his belly, his back was bent like a bow, he trembled very finely, rocked back and forth. Then he nodded.

"How long has it been going on?" I asked.

"Three weeks," he whispered.

"*Three weeks!* Oh, Harold! Why didn't you tell anybody? Why didn't you see a doctor?"

In answer he wept, his dam broken, the tears sliding sparsely from beneath the bottom rim of his glasses like juice being squeezed from a dried lemon.

I turned to Pappy. "We'll have to take him to Vinnie's Cas straight away," I said to her.

Pain and all, he reared up like a cobra. "I will not go to St. Vincent's, it's a Catholic hospital!" he hissed.

"Then we'll take you to Sydney Hospital," I hissed back. "The minute they catheterise you, you'll feel so much better that you'll wonder why you didn't seek help a great deal sooner."

The vision of Harold being catheterised set Mrs. Delvecchio Schwartz howling again. I rounded on her. "Will you get out of here?" I barked. "Make yourself useful! Find some old towels in case he lets go, then hail a taxi—*move*!"

Encouraging him to find his feet but taking his

weight between us, Pappy and I got Harold sort of upright. His agony wouldn't let him straighten up, nor would he remove his hands from his lower abdomen. By the time we got him downstairs, the taxi was waiting.

The junior resident and Sister Cas at Sydney Hospital just stared at Harold when told the nature of the emergency.

"Three weeks!" the junior resident exclaimed tactlessly, then quailed under the glares he got from Sister Cas, Pappy and me.

We watched Harold deposited in a wheelchair and whisked away, then went outside and caught the Bellevue Hill tram.

"They'll give him the works," said Pappy as we climbed aboard. "We won't see him home until he's had cystoscopes and IVPs and God knows what else."

"You don't think it's organic either," I said.

"No, he looks too well. His colour's good, and his distended bladder is the source of his pain. You know what renal cases look like, or stones or pelvic cancers. He must have an electrolyte imbalance, but looking at him? It's not organic."

Oh, Pappy, I wish you'd do general nursing! But I didn't dare voice that thought.

So for the time being, I'm free of Harold, though my worry has increased. Some clinical instinct tells me that this hideously repressed man is edging toward the ultimate repression. Retaining his faeces isn't enough for him any more, the pain and humiliation of that isn't doing it for him, so he's graduated to retaining his urine. But beyond urinary retention, the only thing left to shut down is life itself. Oh, God *damn* Mrs. Delvecchio Schwartz for laughing at him! If she doesn't learn to control herself, one of these days he's going to kill himself. Just pray he leaves it at that, doesn't take Jim or Pappy or me with him. Yet how can any of us reason with a force of Nature like Mrs. Delvecchio Schwartz? She's a law unto herself. Amazingly wise, abysmally foolish. And if he does kill himself, she'll be desolate, penitent, inconsolable. Why hasn't she seen it in the cards? It's there! *It's there!* Harold and the Ten of Swords. The ruin of The House.

**Saturday,
December 10th, 1960**

I invited Toby down for lunch today, and he actually came. He'd needed Saturday morning to buy specialised hardware for his shack, so he had to stay in Sydney because Nock & Kirby's is the only place sells what he wants.

"Saturday's dead anyway, so eat lunch before you hop on the train," I said winningly.

The menu was shepherd's pie made on tuna and mushrooms bound together with a fresh marjoram sauce, the potato topping I'd mashed with tons of butter and ground pink pepper, and I served a salad on the side, its dressing walnut oil shaken with water and old, non-astringent vinegar.

"If you keep on cooking like this, I might just have to marry you the minute I'm famous," he said, mouth full. "This is *good*!"

"As you won't become famous until after you die, I'm safe," I said, smiling at him. "It's fun to cook, though I suspect it wouldn't be if I had to do it every single day like my mother."

"I'll bet she enjoys it," he said, transferring to the easy chair opposite Marceline, who only got a grimace from him.

"If she does, it's because she loves to see her men feeding their faces," I said a bit tartly. "The menu's pretty narrow—steak-and-chips, fish-and-chips, roast leg of lamb, stewed lamb neck chops, curried sausages, crumbed lamb cutlets, cooked prawns from the fishmonger's, then start again—why don't you like my beautiful Marceline?"

"Animals," he said, "don't belong inside houses."

"What a typical bushie you are! If a dog doesn't work the stock properly, shoot it."

"Terminal lead poisoning in the left ear is a good way to go," he protested. "No nonsense, over and done with in a second."

"You're a real loner," I said, taking the chair with the cat.

"You learn to be when you don't get your way all the time, and by all the time, I mean all the time, not occasionally."

"She'll turn to you, Toby, I know it," I said warmly.

"What are you talking about?" he asked blankly.

I looked blank. "Surely you know!"

"No, I don't. Explain."

"Pappy."

His jaw dropped. "*Pappy?*"

"Yes, of course, you drongo, Pappy!"

"Why should Pappy turn to me?" he asked, frowning.

"Oh, really! You may think you hide your feelings successfully, Toby, but it doesn't take a genius to see that you love Pappy."

"Naturally I love Pappy," he said, "but I'm not *in* love with her—you've got to be joking, Harriet."

"But you must be in love with her!" I said, confused.

His eyes were turning red. "That's bullshit."

"Oh, come on, Toby! I've seen the pain in your eyes, you don't fool me for a minute," I floundered.

"You know, Miss Purcell," he said, getting up quickly, "you may fancy that you're a woman of the world these days, but in actual fact you're blind, stupid, illogical and self-obsessed!"

With that parting shot, he stalked out, leaving me sitting with Marceline in my lap wondering what had hit me.

Something is happening to The House, I can feel it, and Toby is just one more symptom. I can't get any sense out of Mrs. Delvecchio Schwartz about either The House or herself, and since his return, Harold is right back in her good books. I suppose he never even knew how she laughed at him, he was in so much pain. When Sydney Hospital referred him to a psychiatrist, he took such umbrage that he signed himself out, came home instead.

Oh, Duncan, I miss you!

Sunday,
December 25th, 1960 (Christmas Day)
I went home to Bronte, though I declined the lounge room couch. I'm working tomorrow, Boxing Day, because there are all sorts of sporting fixtures scheduled for the various grounds to the east of Queens, so we'll have traffic accidents by the score and some victims of drunken brawls. I'm also on duty on New Year's Day, though Ann Smith volunteered to take New Year's Eve because her fiancé is working Cas that night. New Year's Eve is a shambles in every hospital Cas, though it's worst at Vinnie's because half of Sydney pays its annual visit to the Cross to get drunk, strew the streets with litter and vomit, keep Norm, Merv, Bumper Farrell and the rest of the Cross coppers frantically busy.

I gave Willie a bottle of three-star, Granny a stunning Spanish shawl, Gavin and Peter a macro lens for their Zeiss camera, Dad a box of Cuban cigars, and Mum some really pretty underwear (sexy but respectable). The family clubbed in and gave me a voucher to buy heaps of LP records at Nicholson's. Greatly appreciated.

Wednesday,
December 28th, 1960

Mrs. Delvecchio Schwartz grabbed me on the way in this afternoon and invited me up for a Kraft cheese spread glass of brandy. Which irritated me.

"Why are you still using these?" I demanded. "I gave you seven beautiful cut glass tumblers for Christmas!"

The X-ray vision isn't so focused at the moment, she has more of a faraway look, so my question didn't provoke a blaze from her inner lighthouse. "Oh, I couldn't *use* 'em!" she exclaimed. "I'm savin' 'em for best, princess."

"Saving them for best? But I didn't give them to you to put away!" I said despairingly.

"If I used 'em, I might break one."

"But that doesn't matter, Mrs. Delvecchio Schwartz! If one breaks, I'll replace it."

"Can't replace anything what's broke," she said. "The aura's on the originals, princess, them's the seven—good thinkin', to make it seven, not six—what you touched and wrapped up so grouse."

"I'd touch and wrap up the replacement nicely, too," I said.

"Ain't the same. Nope, I'm savin' 'em for best."

I gave up, told her instead about my curious exchange with Toby. "I could have sworn he was in love with Pappy!"

"Nah, never has been. She brought 'im home near five years ago for a quick nooky, then realised I was lookin' for 'im—saw 'im in the cards. The King of Swords. Gotta have a King of Swords in The House, princess, but they're a lot harder to find than the Queens. Men're poor fish, ain't often strong the way women are. But Toby is. Good bloke, Toby," she said, nodding.

"I am aware of that!" I snapped.

"That youse are, princess, but not aware enough."

"Not aware enough?" I asked.

But she changed the subject, informed me that every New Year's Eve she has a party. Quote, a rip-snorter of a bash. It's become a Cross tradition, and everybody who is anybody at the Cross will be there for at least a part of the festivities. Even Norm, Merv, Madame Fugue, Madame Toccata, Chastity Wiggins and a few others of the "permanent" girls snatch the time to attend Mrs. Delvecchio Schwartz's New Year's Eve party. I said I'd be there, but that as I have to work on New Year's Day, I wouldn't be able to get into the real swing of things.

"There ain't no work for you on New Year's Day," she said, "I can tell youse that for sure."

"It's in the cards," I said in a long-suffering voice.

"Got it in one, princess!"

Turns out she wants culinary help, of course. The blokes are instructed to supply the booze, the girls in The House (plus Klaus) provide the food. Mrs. Delvecchio Schwartz herself roasts a turkey—it'll be dry and rubbery, I thought with a shudder. Klaus is down for roast suckling pig, Jim and Bob are doing the salads, weeny saveloys and weeny sausage rolls, Pappy has to come up with spring rolls and prawn toasts, and I am down for the desserts, all suitable to eat with the fingers. Eclairs, fairy cakes, lamingtons and Neenish tarts are my orders.

"Better add some of them grouse Anzac bikkies you make," the old horror added. "I ain't a great one for puddins, but I do like to dip a good crunchy bikky in me cuppa tea."

I laughed. "Go on, you fraud! Since when have you drunk tea?"

"Two cups of it every New Year's Eve," she said solemnly.

"How's Harold?" I asked.

"Harold's Harold," she said, pulling a face. "Lucky thing is that the job he's gotta do for The House is comin' up fast, so the cards inform me. The minute it's done, out he goes."

"No point in telling you that we're losing Pappy as well as Toby," I said, and sighed. "The House is falling apart."

On came the searchlight in her eyes. "Never say that, Harriet Purcell!" she said sternly. "The House is eternal."

Flo came in, yawning and rubbing her eyes, saw me and landed in my lap in one bound. "I've never seen her sleepy before," I said.

"She sleeps."

"Nor have I ever heard her talk."

"She talks."

So I wandered off downstairs, Flo with her hand in mine, to spend an evening only bearable because Mrs. Delvecchio Schwartz had let me have my angel. When I brought her back shortly before nine o'clock (Flo doesn't keep ordinary children's hours, she seems to be up until her mother goes to bed—what would my own mother say about that?), Mrs. Delvecchio Schwartz was sitting in the darkness of her room, not out on the balcony as is her habit in summer. The Glass was on the table before her, and it seemed to gather in every last particle of light from the street lamp outside, the bulb in the hall, an occasional headlight as some chauffeured Rolls delivered a client to 17b or 17d. The moment Flo saw her mother, she stopped absolutely still, the pressure of her hand in mine a silent command not to move. So we stood there in the gloom for what seemed like half an hour while that massive shape sat utterly still, its shadowy face a foot from the Glass.

Finally, with a sigh, Mrs. Delvecchio Schwartz leaned back in her chair, wiped her face with a tired hand. I led Flo forward softly until we reached the table.

"Ta for minding her, princess. I needed to scry."

"Would you like me to switch the light on?"

"Ta. Then come back here for a minute."

When I returned, Flo was sitting on her lap, looking sadly at the buttoned dress.

"It's a pity you weaned her," I found myself saying.

"Had to," she answered curtly. Then she reached out to take both my hands and put them on the Glass, while Flo stared at them raptly, then transferred her gaze to my face in—wonder? I don't know. But I stood there cupping the Glass, waiting for something to happen. Nothing did. The surface is cool and sleek, that's all.

"Remember," Mrs. Delvecchio Schwartz said, "remember that the fate of The House is in the Glass." She removed my hands and put them together, palm against palm, fingers conjoined, the way angels' hands are in paintings. "It's in the Glass."

Friday,
December 30th, 1960

Those bloody cards again! I'm not working New Year's Day after all. Dr. Alan Smith is rostered for duty in Cas all day, so Ann wants to work. I'm not surprised. If he does a double shift in Cas, he'll be buggered, he'll need the haven Cas X-ray will be with Ann staffing it. Our junior's on leave, so we have a temp in her place, a good girl. I wouldn't have consented if Ann wasn't up to the work, but she is, and I've done the pair a kindness, as they will be off duty together for two days straight after.

Sunday,
January 1st, 1961 (New Year's Day)

1961 is almost twenty-four hours old, darkness has fallen. I have been entering this for a year now, and even though I'm so stonkered I can hardly move, I must get everything that's happened today down in my book before the emotions fade. I have found that my exercise book is a sort of catharsis, in that *writing* doesn't go round and round the way thinking about events does.

The New Year's Eve party went off like the hydrogen bomb—a real ripper-ace shindig, as Mrs. Delvecchio Schwartz described it, one arm around Merv, her face beet-red. Though she wasn't drunk, she truly wasn't. Just a little the worse for wear, that's all. Terribly happy, I remember thinking.

The whole Cross came, some for a few minutes only, some for what promised to be perpetuity when I left at three o'clock, helped downstairs by Toby. My memories of it are hazy, I just see snatches, like Lady Richard's arrival in a peroxided wig, five-inch heels and a red sequined tube of a dress split nearly to the top of both hips to reveal smooth, hairless white skin above filmy black silk stockings. His breasts were definitely not falsies, nor was there a sign of a bulge where a man should have a bulge. Pappy told me in a stage whisper that he's rumoured to have gone to Scandinavia to Have The Works. If so, I whispered back, then his urinary tract must be a permanent disaster. Poor old Norm could only stay long enough to give me a sloppy kiss, but Merv used his seniority to hang on longer, flirted outrageously with Mrs. Delvecchio Schwartz. Lerner Chusovich wasn't happy about *that*. Nor, I noticed, was Klaus, who kept gazing at his landlady with naked lust. Jim gave me an expert kiss which I was turpsed enough to enjoy, but it made Bob furious, so I shoved Jim away and concentrated on Toby for the rest of the time. Our little altercation was forgotten, and his kisses, I remember, were right up there with Duncan's, though I didn't kiss him pretending he was Duncan. Toby is definitely Toby.

I passed out on my bed in all my party finery, and was woken about eight this morning by Marceline, whose stomach rules her podgy little life. Toby must have drawn my curtains, a blessing. I weaved out to put my coffee on, drank a good dose of Dexsal to settle my queasiness, and shut Marceline up with top-of-the-milk and a bowl of sardines which stank so much that I had to retch over my sink. Nothing came up, but I retreated to the bedroom until Marceline polished off the sardines.

Flo was on my bed, curled up asleep in the dimness. Angel, my angel! I hadn't seen her or felt her. Things must have been pretty abandoned upstairs for her to seek me out. Or else Harold was in her mother's bed. Oh, yes, he'd been there at the party, drinking brandy on the sidelines, watching Mrs. Delvecchio Schwartz carry on with Merv, muttering, glaring at me, especially when I kissed Jim. "Whore," his lips framed.

As soon as I thought my nausea was gone for good, I went back to the living room and opened my door wide to let in the fresh air, breathed it deeply. The world outside was absolutely silent. No washing flapped on the lines, no sounds of argument or frivolity issued out of 17d's mauve lace windows, and from The House, utter stillness. I'd half expected to hear Mrs. Delvecchio Schwartz bellowing for her angel, but she wasn't. Fairly early morning on New Year's Day must be the quietest moment the Cross experiences, I thought. Every Crossite is out for the count.

But I had to get Flo back upstairs in case her mother woke and became worried. So I went into my bedroom, sat down on the edge of the bed and gathered Flo into my arms, put my cheek on her flyaway hair, cuddled and kissed her. When I was little, that was how Mum had always roused me, and I remember still how lovely it was to come up out of dreamland to hugs and kisses.

She was *wet*. Oh, angel, no! How am I going to manage to get my kapok mattress flopped over the line? was my first reaction. But Flo didn't smell of urine, and it didn't feel like urine, which doesn't dry stiff and hard like Flo's pinny. She hadn't stirred, despite the hugs and kisses. Neither she nor her mother had dolled up for the party, and looking at that snuff-brown fabric, I couldn't see what she was soaked in. I just knew that unique smell. Oh, God!

Quick! Pull the curtains!

Blood. She was wet with blood. My skin squeezed up tight and prickling, but I kept my head, went over her slowly and carefully, lifted the pinny up, peeled the shabby bloomers down to inspect her pubes. Please, God, no! Not that, not that! I was saying over and over, my hands shaking in time to my body. No, nothing. It wasn't her own blood covered Flo from the soles of her feet to her hands—her hands were thick with it, thick. At that moment she woke, gave me a sleepy smile, and put her arms around my neck. I lifted her off the bed and carried her into the living room, where Marceline, having left no scrap in her bowl, was sitting washing herself.

"Darling, play with Marceline," I said through an awful crawling numbness, and put Flo down beside the cat. "I have to pop outside for a minute, angel, so I need you to stay here and mind poor Marceline. Make sure she's a good girl."

I took the stairs five at a time, bounded in one leap across the hall and charged into the room, stopped still as a statue. The blood was a lake that covered the floor under and all around the table, jellified where the lino was buckled into depressions, a thin sheet coating the crests. Someone had tidied up, the party debris was all dumped in the far corner, though the table was piled high with empty dishes and the carcass of that inedible turkey. My eyes took it all in, I didn't seem to miss a thing. The blood hadn't spurted to spatter the walls, but in one place there was a lot of blood on the wall—the wall Flo was currently using for scribbling. It was smeared with great browning whorls of blood, held the imprint of a tiny hand here and there. Bloody little footprints crossed the unmarred lino between the edge of the lake and that section of wall, footprints going to the wall, returning to the lake. Crayons couldn't express her feelings. Flo had finger-painted in the blood.

Mrs. Delvecchio Schwartz lay face down beside the table, dead. Not far from her was Harold Warner, sagged back on his haunches, his hands around the butt of the turkey carving knife where it met his belly, his head flopped down to rest its chin on his chest, as if he contemplated his own undoing.

My mouth opened and I howled. I don't mean that I wept or I cried or I screamed—I made animal noises of horror and despair at the top of my lungs, and I kept on making them.

Toby was the first there, and Toby took over. I suppose he deputed someone to call the police, because I faintly heard him barking orders to people in the doorway, but he never left me. When I couldn't howl any longer he guided me out of the room and shut its door. Pappy, Klaus, Jim and Bob were huddled together in the hall, but of Chikker and Marge from the front ground floor flat there was no sign.

"I've called the police—Toby, what is it?" Pappy cried.

"The ruin of The House," I said through chattering teeth. "The Ten of Swords and Harold. He was here to bring The House down. That was the job he had to do, and if she never knew it from the cards, she saw it in the Glass because I was there when she did. She knew, she knew! But she submitted."

"Mrs. Delvecchio Schwartz and Harold are dead," Toby said.

By the time he got me outside onto the path, every window in 17d was gaping wide, had a head sticking out.

"Mrs. Delvecchio Schwartz is dead," he had to say several times before he got me inside my flat.

Flo was drawn up into a compact cluster of limbs on the floor, curled around the purring Marceline. Toby took one look at her, cast me a horrified look, then went for the brandy bottle.

"No!" I gasped. "I never want to see that stuff again. I'm all right now, Toby, truly I am."

The morning passed in a parade of people, starting with the police. Not my friends from the Vice Squad— these were strangers in plain clothes. Because Toby had taken charge and he refused to leave me, all the activity seemed to happen in my living room. But before they came Pappy took Flo away to give her a bath and change her clothes, while I went to the laundry for a shower, changed my party dress for something sober. Sober.

What concerned the police most was Flo's fingerpainting. It seemed to fascinate them, whereas the crime was clearly run of the mill. Murder and suicide, plain as the nose on your face. They questioned every one of us, looking for motive, but none of us had noticed any change in the behaviour of either Mrs. Delvecchio Schwartz or Harold. I had to tell them how he had stalked me, about his emotional and mental instability, the urinary retention, his refusal to consult a psychiatrist when one had been recommended. Chikker and Marge in the front ground floor flat had decamped, all trace of them gone, not even a fingerprint left behind. But the police weren't interested in them, that showed clearly, though word had gone out to pick them up for questioning. As they were right under the room where it happened, they might have heard it.

"What's obvious," said the sergeant to Toby, "is that the kid watched the whole thing. Once we get her story, we'll know."

I butted in. "Flo can't talk," I said. "She's a mute."

"You mean she's retarded?" the seargeant asked, frowning.

"On the contrary, she's extremely intelligent," I answered. "She simply doesn't talk."

"Is this your opinion too, Mr. Evans?"

Toby confirmed that Flo didn't talk. "She's either superhuman or subhuman, I'm never sure which," he added, the bastard.

On the tail of this, Pappy reappeared with Flo, clad now in a clean snuff-brown pinny, her feet bare as always. The two coppers stared at my angel as if she was a freak, and I could see what they were thinking as if they spoke out loud: she looks like any other five-year-old girl, but underneath, she's a monster.

Yes, Flo is five years old. Today is her birthday and I have her present all wrapped up in a cupboard—a pretty pink dress. It's still there.

Then we got down to the brass tacks of official enquiries, namely, were there any relatives? Each of us had to answer no, we didn't think so. Even Pappy, who has been in The House by far the longest, had to say that no relative had ever shown up, at least as far as she knew. Nor had Mrs. Delvecchio Schwartz ever mentioned any relatives.

Finally the sergeant shut his notebook and got up, thanked Toby for the brandy pick-me-up—ta much, mate, greatly appreciated. You could see that they were glad they'd had a man to talk to, that they hadn't had to deal with a parcel of very strange females on a social basis. Because there *was* a social element—the job's a dirty one, but a good bloke's easy to get on with.

At the door the sergeant turned to me. "I'd be grateful if you could mind the little girl for an hour or so, Miss Purcell. It's going to take that long for the Child Welfare to get here."

I could feel my eyes widen. "It's not necessary to summon the Child Welfare," I said. "I'll be looking after Flo from now on."

"Very sorry, Miss Purcell," he said, "it doesn't work that way. Since there are no known relatives, little Florence"—*Florence?*—"is now the responsibility of the Child Welfare. If we're able to trace a relative, then she can go to that person if she's wanted, and in cases like this, the person almost always says yes. But if we can't trace any relatives, then Florence Schwartz becomes a ward of the State of New South Wales." He put on his natty plain clothes copper trilby and left, his constable behind him.

"Toby!" I gasped.

"Pappy, take Flo and Marceline into the bedroom," Toby said, and watched until she'd obeyed orders.

Then he took my hands, sat me in an easy chair and perched on its arm just the way Duncan used to. *Used to*. Past tense, Harriet, past tense.

"He can't have meant that," I said.

I've never seen Toby so stern, so merciless, so cold. "Yes, Harriet, he did. He meant that Flo is probably without kith or kin. That her mother died in what he presumes was a drunken brawl with her nutty lover, who was not Flo's father. That he personally believes Flo is a grossly neglected child from a very bad home. That he also believes Flo is queer in the head. And that, as soon as he gets back to headquarters, he's going to tell Child Welfare all of it, and recommend that Flo is taken into State custody as of this moment."

"He can't, he can't!" I cried. "Flo couldn't survive outside The House! If they take her away, she'll *die*!"

"You've forgotten the most important factor, Harriet. Flo was there in that room when it all happened, and she used the blood to scribble on the wall. That's an indictment," Toby said harshly.

My beloved friend, to talk like this? Is there no one to take up the cudgels in her defence except me? "Toby, Flo is just five years old!" I said. "What would you or I have done at that age, in those circumstances? Be fair! There aren't any neat statistics to govern such things! All her life she's been allowed to scribble on her mother's walls. Who knows why she used the blood? Maybe she thought it would bring her mother back to life. They can't take Flo away from me, they can't!"

"They can, and they will," Toby said grimly, and went to the stove to put the kettle on. "Harriet, I'm playing the Devil's advocate, that's all. I agree with you that Flo can't thrive away from The House, but no one in authority is going to see it in that light. Now go and get Pappy and Flo. If you won't drink brandy, tea's the next best thing."

They took Flo away from me about noon, two women from Child Welfare. Decent enough women—it's an awful job. Flo refused to co-operate in any way, even after I suggested that they call her Flo, not Florence. I'm willing to bet that Flo is what her birth certificate says— if she has one. Knowing Mrs. Delvecchio Schwartz, Flo mightn't. Angel, angel. She wouldn't let either of the women put a hand on her, nor did she waver as the pair of them coaxed, cajoled, persuaded, pleaded. All Flo did was hang onto me like grim death and press her face into my lap. In the end they decided to sedate her with chloral hydrate, but she vomited it up every time they tried, even when they pinched her nose.

Jim and Bob had come down by this, though I wished they hadn't. The woman in charge looked them up and down as if they were scum, made another black mark in her book about The House, which only had one proper bathroom and toilet to serve four floors. And why was Flo barefooted? Didn't she have shoes? That seemed to worry both of the invaders a lot. When, after the fourth lot of chloral hydrate, Flo left my protection and ran about the room like a bird that's flown inside and can't get out, crashing into the walls, the stove, the furniture, I did my block and went for Child Welfare with my fists. But Toby grabbed me, forced me and Jim to stay out of it.

Eventually they decided to give her an injection of paraldehyde, which never fails to work. Flo collapsed, they picked her up and carried her out with me trailing them, Toby hanging onto me.

"How will I find her?" I asked outside.

"Telephone Child Welfare" was the answer.

They loaded her into their car, and the last I saw of my angel was her still, wee white face as they drove away.

All of them wanted to stay and keep me company, but I didn't want company, least of all Toby's, the most persistent. I shrieked at him to go away! go away! until he went. Pappy crept in a little while later to tell me that Klaus, Lerner Chusovich and Joe Dwyer from the Piccadilly bottle department were upstairs in Klaus's room, wanted to know how I was, what they could do to help. Thank you, I am all right, I don't need anything, I said. My nose was still full of the sweet, sickly smell of paraldehyde.

About three I went into the bedroom to phone Bronte. Mum and Dad would have to be told before the story appeared in the papers, though I suppose a drunken murder and suicide at Kings Cross on New Year's Eve wouldn't rate more than a small paragraph ten pages in. When I lifted the receiver I discovered that the phone was dead—it had been pulled out of the jack on the skirting board. Toby when he put me to bed last night, probably. The moment I plugged it in, it started to ring.

"Harriet, where have you been?" Dad asked. "We're frantic!"

"I've been here all along," I said. "Someone disconnected my phone. Though it sounds as if you already know about it."

"Come home *now*" was all he said—a command, not a request.

I told Pappy where I was going, and hailed a taxi on Victoria Street. The driver gave me a queer look, but didn't say a word.

Mum and Dad were at the dining table, alone. Mum looked as if she'd been crying for hours, Dad suddenly looked his age—my heart twisted because I could *see* he's almost eighty years old.

"I'm glad I don't have to tell you," I said, sitting down.

They were both staring at me as if at a stranger; it's only now, writing this, that I realise I must have looked as if I'd broken free of a coffin. Horror does that.

"Don't you want to know how we know?" Dad asked then.

"Yes, how do you know?" I asked dutifully.

Dad took a letter from its envelope, handed it to me. I took it and read it. Beautiful copperplate handwriting, absolutely straight across the unlined, expensive paper with professionally torn edges. The script and stationery of someone ultra-genteel.

"*Sir,*

"*Your daughter is a whore. A common, vulgar trollop unfit to inhabit this world, but not welcome in the next.*

"*For the past eight months she has been carrying on a sordid sexual affair with a married man, a famous doctor at her hospital. She seduced him, I saw her do it on Victoria Street in the dark. How she led him on! How she paraded her charms! How she wormed her way into his life and affections! How she cheapened him! How she brought him down to her own level and rejoiced! But a decent man can't satisfy her. She is a Lesbian, a valued member of that society of filthy deviants who inhabit her house.*

The doctor's name is Mr. Duncan Forsythe.

"A Concerned Citizen."

"Harold," I said, and put the paper down as if it burned.

"I gather the allegations are true," Dad said.

I smiled, closed my eyes. "Just for a while, Dad. I sent Duncan packing last September, actually, and I can assure you that I'm not a Lesbian, though I do have many Lesbian friends. They're good people. A lot better than the awful little man who wrote this. When did it come?" I asked.

"In yesterday afternoon's post." Dad was frowning. He's no fool, he understood that the way I looked today had nothing to do with an affair over and done with four months ago. "What is the matter, if it isn't this?" he asked.

So I told them about today. Mum was appalled, wept afresh, but Dad—Dad was devastated. Rocked to his foundations. What had he felt for Mrs. Delvecchio Schwartz in that one meeting, to grieve so for her? He kept gasping, squeezing at his heart, until Mum got up and gave him a big nip of Willie's brandy. That put him a little at ease, but it was a long time before I could tell him what I had to tell him, that I was going for custody of Flo. Maybe his profound reaction to the news of my landlady's death had encouraged me to hope he'd be right on my side, but he wasn't.

"Get custody of that freak of a child?" he cried, his voice rising. "Harriet, you can't do that! You're well out of it, and well out of that house! The best thing you can do is come home."

I didn't want to argue, I didn't have the strength to argue, so I got up and left them sitting there.

Poor people, it's been quite a day for them too. They have a daughter who had an affair with an important married doctor, but that had paled into insignificance compared to murder, suicide and said daughter's determination to get custody of a crazy child who can't talk and finger-paints in blood. No wonder they look at me as if I'm someone they don't know.

So much for New Year's Day. Not a nightmare, but a reality.

**Monday,
January 2nd, 1961**
I had the nightmare at five o'clock this morning, choked myself awake to sit bolt upright in my bed groaning for breath, still feeling that rich red lake of blood rising, rising until I stood on tiptoe with my nostrils sinking into it, and Harold screaming with laughter as he watched.

The sun was already on its way, light streamed through my open curtains. I got out of bed, fed Marceline, made a pot of coffee and sat at the table to tell myself over and over that Mrs. Delvecchio Schwartz is dead. People like her are so alive that it's incredible when they die—you just feel that it can't be so, that there's been a mistake. I don't know why it happened, I don't know why she *let* it happen. Because she did let it happen! She saw it in the Glass that last time, and made no attempt to avert it. Yet she was so happy at her party. Maybe she had felt the thing in her brain stirring, and preferred the quickness of Harold's knife.

But I couldn't feel grief, I couldn't weep or mourn. There were too many things to do. Where was Flo? What kind of night had she passed? The first night of her life outside The House.

Job number one was to phone Queens X-ray and inform whoever was in charge of the duty roster at this hour that I wouldn't be in to work. I gave no reason, simply apologised and hung up while the phone was still squawking. No need to do the same for Pappy, she had finished at Royal Queens on Christmas Eve. Stockton loomed.

I got dressed and went to see if Pappy was awake, opened her door to see her fast asleep, closed it, went upstairs. Not to the front room, that I couldn't face yet. Instead I explored the other rooms Mrs. Delvecchio Schwartz had kept for her own use, three in all. A dreary bedroom for herself, its walls almost as smothered in books as Pappy's domain. But what books! Had she really made Harold privy to this secret, or did he not comprehend?

"Now I know how you did it, you old horror," I said, smiling. Scrapbooks stuffed with newspaper clippings about politicians and businessmen and their lives, their scandals, their tragedies, their foibles, the oldest going back thirty years. *Who's Who* of all the English-speaking nations. Almanacs. Court proceedings. *Hansard* records of the Federal and State Parliaments. Anything she thought might come in handy from Australian biographies to lists of societies, associations, institutions. A goldmine for a soothsayer.

Off her bedroom was a cranny for Flo, furnished with an old iron cot stripped to the bare mattress and a chest of drawers—not one picture of a puppy or a kitten or a fairy, not a sign that it had ever been occupied except for the scribbles all over its walls. It looked more like a dead child's nook in an institution than a living child's room, and I shivered in dread. *Why* had she stripped Flo's cot if she didn't know that Flo would be gone? Was it a message that, deprived of her life in The House, Flo would die?

Her kitchen was a poky alcove incapable of producing good food, its equipment ancient, battered, dented, cracked, chipped.

What had made her so indifferent to her own comfort? What sort of woman doesn't care about her nest?

I left to go back downstairs feeling that the mystery grew thicker, that Mrs. Delvecchio Schwartz's death was only the start of an ever-branching maze.

Pappy was moving about, so I told her to come in for coffee and breakfast. Yes, breakfast. So much to do, and all of it needing strength and health.

Jim and Bob called in on their way to work, said they'd stay home if I needed them, but I sent them off. When Toby arrived I was going to do the same, but he wasn't having any of that, he marched in and stood ready to do battle.

"You're going to need me today," he said stiffly, his face very pale, his chin up, his eyes clear and luminous.

In answer, I got up to hug him. He hugged me back, hard.

"Sorry about yesterday, but someone had to do it," he said.

"Yes, I know that. Sit down, we've got a lot to work out."

"Like getting her body for burial, looking for a will, finding out where they're holding Flo, to start with," he said.

But in the end the three of us did the worst job first. We went upstairs and cleaned the front room.

Toby handled the police, and found out that Mrs. Delvecchio Schwartz's body wouldn't be released for burial until after the Coroner made his finding— anything from one to three weeks. Then he went up the street to hunt for Martin, Lady Richard or anyone who might know about things like undertakers, funeral procedures—how ignorant we are of such matters unless we have experienced them, and none of us had, really. Toby's father died in the bush. Mr. Schwartz had died while she was in Singapore, Pappy said, and my own family hadn't lost a member since before I was born.

I phoned the Child Welfare, who, when I couldn't assure them that I was either next-of-kin or even a remote relative, refused to give me any information about Flo except that she was being well cared for at some unspecified place.

"Not Yasmar!" said Pappy when I hung up.

I sat down limply. "Dear God, I never thought of Yasmar!"

"Flo is five now, Harriet, she could be sent to Yasmar."

It was the institution where homeless or problem girls were sent until their futures were sorted out. Currently it was the object of bitter criticism because no effort was made to separate the hapless victims of circumstance like Flo from the hardened, extremely wild and sometimes violent girls taken into custody for everything from prostitution to murder.

So I rang Joe the Q.C. in her chambers and started off by asking about wills, about what would happen if there was no will.

"If there's no will in the house and no solicitor's name, then the Public Trustee will step in. They'll advertise in the law journals for anyone holding a will, and look after the estate in the meantime. Search for deeds as well as a will, Harriet, and I'll see what I can do," Joe said in that crisp, clear voice I imagined would set the rafters of a courthouse ringing.

"Don't go yet," I rushed on. "You can also find me the name of a firm which specialises in child custody cases. If my bones are right, we're not going to find a will, and nor is the Public Trustee. So I'll be seeking custody of Flo."

She didn't answer for a long moment, then she sighed. "Are you positive that's what you want to do?" she asked.

"Absolutely positive," I said.

So she promised to find me a name, and hung up.

Then we commenced to search for a will. Klaus came in from somewhere and helped us open and shake out every book, turn over every page in the scrapbooks, feel the clippings to make sure there was no folded paper underneath. Nothing, nothing, nothing. We did find what appeared to be the deeds to 17 Victoria Street, which was very puzzling. Not 17c, just 17.

"Does that mean she owns *all five* houses?" Pappy squeaked.

"Surely not," said Klaus, staring about. "She is not rich."

There was a big wooden box under the stairs right behind the drum of eucalyptus soap we'd used to scrub the front room, but we hadn't taken any notice of it, assumed it was a tool box. Then desperation prompted Toby to go back to the cupboard and lift it out. He put it on the tiny work bench in Mrs. Delvecchio Schwartz's kitchen, and opened it as if anything from Dracula to a concertinaed paper clown might jump out.

It contained an old but never used blue bunny rug, a huge single crystal of some clear mauve stone, seven cut glass tumblers still in their cardboard cylinders, a white marble model of a baby's hand and arm up past the dimpled elbow, and literally many dozens of little savings bank books.

Toby reached in and took out a handful of the bank books, flicked each one open, studied it in disbelief.

"Jesus!" he exclaimed. "Every one of this lot holds about a thousand pounds, which is the amount you can have in a savings account free and clear, without anybody allowed to ask questions."

In all, we counted over a hundred of them, though we didn't go on opening them. Why, when the answer was plain enough? There was a system involved, simple yet arduous. She never used the same bank twice, which meant that she had accounts in every branch of every bank that Sydney owned. As the last twenty years wore on, she had to go farther and farther afield, until she was plonking a thousand quid in Newcastle, Wollongong and Bathurst banks. What did she do with Flo when she travelled all day long?

"Well, Flo certainly isn't going to want for a thing," Toby said as he packed the bank books neatly into an empty carton, wrapped it in brown paper and tied it with string—she'd saved miles of string as well as sheaves of brown paper, carefully smoothed out, then folded again.

"Flo might never get to see a penny of it or own The House," I said grimly. "The Government might end in collaring the lot—we haven't found Flo's birth certificate."

Nor did we, though we renewed our search with redoubled energy. No will, no birth certificate, no name of any law firm. No wedding certificate either. Nor, it turned out when we quizzed her, could Pappy swear that Flo really was Mrs. Delvecchio Schwartz's child—she'd spent two years in Singapore trying to discover her father's relations. It was after she came back that she brought Toby to The House, so he was no help. Whichever way we headed, we ran into a blank wall. It was just as if Mrs. Delvecchio Schwartz had entered the world fully grown, never married, or had a child. One didn't dream that such things could happen in this day and age, but they could. She was proof of it. How many people existed without the Government ever knowing they did? There were no tax records either, just a simple account book which recorded the minimal rents for 17c. No receipts for property rates, water bills, electricity bills, gas bills, repairs.

"She paid everything in cash," said Klaus, who looked winded.

The last thing we tackled—we had to go through the front room to get there—was the little cupboard outside on the balcony where she kept her Glass and her cards and her heavenly spheres. They were all it contained, not one thing more. We riffled through the ephemeris, examined every horoscope sheet, turned it over, held it up to the light—we even took the tarot deck apart card by card. No birth certificate, no will, *nothing*.

"All right, let's put it all back." I sighed.

But Pappy gasped, grabbed my arm urgently. "No, Harriet, no! Don't do that! Take it all downstairs and hide it in your flat."

I stared at her as if she'd gone mad. "I can't do that!" I said. "These belonged to her, they're part of her estate. The Glass is immensely valuable—she said if she sold it, she'd be able to buy the Hotel Australia."

Toby saw what I didn't. "Pappy's right, take them."

I said no, he growled in exasperation at my stupidity.

"Don't be a fool, Harriet! Use your head! The first people likely to inspect these premises will be from the Child Welfare, and what do you think they're going to say when they find this stuff? Especially with all those bank books. If you want custody of Flo, then her life— and her mother's life!—must look as ordinary and humdrum as possible. We can't stop them thinking the old girl was eccentric, but for God's sake, Harriet, don't hand them ammunition like this!"

We piled the occult paraphernalia into another carton and we fled down the stairs to my flat at a gallop, terrified that we'd hear the door bell ring.

But it didn't ring until five o'clock, which seemed an odd hour for the Child Welfare to arrive. I left Klaus busy at my stove cooking us a meal and went to answer it—we'd locked the front door yesterday, and now we kept it locked.

Duncan Forsythe was standing on the verandah.

"I won't come in," he said. "My wife is waiting in the car."

He looked even worse than he had at Chris Hamilton's wedding—thin and bent, defeated. His hair had hardly any red left in it, but he hadn't salt-and-peppered. Broad streaks of white were mixed in with streaks of grey, very striking. His eyes were exhausted, but they gazed at me with such love that my heart twisted.

I peered over his shoulder and saw the Jaguar sitting within our cul-de-sac with its nose pointed at the kerb right where the Missus could watch everything that happened on 17c's verandah. Taking no chances, the Missus.

"Your wife received a letter written in copperplate on very expensive paper," I said. "It told her that you were in the grasp of a whore—a vulgar, common trollop not fit to live in this world but not fit to enter the next. Its dates were inaccurate, and it implied that we were still seeing each other."

"Yes, exactly," he said without surprise. "It came in this morning's post."

"Further to go," I said. "The one to my father got to Bronte on New Year's Eve."

That did hurt him, he drew a long breath. "Oh, Harriet, my dear! I'm so sorry!"

Oh, how much had happened! I seemed to look at him through a network of strands of pain and worry I hadn't felt until I saw him there, yet none of the strands was pain belonging to him, worry on his account. I had moved on to some other place, and, looking at him, I wondered if I could ever return to what had been *our* place. Before murder. Before they had taken my angel away to die.

So I answered him coolly. "Well, Duncan, if it's any sort of consolation, there won't be any more of these letters. Harold wrote them, and Harold's dead. Now I only have to wonder if old Sister Agatha got one."

"I am afraid she did. She phoned me this morning."

I shrugged. "Too bad. What can she do? Sack me? Not in this day and age, she can't. The worst she can do is take me off Cas and put me on routine chests, but I don't think she's that stupid. I'm too good at my job to waste on routine chests."

He was staring at me as if I was as different from the old Harriet Purcell as I felt inside me. I put my hand on his arm and patted it, making sure that the Missus could see. "Duncan, you didn't have to come and see me, truly. I am all right."

"Cathy insisted," he said, looking hunted. "I am to tell you that she'll ignore our affair and will support both of us by denying the story to anybody who gets one of these letters."

Crikey, what a cheek the woman had! My detachment evaporated as I felt the anger mounting. How dare she patronise him! How dare she patronise *me*! As if her say-so has the power to render anything insignificant! "Big of her," I said. "Mighty big of her." Growl, roar, snarl, out with the claws!

"I've given her my word that I'll never speak to you again."

That was the last straw. I butted Duncan aside with the point of my shoulder and strode to the car, grabbed the passenger's door handle and had the door open before the Missus could find the lock. I reached in, fastened my hand in a French couture shoulder pad, and yanked Mrs. Duncan Forsythe out of her seat, onto the pavement. Then I backed her against the railings of 17c and towered over her—why do tall men always marry women with duck's disease? She was *terrified*! It just hadn't occurred to her that in forcing Duncan to come here with her riding shotgun, she'd meet Jesse James.

"Listen, you," I snarled, my face inches from hers, "stay out of my life! How dare you patronise me! If you'd done your duty and given your husband a bit of nooky occasionally, he wouldn't have strayed. You're only in it for the meal ticket, but you don't pay your debts. I do, and this is a debt I owe your husband for being a decent man and a wonderful lover! It isn't his fault that you've cut his balls off, but you leave him alone, hear me?"

She was gobbling, her face scarlet, her eyes starting out of her head, and by now Madame Toccata was standing on 17b's balcony, and Madame Fugue and Chastity on 17d's balcony, cheering me on.

Duncan had moved onto the pavement, but not to rescue his wife. He leaned against the railings, crossed his ankles, folded his arms and grinned.

"Mind your own business, you silly bitch!" I yelled as I dragged her back to the car. "If you want to be Lady Forsythe one day, then shut your mouth and wear me along with Balenciaga, you skinny little clothes horse!" And I threw her in.

Duncan stood howling with laughter while the Missus huddled in the Jag's passenger seat and cried into her lace hanky.

"Knockout in the first round," he said, wiping his eyes on his own hanky. "God, I love you!"

"And I you," I said, touching his face. "I don't know why, but I do. There's a lot of strength and courage in you, Duncan, there has to be to cope with life and death, maiming and disease. But when it comes to personal relationships, you're a coward. Be everything you can be, and the hell with what other people think. Now take the Missus home."

"May I see you again?" he asked, suddenly back the way he had been that night when we came in from Victoria Street, lit up from within, crackling with life.

"Not now, not for God knows how much time to come," I said. "Harold murdered Mrs. Delvecchio Schwartz on New Year's Day, then killed himself.

And I have to keep my nose clean because I'm going to apply for custody of Flo."

Of course he was shocked, horrified, sympathetic, eager to help, but I could see that he didn't understand why I wanted Flo. Never mind. He still loves me, and that's an enormous comfort.

Tuesday,
January 3rd, 1961

Work today. Brave words to Duncan and all, I can't afford to lose my job. If I can hire some kind soul to look after Flo while I work, between what's left of my salary and the rents of The House, the pair of us ought to be able to live—terrible word!—*respectably* if not luxuriously. At five, she's school age, but what school would take her? I'd have to enquire about special schools, but I've never heard of any in the State system, at any rate. And how would Flo survive in a special school, surrounded by retarded or spastic children? There is nothing *wrong* with her, but she's like that plant which closes up when its leaves are touched. Yes, there's the Spastic Centre at Mosman, it's got a terrific reputation, but would Flo qualify? She's not spastic, she's just a mute.

All questions for the future, when I'd been granted custody of Flo. In the meantime, I had to keep my job and its male charge pay, save as much as I possibly could. If the Public Trustee isn't co-operative— and what public institution ever is?—Flo and I might not even be able to live at 17c, let alone utilise its rents. No birth certificate, no marriage certificate. She had Flo at home on the dunny floor, not in a hospital maternity ward.

There's no point speculating. All I can do is wait.

Sister Agatha carpeted me at nine o'clock this morning, sent a replacement technician to cover my absence. Serious, very serious.

"Do you realise the extent of the inconvenience you caused yesterday, Miss Purcell?" Sister Agatha demanded. "You telephone at ten minutes to six in the morning—ten minutes before you are due on duty!—to say you won't be in. And do you tender a reason? No, you do not. You hang up in Miss Barker's ear."

I stared into the cold blue eyes with this odd vision of the dancing Sister Agatha imposed upon the icicle in the chair, but I couldn't fuse them together no matter how I tried. And of course she was the recipient of a letter from Harold, which wasn't going to help. But it did give me an idea. I knew perfectly well that to explain about Mrs. Delvecchio Schwartz, Harold and Flo would only turn her more against me—respectable women didn't get themselves embroiled in murders and their consequences.

"I am very sorry, Sister Toppingham," I said, "but I was too upset to think logically yesterday morning. This is an embarrassing subject, but I think you will have to know." Embroider, Harriet, lie when you have to. Flo is worth a million lies. "My father

283

received an anonymous letter which accused me of having an affair with Mr. Duncan Forsythe. It is, of course, nonsense. But you must see that it completely destroyed my day. My father demanded my presence at home, and I had to go."

"Hmmmf," she said, and paused. "And did you clear this most disturbing business up, Miss Purcell?"

"With the help of Mrs. Duncan Forsythe, Sister, yes, I did."

Cunning old bitch, she wasn't about to tell me that she was already in the know. Mentioning the Missus did the trick, however. "Your apology is accepted, Miss Purcell. You may go."

I lingered. "Sister, there is one unfortunate consequence of this frightful matter. Um, it appears that there will be legal enquiries, so I may have to leave work at something close to my official knocking off time on some afternoons over the next few weeks. I assure you that I will endeavour to make any appointments as late in the day as possible, but I will have to knock off in time to be where I'm supposed to be."

She didn't like that, but she understood it. No hospital department head ever enjoys being reminded that the staff work a lot of unpaid overtime. "You may keep such appointments, Miss Purcell, provided that you notify me on the relevant days."

"Yes, Sister, thank you, Sister," I said, and escaped.

Not too bad, all considered. Oh, why isn't Royal Queens one of those hospitals like Vinnie's and R.P.A. that never has a quiet weekend? If I were rostered for weekends, I'd have whole days during the working week to do what has to be done. Between Ryde and Queens, I hadn't picked my places of work very well.

**Thursday,
January 5th, 1961**

Joe the Q.C. has given me the name of a law firm specialising in children's work. Partington, Pilkington, Purblind and Hush, in Bridge Street. Straight out of Charles Dickens, but she assures me that there are heaps of Dickensian-sounding law firms, it's a part of legal tradition and most of the partners listed in a firm's title have been dead for a thousand years if they ever existed at all. My pick is Mr. Purblind, but I'm to see Mr. Hush next Monday at four o'clock.

I still can't get any sense out of the Child Welfare, who keep on refusing to tell me where Flo is. She's well, she's happy, she's this and she's that, but if she's in Yasmar they won't admit it. The inquest on Harold and Mrs. Delvecchio Schwartz has been set for Wednesday of next week, so I'll have to think of a brilliant reason why I might need the whole day off. All of us in The House are obliged to attend and answer questions if we're called, though Norm tells me that the Boys in Blue haven't found hide nor hair of Chikker and Marge from the front ground floor flat. Fled interstate is the theory, which means that they might not have been on the game, but they were up to something. Trouble is that without finger-prints, no one knows exactly who they are. Possibly bank robbers. I think they are just seedy people who don't trust The Law.

Something very strange happened last night at about ten past three. We were all in, and all asleep. I was woken by the sound of heavy footsteps thump-ing down the hall from upstairs, for all the world like Mrs. Delvecchio Schwartz doing a small hours patrol. No one else walks like that! Even The House, a stout old Victorian terrace, used to shake when she walked. But Mrs. Delvecchio Schwartz is dead, I saw her dead, and I know that right now the poor crea-ture is lying in a morgue drawer. *Yet she was walk-ing upstairs!* Then came the rumble of her laugh, not the hur-hur-hur, the ha-ha-ha. My hair went straight for the first time in its life.

The next thing they were all clustered at my door. Klaus was beside himself, weeping and moaning, so was Bob. Jim was trying to brave it out, and Toby's face was white. So was mine, not easy for people with dark-tan skin.

I brought them inside and tried to settle them in my chairs, but they twitched, jumped, shivered. So did I.

Only Pappy wasn't scared witless. "She's here

with us," she said, eyes shining. "I knew she'd never desert The House."

"Rubbish!" Toby snapped.

"No, whatever it is, it's real," I said. "We were all sound asleep, and it woke us up."

I put the kettle on, made some tea, and put a stiff dollop of brandy in every mug. Vows never to touch the stuff again are not proof against Mrs. Delvecchio Schwartz.

Then Pappy dropped her bombshell. Our night experience had filled her with a joy I hadn't seen in her since the halcyon days of Ezra. She was sparkling.

"I'm not going to Stockton," she said.

We all stared at her.

"After Mrs. Delvecchio Schwartz passed over," she whispered, "she appeared to me. Not in a dream— while I was reading. She told me that I couldn't desert The House. So I went to see the Sisters at Vinnie's, and asked if I could train there as a nurse but live here. Nuns are so kind, so understanding! They decided that at my age and with my experience of hospitals, I would make a better nurse if I lived out than in. I start at Vinnie's with the next batch of probationers later this month."

This was the first bit of good news since New Year's Eve, and we all needed it desperately. Pappy is strange, very mystical. Yet even after hearing what she had to say, I refuse to believe that it was the real Mrs. Delvecchio Schwartz I heard upstairs. I would rather think that emanations from my lost angel stole into our minds and deluded us.

Where are you, Flo? Are you all right? Do they understand? No, of course you're not all right, and of course they don't understand. With your mother gone, you belong to me, and I'll shift heaven and earth before I'll see you sent to an orphanage. If I can't get you home, you'll die. Your fate is in my hands because your mother put it there. Which is the greatest mystery of all.

Saturday,
January 7th, 1961

A woman from the Child Welfare came today. I saw her standing on the verandah when I returned from the shops, a dowdily dressed woman in her fifties with all the earmarks of spinsterhood, from the ring-less left hand to the whiskers sprouting on her chin. Why don't they ever pluck or shave them? You'd think that a pardonable vanity would push them to it, but at least half of them seem to prefer to wear the whiskers like a badge. It's a good thing that the War freed up women like this to work, otherwise what would become of them? But then again, I suppose the War also cut down on the supply of husbands. Certainly there aren't as many single around my age as there are in the Chris-Marie and upward age brackets. Mind you, Australian men are hard to catch and harder to hang onto. As Chris and Marie have found out, *New* Australian men are a piece of (wedding) cake compared to the Old ones.

This spinster specimen introduced herself and I introduced myself. Miss Farfer or Arthur or Farfin, something that sounded like Arf-Arf in her squeezed-up voice. So I called her Miss Arf-Arf and she answered to it without seeming to notice. As I unlocked the door and she followed me inside, I couldn't see her reaction to the scribbles, the neglected ugliness of The House's public halls. Then, as luck would have it, we emerged into the side passage right at the moment Madame Fugue had chosen to roast Verity.

"You fuckin' stupid fuckin' bitch!" was the only audible bit, thank God, but I suspect it was more than enough.

"What is that house?" she asked as I opened my door.

"A private hotel," I said, and ushered her into my nice pink flat. There she informed me that she had come to inspect Florence Schwartz's past living arrangements. *Past* living arrangements.

"I have been every day since Tuesday, but there is never a soul home," she said peevishly.

Oh, dear. We were off to a bad start and it only got worse. A notebook was produced and duly entered as I explained the nature of The House, its tenants, who we all were, what we did for a crust, how long we'd been here, how well we'd known Mrs. Delvecchio Schwartz and Flo, whom Miss

Arf-Arf persisted in calling Florence. That she had already conferred with the pair who took Flo away was obvious from her questions. Did Flo ever wear shoes? Why wouldn't Flo talk? What sort of hours had Flo kept? What did Flo's mother feed her? Thank God for Pappy's presence of mind over the occult paraphernalia, because Miss Arf-Arf toured the place from top to bottom and left no coverlet unturned or drawer unopened. What would she say if she knew that until shortly before her mother's death, Flo had still been on the breast? Like the soothsaying, our secret.

I refused to let her look in Jim and Bob's flat or in Klaus's room because they weren't in. It didn't please her to be denied, but she was a lot less pleased over Toby's reaction to her request to come up and see him.

"Go to buggery!" he snarled, and slammed his trapdoor.

I left the front room until last, hoping against hope, but of course Miss Arf-Arf wasn't going to miss The Scene of The Murder. *Very* disappointing, obviously. We'd cleaned it scrupulously, so much so that even the crayon scribbles on the walls were barely visible. Of any bloody finger-painting, not a smear or a smudge.

"However, I have seen the police photographs," she said smugly.

I was dying to tell her to go to buggery too, but I didn't dare. With Flo's fate undecided, what I said to anybody from the Child Welfare had to be friendly, candid, sane and balanced. So I ended the tour with the offer of a cup of tea. Miss Arf-Arf accepted.

"Considering the insalubrious location of these premises and the state of Florence's mother's personal accommodations, my dear Miss Purcell, you've made a very pleasant corner for yourself," she said, munching one of my Anzac bikkies. No dunking for her!

I told her that I was going to apply for custody of Flo.

"Oh, that would *never* do!" she said.

I asked her what she meant, and she explained that Florence was being well cared for where she was (no mention of a place—it might have been in Melbourne or Timbuctoo from the way she spoke), so custody wouldn't become an option until after everybody decided that no will or relative existed.

"Which may take many months," she ended.

I looked into her watery blue eyes and understood that if I started to plead eloquently with all the emotional stops out, tried to tell her that Flo would die unless she came home very soon, my chances of ever getting Flo would diminish immediately.

"It's not that they're inhuman, or even inhumane," I said to Toby later up in his airy attic, "it's just that they go by the rules, that individual circumstances are dismissed."

"Of course," he grunted, scrubbing away at a hotel-type picture of a blue gum in a clearing. "They're public servants, Harriet, and public servants don't rock the boat. Everything is decided by the grey ghosts on some committee. Miss Arf-Arf's report will go into Flo's file along with all the other reports, and when the file measures two inches thick, it will go Upstairs for a decision."

"She'll be dead by then," I said, winking away my tears.

He put down his brushes and came across to sit facing me on a hard chair drawn up very close, then he leaned forward and pushed a flopping bit of hair off my forehead. "Why do you love her so?" he asked. "I mean, she's a nice little kid, even if she is a bit strange, but anyone would think that she's your own, the way you talk. You call me obsessed, but Flo is a much greater obsession with you than anything I can drum up."

What kind of answer would make him see the specialness of Flo?

"It's hard for anyone on the outside of affairs of the heart to understand, but the truth is that I just looked at her and loved her," I said.

"No, it's not hard," he said, and shrugged. "It's easy— I'm not on the outside." He gave me a lovely smile and tucked my hair up again. "If you must, Harriet, then go for it with all that spectacular energy and enthusiasm you manage to summon up, even at times like this. But do me a favour, think about your life. If you get Flo, you'll never be free again."

That's true. But there's no contest, which is what Toby will not see. Flo is worth everything to me, even the loss of freedom. I wouldn't walk on coals of fire for Duncan Forsythe or any other man, but Flo? She's my angel. My child.

Monday, January 9th, 1961

I arrived at Messrs. Partington, Pilkington, Purblind and Hush's chambers in Bridge Street exactly one minute before my appointment with Mr. Hush, who, from what his incredibly snooty secretary said, ordinarily does *not* see clients as late as four o'clock. I apologised for inconveniencing Mr. Hush—what a wonderful thing it is to be hospital trained! If the garbageman lectured me about a dent in the lid of my can, I would put my hands behind my back, stand to attention and apologise. It's so much *easier* than attempting things like justification or excuse. The incredibly snooty secretary was delighted at my response, gave me a cat's anus sort of smile, all puckered up, and told me to sit and wait. Law firms, I realised, are in the amateur league compared to hospitals. If I had half an hour to play with, I could have Miss Hoojar jumping through hoops. Interesting that law firms run on spinsters too. Where would the professional world be without them? And what's going to happen when my generation, so much more married, takes over? There'll be private secretaries and department heads trying to cope with sick kids and defaulting husbands as well as the work. Oooooo-aa!

Mr. Hush looks like a butcher. Big and beefy, with purple grog blossoms all over his nose. Right, I decided after one look, cut every scrap of fat out of the meat, skin off the tendons, and give him nothing but good red *muscle*. I launched into my story without a single unnecessary word, stripped it of all its colour and flavour, and ended by saying, "I want custody of Flo, Mr. Hush."

He was terrifically impressed by all this crisp logic— don't tell me I can't handle men!

"Some personal particulars first, Miss Purcell. You are of age? You work?"

"I'm twenty-two and I'm a qualified X-ray technician."

"Can you afford what might be an expensive exercise?"

"Yes, sir."

"So you have private means."

"No, sir. I have enough saved to meet the legal costs."

"Your answer indicates that you have no source of income other than your job of work. Is that correct?"

"Yes, sir," I whispered, deflating rapidly.

"Are you married? Engaged to be married?"

"No, sir," I whispered. I knew where he was going.

"Hmmmm." He tapped his teeth with a pencil.

He then proceeded to tell me that there were three kinds of custody—adoption, guardianship, and the offer of a foster home. "Frankly, Miss Purcell, you would not qualify for any of the three alternatives," he said, wielding his cleaver impersonally. "In this state, considerable research has not revealed one instance of custody of a child being awarded to an unmarried, working woman with no blood kinship. Your youth also predicates against custody. Perhaps it would be wiser to abandon your quest right now."

Fresh iron entered my soul, I glared at him fiercely. "No, I will not!" I snapped. "Flo belongs to me, it's what her mother would have wanted. I don't care what I have to do to get Flo back, and that's honest. But I will get her back! I will, I will!"

He leaped up from behind his desk, came around it *and bent to kiss my hand*! "Oh, what a bonny battler you are, Miss Purcell!" he cried. "This is going to be tremendous fun! I do like shaking the foundations of institutions! Now tell me the rest, because there is a lot more, isn't there?"

I told him as much of the rest as I thought prudent. Yes, I liked him, but not enough to hand over information about soothsaying and breastfeeding. Just about the bank books, the deeds to what seemed the whole of 17 Victoria Street, the lack of documents of any kind from wedding certificates to birth certificates to taxation returns. He loved it so much that he turned even more butcherish. I could see his mind working out a new recipe for sausage made of Child Welfare officials.

So we left it that Mr. Hush would take a personal

interest in items like the search for a will, the effort to trace relatives, the Public Trustee, and any or all parties who might come sniffing around on the trail of truffles like a rather large and possibly illicit fortune.

Thus went my first brush with a law firm, if not with the Law. Between Willie's withdrawal syndrome, Norm, Merv and detectives investigating murder, I must have considerably more experience of the Law than most girls my age who aren't on the game.

It hadn't occurred to me that the people with power over Flo would consider me an unsuitable custodian. That my age, my need to work to live and my unmarried state completely overrode abstracts like love. Which just goes to show how dense I am. The clues were all there in those women from the Child Welfare, more concerned with shoes than love. No, that's wrong. Equating shoes *with* love.

All I know is that if I don't get Flo home, she'll die. Fade away, leaving those with power over her wondering what on earth had happened. Because they genuinely wouldn't know.

Wednesday
January 11th, 1961
The inquest took place this morning. A nothing. All of us were called to testify. I'd worked from six until nine, raced into town in a taxi, then raced back to

Queens in another taxi as soon as it was over. The tale I concocted for Sister Agatha was a police enquiry about anonymous letters, which she accepted without comment. No, we hadn't noticed any particular tension between Mr. Warner and his paramour, Mrs. ? Delvecchio Schwartz. Even Pappy couldn't supply a first name. No, none of us had heard a thing. The absence of Chikker and Marge was duly noted, but the police were of the opinion that they weren't involved. Verdict: murder and suicide. Case closed. We could have Mrs. ? Delvecchio Schwartz's body for burial. *No* cremation! Was that so they could dig her up again if fresh evidence came to light? Or some new investigative test? Yes, we decided.

Someone, possibly through the Missus, had got wind of the affair between Duncan and me, because Sister Cas had a few snide little pots at me. I played dumber than dumb. Let them fish to their hearts' content, they have no hard evidence.

My credibility with Sister Agatha took another pounding when I had to tell her that I wouldn't be in to work at all on Friday. A death in the family, I explained. I don't think she believed me.

Friday,
January 13th, 1961
Battling to get someone buried on a Friday the Thirteenth told me why Sister Agatha didn't believe

me. The undertaker threw up his hands in horror at the very thought, but Toby and I, deputed to be the organisers, refused to budge. What other day of the year would do for Mrs. Delvecchio Schwartz than a Friday the Thirteenth? In the end the only way we could persuade the undertaker was to agree to have a minister of religion officiate, something we hadn't thought she'd want. I think the man deemed us a nest of satanists—Kings Cross and all that, you know. Toby and I looked at each other and shrugged. Maybe it would tickle the old girl no end to be buried with the Church of England rites. Dust to dust, ashes to ashes, etc. Man that is born of woman—our minister wouldn't hear of woman that is born of woman. What a strange world we live in. Riddled with what Pappy calls shibboleths.

You never saw a worse day for a funeral. Sydney bunged on a heatwave, so by nine o'clock it was over a hundred degrees, with a gale blowing from the west like a giant fan across the hobs of Hell. There were bushfires all over the Blue Mountains, so the air was brown, reeked of smoke, rained cinders. All of which petrified the minister, who was convinced that the Devil was laying on a grand reception for one of his most important earthly imps. The hearse left the funeral parlour without incident, followed by the mourners in two big black Fords—Pappy, Toby, Jim and Bob, Klaus, Lerner Chusovich and Joe Dwyer from the Piccadilly pub bottle department. And me, of course. Flo didn't turn up, though we'd notified the Child Welfare. The Mesdames Fugue and Toccata and friends tacked themselves onto the cortege in a huge black Rolls they must have borrowed from a client; when we got to the graveside Norm and Merv were waiting, their police car parked ten yards away between a fallen angel and a rusty iron cross. When the Rolls pulled up, it disgorged Lady Richard on Martin's arm, stunningly gowned in plain black shantung with a cheeky little black pillbox on his mauve hair, face webbed by a wisp of black net. Perfect! Everybody the old girl would have wanted there was there. Except for Flo.

We buried her in Rookwood, surely the world's biggest, most neglected graveyard, literal square miles of it plonked in the middle of the Western Suburbs. Overgrown with weeds and long rank grass, dotted with scrubby bush, a few she-okes, gums and stringy-barks between sparse graves whose ruined headstones leaned at all angles except the vertical.

Toby, Klaus, Merv, Norm, Joe and Martin acted as pallbearers, heaved and shoved and grunted and groaned until they got the gigantic coffin onto their shoulders, then staggered under its enormous weight—it had to be lead-lined, of course, after such a long interlude in a morgue drawer—to the newly dug grave, where they lowered it amid "Shits!" and "Jesus Christs!" onto three four-by-twos laid across the cavity. The minister, who hadn't really seen the coffin until now, stood there gaping while the undertaker had a muttered talk with the grave diggers to make sure they'd followed orders and had excavated a roomy enough final resting place.

The women stood on one side and the men on the other—it was an *Australian* funeral, after all. Jim stood with the men. Very brave we women looked, me in shocking pink, Pappy in an emerald cheongsam, Bob in blue eyelet-embroidered organdie, Lady Richard in his shantung number, and the Mesdames dolled up to the nines in skin-tight black satin, black patent stilettos and dense black veils à la the House of Windsor. The men had all managed to find a tie somewhere (Martin's looked like pea-and-carrot puke), though they'd had the sense to ditch their coats. They did wear black armbands.

How she must have wallowed in it! Just as the minister stood at the head of the grave to commence his obsequies, a hideously hot gust of wind shrieked down like a satanic huff, whipped his skirts up around his face and knocked his glasses off. He nearly landed on the coffin, a plain affair without a flower, let alone a wreath. We had agreed that Mrs. Delvecchio Schwartz would not appreciate such traditional trappings as flowers, since apparently she had not yet properly Passed Over. The nightly gallops down the hall and booms of laughter had lost their novelty by the time we buried her. Nowanights we sort of rouse a bit, sigh, grin, and go back to sleep.

The six men put the straps under the coffin, lifted

it enough for the terrified undertaker to slide the four-by-twos out, then lowered it with more "Shits!" and "Jesus Christs!" into the grave. Once it hit bottom, I stepped forward and dropped the wooden box on top of it. We'd decided that she'd want to have the blue bunny rug, the huge mauve crystal, the marble hand and arm, and the seven cut glass tumblers with her. No one tossed a clod of Rookwood's dismal soil in; we just walked away and left the rest to the grave diggers, who had been standing by in awe.

"Me bloody back's gone on me!" Merv whimpered.

"Heavier in death than in life," Klaus said solemnly.

"Oh, *potties*! I've laddered my stocking!" Lady Richard moaned.

"At least she's in the shade," Toby said, pointing to a gum.

"Memorable!" Joe Dwyer said, wiping away tears. "Memorable!"

We all went home and had a party in Toby's attic.

I wonder who'll bury Harold? Ask me do I care.

Saturday,
January 14th, 1961
I'm having a blue day. Understandable after yesterday. It strikes me as peculiar, that things should have worked out in such a way that we could bury Mrs. Delvecchio Schwartz on a Friday the Thirteenth. The

last one was May, and the next one isn't until October. A sort of an omen, not unlike the appearance of Marceline in my life. Are events really random? I wish I knew.

Toby has disappeared to see if his shack at Wentworth Falls is in the middle of a bushfire, Jim and Bob have tooled off on the Harley Davidson, and Klaus has gone to Bowral with Lerner Chusovich, who felt a bit left out of things because they wouldn't let him be a pallbearer. Such a thin, reedy man. Very shadowy and shy.

Pappy was home, so we had dinner together. This Monday she starts with the rest of the probationers at Vinnie's. Thank God that Stockton has been removed from her equation. Or rather, thank Mrs. Delvecchio Schwartz the phantasm. Pappy honestly does believe that the old horror materialises and talks to her, though I *can't* believe it. Yes, I hear the gallops and the laughs, but I still think they're something Flo is generating.

"Have you taken the Glass and the cards out?" Pappy asked.

"Good lord, no! They're in the Tilsiter cupboard."

"Harriet, she wouldn't like that. The Glass and the cards have to be handled, otherwise they'll lose their power." And nothing would do but that I dragged them out, put them on the table in their dirty silk covers, though I refused to scry or spread.

"I'll handle them occasionally, but no more," I

said firmly. "She told me it was a racket, and all those books in her room tell me it *is* a racket."

"Once upon a time it was," said Pappy, unimpressed. "But that was years ago, before she realised she had the power. The books are still there because she couldn't throw anything out."

"The books were up to date—it's Flo who has the power."

"Perhaps she kept them up to date as part of Flo's inheritance," Pappy said. "Even a Flo has to crawl before she can walk. They're there for Flo to study later."

"What utter rubbish! I'm sure that Mrs. Delvecchio Schwartz knew as well as I do that Flo will never read any more than she can talk," I said. "As to the medium business, I'm hoping you can tell me how Flo and her mother worked."

But Pappy says she can't tell me because she doesn't know, has never seen one of their sessions with a client. Nor, she added in haste (seeing the expression on my face), would any of the clients discuss the sessions. We've had Mrs. Delvecchio Schwartz's phone disconnected, and after several notes of desperate appeal from the clients were gathered off the floor in the front hall, we tacked a small note to the outside of the door saying that Mrs. Delvecchio Schwartz had Passed Over. Which is the end of it. How ghastly, to think of one of those expensive ladies from Point Piper, Vaucluse, Killara and Pymble encountering someone from the Child

Welfare or the Public Trustee on The House's doorstep!

Pappy looks well, tranquil. She's regained the lost weight, is up to the hard labour of nursing training. Though a part of me wishes that she'd mention the lost baby or Ezra, if only to start unburdening herself, another part of me is very glad that she has apparently decided to consign the past to limbo.

Thursday,
February 2nd, 1961

There *are* hidden forces at work! Look at that last word of my last entry, almost three weeks ago. *Limbo.* That's where we live these days, in limbo. Over a month since Mrs. Delvecchio Schwartz died, and still no word about anything. Flo may as well have disappeared off the face of the earth. Though not one single working day has gone by without my phoning to enquire about her, and the people on the Child Welfare switchboard must know my voice at least as well as they know their own, I am no closer to knowing where she is. Yes, Miss Purcell, Florence Schwartz is healthy and happy. No, Miss Purcell, it is not our policy to allow acquaintances to visit our children until their future welfare is assured . . . I am in danger of losing my patience, yet I can't lose my patience. What if they keep a record of my calls, what if one day a sharp and nasty comment from me is used

against me? They already hold my youth, my lack
of money and my unmarried state against me. For
Flo's sake I must remain pleasant and only suitably concerned. Oh, I wish love mattered to official worlds! But it doesn't because it's not a thing
you can see, feel, or weigh. I understand, I do. It's
a lot easier to talk about love than put your back
into it.

From Mr. Hush I hear that so far no will has
turned up, that Florence Schwartz's birth is not listed with the Registrar General, that there are no
records of anyone named Delvecchio marrying anyone named Schwartz. In fact Mr. Schwartz, that shy
and shadowy Jewish gentleman, appears not to exist
at all. Every Schwartz on the electoral rolls has been,
or will be, contacted. New South Wales has been
done, but no Schwartz will admit either to Flo or to
Flo's father. There is no death certificate for any
Schwartz that fits Flo's father! After talking to
Pappy, Mr. Hush thinks that our Mr. Schwartz actually had a different name, under which he was born,
married, and died.

The trouble is that Pappy went to Singapore for
two years—the two years which matter to the mystery of Mr. Schwartz. She remembers that someone
shy and shadowy moved into what later became
Harold's room, but he didn't impinge on her and
Mrs. Delvecchio, as she called herself then, never
even mentioned him. When Pappy came home, there
was Mrs. Delvecchio Schwartz and newborn baby

Flo. Mysteriouser and mysteriouser. Mr. Hush is enraptured.

The Public Trustee is now the guard dog of our limbo, but a most impersonal and indifferent guard dog. We have to pay our rents every four weeks by cheque or money order through the mail, quoting our Official Number. All of us understand that the guard dog is simply waiting for the incredible mess of Mrs. Delvecchio Schwartz's affairs to be sorted out before positive measures are taken. After all, there may be a will in some doddering solicitor's dusty files. We just wait in limbo for some sort of axe to fall.

In a funny way I've grown very close to Toby over these last few weeks. Life's going well for him. Thank God it is for one of us! He got his hotel contract, he's actually found a gallery owner who doesn't rape artists—very unusual, he assures me—and someone in Canberra is waffling about commissioning some paintings for the Australian embassies abroad. Therefore it doesn't matter that the robots are about to take over in his factory. The best news is that, since he only pays three quid a week for his attic, he thinks he'll be able to keep it on as well as his shack at Wentworth Falls. I keep pushing him to let me see this mountain retreat, but he just laughs and says not until after he's put in the septic tank and connected up the toilet. Considerate chap. If there's one thing I hate, it's a long drop. There are great debates about what constitutes civilisation, but

I know my definition—a flushing toilet and hot water laid on to kitchen and bathroom.

You're deteriorating, Harriet Purcell, when all you can find to write about is *sewerage*.

I just hope that I'm not getting too dependent on Toby. As I've always fancied him, I'm a weeny bit afraid that my dependence might give him wrong ideas. He's absolutely right when he says he doesn't get on well with women. He's so—*Australian*. Despite my Dad, Duncan and heaps of other blokes, there's a streak of contempt for women in a lot of Australian men. Look at my big brothers. Typical. About as far from homosexual as men can get, yet if they want to talk seriously or have a wacko good time, they'll choose men to do it with. Women, quote Gavin and Peter, can't talk about anything except clothes, kids, periods and home-making. I've heard them say so a million times. And while Toby doesn't live in the way my Bros do, I always have a funny feeling that there's only so much of himself that he's prepared to share with any woman, even the pretty weird women of The House. I just can't see Toby reduced to a quivering jelly over a woman. He'd hold something back.

The gallops and the laughs continue nightly.

Monday,
February 20th, 1961
I had dinner with Toby this evening, just cold ham,

potato salad and coleslaw from my favourite deli-catessen. Too muggy and sticky for hot food. We don't talk a lot, it doesn't seem necessary to avoid those abstracted silences that have to fall from time to time. When we did talk, it was mostly about Pappy, who is blooming at Vinnie's. What we don't talk about is my angel. Though he did tell me to go for it, I know that in his heart Toby doesn't really approve of so much naked love and passion. So I save all of that for the night marches after the first night march, that of Mrs. Delvecchio Schwartz, gets itself over and done with. Ten past three, on the knocker. The farther Flo drifts away from me, the harder I find it to go back to sleep, maybe because I'm up at half-past four anyway. So I lie there and think of her, try to send her mental messages of love and cheer, will some sort of apparition of myself to appear to her. Fanciful nonsense, but it comforts me, and if any of my thoughts get through, it would comfort Flo. I miss her so much!

This morning I gave up on bed, wandered out to put on coffee. Marceline, who always sleeps on the foot of my bed, is never proof against the prospect of food, so she got up too. Walking around hugging something soft and purring is armour against loneli-ness, I find. But after a while Marceline wanted to get down, and then the minute hand on the big old railway clock on the wall seemed to freeze, wouldn't move. I'd look, half-past three. I'd look again an hour later, half-past three. Maybe I'm running at the speed of light. In desperation I sat down at the table and unwrapped the cards, found my book on the tarot. No, I wouldn't spread. I'd simply start memorising the meanings of each card, right way up and reversed. Maybe if I know the meanings off by heart, if and when I do spread them, I'll see a pattern. It is at least a mental exercise, *something* to occupy my mind. It's been forever since I could read a book, nothing holds my interest. And the exercise did work, inasmuch as the next time I looked at the clock, it said four.

I wrapped the cards up again and took the silk off the Glass, drew it closer. Suddenly I remembered a tiny series of events that concerned the Glass, mostly I think because of Flo's face. Very early last year, when Mrs. Delvecchio Schwartz thrust the Glass at me and invited me to touch it. Flo had gasped, her face a study in awe and amazement. It hadn't really been significant at the time, but I understood now that I must have been the first person Mrs. Delvecchio Schwartz had ever let touch the Glass. Then around about the same time I'd become involved with Duncan, she said something to me about everything depending on the Glass. Just what, I can't remember, though it will be in one of my exercise books. But I do recall very clearly what she said on that last evening when Flo and I had walked into the front room to find her in the darkness communing with the Glass.

"The fate of The House is in the Glass," she'd said,

and put both my hands on it, then joined them together. And Flo had watched with obvious wonder.

Maybe, in that cryptic and oblique way she tackled everything, she was telling me that I had her official permission to use the Glass, that I was her chosen heir to its mysteries.

I got up, switched off the lights and sat down again at the table with my face the same distance from that faintly clouded sphere, just enough light coming in from outside to see. And I stared, fixed the focus of my vision on the inside of the crystal, and kept it there.

"The fate of The House is in the Glass." Well, if it was, I didn't have the wherewithal to see how, because after half an hour of gazing, gazing, gazing, I saw nothing that wasn't already in the room. No visions, no faces, no anything.

I covered it and started to get ready for work.

This evening, as already said, I ate with Toby. We'd finished and I was putting stuff back in the fridge while he washed the few dishes, when the door bell rang. Toby dried his hands on the tea towel and went to answer it. Since Mrs. Delvecchio Schwartz's death, only Toby, Klaus or Jim took door duty. Without her to watch over it, The House was suddenly vulnerable.

He seemed to be gone a long time, so long in fact that I began to worry. Then I heard footsteps coming, his and another's, the low murmur of two male voices.

"Dr. Forsythe wants to see you, Harriet," Toby said, coming in first with scowling face. Oh, I wish he didn't dislike Duncan!

Who walked in with the aloof expression doctors can assume like an extra garment. I got a nod, a slight smile, but no blaze of feeling from his eyes.

I invited him to sit down, with a glare for Toby, who ignored it and remained standing by the door.

"No, I can't stay, thank you. As you probably know," he went on in his best clinical manner, "there is some gossip circulating through Queens about us." When my mouth opened, he waved it shut. "Because of it, one of the registrars in the Psych Pavilion came to see me today to ask me about *my* Harriet Purcell. He'd seen the name on a police report and a Child Welfare report, and he wanted to know if the Harriet Purcell of the gossip could possibly be the same Harriet Purcell. I asked him why he chose to approach me instead of you, and he said he thought it unwise until he had verification from"—a tiny, wry smile—"a sensible man."

"Flo," I said as he paused. "It's Flo."

"She's in the Psych Pavilion, Harriet, admitted there two days ago from a Child Welfare centre."

My knees stopped working, I sat down in a hurry and stared up at him. "What's the matter with her, Duncan?"

"He didn't tell me, and I didn't ask. His name is Prendergast, John Prendergast, and he said to tell you that he'd be in Psych all day tomorrow.

He's very anxious to interview you."

Tears started pouring down my face, the first I'd shed since they took my angel away. Maybe if Duncan hadn't been hampered by Toby's presence, or Toby by Duncan's presence, they might have attempted to comfort me. As it was, when I covered my face with my hands and wept harder, they left me to it.

Just before the door closed, I heard Toby say to Duncan, "Isn't it a pisser that she doesn't love either of us a tenth as much as she does that child?"

Angel, angel, you're on your way home! Now that I've found you, nothing will keep us apart. Child Welfare have put you on my turf, which is a lot closer to home than Yasmar.

Tuesday,
February 21st, 1961

It's pretty new for general hospitals to have psychiatric wards. Only the big teaching hospitals do, and the inmates are not the poor sad chronic epileptics, tertiary syphilitics, senile and other dementias of places like Callan Park and Gladesville. They're all patients whose symptoms are not so firmly based in organic brain damage—schizophrenics and manic depressives in the main, though I'm not very up on psychiatry. When I was doing routine chests I'd get an occasional girl with anorexia nervosa, but that was about it.

So the Psych Pavilion is a new building, the only one not clad in glass with aluminium framing. It's very solid red brick with few windows, and what windows there are have bars. There's a huge steel double door around the back for servicing, but apart from it, the place has just one door, another steel affair with an inch-thick glass panel in it, reinforced with steel webbing. When I got to it just after four o'clock, I saw that it had two separate locks with the insides on the outside. So I had no trouble getting in, all I had to do was turn both knobs simultaneously, but the moment the door closed after me, I saw that in order to get out, I'd need two different keys. A bit like a jail, I suppose.

It's air-conditioned and very nicely decorated. How on earth had they prevailed upon Matron to let them run riot with brilliant colours and fabrics? That's easy to answer. The whole world, even Matron, retreats before Mania. All our defences cannot cope with those who suffer disorders of reason because you can't reason with them. It's a very frightening thought. The four floors are neatly split. Labs and offices on the ground, male patients on one, female patients on two, and child patients up the top on three. The receptionist buzzed Dr. John Prendergast and told me to take the lift all the way up to the third floor, where he'd meet me.

A big teddy bear of a man, curly brown hair, grey eyes, the build of a Rugby player. He ushered me into his office, seated me and went behind his desk, which always disadvantages the visitor. Even as we went through the pleasantries, I realised that he's a cunning bastard. Deceptively mild and dopey. Well, you don't fool me, I thought. I'm not only sane, I'm *smart*. You'll get no ammo from me that might explode in *my* face.

"So to Florence—Flo, you call her?" he asked.

"Flo is what her mother called her. As far as I know, Flo is her proper name. Florence is a Child Welfare presumption."

"You don't like Child Welfare," he said, not a question.

"I have no reason to like Child Welfare, sir."

"The reports say the child was neglected. Was she abused too?"

"Flo was neither neglected nor abused!" I snapped. "She was her mother's angel and the recipient of enormous love. Mrs. Delvecchio Schwartz may not have been an orthodox mother, but she was a very caring one. Flo isn't your average child, either."

After that outburst I forced myself to be calm, self-possessed, alert. I told Prendergast what kind of life Flo had led, about the lack of interest in material comforts, about her mother's brain tumour and odd physical appearance, about Flo's arrival on the dunny floor during a tummy ache, about the doctor who had prescribed the hormone which had resulted in Flo.

"Why has Flo been admitted to Queens?" I asked.

"Suspicion of derangement."

"You surely don't believe that!" I gasped.

"I'm not making any judgements of any kind, Miss Purcell. I think it's going to be weeks before we have the slightest idea what Flo's problems are—how much of her present state is due to what she witnessed, how much of it has always been there. Does she talk?"

"Never, sir, in anyone's hearing, though her mother insisted that she does talk. I've discovered that the reading centres in her brain are either badly impaired or simply not there."

"What kind of child is she?" he asked curiously.

"Hypersensitive to emotion in others, extremely intelligent, very sweet and gentle. She was so afraid of her mother's murderer that she'd bolt under the couch even before he appeared, though no one else except me considered him dangerous."

And so it went, on and on and on, a bit like a fencing match. He knew I wasn't telling him everything, I knew he was trying to trap me. Impasse.

"The police and Child Welfare files say that Flo was present in the room when her mother was murdered. After both parties were dead, she remained in that room without attempting to summon help. And she used the blood to finger-paint on the walls," he said, frowning and shifting in his seat as he stared at me. "You don't seem at all surprised that Flo defaced the room—why?"

I gazed at him blankly. "Because Flo scribbled," I said.

"Scribbled?"

Well, well! No doubt because they regarded both house and child as shockingly neglected, Child Welfare hadn't mentioned the scribbling! They'd missed its significance.

"Flo," I said, "scribbled all over her mother's walls. She was allowed to scribble, it was her favourite—almost only—occupation. That's why Flo and the blood came as no surprise."

He huffed and got up. "Would you like to see Flo?"

"Would I!"

As we walked down the corridor he deplored the locks on the door to the outside world, the bars on the windows. The new drugs were making such a difference to patient behaviour that security measures weren't necessary. "But," he said with a sigh, "general hospital wheels turn very slowly. R.P.A. has abolished its locks, so it's only a matter of time before Queens does."

Flo was in her own little room, attended by a nurse who wore not only the badge of her general training, but a psychiatric one as well. My angel was sitting quietly in her cot, so thin and small in her skimpy little hospital gown that I wanted to weep. My horrified eyes took in the heavy canvas bodice buckled over her shoulders and across her back with leather straps. From the bodice to the underside of the cot, stout ropes held her so that she could sit up or lie down easily, but couldn't get to her feet.

I stood stunned. "Heavy duty restriction harness on *Flo*?"

Prendergast ignored me, went to the cot and let down its side railing. "Hello, Flo," he smiled at her. "I have a very special visitor for you."

The enormous sad eyes stared at me in wonder, then the rosebud mouth broke into a huge smile, and Flo held out both arms to me. I sank onto the mattress, enfolded her in a hug and patted kisses all over her weeny face. Angel, my angel! And she kissed me, stroked me, snuggled against me and looked into my face. Put *this* in your pipe and smoke it, Dr. Bloody John Bloody Prendergast! No one watching could mistake Flo's delight in seeing me.

For a long time I was conscious of nothing except the joy of holding her. Then, looking at her properly, I saw the bruises. Flo's arms and legs were mottled with great blue-black patches.

"She's been beaten!" I yelled. "Who? Who *dared*? I'll have the whole of Child Welfare pilloried!"

"Calm down, Harriet, calm down," Prendergast said. "Flo did this to herself, here as well as at the child shelter. That's why she's tied down. You may not believe it, but this shrimpy little creature tore the calico restriction harness to shreds—not once, but half a dozen times. We had no choice other than to resort to leather and rope."

"Why?" I asked, still doubting.

"Trying to escape, we think. The moment she's free, Flo takes off, literally throws herself at the nearest object. I've seen her myself, cannoning into the wall time and time again. She doesn't care how badly she hurts herself. At the child shelter she went through a plate glass window one floor up. That's why they sent her here. How she didn't kill herself or break anything, we'll never know, but she was badly lacerated." His big, well-shaped hand slid her short gown up a trifle to let me see the neat rows of stitches on the inside of both thighs. "It was either heavy restriction harness or heavy sedation, and we don't like sedation in here. It's convenient for the staff, but it masks symptoms and delays diagnosis."

"Her pubes?" I whispered.

"Stitched too, I'm afraid. We called the plastic surgeons in for a consultation, but they think she'll be fine as is. Whoever sutured her up in R.P.A. Cas did a brilliant job."

"R.P.A. Cas, eh? Then Flo was in Yasmar," I said.

"I didn't say that, nor will I."

"Why wasn't Flo admitted to R.P.A. psych?"

"No bed," he said simply. "Besides, we're the premier unit for small children."

"Anyway," I said triumphantly, "it all proves one thing. This is Flo's way of getting what she wants, and she wants *me*. She was willing to run the risk of dying to find me. That says a lot."

He eyed me speculatively. "Yes, she certainly wants you. Um, would you persuade her to be less frantic?" he asked.

My lip curled. "Not in a fit, ace!"

"Why, for God's sake?" he demanded.

"Because I do not choose to. Why should I help you lot soften her up until she's malleable enough to be sent back to Yasmar? Flo is *mine*. If her mother could speak, I know she'd say so. That's why I'm applying for custody," I said.

"You're young and single, Miss Purcell. You'll never get her."

"So everybody says, but ask me if I care what everybody says. I'll get Flo." I smiled at her. "Won't I, angel?"

Flo closed her eyes, stuck her thumb in her mouth and began to hum her tune through it.

They let me stay with her for half an hour, though Prendergast never let up on me, tried every way he knew to find out what I was hiding. Crafty bugger, he knows there's a lot more to it than I'll admit. Fish away, ace, fish away! You won't crack me. I'm a big old gum tree, her mother said so.

When the secretary emerged from her cubbyhole to unlock the door for me, she handed me a sealed envelope. "Dr. Forsythe asked me to give you this," she said with total lack of curiosity. Like a patient on chlorpromazine. Well, maybe she is.

The note asked if I'd meet him in the coffee lounge underneath the railway station at Circular Quay at six o'clock. An hour hence. I decided to walk, just dream the miles away in a happy haze. No, I don't have Flo yet, but at least I know where she is. After this, Child Welfare will know that I'm a force to be reckoned with, hur-hur-hur. Little Florence Schwartz *wants* me! Even if she's sent back to a shelter, they won't be able to keep me away from her. Dr. John Prendergast may be a nosy bastard, but his report is going to say unequivocally that Florence Schwartz is emotionally dependent on a twenty-two-year-old spinster who has to work for a living. Let the grey ghosts wrestle with that one! Ripper-ace.

As I reached the rather dirty gloom underneath the Circular Quay railway station, I realised that all of this had happened on or next to the day that I looked into the Glass. Is *that* what scrying consists of? Could it be that the scryer doesn't actually see things, but that the act of focusing all that mental energy into an object with exquisitely arranged molecules has the ability to change events? What a thought!

So when I entered the deserted coffee shop, my mind wasn't on Duncan. In fact, for a moment I wondered what I was doing there. Then he came around the bulk of the Gaggia machine, gave me a smile of delighted pleasure, and held out my chair for me. The moment I was seated, he picked up my hand and kissed it, gazed at me with so much love in his eyes that I melted. He can do that to me every time. Oh, why is he such a victim of convention?

"It's a pity," I said, still fizzing over Flo and the Glass, "that a man can't cut himself in half. The half of you that the Missus wants, I definitely don't want, and the half of you that I want, the Missus definitely doesn't want. But I've decided that that is the whole problem with men as far as women are concerned. We only ever want about half a man."

He wasn't in the least offended. In fact, he grinned. "It's wonderful to see you right back on form, my love," he said tenderly. "If an eighth is all you want, then feel free to start dissecting immediately."

I squeezed his hand. "You know I can't. I have to keep my nose clean to get custody of Flo."

Then we both realised that the waitress was standing patiently waiting to take our orders. Listening enthralled.

"I beg your pardon, my dear," he said to her, and ordered two cappuccinos. The girl shuffled away looking as if the Pope had granted her a private audience. Duncan's good manners have the most extraordinary effect on women. Just goes to show we're not used to being treated like delicate flowers.

I told him all about Flo and Dr. John Prendergast, and he did listen as if it really mattered to him. It can't, I know that, except that I know he feels a great deal for me, and I suppose, feeling a great deal, it can matter.

"You have an air," he said at the end of my tale, "of having just completed a walk across hot coals." He studied the palm of my hand as if it held the answer to a riddle. "I wonder why I looked at you and loved you? A millisecond on a ramp, and I was done for. Is it because you belong to the world of

321

Kings Cross? A denizen of an awful old house seething with cockroaches, a walker rather than a driver, a drinker of cheap brandy, a devotee of the bizarre, the tawdry, the frankly undesirable."

"Your tongue, ace," I grinned, "is touched with honey." "No, it isn't," he said instantly, and bit my hand. "Let me come home with you and it'll soon find the honey." The cappuccinos arrived. Duncan smiled at the waitress and thanked her—two audiences with the Pope! "Why did you arrange this rendezvous?" I asked. "Just to see you on your own," he answered. "Mr. Toby Evans seems to have moved into my territory."

"No, he's got his own territory," I said, licking the fluff off my spoon. My happiness flooded back. "Oh, Duncan, the joy of finding my angel!"

"How are you off for money?" he asked.

"Fine," I said.

"If you need it, you know where to come." But he knows I can't accept money from him. Still, it's nice of him to offer. I miss him, I'm never so conscious of it as when I'm with him again, even for a cappuccino at the Quay.

When I got up to go, I leaned across the table and kissed him hungrily, lips and tongue, and he kissed me back, one hand brushing a breast. The waitress was looking at us as if we were Heathcliff and Catherine.

"I'll never be able to stay away from you," he said.

"Good!" I walked out and left him to pay the bill.

They were all waiting to hear about Flo when I walked in. As probationers don't go on the wards for the first three months, our Pappy is home in the evenings too. She'd made a whole heap of Chinese food, which we carried up to Toby's attic because it's the biggest room in the house and the views are marvellous. Funny, that. Toby used to be quite frantic at the very thought of people invading him in case someone left the mark of a rubber heel on his white floor, or chipped the table, or anything. But these days he's more amenable, maybe because we've imposed a few rules of our own, like all shoes off before we go up the ladder, and don't offer to wash the dishes. Truth is, I suspect, that even Toby is missing Mrs. Delvecchio Schwartz, though we hear her every night.

Of course they know as well as I do that I'm actually not a scrap closer to getting Flo than I was before I found out where she is, but it makes such a difference to know where she is, and to know that we can all visit her. I checked that with Prendergast, who of course will be present to hear what's said and see what we all look like, etc. But he won't get any further with a one of them than he did today with me. Crossites are used to keeping secrets from officialdom. No one was surprised that our angel had gone through a plate glass window and no one was surprised that she'd survived it, though Bob cried terribly when I described the lacerations. She has a tender heart. Klaus thought it would be nice to bring his violin to the hospital and play for her— I didn't tell him that I thought there might be objections. Once they hear that bow drawn across the strings, they'll change their minds. I suppose it was the War ruined any chance Klaus had to make music his career, but the world's loss is our gain, and he's such a sweet chap, in love with his budgies. They're *all* so nice.

What we don't talk about when we're together is the future. The Public Trustee, a bit bolder now that almost two months have passed without a will turning up, sent a fellow to inspect The House when only Pappy was home. Oh, the waste! he clucked when he realised that two flats and a room were untenanted. And why were the rents so cheap? So we expect that in another couple of months, maybe sooner, strangers will move into the front ground floor flat, Harold's room, and Mrs. Delvecchio Schwartz's quarters. How can you tell the Public Trustee about front ground floor flats at Kings Cross? There will be sailors everywhere again. Jim reported that she'd spoken to Joe the Q.C., whose considered opinion is that our rents can't be increased without a lot of Fair Rent Board fuss, because the landlady herself had pegged them years ago. It's more the thought of having people in The House who haven't been hand-picked. I mean, the thing is that this is Kings Cross, so the flats aren't really flats and the rooms are pretty awful. *It's under the lap!* Now we've got the bloody Public Trustee peering up our skirts. Once they take full control, there'll be a major earthquake, and they're likely to spend a good part of Flo's bank book inheritance turning The House into something that fits the full meaning of the Act, whichever Act they decide is applicable. They'll probably ban scribbling on the walls.

When the rest departed, I lingered.

Toby hadn't had a lot to say, just sat on the floor with his legs crossed and listened, his eyes going from face to face. They look redder than they ought to, a sure sign that something is on his mind or his temper's ruffled. Some of it, I am convinced, is Flo. Oh, he was always kind to her, but she hasn't the power over him that she has over the rest of us. Toby resists, which may be a part of that Australianness. Let a woman have power over him? Not on!

"Having second thoughts about keeping your room here?" I asked as he commenced to wash the dishes.

His back was to me. "No."

"Then what is biting you?"

"Nothing."

I went round the corner of the sink and leaned against the cupboard so I could see at least a profile. "Something is. Flo?"

He turned his head to look at me. "Flo's none of my business."

"And that's the trouble. To the rest of us, she's very much our business. Why isn't she yours, an orphaned child?"

"Because she's going to ruin your life," he said to the sink.

"Flo could never do that, Toby," I said gently.

"You don't understand," he said through his teeth.

"No, I don't. So why don't you tell me?" I asked.

"You'll be tying yourself down to someone who isn't even the full quid. There's something wrong with Flo, and you're just the sort who's going to spend the next twenty years worrying about her, dragging her to doctors, spending money you don't have." He let the water out of the sink.

"What about the bank books?" I asked.

"That was then. This is now. There isn't a will, Harriet, and governments being governments, the kid will never see a penny of what her mother had. She's going to be a burden resting solidly on you, and you're going to make yourself old before your time."

I sat down in an easy chair, frowning. "So this is about me, not about Flo?"

"There's only one person in this house I'd go to the wall for, Harriet, and that's you. I can't bear the thought of you turning into one of those drab, defeated women you see all over Sydney, with kids in tow and the old man at the pub," he said, pacing.

"Ye gods!" I said feebly. "You mean its *me* you're in love with? Is that why—"

"You're as blind as a fucking bat, Harriet," he interrupted. "I can understand why you fell for

Forsythe the big important bone specialist, but I can't understand why you fell for Flo."

"Oh, this is awful!" I cried.

"Why, because you don't love me?" he demanded. "I'm used to that, I can live with it."

"No, that you're telling me this with no love," I tried to explain. "This ought to be said in a mood I can respond to, but instead you're pounding my head about a kind of love which has nothing to do with any grown man! I can't explain Flo, Toby, I looked at her and loved her, that's all."

"And I looked at you and loved you that day you whopped David a beauty on the verandah," he said, grinning. "And no doubt the big important bone specialist looked at you and loved you the first time he saw you."

"He says so. It was on a ramp at Queens. So we all looked and loved. But it hasn't got us very far, has it? The only one of us prepared to make the total commitment is me, but not to you and not to Duncan." I got up. "It's very mysterious, don't you think?" I walked over to him, kissed the tips of my fingers and put them on his forehead. "Maybe one day we'll manage to sort it out, ace, hur-hur-hur."

**Wednesday,
March 15th, 1961**
Two and a half months since Mrs. Delvecchio Schwartz died, and nothing has been resolved.

According to Mr. Hush, they will soon decide that she died intestate. The whole thing is going to have to go to some sort of child court, because Mr. Schwartz doesn't exist and nor, officially, does Flo. Who continues to stay in the Queens Psych Pavilion being subjected to every kind of test there is from EEGs to batteries of neuropsychological investigations. None of which has told Prendergast and his professor a thing. The EEGs are normal, have a beautiful, high-amplitude, properly modulated alpha rhythm that appears when Flo closes her eyes. They've had fun inventing IQ tests a mute but intelligent and hearing child can answer, except that she won't. The only people she's happy to see are visitors from The House. Though every nurse and psychiatrist and therapist knows her very well by now, Flo refuses to chum up with anyone who isn't from The House.

"Why are you continuing to keep her here?" I asked Prendergast today when I paid my call as soon as work was finished.

"Because she's better off here than in a shelter," he answered, frowning. "At least here she can have her visitors without a fuss. Though the real reason is that Prof Llewllyn and I think we may be looking at a case of what used to be called juvenile schizophrenia, but now is beginning to be called autism. She's not the classical syndrome by any means, but there are characteristic signs. It isn't often that we have a chance to keep a child as young as Flo for so long—parents are always anxious to have them home, no matter how difficult they can be to handle. So Flo is a godsend to us." He looked wistful. "We'd like to give her angiograms, put some air into her brain to see whether she has a lesion in the word areas or some cortical atrophy, but the risks are too great."

"You'd better keep on thinking that!" I snapped. "Try using her as a guinea pig, and I'll go to the newspapers!"

"Peace, peace!" he cried, palms up. "We simply observe."

I feel permanently tired, impotent, despondent. My work hasn't suffered because I won't let it suffer, but the truth is that I am fed up with hospitals. The discipline, the rituals, the constant battle with the women in authority. If you want to fart, you have to get permission. And Sister Agatha keeps a vigilant eye on me thanks to Harold and his letter. No one has ever unearthed a shred of evidence to confirm the rumoured affair between Duncan and me, but they're dying to. For what purpose, I have no idea. I can't be sacked for it, and Duncan can't be made suffer for it. What the place needs is a new scandal with some meat to it, but so far Queens is being unusually well-behaved on the scandal front.

Sister Cas and Constantin are engaged, though they're not planning on marrying before the end of the year. Something to do with Constantin's opening a restaurant in Parramatta, where it can have a decent parking area and offer a menu suitable for the Parramatta populace, a pretty steak-and-chippy lot. Nice.

Naturally the whole place knows that I visit a child in the Psych Pavilion every day, though no one has managed to find out quite why. Gossip is rife among the sisters, including those in psych nursing, but no one's got wind of my custody application.

Which is going nowhere very fast. I have a weekly chat on the phone with Mr. Hush, who keeps warning me that even after all the hearings about Flo are over and she's slipped into an official pigeonhole, I can't expect to get custody. I'm punting on Dr. John Prendergast's report, but Mr. Hush doesn't think it will have the weight with Child Welfare that I want it to. If Flo ends up diagnosed as a juvenile schizophrenic, they may send her to— of all places!—Stockton. This, despite the fact that her psychiatric history has rendered her unadoptable or fosterable! You'd think they'd grab at my offer, but no. I'm too young, too poor and too unmarried. It just isn't fair.

"Harriet," Mr. Hush said to me this afternoon, "you have to understand the official mind. To decide in your favour in the matter of Florence Schwartz would require a kind of wisdom and courage that official bodies don't dare possess. It all boils down to the art of keeping the nose clean. They're too aware that if someone having an axe to grind got hold of such an unorthodox adoption or fostering, there could be a terrific stink, and they'd be blamed. So they will not run the risk, my dear. They simply won't."

Ducky. Just ducky. She's sitting there in her heavy duty restriction harness living from visit to visit, and there's nothing I can do to get her out. Oh, but there have been some wild schemes chasing through my head! The first was to propose marriage to Toby, but that didn't last much longer than the lightbulb flashing on. If Toby condoned a child, the child would have to be his and only his. And a son, not a daughter. I love the man in so many ways—he's straight as an arrow, brilliant, going places, great fun to be with, and very attractive. Part-time, terrific. Full-time, a pain in the arse. Then I had another brainwave which I'm still mulling over. I could kidnap Flo and skip the state, eventually skip the country. Australia is a very big place. If the pair of us headed for Alice Springs or the Katherine and I worked as a domestic in some Outback motel, no one would question Flo. She'd simply spend her time playing in the dust with the Abo kids, who wouldn't mind her muteness in the least—would probably read her thoughts the way her mother had. She'd be a part of a spiritual commune, and when I was off duty, she'd be with me. The scheme has its points.

I have the tarot pack off by heart, though I still haven't tried a spread. That's just an idle remark intended to branch me away from what I'm now going to say. That my hands aren't quite steady, that my eyes are scratchy, that I feel as if the machinery of my body is wearing out or running down.

Ridiculous, I know. It's a mood, it will pass. Oh, if only *something* would happen!

I still gaze into the Glass every night after Mrs. Delvecchio Schwartz wakes me up at ten past three. It was a lovely theory I had when Duncan found Flo, but events haven't confirmed it. So I must assume that Duncan's finding Flo that day was a coincidence.

Friday,
March 24th, 1961
Something odd happened this evening. When the door bell rang shortly after six, I went to answer it because none of the men were home. And there on the verandah stood Madame Fugue from 17d. Oh, dear! What *is* her proper name?

"How nice to see you," I said, compromising.

"Nice to see you too, dahling," she cooed.

"Would you like to come in? Have a coffee?"

She said no, she had to get back next door before business got too brisk, but she was, um, wondering, um, if, um, we had any, um, plans for the vacant rooms? "Some of my girls are interested," she concluded.

How peculiar! Jim and Bob arrived on the Harley Davidson at that moment, and joined me as I was explaining to Madame that the Public Trustee was in control of things, and we hadn't heard yet when they were planning to rent out the vacant premises.

"Fuckin' old women!" she said, and departed,

leaving a strong aroma of Patou's *Joy* behind her.

"Business must be good," I said to Jim. "I believe that stuff costs more than diamonds or truffles."

"Well, she was wearing plenty of diamonds, too, unless you think her earrings and pendant are hunks of bottle," said Jim.

"It isn't fair, is it?" asked Bob a little wistfully. "Good girls like you and camp girls like me are lucky if we get a two-bob box of Black Magic chocolates."

I grabbed at the door knob in shock. "Bob! Do you mean to say that Jim gives you *a whole box* of Black Magic choccies?"

Bob leered to show her Dracula canines. "Jim loves me."

"Well, I'm seriously thinking of asking Madame Fugue for a few tips on how to get started in the game," I said. "The game's one way to earn a decent—oops, indecent— living at home! It would also provide Flo with heaps of uncles."

Jim was frowning, but not at the banter. "You know, Harry, that was a very odd thing for the Madame to do. She has to know that it isn't in our power to rent rooms. I wonder what she was really after?"

"I haven't a clue," I said.

Bob suddenly whooped with laughter. "I wonder what the Child Welfare would say if they knew about 17b and 17d? Ooooooo-aa!"

But they know about 17b and 17d, of course they

know. Jim was right, however, Madame Fugue's appearance was peculiar. What could she have been fishing for? Though I suspect that Child Welfare wasn't as shocked by the brothels next door as Miss Arf-Arf was on her second visit when she saw the winged phallus embroidered on the inside thigh of Jim's jeans. Whereas she was hugely impressed by Lady Richard, on Jim's arm. Alone among us, Lady Richard has gone into traditional formal mourning for Mrs. Delvecchio Schwartz. Still in black, though shortly, he announced, he would be able to wear lilacs and greys. Even, if the occasion warrants it, white.

Tuesday,
April 4th, 1961

Mr. Hush's secretary phoned me at work this morning and asked if I could be in his chambers at two o'clock. Not a request, my instincts said. A summons. Which meant that I had to see Sister Agatha and inform her that I'd have to leave Cas X-ray early. It wasn't a particularly busy day, but that, of course, isn't relevant.

"Really, Miss Purcell," Sister Agatha began in peevish tones, "this downing tools and flying off at a moment's notice has become a rather nasty habit of yours lately. It isn't good enough."

"Sister Toppingham," I said stiffly, "you exaggerate. The occasions when I have taken time off work this year amount to three. January the second, January the eleventh and January the thirteenth. I *did* attend a funeral on that Friday the Thirteenth, as a matter of fact, however inappropriate you may consider the date. I did not ask to be paid for any of those absences, and I am not asking to be paid for the two hours you will lose from me this afternoon. Miss Smith and the junior can cope, it's quiet in Cas. And yes, I know that I am inconveniencing you, Sister, but it is no more than an inconvenience. This hospital will not cease to function at optimum level because I will not be here."

She gobbled just like the Missus. "You are impertinent, Miss Purcell!" was the best retort she could muster.

"No, Sister Toppingham, I am not impertinent. I am merely doing the unpardonable by sticking up for myself," I said.

Sister Agatha reached for a register. "You may go, *madam*. I assure you that I will not forget this."

Oooooo-aa! I'll bet the old bitch won't forget it either. Ah, but it felt good as the Purcell worm turned over!

Mr. Hush's mood was little better than Sister Agatha's. His face looked as if he'd just discovered that the meat chiller had died a minute after he closed the shop for a long weekend.

"I went to see Child Welfare yesterday," he said, "with a view to lodging a formal application to adopt Florence Schwartz. I'm afraid that their reaction was more adamantly against you than I had expected, Miss Purcell. Simply, they informed me that you are not morally fit to have charge of a child."

"*Morally fit?*"

"That is the term. Morally fit. First, there is the matter of the two houses of ill fame which flank your late landlady's premises, in which you intend to rear the child, who is *debatably* her heir. Secondly, one of the Child Welfare officers interviewed Mrs. Duncan Forsythe. Apparently there is a rumour about you and Dr. Forsythe going about, and this officer was apprised of it by a Queens friend. Mrs. Duncan Forsythe left you without a feather to fly with." His face indicated that the meat was badly off. "I'm very sorry, but that is the situation."

"The bitch! I'm going to kill her," I said slowly.

He looked at me sympathetically. "I agree that it would do your heart good to kill her, Harriet, but it won't help Flo, now will it?" The knives came out, he selected one sharp enough not to cause me too much pain. "Child Welfare also notified me that Flo is about to be discharged from Royal Queens. The diagnosis is a nonspecific form of autism, which means that she will be sent to an appropriate institution."

"Stockton," I said hollowly.

"Highly unlikely. Child Welfare is conscious that Flo has a group of regular visitors who are based in Sydney. I imagine she will be sent to Gladesville."

"Exit Flo, neatly pigeonholed." I looked straight at him. "Mr. Hush, I don't care what Child Welfare say, I want that formal application lodged. And every time I'm turned down, lodge another one. For years, if necessary. When Flo is a grown woman, I want her to know that I tried and tried and tried. *If she's still alive, which I doubt. That's the real tragedy.*"

I walked home across the Domain, kicked my shoes off, peeled my stockings off and felt the tough, springy grass fight my feet. Oh, why had I publicly humiliated the Missus? Dragged her out of her car under the Mesdames' noses, chucked her back in after I'd said my piece? Shown her just how small and petty she is? Well, she's had her revenge. Except that I think she'd have done the same even if I hadn't flown up her. But I am going to get the Missus, oh yes. Starting next week. Since I've already been judged morally unfit, what does it matter if I have gentlemen visit my flat? I'll ring Duncan up at home and invite him over for the entire night. If you want to play dirty, Mrs. Forsythe, you're going to find out how dirty dirt can be. Cockroaches . . . I'll catch a giant mortuary jar full of them and let them loose in your poncy little Pommy car. Huge ones that fly, hur-hur-hur. I'll picket the next Black and White Committee meeting with a big placard that says MRS. DUNCAN FORSYTHE DOESN'T GIVE HER HUSBAND ANY NOOKY AND THAT'S WHY HE'S TAKEN UP WITH A MORALLY UNFIT GIRL YOUNG ENOUGH TO BE HIS DAUGHTER.

Nice thoughts. They carried me as far as Woolloomooloo, where I put my shoes on and stopped thinking of things to do to the Missus that I know I can't because they'll rebound on Duncan. However, the cockroaches are feasible. And the invitation to Duncan to spend a night in my arms is a definite. Even better, I'll curse her. B.O. and halitosis. Intractable thrush. Heaps of weight no matter how she starves herself. Wrinkles. Swelling of the feet and ankles so gross that it flops over the edges of her shoes and wobbles. Conjunctivitis. Dandruff. Worms that lay their eggs in the anus so she has to pick her bum in public. Oh, yes! Sicken slowly, Mrs. Forsythe! Die of thwarted vanity! May all your mirrors crack when you look in them, may your haute couture clothes turn into hessian bags and plumber's boots.

That got me as far as the McElhone Stairs, where, halfway up, I stood and cried. Flo, my Flo! Angel! How am I ever going to get you home again?

I was still crying when I let myself in the door, where even through the grey wall of tears I could see how much the scribbles have faded. She's going away from me, I'll have to sit on the sidelines of her institutionalised life, breaking my heart because I can't spend all day every day there with her. I'm young, poor and unmarried. I have to work. I have to go tomorrow and apologise to Sister Agatha. God rot you, Mrs. Duncan Forsythe, with your spiteful barbs. You're in the process of ruining more lives than your spineless mug of a husband's.

I threw myself onto my bed and howled myself to sleep, woke up after dark. 17d's windows glowed iridescent mauve, the usual chatter and laughter floated down, and one screaming fight between Prudence and Constance, who never can get on together. Good luck to you, ladies, I thought as I dealt with my indignant cat. There are worse ways to make a better living. A lot worse ways, Mrs. Bloody Duncan Parasite Forsythe.

Well, it will have to be the kidnap, a flight to somewhere like the Northern Territory, where men are men and women are in short supply. A terrible wrench. I can't even tell Mum and Dad what I'm planning, nor contact them after I find a place to live. Flo and I must disappear off the map. Tell one person a secret, and it's no longer a secret. I'll have to empty my bank account in cash, hide it in a bag under Flo's pinny. Drab clothes. We'll have to look as if we're on the breadline. Flo's own stuff is perfect, but I'll have to rat around in the cast-offs at the Salvos or St. Vincent de Or—joke, hur-hur-hur. Yes, I can do it. Why? Because I'm smart enough to keep track of all the threads in a tissue of lies. My husband deserted me—that's a good, standard story. Australia's chocka with deserted wives. *Buy wedding ring*. My poor wee daughter misses her daddy so much that she won't talk. No, that doesn't sound right—why would she miss a bastard who did the dirty on her mum? She doesn't talk because a bit of her brain went wrong after her daddy hit her in a drunken rage. Yes, that sounds convincing. *Marceline!* My poor old boy had trusted me with his angel—how can I let him down? But I have to—cats don't travel. Or do they? If Marceline has her canvas shopping bag, maybe she will travel. I'll do a dummy run to the Blue Mountains with her. If she copes with that, then I'll take both my angels to the Outback.

. . . This is written later, much later. It must have been nearly midnight when I stopped pacing up and down, plotting and scheming, working out the logistics. I hadn't eaten, but I wasn't hungry. Didn't feel like coffee or tea, didn't feel like a snort of the old three-star. Felt like something Marceline sicked up, actually. At least I don't have to worry any more about Harold and my diaries. The old ones are back in the Tilsiter cupboard.

As I went to the table the Glass caught my eye—well, it's the most eye-catching thing in the whole room. Sitting in its usual spot, glowing pinkly. Fraud of a thing. *Oozing* drama. I was debating whether to scry before I went to bed, instead of after the old girl wakes me up with the nightly gallop and guffaw. Maybe if I did that, the Glass would work for me? Bugger it, no! I sat down with a flop and vowed that never again would I abase myself before a hunk of silicon dioxide. Plain old melted sand.

So I sat there and thought about how horrible everybody had been to me today. Worse by far, they'd been terminally horrible to Flo. And all angry-horrible, not flat-and-depressed horrible. Angry-horrible's unbearable without a head to wallop or some balls to knee. Don't think those awful Child Welfare females don't have balls. They do, and just as big as any other species of rat.

I looked at the Glass, and a weird thought popped into my mind. What is the matter with Mrs. Delvecchio Schwartz? If that's her upstairs every night, then she's still haunting the earthly plane. In which case, *why* is she letting them kill her angel? *Why* has she left such a mess behind? She *must* have known that she was leaving a mess behind! Therefore she must also have left an answer. She was very stupid about some things, but she was also very clever. Only two clues given to me: that the fate of The House is in the Glass; that it depends on the Glass. *Would* she have believed in herself and her powers so ardently that she assumed I'd see everything revealed in the Glass? She put my hands on it, sort of blessed me. But I can't see a thing in the Glass! I've been trying for a month, and nothing. Absolutely nothing.

I glared at the thing fiercely, at its dreamy pink upsidedown rendition of my room. The fate of The House is in the Glass. It all depends on the Glass. I grabbed it and did the unspeakable, freed it from its base by lifting it in both my hands. When I put it down, it started to roll. I steadied it. No vibrations, no peculiar electrical thrills. It's just a very heavy blob of pressure-liquefied silica. The table evidently sloped toward the side away from me, so I shoved the butter dish behind my nemesis and halted it, transferred my gaze to its base. The small circle of padding between it and the black wood isn't silk, it's velvet, the pile squashed and shined by the weight of the Glass itself.

Oh, Harriet Purcell, you drongo! *How could you be so thick?* The answer has been sitting here for four months!

I lifted the base and began to pick at the fabric where it overlapped the wood in a tiny roll, freeing it a weeny bit at a time because the glue was very efficient. But the glue didn't go under the ball, it only held the edges down. And there, beneath the velvet, was a folded piece of paper resting in a shallow cavity that she must have gouged for it with a chisel. A cheap, printed will form of the kind one buys from a newsagency or a stationer's. Diabolical. The time she must have spent devising this final riddle, taking a punt on her whole world, including her angel. She didn't even hedge her bets, she put it all on the nose. *My* nose for a mystery, a puzzle. She wasn't even fair about the two clues. The fate of The House wasn't in the Glass, it was *under* the Glass. One tiny little word. If she'd used the correct preposition, I would have found the will in a day, maybe less. But no, not her. That was too simple, too tame.

The will wasn't very long. It said that all her goods and properties and moneys were bequeathed to Flo Schwartz, her only child, to be held in trust during Flo's minority by her dear friend Miss Harriet Purcell of the same address, who was at liberty to dispose of all income as she wished. And that she consigned the care and custody of Flo Schwartz, her only child, to the said Miss Harriet Purcell, being of the opinion that the said Miss Harriet Purcell would rear Flo as she would want. It was signed Harriet Purcell Delvecchio Schwartz, and there were two witnesses. An Otto Werner and a Fritz Werner, neither of whom I knew from a bar of soap. Brothers? Father and son?

Harriet Purcell! Mrs. Delvecchio Schwartz had been born a Harriet Purcell. The missing generation. But if from Dad's lot, then he wasn't told about her. That's possible, if from her birth she looked *wrong*. Nineteenth century parents were very odd about offspring who looked wrong—would bundle them away to a home, hide them as if a disgrace. It's highly possible that she's a close relative—Dad's sister? He was born in 1882, and she would have been born around 1905. Or what if she'd been born around 1902, while Dad was in South Africa fighting in the Boer War? Dad has twin sisters born later than he, in 1900—a great embarrassment, he always says, laughing. What if, after Auntie Ida and Auntie Joan, there was *another* daughter? Who looked wrong, and was hidden away? This is one mystery I'd be willing to bet will never be solved, though it does answer the riddle of why she was called by the family curse name. An onion, Mrs. Delvecchio

Schwartz. Layer upon layer, and at the core, a child-hood she never mentioned to any of us in The House, even Pappy.

I didn't whoop, yell, scream or holler. Too much has happened to believe this is real. I'll wait until I can show the will to Mr. Hush tomorrow morning.

Wednesday,
April 5th, 1961

I woke at six, feeling very strange. If the author of all the above agony galloped and guffawed at ten past three last night, I didn't hear her. My first chore was to telephone Sister Agatha's office and say that I wouldn't be in to work today. No, no reason, sorry, Miss Barker. Private affairs. Then I pottered around in a delicious daze, gave Marceline extra top-of-the-milk, had several cups of coffee, some scrambled eggs and toast, and got dressed in my new fawny-pink autumn outfit, just out of Lay-by. Every so often I unfolded the will and verified that it did indeed say all those wonderful things. It does. It does, it does!

I was on the doorstep of Partington, Pilkington, Purblind and Hush before Miss Hoojar arrived to open the premises. When she told me disdainfully that Mr. Hush was too busy to see me today, I said I'd wait anyway. Half a minute, a quarter of a minute, I don't care, but I *am* seeing him! I said. So I sat down in the reception area, kept peeking at the will, hummed a tune, flapped magazine pages loudly, and generally made such a nuisance of myself that when Mr. Hush came through the door at ten o'clock, Miss Hoojar was ready to throttle me.

"Miss Purcell refused to leave, Mr. Hush!" she bleated.

"Then Miss Purcell had better come in," he said, sighing, resigned to butchering scrag end of neck instead of fillet steak. "I can't give you long, I'm in court most of today."

In answer, I handed him the will.

"Well, strike me pink and turn me blue!" he said after a quick perusal. "Whereabouts did this turn up?"

"I found it last night, sir, hidden beneath the base of Mrs. Delvecchio Schwartz's favourite ornament."

"Is Harriet Purcell really her name?" he asked, eyeing me as if he suspected me of forgery. Then he subjected the will to a minute examination. "It looks genuine—same handwriting as the bank books, dated a year ago. Do you know the witnesses?"

I had to say no, I didn't, but that I'd ask around. "Does it matter?" I asked tensely. "Is anyone going to argue about it? Contest it?"

"My dear Harriet, I would think that everybody is going to greet the mysterious appearance of this document with a sigh of relief. It is the lady's only existing testament, and in it she acknowledges Flo as her child and unequivocally consigns custody of Flo to you. At law, her commands are our commands."

"But Child Welfare aren't going to change their opinion of me, are they, Mr. Hush?"

"Very likely not," he said placidly. "However, the will lifts the responsibility of Flo from their shoulders. They aren't the arbiters of Flo's destiny any longer—and for that, they'll be very, very glad. I might add that the will also endows you with financial independence. You'll be able to live very comfortably on the estate's incomes, so you won't need to work. You're set."

Then he cleared his throat in a suspicious manner. I gave him all my attention. "As there is no executor named, you'll have to decide who you want to handle matters. You can avail yourself of the Public Trustee, or, if you prefer, I can handle probate. I should warn you that the Public Trustee moves at the pace of a tortoise, and that its fees are quite as hefty as those levied by a private firm."

My cue! "I'd prefer that you handle everything, Mr. Hush."

"Good, good!" The scrag end of neck had clearly turned into fillet steak. "You'll appreciate that I've had occasion to talk to the Public Trustee about the estate. Mrs. Delvecchio Schwartz has over one hundred and ten thousand pounds deposited in savings accounts all over Sydney. The source of these funds has baffled the experts, who cannot prove that they represent earned income. Naturally everybody is aware what goes on in 17b and 17d, but both establishments enjoy virtual immunity from, um, official attention, and the experts have had to take the word of their proprietresses that they pay thirty pounds per week in rent. 17a and 17e, though mere rooming houses, also pay thirty pounds a week. That yields one hundred and twenty pounds a week. A good lawyer can argue it is spent upon upkeep, utilities and rates, as all four places are in tiptop condition— something Mrs. Delvecchio Schwartz's own house does not experience, as I understand. The taxation johnnies are in a tizz-wozz, but unless concrete evidence appears, all they are entitled to do is tax the interest and the rents. If Taxation does decide to challenge, a good team of barristers can tie the case up in court for decades. I will, of course, put you in touch with a firm of accountants and financial managers who can advise you what to do with Flo's principal—it earns mere pennies in savings accounts, brrrr! Birdwhistle, Entwhistle, O'Halloran and Goldberg are the best."

So that's what you were after, Madame Fugue! You were fishing to see how much I knew. But don't worry, you're perfectly safe with me. We can't have all those industrialists and politicians and bankers and judges deprived of the opportunity to get rid of their dirty water in pristine premises, now can we? Um, thirty quid a week? In a pig's eye! Three hundred, more like. But, be warned! I am going to drive a hard bargain on Flo's behalf, dear Mesdames. My name isn't Harriet Purcell for nothing.

This future prospect tickled me so much that I leaned across the desk and kissed Mr. Hush on the lips, a salutation he returned with interesting gusto. "Sir, you are a sweetie!"

He giggled. "I must confess I've always thought I was, but it's nice to have confirmation. It would be best if you leave it to me to arrange for Flo's release. In the meantime, I'll make sure that you have enough money to live on until probate is granted. You'll have Flo back well before that day."

I caught a taxi out to Queens, though I didn't go straight to Sister Agatha's office. I went to the Psych Pavilion and caught Dr. John Prendergast on his way to a conference.

"John, John! Mrs. Delvecchio Schwartz left a will which names me as Flo's guardian!" I yelled. "Child Welfare will be handing her over to me very short-ly— yippee!"

His face went very teddy bearish. "Then we'll keep her here for you." He picked me up like a feather and whirled me around and around. "Since I'm not keen on nurses," he said, leading the way to Flo's room, "the story of my life is that every woman I fancy belongs to a patient, and is therefore out of bounds. You are about to depart from this category, so I don't suppose you ever have a spare evening for dinner with a rather less nutty than usual psychia-trist?"

"You've got my phone number," I said, looking at him with a fresh eye. Hmmmm. My horizons are expanding. A Rugby front row forward type. Variety, she had said. Keep them all different, princess, and you gotta have a virgin before you die. Though I very much doubt that John Prendergast is a virgin.

Flo greeted me with open arms as usual, but I greeted her with hugs and kisses by the dozens. And a few tears. "Darling Flo, you're coming home with me soon," I whispered into the ear close to my mouth.

The biggest smile in the world lit her weeny face up, she threw her arms around me and squeezed me fervently.

"No fool, our Flo," said John Prendergast without surprise.

"Autistic, my foot!" I snorted. "Flo is unique. I think God is very tired of the mess we've made of things, so He's inventing a new model. It's speech gets us into so much trouble. But if we can read each other's thoughts, lies and duplicity go out the window. We'll have to be what we really are."

Next on my list was Sister Agatha, who had definitely girded her loins for battle, judging from the expression on her face when I erupted into her office. But I didn't give her the chance to open her mouth, the sour old biddy.

"Sister Toppingham, I quit!" I declared. "Today is Wednesday and I'm not here. I'll work tomorrow and Friday, then I'm gone!"

Gobble, gobble, gobble. "I require two weeks' notice from you, Miss Purcell."

"Hard cack, ace, you're not getting it. On Friday afternoon, I am goney-gone."

Gobble, gobble, gobble. "You are impertinent!"

"Impertinence," I said, "increases both exponentially and synchronously with financial independence." I blew her a kiss and blew out of there. Goodbye, Sister Agatha!

Then it was off to Bronte in another taxi to break the news to my very worried family.

I'd chosen my hour deliberately. Dad and the Bros were at the shop, only Mum and Granny would be home. What a pity Granny isn't Dad's mother. Then we'd get the truth. But Dad's parents Passed Over—I'm catching the disease—before I was born. The patch of Potty grass, I noticed on my way in through the back door, is poisonously green and lush. Willie was taking in the sun.

"Da daaaa! You are looking at someone so rolling in riches that she doesn't need to work!" I announced as I walked in.

Mum and Granny were sitting having lunch. Bread, butter, a tin of IXL apricot jam and the teapot. Both of them looked oh so glum—debating events at 17c Victoria Street for the umpteenth time, I guessed. Love affairs with married bone surgeons, murder and suicide, missing children, a daughter gone gaga—not any parent's or grandparent's idea of heaven.

When I trumpeted that, they sat up in a hurry.

"A cup of tea, dear?" Mum asked.

"Ta, but no," I said, went to the sauce cupboard and dug Willie's bottle of three-star out from behind the Worcestershire, P.M.U., tomato and Camp Essence of Coffee and Chicory. "I'll have a snort of this. Brandy," I went on as I glugged some into Stuart crystal, "is good for the soul. Ask Willie. You know, Mum, you ought to save the old Kraft cheese spread glasses, they're indestructible and they don't look too bad with those tulipy things painted on them." I sat down and tilted the posh glass at them. "Bottoms up, as the bishop said to the choir boys."

"*Harriet!*" Granny squawked.

Mum's shrewd. She relaxed. "It's all sorted out," she said.

"That it is," I answered, and told them the whole story.

"Harriet Purcell!" Mum breathed at the end of it. "I wonder if she is Roger's sister? It would account for a lot."

"If she is, then neither Dad nor Auntie Joan and Auntie Ida know," I said, "but feel free to speculate. Maybe one of them will remember an unfathomable remark their parents made yonks ago. Or mysterious absences from the family fold occasionally to visit some place spoken of in whispers. Ask Auntie Ida—she's got a memory like an elephant and she's into gossip—typical old maid."

"Won't you be sorry to give up X-ray?" Mum asked.

Poor Mum, she would have loved to have had a job of work aside from domesticity, but it didn't happen in those days. I believe she did once apply to train as a nurse at R.P.A. in about 1920, but Granny put the kybosh on that quick-smart. Mum's a lot younger than Dad. Maybe that's why I like older men? Pappy would say so, certainly, but then, Pappy can find something Freudian in a hole piped in cream on top of a jammy cake.

"Mum, I've had it up to the back teeth with gainful employment," I said. "The work itself is terrific, but the people in charge are straight off the Ark. Believe me, I don't intend to be idle. I'm going to have a lot to do, between supervising the unruly tenants, trying to work out a way of communicating with Flo, and getting the best return from Flo's money."

"Well," Mum sighed, "it's not difficult to see that you're on top of the world, dear, and so am I for your sake." She coughed delicately and went a little pink. "Um, what about Dr. Forsythe?"

"What about him?" I asked, very offhand.

Her courage failed her. "Um, nothing, I suppose."

On the way out, I went down to where Willie's cage was sitting in a sunny corner. From his crusted breast feathers, still on the porridge-and-brandy. Discriminating bird.

"Hello, my gorgeous chap," I cooed.

He opened one eye and looked at me. "Get stuffed!" he said.

"Watch it, ace!" I said.

I was three paces away when he replied. "Watch it yourself, princess!"

When I spun around, stunned, he was dozing.

I laid on a feast in my living room—smoked eel, potato salad, coleslaw, shaved ham, crusty French baguettes, butter neither too hard nor too soft, about a ton of Greek rice pudding, and all the three-star we could drink, given that everybody has to work tomorrow. Lerner Chusovich was visiting Klaus, so he came, and I'd phoned Martin to bring Lady Richard, who arrived in subtle lilac alleviated by a red wig. Martin, much to our relief, has finally given in and been fitted for dentures at the Sydney Dental Hospital, where they cost nothing because the patients are guinea pigs for the students. The mouthful of teeth has made a great difference to his career, as he is colossally handsome, as graceful as a weeping willow, and as charming as George Sanders when handling the ladies who are now flocking to have him take their portraits. Move over, Annigoni! I also invited Joe the Q.C. and her friend Bert, and later Joe Dwyer arrived from the Piccadilly with two bottles of Dom Perignon. I had debated whether to ask the Mesdames, but decided that they could stew for a few more days. Chastity Wiggins just invited herself after she heard the screams of joy from her window, so I made her promise that she'd keep the news to herself.

"The first thing I'm going to do," I announced to the assembled mob, "is make a few changes to The House. A bathroom and toilet on every floor, fresh coats of paint, decent lights, new linoleum and some rugs, new fridges and stoves, a couple of washing machines for the laundry plus a Hills Hoist clothes line, and *no gas meters*! I'm going to have a decorating scheme that makes Flo's scribbles look deliberate—avant garde ultramodern. I may be *in loco parentis* for Mrs. Delvecchio Schwartz, but we operate in different ways. My way is comfort, modernity and nice surroundings."

"It will be difficult," said Jim, frowning. "The Council is not very co-operative about renovations."

"As I don't intend to inform the Council, Jim, it's irrelevant what the Council thinks. I'll do everything under the lap."

"The Werner brothers!" said Klaus and Pappy together.

"They can do everything you want, Harriet," Klaus explained. "They smuggle the bits and pieces in after dark."

So there you are. Fritz and Otto Werner have surfaced. Dear Mr. Hush *will* be pleased!

"What about the empty flats?" Bob asked.

"We'll wait until they've been done up, then I'll handpick the new tenants," I said, and lifted my glass of bubbly. "Here's to Flo, to Mrs. Delvecchio Schwartz, and to The House."

As the noise settled down and people began to clump, Toby joined me on the floor in the corner.

"I'm surprised you didn't invite Norm and Merv," he said.

"Norm and Merv belong in the Fugue and Toccata category, Toby. I'll tell them when I'm good and ready." I drained my glass—bubbly isn't really a patch on three-star—and put it down. "Are you going to forgive me for taking Flo on?" I asked.

Gone red with love, his eyes caressed me. "How can I not? She's your own flesh and blood, it seems, and that I understand. Besides, you're not going to suffer because of her. The old girl came good in the end. What a place to hide a will!"

I nestled against him, my hand on his upper arm discovering nicely bulging muscles. "You'd have liked to hear me telling Mr. Hush that I found it concealed in her favourite ornament."

"I'll give you this, Harriet, for such a rambunctious, noisy sort of woman, you're mighty close when you want."

"What Mrs. Delvecchio Schwartz did for a crust is no one's business except The House's."

"I've connected the septic tank," he said, pushing the hair off my forehead. "Want to come up to Wentworth Falls and have a look this weekend?"

"With knobs on, ace, with knobs on. Hur-hur-hur."

Pappy helped me tidy up when I asked her, pushed Toby out the door protesting.

"How much of this did you know?" I asked her.

The almond eyes elongated, the rosebud mouth curved into a faint smile. "Some, perhaps, but by no means everything. One always had to make deductions, and often more from what she didn't say than said. What I did know was that from the moment I told her I had met a Harriet Purcell at Queens, she never let up on me until I brought you home. So I realised that your name held some significance for her, but what, I had no idea. If anyone got the message, it was Harold. *He* knew that you stood higher in her affections than the rest of The House put together, though I don't think for a moment that she told him a thing. But he loved her, poor little man, and after almost forty years of having his mother to himself, he couldn't accept sharing the woman who had taken her place. He knew she loved you even before you turned up in the flesh, and it ate at him more and more as he watched the two of you together. I think you were right to fear him. I think that for a long time, it was you he planned to murder, not her. Though I'm sure he never planned what did happen. We'll never know what passed between them that night, except that I'm sure she threw him the ultimate insult. The knife was there, he picked it up and used it. But no, I don't think he intended to."

"*Did* she see it in the cards or the Glass, Pappy?"

"You'd know that better than I, Harriet. What I do know is that she wasn't a charlatan, though she may have started out that way. She could see things, especially in the cards when they concerned The House, and with Flo when it came to her clients. Those women swore by her, and they weren't consulting her on private matters. They consulted her to inform their husbands what was going to happen to the stock market, to money, to how the Government's actions might affect commerce. They paid her a fortune, which means that what she told them had to be absolutely accurate. And though we found scrapbooks full of clippings about these men, we found no books on economics or business trends."

"It's the fact that she submitted so tamely really gnaws at me," I said.

"She believed implicitly in destiny, Harriet. If her time to Pass Over had come, she would have accepted it simply and naturally. What's more, it started just before the New Year of 1960—that's when Harold and the Ten of Swords first appeared. She hadn't even heard your name then, though she turned you up in the cards at the same moment as Harold and the Ten of Swords. You were her salvation, the Scorpian Queen of Swords with the massive Mars. All she said to me was that you would preserve The House."

So there you have the Papele Sutama Theory. I am *fairly* comfortable with it.

Monday,
April 10th, 1961

I came back from Wentworth Falls this morning by train, leaving Toby behind to carry on with his construction. Like me, today is his first day of independence; we both finished at our places of work last Friday with neither fuss nor fanfare.

When I set eyes on Toby's refuge, I was amazed. I'd expected what he'd called it, a shack, but instead I found a truly beautiful, very modern small house well on its way to completion. There had been an old dead house on the site, he explained, and it yielded him enough lovely old sandstone blocks to make his foundations, footings, floors and the piers between his windows as well as the few internal walls. His money had mostly gone into the glass, a corrugated iron roof and fixed fittings.

"I modelled it on a Walter Burley Griffin House on top of the crest at Avalon," he said, "which belongs to Sali Herman. I don't have its water views, but I do see the mountains and forests forever. Nice, to think that this part of the country's so rugged no one logged it out in the old days, and now they can't log it at all, thanks to government embargoes."

"You'll get the afternoon sun," I frowned. "With all this glass, it will bake you."

"I'm putting a very wide verandah on the western side," he said. "In the evenings I'll sit out there and watch the sun set over the Grose Valley."

He'd done all the building himself, with a little

help from Martin and the rest of the Cross camp scene.

"I'm a bushie," he explained. "Where I come from, you can't just ring up a plumber or a chippie or a stonemason. You learn to make do with your own pair of hands."

The place was terribly overgrown, but there was the remnant of an old apple orchard, right at this moment loaded with fruit. I made such a pig of myself that I was exceedingly grateful for the flushing toilet and its septic tank, which he informed me he'd got working by chucking a dead rabbit into it. The things you learn!

We just went to bed together after we'd eaten and he'd washed the dishes—some things will never change, he's still the most obsessive man I know. Manna from heaven for me! I'll never have to do any of the housework. Just a spot of cooking.

I'd wondered what sort of lover that would make him, but I needn't have. He's an artist, he appreciates beauty, and for some reason he thinks I'm beautiful. No, I'm not, but beauty is in the eye of the beholder, as they say. What *are* Mum and Dad going to say when nudes of Harriet Purcell pop up in art galleries? The lovemaking is delicious, but I really think he's more interested in painting me. Of course as he grows more famous he's going to lose his clinical eye and branch out into stuff that only the high art connoisseurs will appreciate, I suspect, but they're the ones who pay the biggest bikkies anyway. I still like the smoking slag heap in the thunderstorm. And his portrait of Flo, which he's given to me. He never did get around to painting Mrs. Delvecchio Schwartz, though he doesn't seem to be sorry about it.

He's a lovely hairy man, which would please her. Not black hair like Mr. Delvecchio, but dark red. As I suspected, muscular and strong, and not at all disadvantaged by his lack of height. He says it makes my breasts more accessible. I prowled the tangles and snarls, combed the you-know-where with me tongue, hur-hur-hur.

"But you mustn't think," I said to him as I packed my little weekender bag and prepared to make the four-mile traipse to the railway station, "that you own me, Toby."

His eyes were dark, probably because dawn was barely breaking. "You don't need to tell me that, Harriet," he said. "I've said it before, and I'll say it again now. In some ways you're very like Mrs. Delvecchio Schwartz. No man can own a force of Nature."

Good bloke!

The big C–38 steam engine was just approaching the station when I crossed the bridge over the line, and I stopped to lean over the parapet, get massive clouds of black coal smoke and soot in my face. She'd come down from Mount Victoria, the gorgeous beast. I love steam trains, spent the whole trip home leaning out of the window to get the sound and smell of her pushing those con-rods around, work, work, work. The Government is switching to diesel locomotives, which are *dismal*. You never see any evidence of the power. I adore power on display, including that in muscular men.

Friday,
April 21st, 1961

Flo came home today, clinging to my hip like a monkey, all wreathed in smiles. When she saw fat Marceline she wriggled down and was off to play, just as if those months in the child shelter and Queens Psych had never happened. As if she had never scribbled in blood, or gone through a plate glass window, or compelled innately kind people to tie her down.

I am still flummoxed. *Does* she talk? She understands every word I say, but I haven't been the recipient of a single beam or pulsation of telepathic communication. I had hoped against hope that I would once she was back home and accepted that her mother is no longer a part of her life. Nonsense! She accepted it the night her mother died.

The Werners have proven treasures. They make a living by doing odd jobs under the lap and taking cash payments for them. Experience has shown that they're as competent jacks-of-all-trades as Toby, so we've come to an arrangement. I've given them free tenancy of the front ground floor flat and I give them plenty of cash for the work they're doing and the work they'll continue to do in perpetuity. The five houses of 17 Victoria Street now have a pair of live-in handymen to keep them in good trim. Lerner Chusovich has my old flat for the same rent because he can smoke his eels in our backyard without the neighbours bitching. It isn't pink any more. Lerner likes smoked eel yellow with black woodwork.

Toby and I discovered how to put ablution conveniences on the floor Jim and Bob share with Klaus. We're having the Werners take a bit off Klaus and a bit off Jim and Bob. They open onto the landing, where Otto worked out how to put in two separate toilets, even if only one bathroom. Lashings of hot water from a big system and a shower stall as well as a bathtub. I found ceramic tiles painted in budgies for the walls—Klaus is ecstatic. Toby's room is so big that the Werners just extended his kitchen area and added another screen to hide the result, but the ground floor still has to trot down to the laundry. Fritz and Otto tend to pee into the soil around the hideous frangipani in our minute front garden if they're caught short, but the tree has improved out of sight on the urea-rich diet, so I decided to leave them to it. We now have perfumed frangipani float bowls on our tables.

Though at first I shrank from it, in the end I bit the bullet and took over the whole of Mrs. Delvecchio Schwartz's floor for my own quarters. However, with new paint (mostly pink), some carpet in the living room and bedrooms, and decent furniture, I've lost my fear of it. Every house must have awful things happen in it from time to time, and I'm finding a strange comfort in being where she used to be. *Used to be.* That tense you can't get away from.

This sounds as if the work is finished, but it's not. That will take several more months, so there's a lot of plaster dust around, and toilets and bathtubs and sinks and stoves and showers and hot-water systems clutter up the halls, while the backyard is stacked with wall and floor tiles. The Werners just smuggle the lot in through their French doors onto the front verandah.

I'm just so happy, now that my angel is home.

I ought to record that my love life has sorted itself out beautifully, at least to my way of thinking. Weekends are Toby's. He and I go up to Wentworth Falls. In future Flo will come with us. Toby wasn't too thrilled about that, but I told him it was either both of us or neither of us. So he pulled a face and said he'd take both. About Duncan, he's not, um, *pleased.*

Duncan has Tuesday and Thursday nights with me. He came to an arrangement with the Missus, who is suffering dreadfully from the Harriet Purcell Curse. No dandruff or intractable thrush, though. She's developed a neuropathy in her legs—not mortal, just makes her life a misery. I think Duncan was a bit appalled at my total lack of pity for her, but I daresay I have to make allowances for the fact they've lived together for fifteen years. I told him to give her a message from me—if she's decent and understanding and does *not* feed his sons a morsel of poison about their father, I'll lift the curse. She can't play tennis, has to walk with a stick, and between the ACTH they've put her on and the lack of exercise, her weight's going through the ceiling. She'll soon be an XL and she wears lace-up flatties with rubber oedema stockings. Hur-hur-hur.

About John Prendergast I'm not sure yet, so the fortress has not fallen. Much though he denies it, I have a strong suspicion that he looks at me a bit like a patient with some peculiar sort of psychopathy. That's the whole trouble with psychiatrists, they are never completely off duty. He probably analyses his performance in bed into the bargain. So I let him buy me an occasional meal and lead him ten times around the mulberry bush.

Wednesday,
May 17th, 1961

We are baffled, bamboozled, buggered if we know. Flo has been home for a month now, and she won't scribble. There are freshly painted half-walls everywhere in my quarters and the communal passageways and landings, I bought her more crayons to add to her collection, and I tell her a hundred times a day that she's welcome to scribble to her heart's content. All she does is nod, smile, step over the crayons and wander off to watch Fritz and Otto as they work, hand them washers, nails, screws, bolts, trowels. Always the right thing for the job. They're fascinated by her.

Oh, she still clings to my legs, sits on my lap, hums her tune. The snuff-brown pinnies are things of the past, but I have not made her wear shoes and the dresses I've bought for her are fairly plain. To Flo, colour is for crayons, though not any more. These days she walks up to the shops with me, something she never did with her mother, so sometimes I wonder if, out of sheer ignorance, I've thrown a spanner into how Flo and The House work. My one barometer is Flo herself. If Flo likes it or seems to enjoy it, we do it. Certainly she loves her weekends at Wentworth Falls, packs her weeny port on Friday nights and makes sure that the canvas dillybag is aired out for Marceline. Poor Toby! Not one, but three women.

Little though I liked the thought, I've made Harold's room my bedroom, and put Flo in her mother's old bedroom. That cranny Flo used to be in is now the linen closet and the Delvecchio Schwartz reference library. I wondered if I was removing myself too far from Flo, but luckily Marceline took care of that by transferring to Flo's bed. She sleeps, my angel, so sweetly and soundly, never stirs, never seems to have bad dreams.

The nightly gallops and guffaws ceased the moment I found the will, but I'm still far from positive that Mrs. Delvecchio Schwartz has properly Passed Over. When I went that first night to Harold's room, my hair on end and my skin solid goose pimples, I heard a soft sigh as I closed the door. Not her sigh. Harold's. Like a goodbye forever.

Then her voice said "Youse done good, princess. Ripper-ace!"

Something fluttered and flapped. One of Klaus's budgies. I looked at it, it looked at me, then I held out my hand and it hopped onto my finger, jigged up and down gleefully.

"Oh, thank heavens!" Klaus cried when I presented the bird to him. "My little Mausie flew out the window the moment I opened it. I thought I'd lost her for good."

"No worries, ace," I said. "You're not going to get rid of little Mausie *that* easily. Will he—eh, Mausie?"

All the above notwithstanding, Flo won't scribble, and it has all of us beaten. Jim and Bob, Klaus and Pappy spend hours with her and the crayons, coaxing and cajoling. Even Toby has succumbed to Scribble Mania. He went out and bought several blocks of butcher's paper and showed her how to scribble on those, but she just looked at me sadly and dropped the pink crayon he offered her.

Thursday,
May 25th, 1961
It's taken a long time, but the Mesdames Fugue and Toccata are finally sorted out to everybody's satis-

faction. They stuck to their story that they only paid thirty quid a week in rent, I blew a succession of raspberries, and so it went for a long time. But today we agreed on four hundred quid a week from each of the ladies, thirty of it on the official books. Though I am fond of the Mesdames, you can't run a very superior brothel catering to all sorts of tastes above and beyond the usual without also being as tough as a pair of old boots. They are *tough*. So for a short moment they tried pulling a few Council strings to get me into hot water, but I simply sent each of them a weeny Kewpie doll with china-headed pins shoved up their fundamental orifices, back and front, and a third in the mouth for good measure. Oooooo-aa! The message was correctly interpreted, the Mesdames gave in.

It seems to be a watershed. Today I spread the cards for the first time, after Flo had gone to bed, and The House lapsed into silence except for Klaus's violin.

The House is happy. The Queens of Swords are very well placed, so are the King of Pentacles and the King of Swords. Only the Page of Swords—Flo—isn't perfectly at peace. It's the scribbling, it's got to be the scribbling. There isn't a card with a meaning I can pick as related to scribbling, but it all began to settle into place when I turned up the Six of Cups, reversed. Something is going to happen soon. Especially as the next card was The Fool—an unexpected appearance? Then three Nines and four

Twos—conversation, correspondence, messages. Oh, pray all this says communication is on the doorstep!

Saturday,
June 3rd, 1961

It's the start of winter, and it's raining so hard that Toby and I have had to forego our weekend at Wentworth Falls. Flo and Marceline have been wandering around all morning looking thwarted. Though the front door is unlocked again these days, I put them under stern orders not to open it and go onto the verandah.

We were all gathered in my living room drinking coffee and planning what we were going to have for lunch. How nice this is, I thought, feeling a wave of well-being wash over me. Thank you, Mrs. Delvecchio Schwartz, for giving me the opportunity to be who I am meant to be. You are ripper-ace, princess, ripper-ace. Oh, just when *are* you going to Pass Over properly?

Suddenly Flo stopped scuffing her feet through the carpet, raced to her crayons, chose three like lightning, and started to scribble on the wall. Flesh pink, then a pale, ashen blue, then a lot of dark purple.

And I knew. "A strange woman with blue hair and wearing a dark purple dress is coming up the stairs," I announced.

No one moved. No one said a word.

A knock on the door made the lot of them jump. Toby leaped to open it. A strange woman with blue-rinsed hair and wearing a dark purple dress was standing on the threshold.

"I do beg your pardon," she said, hesitating, "but I'm looking for Mrs. Delvecchio Schwartz."

They all pointed at me.

"That's her," Toby said, wriggling his brows at the rest, who rose to their feet in silence.

"I am Mrs. Charles Pomfrett-Smythe," the stranger said, "and, um, I was wondering if—?"

"Come in, come in," I said as the others filed out. "It's a terrible day out there, princess."

"Indeed it is," she said, sitting opposite me on a pink velvet chair drawn up to the walnut table. "However, my chauffeur carries an umbrella."

"Good help is worth hanging onto," I said, patting the Glass.

Mrs. Pomfrett-Smythe gazed about. "I hadn't thought, from what Elma Pearson told me, that your house was so pretty," she said.

"Things change, princess, things change. A sudden abscissal astringency necessitated a new décor in order to return the chondral energy fluxes to normal," I said smoothly. "So it was Mrs. Pearson put you in touch, was it?"

"Not exactly, no. Everyone seems to think that Mrs. Delvecchio Schwartz has Passed Over, but I'm so desperate that I thought I'd try anyway," she said, removing her dark purple kid gloves.

"There is *always* a Mrs. Delvecchio Schwartz. I am the, um, second edition. This is my daughter, Flo."

"How do you do, Flo?" she asked nicely.

Flo stuck her tongue out, not rudely, but in that way small children do when they are weaving around Mummy's legs trying to see the stranger from all angles.

"What's wrong, Mrs. Pomfrett-Smythe?" I asked.

She grabbed her gloves convulsively. "Dear Mrs. Delvecchio Schwartz, it's my husband! He took a chance on a particular stock—something to do with funny little gadgets that act like sheep culling gates, only not with sheep. With electricity, I think," she said, very distressed.

"Sheep culling gates?" I asked blankly.

"Perhaps you don't know how they cull sheep in the country, but I do—my father was a grazier. The gate swings between two stockyards, and whoever is on the gate can send a sheep into either of the stock-yards," she explained. "After my husband bought his first lot of stock—share stock, not sheep—he did some research and put everything he has into buying more." She was growing more and more flustered, from which I deduced that the chauffeur with the umbrella was in danger of being lost, along with the limousine he drove, and the mansion in Point Piper.

"How about a nice cup of tea?" I asked soothingly.

"Oh dear, I'd love one, but there isn't the time!"

she wailed. "I had to come at once because he's had an offer for the stock, and he has to give his answer by two this afternoon. I think he's still keen on keeping it, but all his friends and colleagues are convinced he's going to lose everything, so they're pressing him to accept." She started pulling her gloves through her hands and stretching them in a way Lady Richard would have deplored.

"Such a terrible dilemma," I said.

"Yes!" Stretch, stretch, stretch.

"What baffles me, Mrs. Pomfrett-Smythe," I said, frowning, "is why an eminent businessman like your husband is seeking his answer from a soothsayer. I mean, you've never been here before."

"He doesn't know I'm here!" she cried, utterly ruining the gloves. "He left the decision to *me*!"

"To you?"

"Yes, to me! He just doesn't know what to do, and whenever he doesn't know what to do, he leaves the decision to me."

The lightbulb flashed on. "So if you make the wrong decision, he has someone to blame."

"Exactly!" she said wretchedly.

"Well, we can't have that, princess—can we, Flo?"

Flo carefully chose four crayons from her repository and went to the wall. This, I realised, was the tricky bit; Mrs. Pomfrett-Smythe's attention had to remain focused on *me*, which meant some sort of mediumistic behaviour—a trance, certainly, mutters and moans, definitely, but how does one produce

371

COLLEEN MCCULLOUGH

ectoplasmic drooling? Bubble gum and soap? Research, Harriet, research!

For today, I flopped back in my pink chair, sighed and sagged, gave little screechy squeaks. And squinted at Flo through half-shut eyes. She took the dark purple crayon first and scribbled. Mrs. Pomfrett-Smythe. Then she produced some wavy-edged rectangles in bottle-green. Money. Lots of bright yellow circles. Gold coins. And finally a pyramid of tiny pale ochre dots. A sand heap. Now that I know, it's easy. Flo's words are colours and shapes. As her drawing skills improve, it will be manifest. But the real miracle is that Flo can see the right answers to all the questions "me ladies" ask. Can see the torment in a soul, can see into every heart. Can see murder coming. My weeny angel, God's new experiment. Well, with me, she's safe. That's what Mrs. Delvecchio Schwartz understood. Knowing, I think now, that she herself would soon be ill-equipped to cope with all that Flo is going to become. She'd passed the task to a younger, better educated Harriet Purcell. Today I realised at last why the first Delvecchio Schwartz submitted to her fate so tamely. We're there for our angel; she's the one who really matters.

When Flo dropped the crayons, I groaned and emerged slowly from my trance. Mrs. Pomfrett-Smythe was staring at me as if I had sprouted an extra head.

"Princess," I announced, "you tell your husband to hang onto his funny little gadgets for dear life. What the world has been waiting for is a way to sort the electrical sheep from the electrical goats. These funny little gadgets are sheer dynamite." I stroked the Glass. "Silicon! *Amazing* stuff."

"Are you absolutely sure, Mrs. Delvecchio Schwartz?" she asked doubtfully.

No, Flo is sure, I thought to myself. The sheep culling gates are transistors—very newfangled, but I'm technically trained. There are a few medical machines made out of them, and even a computer or two. Canny Mr. Pomfrett-Smythe! Clearly he's latched onto some staggering advance in them, so maybe the days of vacuum tubes and thermionic emission are numbered?

Then I had another thought: are Mr. Pomfrett-Smythe's friends and colleagues plotting to buy him out?

No sooner had I wondered this than Flo took a pea-green crayon and scribbled a sort of liver shape, followed that up with rays of jaundice-yellow. Yep, that's the story. And Flo just read my thoughts, *answered my unspoken question*. The break-through at last! Flo has admitted me to her mind, she and I just became one. I am vindicated.

Mrs. Pomfrett-Smythe was still looking at me enquiringly, her question still hanging in the air.

"I am absolutely, positively, definitely sure," I said

with utter conviction. "What's more, you can give him a tip from—use my name!—Mrs. Delvecchio Schwartz. A wise man ought not to believe everything his friends and colleagues say."

"I will, I will!" No idiot, Mrs. Pomfrett-Smythe; she got my drift. The pale purple kid handbag flipped open. "Um, how much is that?"

I made a grand gesture. "No charge the first time, princess, but from now on, I'll charge like the Light Brigade." Charge her for today? Not on your nelly! On Monday I'm going to open two share portfolios, one for Flo and one for me, and our first punt is going to be on Mr. Pomfrett-Smythe's funny little gadgets.

My first client was gazing at me in awe and vast respect; then her eyes went to Flo, displayed only the tender admiration women feel for a beautiful child.

"I'd appreciate it," I said, getting to my feet, "if you give Mrs. Pearson a ring on the phone and tell her that the one and only Mrs. Delvecchio Schwartz is open for business in her new incarnation. The magnetic mu is less than one again, and the vectoring of the equanimities is complete. Things have returned to normal at The House."

Flo and I ushered her down the stairs and out onto the verandah, where we waited for the smart-looking chauffeur to dash across, his umbrella at the ready.

"Angel," I said as we waved the Rolls goodbye through the rain, "let's keep your blossoming drawing skills our secret, eh? The clients are going to start Rolling—hur-hur-hur—up in droves shortly, and we don't want to let them know how we do it, do we? Mrs. Delvecchio Schwartz has to stay unique—she's your shelter from a world that isn't ready for you."

And just like that I looked into her mind! Blurred outlines of institutional furniture flying past, the shock of pain as she threw herself against something, the myriad shards of an exploding window, the concerned yet uncomprehending faces. But all that, I understood, was as nothing before the love she harbours for her two mothers, the two Mrs. Delvecchio Schwartzes.

She smiled at me, nodding vigorously. Our secret.

"I wonder," I asked as I put my hand on the door, "if the first edition is ever going to Pass Over properly? What's your opinion, angel?"

Flo took three crayons—yellow, blue and green—from her pink pocket and drew a cockatoo and a budgie on the glossy white wall between 17d and The House.

Somehow I think that Mum isn't going to be a scrap surprised when I ask her for permanent custody of Willie; undoubtedly it's already been arranged.